'My son, go find a fitting kingdom;
Macedonia is too small for you.'
Philip of Macedonia to his son, Alexander

'... and if you're still not convinced that I have won the
kingdom, fight me for it again, I shall be ready. But don't
run away, for I will follow you to the ends of the earth.'
Extract of a letter from Alexander to
Darius, King of Persia

'Tempus edax rerum'
– (Time destroys everything)
Ovid

Saying is written in gold above the door in the Sending
Room at Tempus University, Institute of Time Travel and
Study.

Prologue

There are several tombs purported to be of Alexander the Great. Only I know the real one. I will tell you this much: it is a simple tomb carved in hard stone. Inside, there are the relics of a legend. There is a gold cup in the shape of a winged lion. There is a large round shield, supposedly magic, that once belonged to the great hero, Achilles. There is a long braid of pale hair. There are many well-read letters in an ebony box, for he loved mail, and there is an ancient scroll that, when carefully unrolled, reveals a copy of the *Iliad*. He was never without it.

He was buried alone, since he died before any of us. For that, I will always curse him. My prayer had ever been to die before him. We would have all preferred to die before he did, for we all loved him. He was our sun, our god, and the reason we lived. Without him, the world appeared much darker and smaller somehow, than it had before.

Alexander: the name is a whisper in the room, merging with the shadows. There is still an echo of him; an echo that lasted for three thousand years. Sometimes I can almost feel him standing next to me. Blue light from the glass lamp makes strange shadows on the wall, and I pause as I write this. Night is falling, and soon lions will come to the water to drink. I love to sit on the porch and watch them. My terrace is set well back from the lake, but on a hill, so I can see all the way down the coast to the river, and sometimes I can catch a glint of the sea beyond. It is a timeless place; a place where the gods have their banquets, and where man and beast still live in perfect harmony. It will change. All will change.

I am getting old now, and my hand sometimes trembles and refuses to hold the pen. Getting old bothers me more than I thought it would, but the thought of dying holds no fear for me. I even look forward to it, for, you see, how can I be afraid to die? In three thousand years, I will be born again. I will win a prestigious award and choose to interview a legend. In three thousand years, I will return to Alexander, and the story will go on. The story will never end. I am looking forward to meeting Alexander again.

Chapter One

I could not, would not, go back in time with my head shaved. But the fashion consultant ignored my protests, put the razor to my head, and swept off my hair.

That should have been a warning, but all day long I'd ignored the signs. To begin with, I couldn't get any of my so-called friends from Tempus University to come and pick me up. They'd stopped speaking to me when I'd been chosen for the prize. It shouldn't have bothered me. I'd never had friends before, why did I need them now? Well, they would have come in handy for a ride. The only flat I could afford after giving my money to a charity foundation was in a crappy section just outside town and there was no zip-tram nearby. When I called a taxi, he'd refused to drive up to my door and I had to walk through the garbage-strewn streets to the main station.

When I finally got to the University, the fashion consultant gave me a dress to wear that felt like it had been woven from nettles and the most uncomfortable sandals in the world. The sandals, the fashion consultant informed me, were made by a shoemaker-slash-historian from plaited grass imported directly from the Euphrates riverbanks.

Just after I'd finished dressing, the smug fashion consultant shaved me bald and gave me a most unflattering wig. Then, in another room, a surgeon gave

1

me a shot that would temporarily protect me from all the known illnesses of the time, including pregnancy and rabies. Then he implanted my tradi-scope right above my left ear, missing the first time, and giving me a fearsome headache. I didn't complain. Besides, I needed the tradi-scope to understand all the languages I would meet.

Finally, when I was deemed dressed and coifed appropriately for 333 BC, the fashion consultant escorted me to the very centre of the Institute of Time Travel and Study, where I climbed onto the massive seat carved from a block of pure quartz crystal that would send my atoms spinning through time.

A nurse paused next to me and looked at the glowing screen by the cylinder of frozen nitrogen. 'Only a few more minutes before you get vaporized,' she said, and smiled.

Everyone in the room was waiting for me to fail at my undertaking or to show some sort of weakness. I leaned back in the freezing chair and pretended to yawn.

Above all, a time-travelling journalist must be in control of his or her emotions. Emotions clouded judgment. Emotions were marks against you at Tempus University. Sentiments were stomped out and clinical thinking was put in their place. I was trained to observe and to ask pertinent questions, all the while remaining detached. The Time Travel Institute was not about to spend millions of dollars to send people back in time to have them fall apart and blather.

Lightning crashed and thunder shook the building. On the glass dome above my head, rain poured like a waterfall, the sound deafening. More lighting jagged across the sky, and the white-coated scientist standing next to me glanced upwards. 'Right on time.' He checked his watch and then motioned curtly to a nurse standing nearby. 'Four minutes.'

I shifted, my bones aching. The ice-cold, quartz-crystal chair beneath me seemed to vibrate with every lighting flash. Time travel uses lightning, and takes so much power that only one individual can voyage each year. The entire planet's energy system dims for the hour it takes to send the voyager. The renown of the programme and its consequences are such that none can ignore it. In a short time, I would be among the most famous people in the world.

The programme had been invented in 2300 by scientists working for a private company based in Tempus University. At first, only inanimate objects, especially those made of quartz crystal, could be sent back in time. When it was perfected in 2900, Tempus University started their reporting programme. Because their time in the past was limited, researchers and historians had to make the most of it. It was decided they should act as journalists and concentrate on interviewing famous people. Some early experiences were resounding successes; Shakespeare, Julius Caesar and Marie Curie gave fascinating interviews. Others were failures. Jesus, for example, remained elusive. Some trips simply didn't work out because the journalist was in the wrong place or the wrong time; but they usually came back alive.

To be chosen for the programme was akin to winning the lottery – the chances against you were millions to one. But that never bothered me. When at last I knew what I wanted to do, I went after my goal with a single-mindedness that would have put even my mother to shame. When I was chosen, the looks my fellow journalists gave me could have cut glass. Those I believed to be my friends turned out to be bitterly jealous. That shouldn't have bothered me. Emotions were something I'd long ago learned to suppress.

But right now I was having a hard time. The visions I'd had of arriving back in time dressed in long, silk robes, my beautiful hair brushed into an intricate fashion, had shattered with the buzz of a razor and the sight of the shoddy sandals. I clenched my fists and tried to think of something else. But the something else was the present, and I was even more uncomfortable with that.

Looking upward, all that was visible was the glass dome and the water pouring upon it like black silk. Lighting flickered eerily across the night sky and, a moment later, thunder boomed. I watched as scientists and nurses bustled about taking their endless measures, whispering, checking the magnetic poles, and muttering into microphones. The chair beneath me was growing colder by the second, and next to me a chrome cylinder full of liquid nitrogen gave off freezing vapour.

'Almost midnight.' The nurse stepped closer. 'Not nervous yet?' Her look said clearly she was hoping for me to fall apart.

I didn't answer. Silence is a shield. That had been the first lesson I'd learned. My upbringing set me apart from anyone I knew because of the fortune my parents possessed, and because I'd been unwanted. I was punished if I made noise, so I learned to keep quiet, and I

4

wandered around our vast domain silently and alone until I was old enough to be shipped off to boarding school. Most of my mother's friends had no idea she had a child.

My second lesson was harder. When I was sixteen I graduated from finishing school, and my mother decided to take control of my life. She married me to a man twenty years my senior, the Baron Thibault de Riveraine.

I'd never been an easy child – I'd inherited my parents' tempers from both sides along with their stubbornness and, I'm afraid, their emotional aloofness, but it never occurred to me to protest my marriage. At the time, I thought I was escaping my mother.

My husband turned out to be worse. He was cruel, humourless, and violent. I was a virgin. He raped me on our wedding night and was brutal every night thereafter. He was careful not to bruise my face – I was his trophy wife and he liked to show me off. I left him after six months, dropping my suitcase out the window and climbing down after it like a thief in the night. It took me nearly a year to recover my self-esteem and face him again. I contacted a lawyer to arrange our divorce. My husband agreed because I'd threatened to expose him. When we finally did meet, my husband lost his temper and punched me.

The fight happened in the presence of my mother, the judge, and our two lawyers. My mother had come to court hanging onto my husband's arm, her mouth twisted in scorn at my stupidity. I wanted a divorce and half my husband's fortune. My husband said I could have neither.

I got both, along with my title, Baronne Riveraine. I didn't want the title, and that was the reason my ex-husband punched me. Or, perhaps it was my laugh when the judge asked if I was sure I wanted the divorce. Whatever the cause, for the first time ever I dared hit back when he hit me. My fist flew and broke Thibault's nose with a satisfying crunch. My mother screamed, the lawyers gasped, and I walked out of the courtroom with a black eye, a fortune, and a new goal in life. I was eighteen and I knew exactly what I wanted to do. I wanted to go back in time and meet my childhood hero, Alexander the Great. I applied to Tempus University and graduated with honours.

My attention shifted to the time-sender, a tall, severe man in a white lab coat. 'Don't move,' he said. 'The tractor beam must be set for your exact weight and mass.'

'How does it work?' I asked.

The scientist snorted. 'I can't tell you how, you won't understand anyway. Suffice to say that you choose any person in any historic time and we send you to him or her. You are outfitted with the tradi-scope, so you speak and understand any language and idiom of that time. We provide the science, you provide the legwork.'

'I've been trained for all that, you know.' Across the top of the screen I saw numbers start to flash.

He snorted. Obviously he was sure my title and fortune had paved my way to this chair. If he read the papers, he'd know that after I'd paid for my education, I'd given my fortune away to a charity foundation. But I wasn't going to tell him. I couldn't care less what he thought.

'One minute and counting,' came the electronic voice. The nurse leaned over and spoke to me.

'What did you say?' I asked, keeping my eyes on the

glowing needle inserted in my arm. My temperature was dropping rapidly; soon my blood would freeze. My atoms were being disconnected for their voyage into the vacuums of time. Pain bloomed, spreading from my arm to the rest of my body. My teeth began to chatter, and I wondered if I'd die. Some people did. I must have uttered a slight moan. The nurse looked at me sharply.

'I was wondering why you chose Alexander the Great,' she said. Then my vision darkened and I couldn't answer, but I knew what I would say if I could.

I'd decided to interview him for several reasons. So much had been said about him, yet hardly any writings remained by his contemporaries. He'd been glorified, vilified, deified, and his myth existed in all the known languages on earth. He was represented in the four major religions.

I was curious to learn about the young man's charisma and leadership qualities. What had made him so special? The final reason I wanted to see him was a burning passion I'd nurtured since high school for the enigmatic king. That, however, was not on the application I'd sent to the Institute of Time-Travelling Journalists. If they knew I'd turned down dates because the man didn't measure up to my ideal of Alexander, they'd never have chosen me. An interviewer has to be able to hide his feelings. Clearly I'd succeeded. No one had realized the extent of my infatuation. I wasn't worried about it. I was confident I would be able to control my emotions – after all, I was a modern, well-educated woman.

Alexander had already been interviewed – as had most

of the people who'd made history. However, the timing had been different. The interview had been held just before his death, and he'd been delirious with fever. He hadn't said anything of interest, and no one had gone back to see him again. Afterwards, for some reason, he'd been classified as a dangerous subject. Most first-time time-travelling journalists chose an easy interview. I wanted the prize, though, so I'd gone with the risk and it had paid off. I'd been chosen over thousands of other candidates.

Interviewers had to be careful never to give away the fact they were from the future, and they had to make sure that they didn't alter history. The time one spent in the past was severely limited, only twenty hours. We took vows. It's all very 'Boy's Club' and 'Scout's Honour' sort of stuff. Cross your heart and hope to die. Prick your finger and dab a drop of blood on the dotted line, right next to your signature. You see, the time travelling programme is so precise that if you change history, even the slightest, the scientists simply erase the part you changed, and in doing so, erase you. What's more, if you don't make it back to your rendezvous, you are left there to die. Your tradi-scope is disconnected, so you lose the power to understand and speak the languages of that time. Most people don't last a week under those conditions, especially during wars, plagues, or intrigues. In the past, spies were executed without a trial, usually on the spot.

I was going back in time. I'd filled out my contract and meant to honour it. I also meant to come back and win another journalistic prize. Once tasted, success is intoxicating – and perhaps I was hoping I could prove to everyone that I was not just a spoiled little rich girl. I sought something that I'd never received: approval.

I clenched my teeth as intense pain exploded in my arms and legs. My chest grew tight, making breathing difficult. A solid wave of ice seemed to flow through my body. I tried to open my eyes, but all I saw were flashing white lights. I screamed then, and my last thoughts were that I was dying, that I'd failed, and that no one in that room, or anywhere on earth, would give the slightest damn.

I woke up beneath a small pomegranate tree. It was early morning, the sun was just rising and mist obscured the tops of the hills. My teeth chattered with cold, and my hands were pale blue and wouldn't work. I lay there, shaking, until the sun's rays finally thawed me out. When I could sit up, I had to brace myself against the tree trunk. I rested, waiting for the waves of dizziness and nausea to subside. Drops of blood ran down my chin and landed on my hands. It was just my nose. I pinched it, and waited. My head was clearing, and to my relief I found I could stand.

The sun was a pink disc on the horizon, and the mist started to dissipate. I straightened my shoulders and took a deep breath. I'd made it this far. I stood up, brushing the dirt off my robe with my tingling hands. I fingered the sash. It marked me a vestal virgin and would hopefully protect me from the common soldiers.

My head itched, my dress scratched, and every step I took with the flimsy grass sandals hurt. And I hated my stupid wig. It was the Egyptian style, reported to be the fashion rage that decade in the Tigris delta. I sincerely hoped so – I'd hate to be executed for lack of taste. In any case, I'd find out soon enough.

I waited until the sun rose fully, then made my way eastwards over low hills toward where streamers of smoke reached to the sky. Dew sparkled on the grass, wetting my feet. The air was incredibly pure, sweet and potent. I filled my lungs with it, drawing huge breaths. I'd never inhaled a breeze such as that. It was intoxicating. I inhaled the air as I walked, gulping it heartily. My journalist mind was busy ticking off details for the article I was to write. The pristine air, the diamond-bright dewdrops, the groves of date palms, and the scent of freshly ploughed fields were all part of the unfolding scene. It was still early, and the sky was pale blue. Smoke from campfires spiralled upwards and was lost in the mist. Faraway mountains faded into a lavender haze. The morning air was fresh and cool, but the shimmer on the horizon announced a brassy heat. It was going to be a scorching day.

My article would start with a description of the opalescent colours of the hills, then … I tripped on a rock and winced, the pain bringing me back to the present. I inspected my toe, shaking the dew off my foot, then sniffed. The smell of woodsmoke and garlic wafted through the air, along with the sharper odour of sweat and the sound of many voices. I crested the last hill and stopped, dazed. I hadn't truly realized what I had done yet, or where I was. Imagining the camp was one thing, actually seeing, hearing, and smelling it was another. I had arrived.

The encampment was a sprawling affair near the banks of a river. I'd read that Alexander had forty thousand men with him. Unbleached linen tents were set up in orderly rows in a level field; behind them were horse corrals. Soldiers swarmed around like ants. After watching closely, I saw an order to their movements. Some men were taking care of weapons – there was a veritable thicket of long spears alongside the tents – checking shields, or sharpening swords. Other soldiers were in the shade playing with what looked like dice. They were talking, laughing or even singing. I heard music from flutes.

A strong smell of garlic and onions permeated the encampment. There were also the odours of smoke, acrid sweat, freshly cut wood and baking bread. The camp was surrounded by guards and was full of soldiers, but I saw other people as well. Merchants hawked their wares, slaves bustled about, and pot-bellied children played noisily. On the banks of the wide, shallow river, women were washing clothes and chattering in shrill voices.

I walked down the hill and entered the camp. Nobody paid any direct attention to me, but the sentinels followed me with their eyes, spears gripped tightly in their hands. For all their apparent relaxation, they were on the *qui vive*.

I strolled down a well-trodden path following the riverbank and smiled in a friendly fashion to a young woman carrying a jug of water on her head. She smiled back and said something to me that set my tradi-scope working. They work well, but they have to be prompted by sound. So, for a few annoying seconds, there was an infernal buzzing in my head while the tradi-scope chewed up the woman's words, digested them, and spit them out. She'd said, 'Lovely morning for a walk.'

'Very nice,' I agreed. My own words came out of my mouth in her language, thanks to a complex bio-implant in my cerebral cortex. It was a shock at first.

'Are you one of the temple virgins?' she asked.

'I'm not a temple virgin. I'm an onirocrite.'

Her eyes widened. *Onirocrites* interpreted dreams. They were also exempt from most of the mundane sacrifices. It wasn't a bad choice for someone from the future.

I waved and continued along the path. I wanted to go directly to Alexander's tent. He was reputed to be easily approachable, well educated, and interested in omens, portents and dreams. The biggest tent was set off by itself between two tall palm trees. I thought it must be Alexander's, so, after taking a deep breath to clear my head, I went towards it.

There were three guards outside his tent. They were sitting on a mat made of woven grass, playing a game with bleached knucklebones. Bright coins glittered in the middle of the mat, and after each throw a new one would be added or subtracted from the pile. The guards barely glanced at me when I arrived.

'Is Alexander here? May I speak with him?' I asked.

'He's in the tent; let me announce you. State your name and business.' The guards were all professional. They seemed to be absorbed in their game but had subtly shifted position as soon as I'd arrived, so that I could neither advance nor retreat.

'I can't tell you my real name,' I said truthfully. 'But you can say that an onirocrite is here to speak to him. I've travelled all night.'

After a second's hesitation, the guard lifted the tent flap and disappeared inside. The heavy cloth was nearly soundproof. All I could hear was an indistinct murmur of voices before he came out again.

'Iskander receives the onirocrite,' he said, holding the flap high for me.

I ducked and entered. My eyes took a second to get used to the gloom. Then I saw him. Alexander was sitting cross-legged on a beautiful rug. A bowl of pale green grapes was next to him, and he was idly picking through them, choosing the smallest and sweetest to eat.

He was wearing a short, pleated tunic made of bleached linen. His feet were bare, but a pair of leather sandals lay on the floor next to him. Otherwise, he wore no ornaments and his tunic, though finely woven, was plain. He had many scars on his legs and arms. Most looked like they had been made by swords. They'd healed well, but one on his wrist seemed recent. As I watched, he rubbed it a bit; perhaps it still pained him. His hands were square and strong with the tendons showing on the backs. His fingers were long and his nails trimmed very short. On the inside of his arms I could see the tracing of blue veins. Though he was tanned, his skin was nearly translucent in some places; there were lavender shadows beneath his eyes and on his temples, and in the hollow of his throat I could see a pulse beat.

My first impression was that he was dangerous. He gave off an aura of energy. His movements were controlled. His gaze was direct yet hooded. He had long, brassy gold hair tied back from his face with a leather thong. His hair was dyed, which was not unusual for a man in that time, but it was impossible to say what the true colour was, perhaps a reddish-gold, or a warm brown. His eyebrows were dark, thick, and arched across a wide, clear brow. His eyes were canny; I was reminded of a South American jaguar. Then he tilted his head and I saw that one eye was blue-green and the other brown. It was disconcerting. He looked both wary and assured. Without breaking his gaze, he popped another grape into his mouth.

Before I realized how he'd done it, he was standing in front of me. His movement had been so fast and fluid I hadn't even registered it. I took a step back.

'Did I startle you? My pardon.' His voice was a comfortable tenor. He smiled for the first time since I had come in, showing white, even teeth with a slight overbite, and he motioned towards the rug. 'Please sit down. I was told you'd walked all night. Would you care for a drink, or something to eat?'

'Both, please, thank you. Is this your breakfast?'

He looked amused. 'No, it's just a snack. I've been up since before dawn. I eat breakfast when the first rays of the sun pierce the night's gloom.'

I looked around the tent and found it Spartan yet rich. Only one rug, but it was sublime. Just one bed covered with richly embroidered cushions. A low table of carved wood, inlaid with ivory and jet, stood in the corner. On top of it were writing materials made of bone set with gold. A delicately moulded glass lamp hung from the tent pole overhead. The fruit bowl was carved from a block of apple-green jade.

I sat cross-legged on the rug and waited for him to sit,

but he paced back and forth in front of me, further heightening the impression of a caged feline. I wondered if I should speak or wait until he spoke to me. I was irritated to feel myself getting flustered. Then Alexander sat down next to me with a fluid movement and I stifled an exclamation.

'What can I give you? Grapes? Some wine?'

'That sounds fine,' I said, my fingers itching for a pen so I could write down all my impressions. But I had to wait until I got back. Until then, I was supposed to make a mental note of every word and action.

He chose a grape for me and gently put it into my mouth. It was one of the most sensual gestures anyone had ever made to me. I felt faint, and, when he leaned over and kissed me, I toppled over onto the rug with hardly a whimper.

Alexander obviously thought I'd come to see him for only one reason. I guess he was smothered with women throwing themselves on him, but vestal virgins? My body was saying, 'Yes! Yes!' My head said, 'Ashley! Get a hold of yourself this instant!' I sat up and pushed him away. 'Sorry, I can't do this,' I said.

His expression of surprise was comical. 'You mean, you really *did* come from the temple?'

'Can we talk?' I avoided the question and took a bunch of grapes.

'Not those,' he said, plucking them from my hand and putting them back into the bowl. 'Those grapes are poisoned. I keep them in case an enemy comes. So, what do you want to talk about?' His brow furrowed, then his face cleared. 'Ah, yes, I recall. You're the onirocrite. So, what dreams have you had?'

'I dreamt that I came to your tent while you were sleeping. In your sleep you were calling out my name, the secret one that I can't tell to anyone except the goddess. When you woke up you saw me. You said that I must come to you because you had a dream that you wanted me to interpret for you. You also said that it was a waking dream.'

He looked interested. 'Really? And just what is a waking dream?'

'It's like a wish,' I said. 'It's what you want to do with your life. Can you tell me about it?' I was hoping for grist for the prize-winning article that I was going to write when I got back. No one knew why Alexander had decided to conquer Persia and travel as far as the Indus River. It was a mystery, and I'd decided to solve it.

Instead of answering me, he lay back on his bed, put his arms above his head and stretched, showing off his lean body with its beautiful, flowing lines. 'That's too bad,' he said. 'I was hoping you were one of the virgins who didn't want to be sacrificed. There are lots of them, you know,' he added, looking at me sideways out of his magnificent eyes. 'When they don't want to be sacrificed they simply cease to be virgins, if you get my meaning.'

'I do,' I said, 'and I'm flattered. But can we get back to the subject of my visit?'

'A single-minded woman,' he sighed. 'You remind me of my mother. She's terribly stubborn. She hated it when I sucked my thumb, so I did it for years just to spite her.'

'Well, that explains your teeth,' I said, vexed to be compared to his mother.

He looked at me, his expression unreadable. I started to think that maybe conversations about his mother weren't the best idea, but all he said was, 'You want to hear about my dreams, is that it?'

'Please,' I said, concentrating on his next words.

'Very well.' He stood up, poured two glasses of wine from an earthenware pitcher, and sat down next to me again, handing me one. The wine had a faint spicy note.

I was feeling smug. The article was going to net me a huge prize. I could just imagine the accolades. I was going to be famous; I couldn't wait to see the faces of those who'd been waiting to see me fail. 'Cheers,' I said, and sipped. The drink wasn't bad. It was young grape wine with spices and a trace of honey. It had been watered down so it was refreshing.

He raised his eyebrows. 'Cheers?'

'Here's to your health,' I amended.

We sipped our wine in silence for a few minutes while he studied me. Finally he put down his glass and shook his head.

'There's something strange about you,' he said, 'though I cannot say exactly what it is. You are impressed, I sense this, and you are interested. But, you are not afraid. Perhaps it is your lack of fear I detect the most. I am extremely attuned to fear; my father beat it into me. But it goes deeper than that.' As he spoke, he wound his body around me, pausing now and then to touch my cheeks, my neck, or my breast. 'I get a very peculiar feeling from you. There is a coldness, a frost that emanates from your very bones.' He paused and ran his hands lightly down my sides.

'I don't know what you mean,' I stammered. 'I've wanted to meet you since I first heard about you. It was a dream, and now it's come true.' The passion in my voice startled me. I frowned, struggling to keep my emotions in check. This was not the cool, calm, collected Ashley I knew.

Alexander took my hand, stroking the inside of my wrist before pressing it to his mouth. 'I want to bite you,' he said. 'I want to shake you out of your indifference. I want to hear you scream.' He stared at me, a fierce expression in his uncanny eyes. 'My mother is cold like you. She's as cold as the ice on the mountaintops.'

I shivered. 'I'm sorry if I appear cold. It was my parents' fault. I had to stay quiet, otherwise I was punished.'

'Perhaps that's it.' He tilted his head and looked at me. I felt the blood rush to my cheeks. There was such intensity in his gaze that I had to struggle not to drop my eyes.

'Did you know that of all the living things on this earth, only man can look another man in the eye? My teacher, an old Greek, taught me that. He is a very intelligent man. He said that the world was round like an orange, and that the stars we see at night are in reality other earths, like this one, or suns. Is that heresy, do you think, or is it truth? I would like to know the answer to those questions and to so many more. I want to see the ends of the earth where the water drops off into a great chasm. Of course, if my teacher is right, I shall never find that. Instead, I will end up where I started out.' He sighed, then leaned over and lifted a corner of the tent to peer outside. 'It's getting near midday, I have to go see my troops. Will you stay, or will you go back to your temple?'

'If you please,' I said humbly, 'I'd like to stay.'

'I please.' He smiled then, and I realized that his face had more expressions than anyone's I'd ever seen, including the great actors and mimes. His smile seemed to bloom from within, to reach out and caress me, and to bind me to him.

Anyone on the receiving end of that smile, I thought, would walk straight off the edge of the world if Alexander asked him to.

Chapter Two

I walked around the camp, then found the latrines and used them. Very primitive, but at least they existed. The village was just under a kilometre away, so I decided to go across the fields to have a look.

The centre of the village consisted of a temple, a marketplace, and several windowless buildings for storage. Dwellings were mud and wattle, with stone foundations. Most roofs were thatched. The streets were dusty and probably muddy when it rained. There was no particular arrangement to this town. Houses were set down haphazardly and the streets were simply winding paths. There were sewage ditches along the sides of the larger streets. They smelled rather ripe. The best buildings in town, the temple, a courthouse, and a bakery, were adjacent to the central marketplace. The warehouse was full of bales of wool and huge clay amphorae containing oil, wine and grain.

I poked around everywhere, curious. No one minded. The village was busy. Some men were making clay pots under an awning. Women were standing in line in front of the bakery waiting to bake their bread. At a rough table near the fountain a man was setting out fish to sell.

Children were everywhere. The older ones had loincloths or wore simple shifts tied at the waist with colourful yarn belts. They played leapfrog, knucklebones, hopscotch. Girls clutched painted dolls made of clay or wood.

I was parched, the dust made my teeth grate. I saw someone drinking from the fountain. The water came straight from a spring and was very cold and sweet. After the people drank, they made a sign with their hands. I made the same sign, though I wasn't sure what it meant.

The sun was getting hot, so I drifted back towards the army camp. My feet raised little clouds of dust as I walked and the sun beat down on my head. I had no hair, I'd left my wig in Alexander's tent; so, by the time I got back, I had a nice case of sunburn.

The guards stepped aside and lifted the tent flap up for me. Alexander wasn't back yet. I felt odd, alone in his tent. I thought perhaps I'd wait outside, but the air was hot. With a sigh, I retreated back into the coolness of the interior.

Once back inside, I tried to put on my wig, but it hurt my sunburnt head too much. It was made according to the pattern of the times, that is, real hair knotted onto a rough linen mesh and attached with string under my chin. I hated it, and wished I hadn't let myself be talked into shaving my head. Only two or three other women in the village were shorn, all the others had their own hair. They wore it plaited in many fine braids and decorated with glass paste pearls. Some of them had very short hair, others had it very long and none of them would have gotten more than a perfunctory glance in modern times. I was going to have a long talk with the fashion consultant when I got back to my own time.

I poured myself some of Alexander's wine and drank

it. Then I had some more because I was thirsty and hadn't eaten all day. I didn't touch the grapes because I'd forgotten which bunch was poisoned, and they all looked alike to me. I didn't dare ask anyone to bring me food. I was a precarious guest, uninvited, and unsure of my welcome.

My head started to ache so I lay down on the rug. My feet were sore from all the walking in my horrible sandals. They were made of grass, which has a sharp edge to it. I had little, stinging cuts between my toes, and my ankles were rubbed raw.

I stared blearily at my scratchy wig, up-ended on the floor, and my uncomfortable sandals, temptingly near the brazier. I wished that the fashion consultant was sitting in front of me, so I could bite her and hear her scream.

I drifted off to sleep with that comforting thought in mind, a half-smile on my face. I dreamed I was in the mouth of an enormous dragon. He was holding me in his jaws as delicately as an egg, but I knew that if he wanted he could close his mouth and crush me. The dragon's mouth was wide, and long, pointed teeth surrounded me. I was trapped and I could never get out. However, the dragon wasn't sure what he wanted to do with me. I couldn't speak to him, but I could sense his thoughts. He wasn't sure if I would make a good breakfast, lunch, high-tea snack, or if I would be better as a companion to talk to, or even as a sort of bauble to look at. A toy perhaps to play with? Dinner?

'Dinner!' I woke up with a cry. I was no longer alone. Alexander was sitting in front of his table writing on a clay tablet. He looked up at me and grinned.

'So you're hungry?'

I rubbed my aching head and groaned. 'How long have I been sleeping?'

'An hour, perhaps less. I didn't want to wake you because you snore so peacefully.'

'Do I really?'

'You do. But I don't mind. I have heard I snore too.' He tapped his large, aquiline nose. 'It's a sign of good health.'

'Listen, Iskander, I'm sorry, but I'd like to take just a few minutes of your time and ask some questions. I hope you don't mind this new tactic; it's called "not having much time left and being in a hurry".'

He looked amused. 'How interesting. A "tactic". Perhaps I shall learn something. Ask away, by all means.'

'What are your ambitions? I mean, besides seeing the ends of the earth?'

He stared at me. 'How did you know about wanting to see the ends of the earth? Who told you that?'

'Uh …' I didn't like the look in his narrowed eyes. In a minute he'd call for his guards and have me executed for spying or something. I tried to think of something to say.

Then Alexander snapped his fingers. 'That's right, you're an onirocrite. You must have dreamed about that. My immediate ambition is to finish conquering the Persians. We've passed Gaugamela, and we're heading towards Babylon. Then I will go to Alexandria and make her the most beautiful city in the world. I will rule Egypt, Greece, and Macedonia. I will give Babylon to my mother – maybe that will keep her busy.' His smile was like quicksilver dashing across his face.

I was surprised. 'And what about the rest of Persia, and India?'

His expression was thoughtful. 'I never thought of those places. Why do you ask?'

I frowned. There were strict rules to time-travel journalism, and one was you couldn't give anything about the subject's future away. Alexander was supposed to go to the ends of Persia and into the heart of India. He just didn't know why yet, I supposed. Disappointment was a bitter taste in my mouth. 'I'm just curious. I got the impression from my dream that you were interested in India.'

'No. I'm interested in Alexandria,' he said bluntly, and went back to his writing.

'Don't you have parchment?' I asked, pointing to the clay tablet.

'Yes, but I like writing cuneiform on clay. It's a very satisfying sensation.'

'How many languages do you speak?' I asked, desperate for information.

'Well, now that's a good question.' He scratched his temple thoughtfully with the nib of the reed, leaving a faint, red mark of clay. 'Greek of course, and Egyptian. Macedonian, Persian, and some of the mountain dialects the barbarians use. They say I pick up languages quickly.'

'Ah. And where is Nearchus?' I asked.

He stopped writing and looked at me with a frown. 'Why do you ask? Do you know Nearchus?'

'No, but I know he's very close to you. Has he gone ahead to scout?'

'Nearchus doesn't scout.' Alexander stood up and

walked towards me, stepping on my wig. 'Sorry,' he said, kicking it to one side. 'No, Nearchus has gone to see about the boats. I have a naval army. Nearchus is fascinated with the sea. I'm going to tell you something nobody else knows; I get seasickness.' He nodded. 'It's true. I admire Nearchus because he never vomits when he goes out on those infernal boats. I've put him in charge of the navy. It keeps him out of trouble, too. He's quite possessive of me and I suspect him of trying to poison my wife.' He shrugged. 'It was either Nearchus or my mother, I'm not sure which, but at any rate, the girl's still alive.' He paused and stared at the clay tablet, then shook his head. 'It's quite amazing to have a city named after oneself, don't you think? I never would have thought of it myself, but Nearchus insisted, so there it is. Alexandria. A lovely city.' He spoke dreamily, and went back to his table and started writing again. He was the kind of person who couldn't sit still for more than a few minutes.

I picked up my wig and looked at it. It was bent out of shape. If I put it on now I would look like one of those fancy chickens with feathers popping out all over their heads. I sighed and tried to straighten it out anyway. The interview was not going as I'd planned. I tried to think of a pertinent question but gave up. I looked at Alexander sitting at his table. His face was grave. Light from a small opening in the tent fell on the clay tablet so that he could work, and it showed his pensive expression. His face was all angles, and yet it was so well put together it was harmonious and noble. His nose was long and high-bridged. His profile looked like the one on a Greek coin. Was his fame such that he was already on coins? I asked him.

'No, that's my father. Surely you know that? Or are vestal virgins so protected they can't even touch money?'

'We're fairly well guarded,' I said sadly. I *was* sad. I knew that my time was running out and that I had to leave soon. I knew that he was on the most glorious part of his campaign, and soon he would conquer Persia, Bactria, Sogdia, part of India, and then return to Babylon. However, his reign would end when he was only thirty-three, and that, to me, was the greatest tragedy. That this young man would die so early was heartbreaking. He seemed so vital, so full of life and energy, even when sitting motionless behind his desk. He made me feel as insubstantial as mist. I wanted to touch him, to feel his arms around me. I needed him to make me real. A tremor ran through me. Was it because I was so far from my own time that I felt hollow? The words of one of my classmates came back to me. 'Permafrost,' she'd called me. I bit my lip. For the first time in my life, I wished I could show just one iota of the feelings inside me. I *did* feel things. When I looked at Alexander, there was a shiver inside me that I'd never experienced. It started at my toes and rose to my belly, where it seemed to blossom like a flame. Then it travelled to my chest, making it hard to breathe. I had no idea what was happening to me. Maybe it was only the flu.

I looked at him, and he stared back at me with his uncommon eyes. Something stirred in my heart, and my feelings must have showed. He moved with his usual quick grace and was beside me in an instant. His arms were around me and I forgot everything else. I forgot my resolutions, my sore feet, my interview, and my vestal virgin act. I clung to him and I didn't protest when he took my robe off and flung it to the far side of the tent.

He made love with the same fierce concentration he gave to everything else. It was like a storm that mounted in the heavens and then let itself out in a rush. I don't mean to say it was over in a flash, but the very intensity of it made it impossible to sustain for very long. At first he was gentle. He didn't hurry. He was absorbed in his movements, attuned to my slightest reaction. I tried to concentrate, but each time his skin touched mine my thoughts scattered and waves of pleasure blinded me – I closed my eyes and pressed myself closer to him, every nerve in my body tingling. Then a frenzy overcame us. When he cried out, I felt my belly convulse. Afterward we both trembled in each other's arms. My body quivered and his answered mine. Our hands were entwined.

I tried to analyze my emotions, but they were too new. I'd never felt like this before and it dazed me. I tried to recover my detachment. To my relief, my heart slowed, my breathing evened out, and I was able to think again.

Alexander rolled over and looked at me from beneath ridiculously long lashes. His eyes were shadowed and his regard was serious. 'Was it the first time for you?' he asked.

'No.' I moved my hips, feeling a slight ache. My tongue probed my lip and found it swollen. 'It's been … such a long time,' I said. I wanted to laugh, or cry. But the emotions stayed bottled inside me. I wanted to tell him that he was the first person to ever make love to me; my husband had only taken me by force and I'd never wanted to try with anyone else. But the words stayed locked in my throat. All I could do was sigh and put my hand lightly on his cheek.

He took it and kissed my palm. 'I will be gentler next time.'

The thought that there would be a next time brought a flush to my cheeks. He chuckled softly and gathered me into his arms. I wanted to stay there for ever, wrapped in his strong arms, but it was so hot that we couldn't lie together long.

We slipped out the back of the tent and dashed to the river. I think perhaps the whole camp saw us, but no one made hooting noises or catcalls, as they would have if a modern-day army general suddenly took it in his head to go skinny-dipping with a lady in the middle of a war campaign. In fact, they were very polite and pointedly abandoned the area, leaving us in peace.

We floated in the water. Sometimes we'd come together and touch, and then we'd separate and float. After about a half an hour we made love again, in the water this time. It was wonderful. I liked the way his eyes got darker when he was aroused. He also proved to be a dramatic kisser; I could have spent all day kissing him and never tire of it. I told myself it was 'just research', that the warmth I felt when he held me, and the tingling that grew in my belly whenever he looked at me, were just signs of clinical investigation. I'd never made love before, I told myself sternly, so it was normal that I was curious about it. My training reasserted itself.

'Tell me about your teacher, Aristotle,' I said, trying for more information for my article.

'He was a bit mad, but in a nice way. He loved to take walks down by the ocean, and he'd give me all his lessons with a long stick in his hand. He used the stick to draw diagrams in the sand, or to hit me over the head if I didn't pay attention.' He grinned. 'I'm afraid I wasn't very attentive.'

'What was the most important thing he taught you?' I asked.

'He told me to watch out for poison. I think that's one of the most practical things he taught me. He also taught me to withstand my mother. It wasn't easy. She's part-goddess, you know, and she's got a terrible temper.'

That wasn't what I'd expected. 'Does that make you part-god?' I asked, drawing my finger lightly down his forehead, his nose and over his full lips. He seized my finger between his teeth and bit down gently. Then he teased it with the tip of his tongue.

He took my finger out of his mouth. 'Maybe. I don't know. Aristotle said it was twaddle, and that Olympias just liked to put on airs. She admired him. Do you know why? Because he was the only one who never took her seriously.' He stopped talking and grabbed my shoulders. 'Enough about me. Who are you? Where are you from? What do you want from me?' He gripped me hard enough to make me wince, but he didn't let go.

I thought about the day I broke my ex-husband's nose. The day I finally knew exactly what I wanted. I wanted to go back in time and meet Alexander the Great. And here I was. 'Where I'm from is not important,' I said. 'I've been in love with you since I the day I first heard about you. And I wanted to meet you, to actually meet you in person.'

'You've been in love with me?' He let go.

Love? I'd just said 'love'? I felt a rush of heat wash over me as my predicament hit me. 'What's wrong with that?' My cheeks burned. I'd never told anyone I loved them, and Alexander simply looked surprised. I was expecting something else, as usual.

'Love, what a strange emotion. Aristotle used to say that love was a secondary emotion, that it was linked to the humours and should be quenched as much as possible. But then again, he was a dried-up old man with a sour wife, so what did he know? Love. I never thought much about it. I think I love my horse. Have you seen him? I must show him to you, he's amazing. I admired my father, and I hate my mother, so, according to Aristotle, I love her too, because he told me the two humours go hand in hand. But how can you love me without knowing me? Without seeing me? By just hearing about me?'

'I don't know,' I confessed. 'But ever since I can remember I've loved you. I turned down so many suitors because of you I became known as the "Ice Queen".'

He looked thoughtful. 'Yes, that suits you. You had that coldness about you when I first saw you. Not now, of course – now you are more of a volcano princess.'

I dunked him under the water and he came up sputtering and laughing.

'I have a proposition for you, my little volcano. Come with me. Be my consort. I will even marry you if you want. You'll be my second wife; I have one already. She's a barbarian princess who stayed with her family. I married her for political reasons; I shall marry you for love. What do you say? Shall we? It will be unique, and I will write a letter to Mother tonight. It will make her so angry she'll probably call down a plague upon us, or something. What's the matter? Why did you shiver?'

'I'm chilly. The sun is setting.' I pointed to the darkening sky.

'We'd better go inside. The mosquitoes are dreadful, they come out in swarms.'

I shivered again. He would most likely die of malaria, given to him by a mosquito. One buzzed around my head and I slapped it away. We climbed out of the water and he held up a white linen robe and wrapped it around me. He had one too.

'My soldiers left them for me,' he explained. 'I usually bathe in the evening.'

'With a woman?' I asked, stunned by a sharp pang of jealousy. I had definitely lost my mind and fallen apart.

'A woman or a man. Sometimes both.' He put his arms around me and hugged me. 'But you're the first to tell me you loved me.'

'What about your mother?'

He grimaced. 'I think I heard my mother say "I love you" once, but she was gazing into a mirror at the time, and I believe she was talking to herself, not to me. To me she'd say, "Iskander! Take that thumb out of your mouth and stop whining."!' He shook his head. 'I never whined, ever.'

'Of course you didn't!' I put my hand on his shoulder and we walked back to the tent. My heart was breaking. I had to leave soon and I didn't want to. I wanted to spend the rest of my life with Alexander; he made me think of

31

the sun. He was so brilliant. He was so perfect physically, so sharp mentally, so forceful and proud, and yet he had something vulnerable that shone in his smile and in his parti-coloured eyes. I took a deep breath and berated myself. My trip, so far, had been an abysmal failure. I dug my fingernails into my palms.

When we got to the tent he took a linen towel and rubbed me dry, and then he smoothed perfumed oil over my body so that I was soft and scented. A soldier came in, placed a tray of food on the table, and left without a word. But Alexander called out, 'Thank you!' I swear the man blushed.

'Everyone is in awe of me, now that I've beaten Darius,' he said, taking a piece of grilled squab and wrapping it tenderly in marinated grape leaves. He popped it into my mouth. 'You can be my poison taster tonight,' he said cheerfully. Then, seeing my eyes widen, 'No, I'm just teasing. My servants prepare my food, and it's been tested already.'

I swallowed and smiled bravely. 'I'd be honoured to die in your place.' Well, I already knew it wasn't poisoned.

'Oh, what a sweet little dream weaver you are!' he cried. 'Well, not so little. You're almost as tall as I am. The barbarian girl, if you can believe it, towers over me. She looks like a bear. She has more hair on her body than an Egyptian ape. Fascinating. She even has a little beard, which I asked her to shave, seeing as I shave mine. She looked much better with the beard, actually.' He chuckled. 'But she's a nice girl. She can throw a spear farther than Nearchus, and she told him that if she caught him sneaking around her tent again she'd cut off his balls and stuff them down his throat.'

'Nice girl,' I agreed.

'Nearchus is jealous, you see.'

'I hope I'm gone before he comes back, then,' I said. 'I'm not good at defending myself.'

'Oh, don't bother about him. I'll send him off on another trip. Maybe to India, how does that sound? You gave me the idea. I'll tell him not to come back until he can speak in their language. Fluently. He'll be gone fifty years. He has no ear at all for languages. He picks up the swear words fast enough, though. I suppose it's a sailor's thing.'

We stopped talking for a while and ate dinner. The food was delicately prepared and very good. I especially liked the persimmons. They were cooked with a spicy honey sauce. We lay on the rug and fed each other, licking each other's lips and fingers, and ended up making love again.

Afterwards, we just stared at each other. I wanted to remember each plane of his face, each curve of his body, each muscle, each bone, each expression. I touched his mouth, his nose, his hair, and he lay there purring like a cat. His magnificent eyes, with their sweeping dark eyelashes, were half closed. He was relaxed to the point of bonelessness, but I could sense the energy running like an electrical current through his veins. That energy would drive him all the way to India, and he would conquer the biggest empire the world had ever known. The warmth emanating from him surrounded everyone who came into his sphere. I saw his soldiers react to it. He was a warrior, with a warrior's reflexes, yet he had a philosopher's mind, curious and far-reaching. He was also physically imposing and inordinately handsome. The combination was seductive. He was the sort of person people would die for, and I had fallen under his spell.

I'd never been in love before. I never even considered the possibility. I'd always assumed my heart was as frozen as my icy-blue gaze. Now I was lying next to someone whose presence made my heart pound. It was disconcerting. I wasn't sure if I was in a hurry to leave, or if I wanted this evening to last for ever. I was confused, and for the first time in my life, felt vulnerable. A strange longing came over me, but for what, I could not tell.

We lay on the rug as night crept over the river valley. Purple shadows slid down the mountainside, then the stars came out. We looked through the opening in the top of the tent, and he pointed out the constellations.

'There's the swan, and the great hunter, Orion, with his dog. Underneath is the Lion, my sign. Over there is the virgin, Hestia, your sign.' He paused and propped himself up on his elbow. 'You weren't really a vestal virgin,' he said, reproach in his eyes.

I blushed. 'I'm sorry, but I had to wear a costume that would allow me to pass unmolested through the army lines.'

'My soldiers would never molest a woman. They don't need to, for one thing. The women all give themselves freely. They seem to like our fair colouring, and they beg for babies.' He shook his head. 'No, you didn't disguise yourself for that reason. You did it so you could be sure to see me. I *am* interested in dreams, you know. I dreamt about a dragon last night. As long as you're here, and pretending to be an onirocrite, I'll tell you all about it.

'I dreamt I was a great dragon. I was covered in gold and green scales, and as I flew through the air, I kept my eyes open for something to eat, because I was very hungry. Are you getting all this?'

I had gooseflesh, but I nodded. 'Yes, go on.'

'Well, I saw something interesting and I swooped down to see what it was. Can you guess?'

'Me,' I said.

'Why yes, that's right! I saw you. But you were not dressed as you are now.' He glanced at my nakedness and cleared his throat. 'I mean, you weren't dressed as a priestess. You had on a strange dress that hugged your legs and arms with a very intricate pattern, all in reds and purples. It was a very rich cloth, so I thought you must be a princess. Your hair, by the way, was down past your shoulders and quite amazing. I never saw hair that colour, as pale silver as the moonbeams. At first, I thought you were very old, because your hair was so white, but then I saw you were very young, and your hair was like the shining stuff the people in the east call "silk". Your eyes were twin sapphires from Kashmir. You were such a treasure I didn't think. I swooped down, caught you in my mouth, and flew back to my cave.

'I was in a dilemma. I was terribly hungry and you were soft and sweet. However, I wanted to talk to you, because I could sense you held the key to my future. Then, just before dawn, I woke up. I woke up, and do you know the strangest thing of all? In my mouth, I found a pearl. There's certainly a very simple explanation for that.

Perhaps it came from the oysters I'd eaten that evening, or perhaps Hera, the queen of the goddesses, played a trick on me. But whatever it was, look, here it is. Can you explain this?'

He reached over to the table and picked up a single, glowing, white pearl. It was one of the biggest, finest ones I'd ever seen.

'Do you chew your oysters?' I asked.

'No, I love them, but I can't bear to chew them. That must be the explanation. Now, you tell me, what is the future? Will I succeed? Will I see the edge of the earth?'

I rolled over on the rug and looked for my clothes. 'I'd love to stay and chat,' I said, 'but I have to go home.'

He took my wrist and held me. 'No. You're not leaving. My dream was quite clear. It was almost as if I were awake. And I saw you, as you really are, not disguised. I insist you stay until I solve the mystery.'

'What mystery?' I gave a nervous laugh. 'You ate an oyster that didn't agree with you and had some bad dreams. It's a common complaint. Take some bicarbonate and stay away from rich food for a few days.'

He pulled me down on the rug and rolled over, pinning me beneath him. 'You are my prisoner. There are several other little mysteries I'd like to clear up, and one of them involves your tongue.'

'My tongue?' I was confused.

'Yes. I spoke to you in five different languages and you replied in each one. I even used the language of the barbarians and it posed no problem.'

'Oh, that!' I smiled. 'That's easy to explain. I had a very good tutor when I was young. I learned many languages. You're not the only one with a gift for tongues.'

'And how did you know my teacher was Aristotle? I simply mentioned an old Greek, and you spoke his name.'

'Everyone knows you were taught by Aristotle,' I said. 'Now let me up, I must go.'

'You said you loved me.' He said this in a soft whisper, so low I nearly didn't hear it. My skin prickled.

'Does it matter?' I asked. 'You have an empire to conquer. Your army awaits. What place would I have by your side? You have places to go, cities to destroy …'

'I never destroy cities.' He spoke sharply. 'I build them.'

'Sorry, it was a slip of the tongue.'

'Slip it in here then,' he murmured, and his mouth fastened on mine. We kissed, but I knew I had to leave immediately.

Time travel involves minute planning, and I had to go back to the exact place I'd arrived to be picked up. If I didn't, I would be left behind. My tradi-scope would be shut off, and I could never return to my time.

I was faced with a terrible dilemma, but it was necessary. I couldn't change history. It is the first thing a time-journalist learns. We learn to hide our feelings, to smother them, and to look at everything dispassionately. I'd easily mastered those techniques. What astonished me was how quickly I seemed to forget.

I managed to wriggle from his grasp. It was dark and I had to grope around the tent to find my robe. I tucked the hated wig into my belt – I had to bring everything back or it would be docked from my pay check. I put the sandals on and winced as they rubbed against my sore feet. All this time Alexander was still, his eyes following me, his mouth drawn in a thin, unhappy line. When I was dressed he got to his feet and very formally walked me to the edge of the camp. He was naked, but he could have been wearing full military regalia from the way he held himself. He let go of my elbow when we reached the edge of the campfire's orange light.

'Shall I see you again?' he asked.

'No, I'm sorry.' I leaned against his chest. My heart was aching worse than my feet, which was a blessing, because otherwise I would not have been able to walk all those miles back to the checkpoint. My trip had been a fiasco. I had no idea what I'd write about. Alexander hadn't told me anything. When I got back, I'd be the laughing-stock of the world, but that didn't matter. What mattered was I was about to leave behind the most incredible man I'd ever met.

I hadn't known I'd had a heart until it broke.

He pressed the pearl into my hand before I left, and I clutched it. We weren't allowed to bring back souvenirs, so when I arrived at the little hollow where I was to be picked up, I buried it beneath the pomegranate tree. A lone tear trickled down my cheek and dropped on the earth. I wondered what it would grow.

Plant a pearl by the light of the moon, water it with tears …

A pale blue light seemed to come from nowhere. It encircled me and I could feel its coldness icing my blood and freezing it in my veins. My tears froze on my cheeks, and my teeth started chattering. Frost bloomed on my

38

skin. Then I felt my chest being squeezed and my breath being forced out of me. The night seemed to swirl around in my head, and the stars stabbed me with their icy brightness. My heart was aching and I couldn't breathe. I lost consciousness. The journey home had begun.

There was a babble of voices that my tradi-scope couldn't seem to handle. It whined and buzzed in my ears. I opened my eyes, expecting to see the cool, white Receiving Room at the Time Travel Institute. Instead, I saw flickering torches and the face of my lover bent over me, his eyes dark with worry.

'Have no fear. I found you on time. I should have known, I should have guessed. But he won't get you back, I saved you from him.'

'Saved me from who?' I gasped.

'From Hades, of course! But it's all over now; the cold demon has been driven away. When I saw you kneeling beneath the pomegranate tree, I recognized you. Persephone, sweet daughter of Demeter, will you stay by my side? I need you more than your cruel husband. And even he, the god of the dead, holds no terror for me.'

I tried to lift my head, but the shock was too great. I thought, *I must be dreaming*. And then I knew nothing.

Chapter Three

I woke up with the sun shining on my face through a hole in the tent. I groaned and sat up. It was true then. It wasn't a nightmare. Somehow, Alexander had torn me from the Time Traveller Tractor Beam. It must have been a fearsome battle; I knew the strength of that particular magnetic field. I felt bruised all over.

I shaded my eyes, searching for Alexander, but the tent was empty. I stood on wobbly legs and staggered over to the doorway. My muscles were stiff and my bones felt fragile. In front of the tent flap, three soldiers were playing dice. I nodded to them and they nodded back. One of them spoke to me, and I realized with horror my tradiscope was no longer functioning. I couldn't understand a word he said. I gasped and reeled backwards into the tent.

What would become of me? I tried to calm myself. I did speak ancient Greek after all; I also spoke English, Italian, French and German. I hadn't been joking when I said I had a good ear for languages. Alexander spoke Greek, of course. I simply had to start learning Persian, Phoenician, Egyptian and Sumerian. I wiped my sweaty hands on my dress. I would panic later, I thought. I went back to the soldiers and motioned eating and drinking. One sprang to his feet and trotted towards the mess tent. He came back a few minutes later with a pitcher of wine and a large piece of unleavened bread.

My head was aching so I lay down on the bed and tried to rest. I also tried to remember if anybody had ever survived being left behind, or if anyone had ever been kidnapped. I couldn't think of anyone. Actually, I couldn't think at all. I was paralyzed with a sort of panic that made rational thought impossible. Instead, all sorts of weird things crossed my mind, such as *what shall I wear*? Whom can I trust? When can I get home? And, *what will my mother think*? On a purely mathematical level, I was now over three thousand years older than my own mother. It was a sobering thought, so I drank some wine.

I decided the best thing to do would be to get drunk and go throw myself in the river. That way, I would be sure not to give away any secrets from the future, and I wouldn't risk changing history. I drank more wine and things didn't look so bad. Actually, they became almost funny. One or two cups later they were downright hysterical, and I was giggling when Alexander came into the tent.

He tossed his bronze breastplate onto the bed and threw himself on the floor beside me, a wide, white grin on his tanned face. 'What's so funny?' he wanted to know.

'Oh, nothing.'

'It's the relief, Isn't it? Knowing you don't have to go back to the underworld. It must be a freezing, cold place, because you were like ice when I grabbed you. He almost succeeded in tearing you away, but I wouldn't let go. I screamed that he'd have to take me too, so he released you.'

'Did you see him?' I asked, interested.

41

'Your Greek is strange today,' he said frowning at me. 'No, I didn't see him. Just a blue light. It must have been his minions. I would have been no match for Hades.'

'Well, he's punished me already,' I said. 'He's taken away the gift of tongues, so now I only speak Greek.'

'And a poor Greek it is,' he said pityingly. 'He's left you sounding like an actor playing a Mesopotamian whore.'

I winced. 'I'm sorry. It'll get better. I'm still trying to catch your accent.'

'I have no accent,' he told me gravely. 'Well, it's of no importance, I have you now, and that's all that counts.' He grinned. 'Won't Mother be jealous of you! She, who claims to be descended from Achilles and Thebes. You are the daughter of Demeter! I can't wait to see her face. Aristotle will love you, I'm sure. He loves anyone who can humble Mother.'

'I get to meet Aristotle?'

'Why yes, when we marry. It will be a big wedding. I want to do things right this time. You are the daughter of a goddess.' His face lit up. 'Will your family want to come, do you suppose?'

'No, I doubt it,' I said. The alcohol was making this conversation even more bizarre than it already was. 'They don't like weddings, and anyway I'm not anyone very important, I told you that.'

'It's just as well. When the gods meddle with our lives it usually ends in disaster. Look at poor Midas.'

I wondered if he was joking, but he seemed perfectly serious.

'The sad part is,' he said, and stopped.

'What? What's the sad part?'

'Well, the fact that I'll get old and you won't. You have the gift of immortality and I don't. However, when I get old and decrepit I'll let you go. I won't make you watch me die.'

'Oh, Iskander!' I cried. I swooned into his arms and then the wine won. I fell asleep, and probably snored loudly, until late in the afternoon.

When I woke, my head was splitting. I never want to have another hangover brought on by honeyed wine. I was alone, but as soon as I stirred, a Greek guard poked his head in the tent and told me that Alexander was waiting for me at the riverside. I went to the swimming hole and there he was, lying on the beach. He was dressed in a linen tunic with a stiff, pleated skirt. It should have looked ridiculous, but he would have looked regal dressed in a pink Easter Bunny suit. Four slaves were standing over him, each holding a pole. The poles supported a canopy that kept the hot sun off. He saw me and got to his feet.

'Did you want to see me?' I asked.

'I wanted to show you my horse. Come.' We walked to the stables, the four slaves keeping step with us. I liked having the shade over our heads, but I hated the idea of slaves, so I whispered to Alexander that maybe they could go sit down for a while.

He looked at me as if I'd gone mad. 'They spend most of the day sitting. Poor chaps, they'll die of boredom. Come on, we're almost there.' He gave a piercing whistle and was answered by a wild whinny. 'That's Bucephalus,' he said proudly.

The horse was smaller than I'd expected; more

compact than the horses I was used to seeing. His back was short and strong, his neck was very thick and he had hardly any withers. His tail swept the ground, and his mane fell past his massive chest. He was reddish brown, with a black muzzle. His mane and tail were black as well.

Thousands of years of domestication have rendered modern horses as interesting and intelligent as rutabagas. Bucephalus was different. His brain was still canny with all the instincts of a wild animal, and it showed in his broad forehead and large, bright eyes. He looked at me, and I could see his mind working. He looked at Alexander, and his eyes softened, and all his love shone in a warm light. He whickered and pushed his nose under Alexander's arm.

'Hey, Buci, hey boy.' Alexander's voice was rough with emotion, and he scratched the horse behind his small, pointed ears. He fed him some tidbits and then patted him on the neck.

'Are you going to ride him?' I asked.

'Do I look like I'm dressed for riding?'

He looked like he was going to try out for the cheerleading squad, but I didn't say that. 'No, but don't you have to exercise him?'

'He's had enough exercise. We've been in three battles in as many months, and now we're resting. It isn't as calm as this all the time, you realize. We're taking a break. In ten days we'll be on the move. Nearchus will be back with news from Athens, and we'll make our plans.'

'Where are you going next?' I asked.

'Babylon. And then we marry.' He smiled at me. 'We

have to plan our wedding. Shall I invite my mother?'

'She'll never get the invitation on time,' I said.

He was surprised. 'Yes she will. If I send a message tonight she'll get it in four days.'

'How?'

'By bird, of course.'

'Of course.' I hadn't given much thought to the methods of communication of the time. I realized I had a lot to learn. 'Will she want to attend?' I asked.

'Who knows? We'll give her time to come, though. You'll hate her, Persephone,' he said with a grin.

'Another thing,' I said. I wasn't sure how to bring this up but I had to. 'My name isn't really Persephone.'

'It's not?' He raised an eyebrow. 'What is it?'

'It's Ashley.'

'Ashley? What sort of name is that?'

'It's the one my mother gave me, and I've gotten used to it. No one calls me Persephone,' I said.

'Ashley, ashes, ash. Was it because she was goddess of the hearth? No, your mother is Demeter, goddess of the harvest. Ashley. Well, I suppose I'll get used to it. Iskander and Ashley.' He rolled my name around in his mouth and seemed to like the taste of it. 'Hmmm, it's nice. Ashley. Ashhhhhhleeeeeeey.'

'Oh stop it.' I swatted his butt.

'Assssssshhhhhhhhllllllleeeeeeeeyyyy.' He stuck his tongue out and ducked behind one of the impassive slaves when I lunged at him. 'You are so slow!' he exclaimed.

I dived at him again, but missed. It was annoying. I dashed after him – after all, I was no mean sprinter and I'd racked up some running medals in school. He ran backwards and outdistanced me as if I were standing still. I was perplexed. He seemed to defy the laws of gravity. *And* dressed in a skirt.

We were near the river and the running had made us hot, so we stripped off our clothes and plunged into the water.

'Last one to the opposite shore is a rotten egg!' I called and started across. I swam well. Being a member of a posh country club had its advantages.

He swam past me and pushed me underwater before streaking away.

'Damn him,' I muttered. Was there nothing I could do better than he? I finished the race alone, watching him as he splashed on the far side of the river. I slowed to a leisurely breaststroke to watch him. He glowed in the sunshine. His head was crowned in gold. His body seemed made of ivory and rose. The clear, amber water surrounded him like a setting for a precious jewel. I stroked against the current, letting myself drift a bit downstream so I could get a better look at my future husband, Alexander the Great.

I didn't see the crocodile until it was nearly upon me. I screamed. It was terrifying – fifteen feet long and covered in black and yellow scales.

Alexander heard me and turned his head. I kept my eyes on Alexander all the while backstroking frantically away from the beast. There was a moment when Alexander's body left the water. Then he disappeared under the surface. The crocodile was coming at me, propelling itself with its strong tail; its body weaving back and forth, mouth open, showing jagged rows of teeth.

Suddenly, it seemed to stop and swim backwards. A terrific wave broke over its head, and Alexander was sitting on the creature's back, his hands locked under its jaw, his legs wrapped around its middle.

The crocodile opened its mouth wide and hissed, it bucked and twisted. Alexander was lost in a thrashing froth of white water. I found my voice and screamed.

His guards were never far away. They came hurtling to the riverside and threw themselves into the water. Knives glinted in their hands as they jumped into the fray. Most of them, I saw, were grinning.

The crocodile had no chance against five trained soldiers. It was soon floating belly-up in the river while the men pushed it upstream, singing a loud, probably bawdy song. Alexander sat on its stomach, riding it in triumph, waving his arms and singing along with the others.

I couldn't believe my ears. He was totally tone deaf. His singing was an ear-splitting cacophony. I smiled in grim satisfaction. I had perfect pitch.

After the soldiers, still singing, had lugged the crocodile away, Alexander and I sat in the sand. I felt shy. Not because I was nude, sitting under a canopy held up by four huge Nubians, and I'd just been saved from a monstrous crocodile. I was shy because I had started to perceive the enormous gulf that separated us. The gulf was more than just time, more than cultural or physical. It was there because I'd grown up in a society where everything was controlled and regulated – where fake feelings were served up in cellophane packages such as movies, and real emotions were throttled or turned into derision. People didn't burst into song because they had wrestled with a crocodile. They didn't have the candid expressions these men had. People in my time had stony faces and avoided eye contact. They didn't touch each other, and they didn't speak unless spoken to. People here wore their emotions on the outside, they spoke their minds, and they expected me to do the same.

I couldn't. I realized that I would never be able to fit in. I was troubled for the rest of the evening, and during the dinner I observed everyone, but never joined in the conversation. Alexander watched me. Once I thought he would ask me something. He opened his mouth, then frowned and shut it. I felt something, but didn't know if it was disappointment or relief.

I drank more than I should have that night. I don't remember going to the tent, or falling asleep. Perhaps it was the shock. I felt as if I were floating above everything, as if I could see through everyone. Mostly, though, I felt as if my own body were transparent, and that I had no more substance than a ghost.

Dawn poked rosy fingers into the tent, and I opened my eyes and tried to focus them. It seemed that my head had been hurting for three days, and I wondered where I could find some aspirin. Alexander looked fresh and fit. His eyes were clear and he sat cross-legged on the floor while his slave shaved his cheeks.

'Do you want him to shave your head?' he asked.

I reached up and felt my stubble. 'No thanks, I think I'll let it grow.'

'Wise choice, but you'll get sunburned if you refuse to wear your wig.'

'My wig,' I wrinkled my nose. 'Where is that damn thing, anyway?'

'I think they used it to start the fire last night.' He sounded amused.

'Good riddance.' I rolled over on the bed and stretched. 'Breakfast?'

'The sun is rising, and I must go and show myself to my troops.' He sounded regretful, and he kissed the tip of my nose. 'You can go to the village and buy yourself some robes for the wedding.' He lifted the lid of a wooden box and gave me some coins. 'That should do. Get something nice.'

'But it's barely dawn,' I protested. 'Everyone will be asleep.'

'No, it's market day. Don't come back with any live animals, though, I can't bear women who have pets.'

'Your mother?' I guessed.

He nodded, his face dark. 'She had a parrot that sat on her shoulder. If we got too close to her, it would leap at us and bite our noses. My sister was almost disfigured.' He shuddered.

'My mother had a spaniel. If I got too close, it would growl and she'd say, 'Ashley, don't upset Hector!'

Alexander burst out laughing. 'I didn't know the goddesses had pets. What's a spaniel? A sort of dragon?'

I choked and shook my head. 'No, no, it's a dog. A little dog,' I put my hand a foot from the ground. 'Like this.'

'Why didn't you kill it?'

'I couldn't! Did you kill the parrot?'

'No,' he smirked. 'My sister did. She poisoned the

beast.'

'How dreadful! How did she manage that?'

'She put poison on her nose. Mother was furious. Poor Nike.'

'Nike?'

'Thessalonike. My sister. I call her Nike. Her husband, Cassander, is a nice enough fellow. When Nike married him she made sure Mother didn't come to their wedding. She was afraid Mother would try something foolish, like poison, to avenge her parrot.'

'What a family,' I muttered.

'Oh, our growl is worse than our bite,' he said.

The slave came back with a tray holding a bowl of yoghurt and some fresh fruit. Alexander thought it was funny when I tried to talk to the slave.

'He won't answer you,' he said. 'He can't talk.'

'Oh, what language does he speak?'

'None now. They cut off his tongue at birth.'

'Poor man! It's criminal!'

'They didn't only cut off his tongue,' he said, winking at the man who stood impassively. 'They cut off his …'

'Don't say it!' I held up my hand. Alexander, I'm going to tell you something very important. You must not own slaves. Slaves are human beings, just like us.'

He frowned and reached over to touch my forehead. 'You have no fever.' He sat back and shrugged. 'Of course they're human beings. But what should I do with poor Brazza? He has no family, no tongue with which to speak, no testicles to engender babies – should I just turn him out?' He addressed the slave in a guttural dialect. The slave looked shocked, then amused, and stuck his chin into the air, tipping his head back. 'See? He doesn't want to leave. Now finish your breakfast and go to the village. I have to see my generals now.' He kissed me softly on the lips, and went.

The village was swarming with people. Everybody was up and about. It made sense when I thought about it. The afternoons were blazingly hot, and only in the morning or evening could one stay outside very long.

There were little stands set up everywhere. Some sold wine, others food. There were animals, birds, fish, gold, silver, and bolts of brightly coloured cloth. Everyone mingled, the rich and the poor, the beggars, the soldiers, the whores, and the priests. There was a group of vestal virgins, surrounded by their eunuchs. They were admiring a man juggling oranges and knives. He would cut the oranges as he juggled and he passed the pieces to the virgins, never once dropping anything. A small monkey sat on his head and shrieked.

Everyone was shouting or laughing. There were no written signs, so wares were advertised by criers. An important-looking man with a long scroll stood on a block of carved marble and read something in a loud, singsong voice. When he finished reading he'd take a drink from the wineskin slung around his neck and start all over again. I guessed he was the morning news. There were people speaking Greek, Phoenician, Persian, Coptic, Egyptian, Arabic, and at least five or six other languages. Translators rushed back and forth, translating prices and news for a few coins. I found one who spoke Greek, and asked him to come with me.

He bowed and said his name was Nassar. He was a small man, black-haired and wiry. He wore a rectangle of unbleached muslin draped around his shoulders Greek-style.

'Can you tell me what he's saying?' I asked, pointing to the man standing on the marble pillar.

'Certainly. He's telling everyone the latest news.' He frowned. 'He's saying Plato died.'

I did some mental arithmetic and frowned. 'That's the latest news? He died thirteen years ago.'

Nassar listened some more and shook his head. 'No, I got it wrong. He's saying that tonight at the amphitheatre there's to be a play by the late Plato. His accent is terrible; I wonder how much wine he's drunk.' He listened some more, frowning. 'He says Nearchus will be returning with the other half of Iskander's army in three days. Ah, now that's interesting. There is to be a virgin sacrifice to appease Hera; apparently some girl has made her jealous again.'

'What happens when Hera gets jealous?' I asked.

'Oh, war, famine, exploding volcanoes. The usual. My guess is one of the temple virgins made the head priestess jealous, but then again, I'm an atheist.'

'But that's awful! That poor girl! I thought human sacrifice was an abomination.'

'We're not in Greece any more,' Nassar shrugged. He had a very eloquent shrug.

'When's the sacrifice?' I asked.

'In three days.'

'I'll have to speak to Alexander about that,' I muttered. 'He's supposed to be bringing Greek culture to the rest of the world.'

'Now he's saying that there's a sale on parrots near the temple.'

'I need a wedding dress,' I told him.

He glanced at my vestal virgin attire and grinned. 'Did the news about the sacrifice make you nervous?'

'Wouldn't it make you nervous?' I asked him.

'If I were a virgin, yes. Now, over here we have cloth from Egypt, nice cotton, and some fine linen. There's silk if you can believe it, all the way from the land of the yellow devils.'

I fingered the silk and the cotton, both were very expensive and of poor quality. I ended up buying some fine linen. I found some that had been dyed a rich crimson and I bought a yellow sash to tie around my waist. I also decided I needed a head covering, so I bought another wig, but this one was very simple and light, consisting of a thin braid wrapped all the way around the crown.

'Good choice,' said Nassar when I paid for it. 'Finest quality hair from Indus. The braids are taken from dead soldiers. They never cut their hair there, you know.'

I gagged and tore the wig off my head. Holding it delicately with two fingers, I went back to the wig stand and traded it for a simple turban made of bleached cotton.

'You're a strange girl, you know,' said Nassar.

'That's what I've been told,' I said.

'Look! Honey-roasted nuts!' Nassar had a sweet tooth. I bought him some nuts, and he followed me, happily crunching, while I wandered about the marketplace. Then he wiped his face with the hem of his robe. 'Now what?' he asked.

'Now I go back to camp. You'll have to come with me; I don't have any money left to pay you.'

He nodded and we trotted back to the encampment. He faltered when we arrived and tugged on my arm. 'That's Iskander's tent,' he whispered.

'I know. That's who I'm marrying.'

His eyes widened. 'Iskander?' I shot to dizzying heights in his esteem. 'Does he need a translator?' he whispered.

'No, he doesn't, but I do. How many languages do you speak?'

He counted on his fingers then bent down to look at his toes. I caught his arm.

'All right,' I said. 'If I can, I'll hire you. What's your rate?'

He wriggled his nose like an excited bunny. 'Food and lodging, writing instruments and a few coins now and then. I write letters too, and if I can work in Iskander's army I'll make lots of money.' He rubbed his hands together, and then looked worried. 'But what if he says no?'

'Why would he say no?' I was amused.

'Because I'm from Babylon. Everyone knows Iskander is on his way there to conquer it. He may think I'm a spy.'

'Are you?'

'No! I'm apolitical,' he said proudly, 'and an atheist. I embrace all the latest philosophies from Athens. Personally, I can't wait until Iskander conquers Babylon, I was getting tired of it. A city needs change to thrive. We haven't had any excitement since Nebuchadnezzar. I'm named after him, you know. Nassar is just my nickname.'

'I'm impressed.' I waved to the soldiers guarding the tent and they stood at attention as I drew near.

'Iskander is waiting for you,' one said.

'Oh, thank you.' I thought of something. 'What are your names, please?' I asked.

'You address us according to our rank,' said the Greek soldier. 'I am captain of the guards, and these are my sergeants. My name is Lysimachus.'

I was startled. I had heard of him in my history classes. 'Thank you, Captain.' I ducked under the tent flap the sergeant was holding aside.

'How was the market?' Alexander was sitting behind his table, looking at a beautifully drawn map of the area. Every now and then he'd take a piece of straw and poke it through the parchment, making a tiny hole. Then he'd hold the map up to the light and squint at it.

'Nice, very nice,' I said. 'I met a translator and he worked for me all morning. Do you mind giving him some money? I spent everything you gave me on a wedding dress.'

He took a couple of coins and gave them to me. 'All right, speak your mind, woman.'

'Speak of what?'

'Whatever it is you want to ask. I sense your uncertainty.'

'Oh.' I uncrossed my feet. 'Well, I was wondering if we could keep Nassar. He's a good translator. He speaks many languages, almost as many as you. He said he'd be happy to write letters for your soldiers.'

'Hmmm. Maybe. What's the problem?'

'He's from Babylon,' I said. 'He's afraid you'll think

he's a spy.'

'He probably is.' He shrugged. 'But I don't mind. Spies are as numerous as mosquitoes around this camp. Where's the dress?'

'I can't show you, it's bad luck.' I hesitated, then blurted, 'Iskander, there's more. You have to put a stop to human sacrifice. It's not right. There's one scheduled three days from now!'

'No problem,' he grinned and stood up, stretching. 'I'll just slaughter all the priestesses and the priests at the temple. That should take care of it for a while.'

'No, no!' I stamped my foot. 'That's not what I meant. Give an order or give a speech. You have charisma and power enough to influence them.'

'I was just teasing.' He shook his head. 'You must take me for a barbarian. I suppose the gods live differently – no slaves, no sacrifices – but we're on earth now, and you'll have to get used to some things.'

'I'll try to settle in, but Rome wasn't built in a day,' I said.

'Rome wasn't built in a day,' repeated Alexander, savouring the words. 'I like that.' He smiled. 'Do the gods have many sayings like that?'

'Many,' I said seriously. 'Oh, Alex, can we go to the theatre tonight? They're doing something by Plato.'

'Why not? Plato's dry, though. I hope they also have some comedy.'

'Plato's dry?'

'I could barely get through his *Republic*, no action.' Alexander cocked his head and stared at me. 'Did you call me Alex a moment ago?'

'Alex? I guess so, is that all right?'

'My sister used to call me Alex. I like it. But don't call me that in front of my men.'

'OK.'

'What does Oh-kay mean?'

'It means sure, all right, yes.'

'In what language? I've never heard it?'

'Well, I'm not sure. It must be something left over from the gift of tongues. Never mind.'

Alexander sat down again. 'There's something so strange about you,' he said, and he sounded almost sad.

I looked at him and wished that I could tell him everything. But I knew that if I changed the course of history, the people at the Time Travel Institute would activate their infernal machine and erase me from time, as easily as Alexander was taking out the small villages on his map with the poke of a stick. I would cease to be. I didn't want that to happen.

Marrying Alexander might change a few things, but nothing radical. Alexander had had numerous wives; supposedly he married one woman in every city he conquered. No one knows for sure how many he married. Officially, there were Roxanne and Darius's daughter. However, marriages at the time were not like our marriages. They weren't written contracts. They were often, as he'd said, politics. His heirs would be the boys or girls he cared to claim. Alexander had been born to his father's concubine.

I wasn't worried about suddenly appearing in the history books. The written word was rare. I was in an aural society, where speaking was more important than writing; where people chose what they said with care. Pledges were made orally, and they held as much power as a document would centuries later. When someone asked a question, he listened carefully to the answer because survival could depend on what was said. Stories were told, but lies were few. People in this time picked up every nuance in speech. When they talked, it was to communicate. They would gather and discuss religion and philosophy, and the latest way to make purple dye. Everything interested them. They had come to a point in history where the world was changing and people were travelling more than ever. New ideas were coming from the four corners of the known world, and all ideas were considered. Everyone embraced everyone else's notions. They were new, different, and amusing. It was a time of expansion and people were ready.

Alexander's army had been carefully chosen. As a soldier, he wanted fighting men. However, as a keen politician, he wanted men who would impress people in other lands. He wanted his men to be educated, so he would often talk to them about the things he'd learned from Aristotle. And the men listened. Most were young men eager for travel and change, open-minded and curious. They remembered his words. Afterwards, when they were left behind in a garrison town, either because they had been wounded or had been married to a local girl, they continued Alexander's mission. They repeated everything he'd told him, and people listened and told their families and friends. So, much faster than you would expect, Greek civilization swept across Asia.

With Alexander's army were doctors, biologists,

priests, merchants, historians, minstrels, actors, whores, soldiers' wives, children, and diplomats. And then there was myself.

I was an only child of elderly parents; a freak accident that my mother, well into menopause, could never explain. She found she was pregnant when it was too late to do anything about it, and she resigned herself to being a mother at an age when most women are grandmothers.

To say I was an embarrassment would be an understatement. My mother hardly dared tell her closest friends. I believe most people thought I was the cook's daughter. When I was old enough to be toilet-trained, I was shipped off to boarding school. I came home for vacations and wandered around our huge, empty house alone. I had no friends in the neighbourhood, and my schoolmates were never allowed to visit. Summers were the worst. Our house was the biggest one in the village, my parents were the richest people, and the other children hated me. My mother had our chauffeur drive me to the country club for my lessons every day. I had swimming lessons, golf lessons, riding lessons, and tennis lessons. At home, there were piano lessons, and I was tutored in French and Italian. Everywhere I went I was alone, except for my various tutors and our ancient chauffeur, whose only attempt at conversation was to ask me every day if 'Mademoiselle was well.'

My father died of old age when I was ten. I dressed in black and paraded down the street behind the hearse to the cemetery. It was the first time I'd ever walked through the village. I walked behind the hearse, alone. My elderly mother rode in the car. I must have looked ridiculous, but the people lined up along the streets nodded sympathetically to me. I remember seeing them and wondered where the parade was. When I realized I was the parade, I was glad of the black veil hiding my face.

At the cemetery, my mother and I stood in front of a huge crowd of mourners. I didn't cry. I had already learned to smother my feelings. The mourners walked back to the house where a huge banquet was set up on the lawn. It was mid-July, and the whole atmosphere was like a garden party. Except for the black clothes, you would have thought it was a fiesta.

After my father's death, my mother took a bit more interest in me. It was the sort of interest one takes in a rough gemstone. She decided to polish me and put me in the best setting she could find. That's how, when I was only sixteen years old, I found myself married to a French Baron.

Married. I had been standing still, thinking about all this, while Alexander watched me. He had stopped poking holes in the map and his eyes had their jaguar look.

I blushed. 'I'm sorry, did you say something?'

He shook his head. 'No, but some day you'll tell me about it. You're face is thawing, my Ice Queen. You are turning into a human being.'

I went outside and told Nassar he could stay. He was overjoyed and kept kissing my feet, which I found embarrassing. I gave him the coins and he tucked them in his belt. Then he bowed a few more times and danced off towards the village. Before he left, I asked him what time the play started.

'At sunset,' he said, and waved.

I hesitated to go back into the tent. For one thing, I didn't want to disturb Alexander who seemed to be concentrating on his task, and for another, I wanted to be alone. I needed to think. I wandered towards the river, but there was a crowd of men and women on the banks. The fields were full of farmers and under nearly every large tree someone was sitting in the shade. I ended up at the stables. I liked horses, even after years of boring riding lessons.

Alexander's horse snorted at me. I was afraid to touch him, he looked so wild. There were tamer-looking ponies in the corral, so I leaned over the fence and scratched their necks. They were shy at first, but soon crowded around me. Their eyes were so intelligent they looked like large dogs. Dogs have expressions and so did these ponies. One in particular was very sweet. She was a pale grey filly with a white mane and tail. I wondered if I could take her for a ride, and I went in search of a groom.

The man in charge was Greek. He told me there was no problem if I wanted to ride the grey pony. He put a bridle on her, and I examined it. It was made of wide, thick leather to protect from sword cuts. The bit was a simple snaffle with a pretty, braided rein looped through two metal hoops on each side of the pony's mouth and tied in a knot. The reins were short but easy to handle. There was no saddle; instead, a sheepskin was thrown over the pony's back and cinched with a wide leather band. Over the sheepskin went a felt blanket. A breast strap was attached to the girth to keep the whole affair from slipping backwards. There were no stirrups, but I didn't think I'd need any.

The pony, calm and almost sleepy in the pen, turned into a racehorse when I got on its back. It wheeled around and galloped off towards the hills.

I was left sitting in the dust, staring after its floating white tail. The groom didn't seem perturbed. He pursed his lips and whistled. The pony whirled around again and galloped back, snorting and prancing in front of the groom. He handed me its reins and told me to squeeze with my knees and not to worry, when the filly got tired she would slow down. I got on again and off we went.

I didn't try to steer. It wouldn't have mattered where I went, and the pony chose a shaded road that led towards a large wooded hillside. The pony galloped for about five minutes, which put us quite a way from the camp, and then it slowed and let me take control.

I experimented with stopping and turning her, and I was impressed. She stopped so suddenly I nearly pitched over her head and she turned on a dime, literally. I picked myself off the dusty road and whistled, and the pony trotted over to me and stood while I climbed back on. Then we headed towards the woods. I needed to think and I was hoping to find a spring; my throat was parched.

Behind me, the plains near the river had been planted recently with the winter wheat, and light green shoots were sprouting in the dark earth. Date palms grew in tall groves. White, curly-haired goats grazed beneath them, their soft bleating echoing through the blue shade. The road I was riding on was pale yellow, and dust rose in a talcum cloud with every step. A wood ahead of me seemed inviting. Pine trees and olive trees cast cool, dappled shadows.

We picked our way through the forest, the docile pony weaving around the trees until we came to a small clearing. I spotted a simple stone temple marking a burbling spring. I lay on my stomach and drank deeply while the pony plunged its nose in and drank too. Afterwards, I tied the pony to a shady tree and walked around the meadow gathering flowers. When I had a colourful bouquet, I placed it near the spring then sat under a tree.

The spicy pine scent was soothing and the buzzing of bees and the liquid chirping of birds soon lulled me to a half-sleep. I felt as content as I'd ever felt in my entire life and wanted to savour it, not ruin it with useless worry about my predicament. However, my mind was unable to relax. My body was slumped against a smooth tree trunk, but my mind was crashing against the bars of the time-cage in which I was caught.

I had to accept the fact that I was trapped. I would have to live the rest of my life here, in this age and time, and I could do nothing, absolutely nothing, to change what must happen. I had to let events wash over me. I also had to shake off the strange, dreamlike state I had been in ever since I'd arrived. Somehow, the cold was still steeped in my bones, and my mind seemed half numbed.

When I'd managed to convince myself I was sitting in a meadow, and there were, in fact, a pony, a temple and a spring, I started to work on convincing myself I was in Mesopotamia in the year 333 BC.

I tried to remember all the pertinent things I'd need to know. We were in Mesopotamia, and we were heading towards Babylon. Alexander was not Greek, but from

Macedonia. His father had conquered Greece and then had been assassinated.

I closed my eyes and tried to stop shaking.

Religions were important, and in Athens, Socrates had been put to death because he had been impious. Paradoxically, atheists were tolerated. They even mocked the gods in certain comedies. Not here, though, not in Alexander's army. There was a herd of pure white cows and pitch-black bulls used for sacrifice. The black bulls, if I remembered correctly, were for the god of the dead, Hades – my supposed spouse.

I paused and managed to relax my jaw. The spasms were ebbing, my stomach was unclenching and I found I could open my fingers. The stick fell from my hand. What I knew was not enough to survive. I had only planned to stay for twenty hours.

I gasped and doubled over, my whole body writhing with cramps. They had told me what might happen if I didn't come back. It was something to do with the space-time continuum – mass from the future coming back to the past. When one stayed a very short time, a day for instance, there was no need to adjust. My mass took up just a bit of space and the elasticity of time allowed for it. However, if my mass stayed then the space would try to reclaim its former shape. I didn't belong here. There was a chance that everything would shift and I would find my place here. Until then there were waves of pain and dizziness as my mind was pulled towards the future and my body's atoms fought to stay in this timeline.

Blood spattered onto my hands and soaked into the ground as my nose started to bleed. I sat up and spat the blood out of my mouth. I peered through dazzling sunshine towards the spring. The sound of the cool water gurgling became a roar in my ears. Another wave of cramps rushed over me. The earth next to me dipped, as if an invisible weight had settled on it. I knew it was just the mass evening itself out. Soon it would be done and I would either be absorbed into the timeline, or left here.

My mind balked. I drew my knees up against my chest and huddled. My mind was trying to process all the information and it was having a hard time. The part about being trapped bothered it, as did the possibility I'd be erased if I made a wrong move. Then the pain stopped, the headache disappeared and the sunlight ceased to stab my eyes. My muscles all relaxed at once and I sprawled onto the soft ground, into the hollow that the earth had made for me. The earth had let me stay.

I stood up and shook myself. I had to stop separating my mind from myself. I had to …

I had to stop right where I was and not move a muscle. A very small snake was curling itself into a tight coil just inches from my right foot. It was a pretty snake, as snakes go, but I knew nothing about them and distrusted its bright colours. I froze. The snake darted its tongue at me, and I started to shake. I don't know how long I would have stayed frozen like that, but the snake became bored and slithered away. I walked back to my pony and leaned against her withers. She seemed to sympathize, nuzzling my shoulder and whickering. When I stopped trembling, I washed my face, drank deeply, untied the pony, and rode slowly back to the camp.

Chapter Four

Alexander had gone to see his soldiers, so I lay down on the bed and had a nap.

When I woke up Alexander and I went for our evening swim. We washed each other's hair, and I plucked a willow branch and proceeded to clean my teeth. I had been cleaning them this way since I'd arrived, although I would have liked some fresh mint toothpaste to go along with it. I was just starting to nibble at the wood, to make it softer, when Alexander asked me what I was doing.

'I'm cleaning my teeth,' I explained. I showed him how it was done, and told him I did it three times a day.

Alexander raised his eyebrows. 'We use little brushes and put paste made of chalk and lemon juice on them. The Egyptians use urine, white wood ashes and ass's milk,' he added. 'What does your mother use? What do you use in the underworld? Are there trees there? It must be dreadfully cold.' He stopped talking and waited for me to answer all of his questions in the order he'd asked them.

I hadn't known about their toothbrushes. I was put off by the description of the Egyptians' toothpaste, though. 'My mother had little brushes that we used; the ones she liked had hog's bristles. And as for the underworld ...' I stopped and groped for something to say about that, '... well, it's cold in the wintertime and hot in the summer.' I left it at that and he seemed content. Except for one thing.

'What about the trees?'

'Oh. Well, no, there are no trees underground.' I frowned. This was getting tricky. 'You know, I can't talk about any of that, I hope you'll understand.'

He nodded. 'I should have known. I won't ask you any more about it. It must have been dreadful and you want to forget it, is that it?'

'Exactly.' I smiled and then swam against the current. 'Shall we get dressed for the theatre? I don't want to be late.'

'No, I don't want to get dressed just yet.' He drifted alongside me and rolled over in the water like a playful dolphin. I noticed his erection and grinned; he was about as subtle as a tank. We splashed about in the water together. It was fun swimming against the current and making love at the same time. I started giggling and nearly choked and he found that hilarious. He held me up and then moaned, putting his face in the crook of my neck. The current took us downstream, and we had to wade back to our beach.

He caught me watching him, and his face shifted. He smiled and shook his head. 'You mustn't look at me like that,' he said gravely. 'The gods will be jealous and they'll take you away again.' He caught me by the arm and pulled me to him, holding me tightly. 'I don't want to lose you,' he whispered in my ear. 'So don't tempt the gods, please.'

For once, I thought I knew what he was feeling, so I nodded, my face against his broad chest.

We dressed for the theatre. I wrapped linen around

myself like a sari, tied a yellow sash around my waist, and then wincing, put my sandals on again. My feet were not getting used to them.

Alexander looked imposing with a white, pleated dress skirt and his military tunic. He slipped his breastplate on, then shook his head and took it off. 'A bit ostentatious,' he said. Instead, he took a deep purple cape.

'Very handsome,' I told him.

He asked me to plait his hair into one long braid. His shoulder-length hair was naturally wavy and thick, and I wished mine would grow in faster. My stubble looked like hoarfrost on my head. I put my turban on.

He kissed me before we left. He grinned at me, our foreheads touching. His was warm, mine cool.

'Shall we go, my snow queen?'

'We go, my sun prince,' I answered, and our hands entwined as we walked down the road towards the setting sun. There was a marvellous feeling growing in my chest making it hard to breathe, but even harder to stop grinning.

The theatre was crowded, but we had the best seats. First, one of the actors read a discourse from Plato's *Republic*, in Phoenician, so I didn't get a word of it. Then Alexander went to the stage and took a bow. He gave a long speech, also in Phoenician, and I had no idea what it was about, but I guessed it was a harangue on Greek culture. The people raised their arms into the air and snapped their fingers, which was their way of applauding.

Afterwards there was a tragedy, and then a comedy.

The tragedy was *Oedipus Rex*.

Unwittingly, Oedipus killed his father and married his

mother. Then he tried to find out why the gods were forsaking the city. No one would tell him. When he discovered the truth, he put out his own eyes and became a beggar.

Everyone cried; some even sobbed aloud. I was embarrassed by the noisy outburst of emotion, and shrank into my seat. Alexander turned to me with tears on his face. When he saw my frozen expression he looked startled for an instant, then shutters seemed to come down over his eyes. He turned back to the play, and I breathed a sigh of relief.

Afterwards, there was an intermission, and vendors swarmed over the amphitheatre offering food and drinks. Alexander bought me some honeyed nuts, and we drank watered wine that one of the soldiers carried in a goatskin. A section of the theatre was reserved for slaves, and I caught sight of Brazza, the mute, happily munching on nuts.

Nassar was near the stage translating for some merchants who looked like Egyptians. He saw me, his face brightened, and he waved.

Then the actors came back on the stage, and the second half of the evening began. It was the comedy. Some women and children left, and I remembered that comedies could sometimes turn lascivious or impious. People with high moral standards departed after the tragedies.

Most people stayed.

It was Plato's *Banquet*, which I'd never seen. I recognized the famous harangue *In vino veritas*, and the crowd was helpless with laughter at the actors' drunken antics. The play was not a straight comedy, it seemed to have more to do with love than wine, and I was nearly moved to tears in the end. Everyone else did cry. I sat there feeling out of place, but I was used to that.

Afterwards the actors took their masks off and came to meet Alexander. He praised their interpretation, even reciting several speeches by heart. More people came up to him, and he smiled and answered questions. His magnetism drew them. They crowded around him. He didn't seem to notice. He was the same with everyone, be they slave, infant, or Queen of Egypt. He treated everyone with the same grave consideration. The people adored him.

When the crowd thinned, we strolled back to the camp, the soldiers walking behind us. Alexander had his arm linked through mine, and every now and then we'd stop and he'd point out a constellation.

The soldiers stopped when we did and walked when we walked. Alexander spoke to them as if they were all equals, and they looked at him in open admiration. He didn't notice.

He did notice when I started limping, though.

'What happened to you? Let me see your feet.' He motioned for a torch and looked at my sore feet, making clucking sounds as he did. 'What awful sandals, where did you get them? I've never seen worse. Why don't you get some leather ones? Lysimachus!'

The captain of the guard came over. 'Yes, sir!'

'Captain, you will get some sandals for this woman tomorrow.'

'Yes, sir!' He saluted.

Alexander had two soldiers make a hand-chair for me,

and they carried me back to the tent.

'I can't believe you wore these!' he kept exclaiming.

'They were given to me,' I explained.

Alexander couldn't get over it. My itchy linen robe had been the very finest quality, thanks to the machine that wove it, but my shoes had been a dismal failure and he was disappointed in the gods' choice of footwear.

I tried to explain that the gods had nothing to do with my sandals but fell asleep in the middle of my sentence. It wasn't that important anyway, I thought.

There was a new pair of sandals on the rug the next morning. They fitted perfectly. My old ones had disappeared, and I didn't find out where they'd gone until I went into the village and passed by the temple. There, on the altar, were my sandals.

Fresh flowers, a bowl of warm milk, and a small snail made of clay surrounded them. A young girl in temple robes sat next to them murmuring a prayer. I tried to speak to her in Greek, but she didn't understand me. I pursed my lips and went to find Nassar. Maybe he could explain.

Nassar was writing a letter for a tough-looking soldier. They were both sitting on a mat made of reeds, and every once in a while Nassar would throw his pen away and break off a reed. He would sharpen it quickly with his teeth and I realized with a small start that his front teeth had been carefully cut at a bias to trim reeds into pens. It was interesting and I resolved to have him explain how it was done. He dipped the reed into a little clay pot of ink and wrote on a rather cheap piece of papyrus. A dozen rolled-up letters were lying beside him, each one flattened and sealed with a blob of wax. He'd been busy all morning. When he finished the letter he rolled it up, tied it with a piece of grass and sealed it with hard wax. Then he flattened the whole thing with his fist, wrote the address on the outside, and placed it on top of the pile.

'Next?' he called out in his nasal voice.

'Good morning, Nassar,' I said as I approached.

He held his arms up in a stiff salute and then bowed, touching his forehead to the mat. 'Hail, Demeter's daughter,' he intoned.

'Don't do that!' I was upset. 'Who told you that, anyway?'

'Oh, everyone knows,' he said smugly.

'Well, I'd like you to come to the temple with me to see about a pair of shoes,' I said.

'Oh! The Sacred Sandals! I should be honoured! May I touch them, O daughter of Demeter?'

I closed my eyes and counted to ten. 'They aren't sacred sandals,' I said. 'And of course you can touch them. There's been a mistake.'

'They weren't your sandals? The captain of the guards took them to the shoemaker early this morning to have a copy made in leather and gave the originals to the temple. It is not a coincidence that the goddess of the harvest, Demeter, guards this town. It was why you were sent here. Now that Iskander has rescued you, the harvest is sure to be fantastic this year.'

'But isn't the village protected by Ishtar?'

'It was, but it's becoming Hellenicised. Now it has adopted Demeter, goddess of the harvest, because of what Iskander said last night in his speech.'

'His speech? What did he say?'

'You should have asked me to translate,' he said, reproach in his voice. 'He said he was glad to be there and that he hoped the play would be entertaining, that he and his soldiers were very happy in the village, and he was honoured everyone had made them feel so welcome, and how the two cultures would complement each other.' Nassar took a deep breath, like a swimmer, and plunged in again. 'He said that the gods of Greece were stronger than our gods so we'd do well to adopt theirs. He said you had been sent as a sign and that he'd saved you from Hades himself, so Demeter would for ever be grateful. He said that as a goddess you would personally see to the welfare of the village.' He finished in a rush and smiled at me. 'I'm no longer an atheist,' he said proudly. 'I believe in you. Why, if I want, I can actually touch your sandals.'

I closed my eyes again and waited for the wave of pain that was sure to come. Pretending to be a goddess must rate among the three top reasons for erasing a time-travelling journalist. After a few seconds I opened one eye, then the other. Nothing had happened. I was still sitting in front of Nassar, and he was watching me with a rapt expression on his narrow, rat-like face.

'Did your mother speak to you?' he whispered, his eyes wide.

'No. No, she didn't. Excuse me, Nassar, but I think I'll just go lie down. I have to think about all this.' I stood up, shivering with disquiet, and walked back to the tent where Alexander was having a game of dice with a tall man I recognized as the village priest. I wondered if I could sneak away, but they turned and saw me.

'Oh! There you are!' cried Alexander, standing up and

holding out his arms. 'I was worried. Did you find your new shoes? Yes, I see you did. The village priest has come to thank you for your sandals. In exchange, he has agreed to forsake all virgin sacrifices. Isn't that wonderful? Your mother will be thrilled.'

'I'm sure she will be,' I said with the utmost truthfulness. Then I went into the tent and collapsed.

Alexander came in to join me about an hour later. He stretched out on the bed next to me and tickled my back until I finally turned to face him.

'Is it so very difficult?' he asked me, his face a study in sorrow.

'What?'

'Living with mortals. I'm sorry if you're unhappy. I wasn't thinking when I snatched you from Hades' grasp. I thought you wouldn't want to go back. I admit to being selfish, I wanted to keep you by my side, but I didn't think of the consequences. Will they be terrible? Will your mother put a curse on me? Is it too late for you to go back?'

I thought about what to say. Alexander folded his arms beneath his chin and waited patiently. Today, his eyes had the candid stare of a lion.

'I can never go back,' I said, 'at least not in your lifetime.'

'You're bound to me for my lifetime,' said Alexander. He said it as if he were pronouncing vows and I shivered.

'I did want to go back. But some of it was my fault because part of me wanted to stay here with you, and I was lost because I couldn't make myself clear.' I was silent again, watching him. His stare never wavered. 'My mother will not put a curse on you,' I said. 'You will never have to worry about that.'

'But what about Hades?' he asked. 'I've cheated him out of a bride.'

'We won't have to worry about him either.'

'Am I so important?' He was serious.

'You are extremely important,' I answered.

'I must be careful then, not to draw the gods' choler upon me. You will guide me.'

I shook my head. 'You must not change in the least,' I said. 'You have to go on as if I weren't here, and do exactly what you always planned on doing. It's not my presence that will change anything. And I can't advise you, I … I made a promise.'

'And I will make one to you. You will never regret being captured by Iskander of Macedonia. I pledge my army to protect you and my heart to hold you.'

He rolled over on the bed and reached into the green jade bowl full of fresh fruit. 'Here, have a grape.'

He fed me grapes and we kissed. I loved kissing him, he gave it all of his attention, and it was a particularly intense experience.

He broke off every now and then to ask me questions.

'Can you be injured?' he asked.

'I can die,' I said.

'You're trapped in a mortal body now?' He was fascinated.

'I am as mortal as you.'

'How interesting. I suppose that when your body dies your spirit returns to the gods and you take your natural form.'

I winced. 'Something like that.'

We kissed some more, then: 'Will you die before I do?' He sounded worried.

'Perhaps. If I'm wounded or get sick.'

'Won't that be a new experience for you? No, I'm being foolish. The gods have walked among us often and I suppose you have come previously as well. If you die before I do, I shall give you a magnificent tomb.'

'No!' I spoke quickly. 'No. If I die before you, promise not to do anything to attract attention. Simply burn my body and scatter the ashes.'

'Are you sure?'

'Positive.' I kissed him some more then began to tremble. I was frightened. Strange as Alexander's words were, they showed me the reality of my situation. I wasn't going anywhere, and in two days Nearchus was coming back with half of Alexander's army, and he would likely try and kill me.

'Why are you shivering?' He tipped my chin up and gently kissed my cheeks. 'Do you miss your mother?'

'No.' At least I could always tell the truth to him, however he cared to interpret it.

Nearchus arrived with the clarion cry of trumpets and the crash of cymbals. He was a tall man, well made and haughty, with shining golden hair he didn't need to dye. He walked across the uneven ground and knelt at Alexander's feet. Behind him stood the army, the sun glinting off their spears and shields. The men were silent. I'd expected something noisier, less disciplined, but then I realized Alexander had shifted back into the soldier-mode.

He was no longer resting, and the army had become a fighting force.

The two halves of the army melded together like molten bronze. Tents were set up and the camp expanded, but it was done effortlessly and in a silence that let the sound of children's clear voices shine through. The children had gathered to watch the soldiers.

Another man stood out from the crowd. Unlike Alexander and Nearchus, his hair was cut very short and it was dark. His complexion was olive, his features neat and smooth. I noticed him because he was trying so hard to go unnoticed. He blended into the air around him, into the soft murmur of voices and the quick movements of the soldiers. Nothing he did was designed to call attention to himself. Perhaps it was for that reason I saw him before Alexander did.

Alexander had moved to my side. His actions were unconscious, but his mind worked superbly on both levels. The soldiers knew who I was purported to be, and they looked sideways at me, showing the whites of their eyes like spooked horses.

Nearchus stood next to Alexander, and his face, when he turned it towards me, was grave and respectful. His eyes were dark blue and flat, like wet slate. They gave little away.

However, the other man looked at me with eyes as bright as amber glass. 'Who is that?' I asked Alexander.

He followed my gaze and blenched. 'Plexis,' he breathed. To Nearchus he said, 'Plexis followed you.' It was a statement. His voice was blank.

Nearchus seemed to shrink. 'I have letters.'

'I'll read them later. What does he want?'

'To find out what you're planning to do, I suppose.'

Alexander considered this then asked, 'Why now?'

'Because he'll have to know sometime. He has a lot at stake in your army.'

Alexander nodded. 'A lot indeed.' He stepped forward to greet the dark-haired man. 'Plexis,' he said.

The man bowed low to him, then to me. He faced Alexander and spoke to him in a language I did not understand. Alexander replied in Greek, which seemed to annoy Plexis.

'We are not alone,' Alexander told him. 'The gods themselves are with us.'

'Beware the gods' favour,' said Plexis, in Greek now.

'Perhaps I have been punished enough,' said Alexander in a voice I didn't recognize.

'I doubt it,' said Plexis, earning an in-drawn breath like a whistle from Nearchus.

Alexander simply shrugged. 'We shall see,' he said. Then, in a low voice, 'Will you ever forgive me, Plexis?'

The dark-haired man didn't speak, but the pain in his eyes seemed to answer for him, and Alexander turned with a curse and disappeared into his tent.

Plexis stared after him. 'Iskander,' he said softly. The look he gave me was assessing. He smiled at me, but I didn't smile back. I had long ago learned to tell smiles apart. His said, as clearly as words, 'Whoever you are, if you get in my way I will destroy you.'

I gave him my frostiest stare, the one that cowed even my mother, but his smile didn't waver.

He bowed and left us, walking towards the village with

a light step. I caught my breath and looked towards Alexander's tent. Something was going to happen, and I wasn't sure what it was. I hoped it wasn't what I thought. The name Plexis meant nothing to me, which was, I reflected, either a very good sign or a very bad one. I resolved to watch him carefully.

That evening there was a banquet. Alexander managed to drag it out until the early hours, calling for more songs, more stories, and more games, until everyone was hoarse and falling from exhaustion.

Nearchus had excused himself rather early, but Plexis stayed with us. He didn't sing or tell jokes. He seemed to drink a prodigious amount of wine and never get drunk. My own head was swimming, but I kept part of it clear to watch him. Alexander seemed to have no compulsion to do so. He drank steadily, until, when the sky started to pale, he pitched forward onto the ground and three soldiers carried him back to his tent. Plexis helped, and then without asking me, lay down next to Alexander, holding his head next to his breast. Alexander swam out of his sleep and tried to extricate himself, but Plexis held on tightly, crooning to him in a low voice. He was not speaking Greek. Before he passed out again, Alexander moaned and cried out, as if in great pain, 'No! Cxious! I've atoned for my sins!' I couldn't see what had happened, but Plexis started cursing.

I wrapped myself in Alexander's cloak and slept fitfully on the rug.

When I awoke, Plexis was gone.

Alexander woke up in a cheerful mood, seemingly unaffected by the party, but I was hung-over and shaky. I wanted to ask him who Plexis was, but it was not the time or the place.

Befitting my rank as daughter of an authentic goddess, I was draped in purple wool and sweltered in the front row to welcome Nearchus officially and bless the army.

I couldn't wriggle out of that one, but I'd managed to convince Alexander that the village priest was supposed to do all the talking, since my Greek was atrocious just now.

Nearchus stood next to me. He was very good about hiding his feelings but I was an expert, and no one living in that century could hide his feelings from me. His eyes shifted ever so subtly towards Alexander and his lips narrowed imperceptibly – except that I saw. My own face could have been carved from ice.

Wool covered me from head to foot; Alexander had draped me according to Athenian custom. The large rectangle of cloth was crossed right over left with the points hanging down in front and back. I held it together from the inside with my left hand, freeing my right hand. I raised it in a solemn salute. Nearchus saluted me in return. His movement was brusque, almost to the point of rudeness. Almost. The fear in his eyes gave him away.

Alexander gave a ceremonial speech for Nearchus, and a kiss, which was less ceremonial, but not enough so to appease Nearchus. Then he let the village priest speak.

The priest made a very long speech, which glazed everyone's eyes and brought on a plague of yawns. After what seemed like hours, a white goat was dragged to a flat rock, and I was handed a knife.

I had been watching Plexis, who stood in a place of honour next to Alexander. He didn't act bored, or interested, or anything. He was simply 'there,' and it was his lack of any emotion that was the most unsettling. I realized that I must seem like that to everyone around me.

When the priest handed me the knife, I was startled out of my reverie. Horrified, I stared at it. I'd never killed an animal in my life. I could hardly step on an ant without feeling queasy. The sight of blood made me faint. Everyone was looking at me now, expectant. Plexis stared at me, the faintest hint of a sardonic smile tugging his lips.

I raised the dagger and swore at it in English, figuring that would sound mysterious. Then I closed my eyes and tipped my head, as if I were listening to some tiny voice from beyond. I nodded, opened my eyes, and handed the knife back to the priest. He looked confused and glanced at Alexander who in turn looked at me, frowning.

'What is the matter?' he whispered.

'I can't kill anything,' I whispered back.

His face cleared and he nodded imperiously to the priest. 'Go ahead, the knife has been purified.'

The priest killed the goat, the blood spurted out over my feet, and I fainted. Everyone was most impressed and quite happy with the ceremony, for fainting was taken as an excellent omen. The goat's liver was intact – no lobes missing – which was another good omen. And a sudden shower blew over the mountains, which made everyone absolutely ecstatic, rain being the ultimate blessing from the gods.

I was carried back to the tent.

Nearchus and Alexander sat on the floor and talked in low tones, while I was laid out on the bed. Brazza took the horrid, itchy wool cape off me and cooled me with a large fan made of fragrant sandalwood. I felt much better.

After a while Nearchus went away. Brazza left in response to a small nod from Alexander, who sat down by my side and ran his thumb down my forehead, down the bridge of my nose, and over my lips.

'You can't kill,' he said quietly.

'No, I can't.'

'Can't, or won't?'

'I'm not sure,' I said. My head hurt; nothing new there. I wished for the thousandth time that aspirin had been invented. 'Who is Plexis?' I asked.

He sighed and looked down at his feet. 'Don't you know?'

'No, I never heard of him.'

His eyebrows lifted and his face seemed to loose its edges. 'His name is Hephaestion, but we always called him Plexis. He was my best friend.'

'Was?'

'I killed his brother.' He looked past me to the doorway, and his eyes were bleak. 'I killed his brother in a fit of rage. After that, I swore I'd never lose my temper again. Plexis has appointed himself as a moral guardian, if you like, to my promise. He's also invested all of his fortune in my army. If my venture fails I will ruin his entire family.'

I didn't try to comfort him. There was something in his voice that told me he was beyond that. Instead, I asked him why Nearchus had winked at me before leaving the tent.

Alexander rubbed his temples. 'Nearchus is sceptical about your divinity. He doesn't believe anything, don't worry. I have a pile of letters to read. Why don't you go to the river and wash off the purple dye? Go find Brazza, he'll give you something for that.' He finished speaking and turned away, sitting with his back to me. I thought I saw his shoulders shaking.

I glanced at my body and saw that the sweat had caused the dye to run, and my chest and belly were blue. Outside, I found Brazza near the stables, and he gave me a handful of something like soft soap. It made a nice lather, but it smelled like a sheep. To take the sheep smell away, I swam for nearly an hour, then I went to the riverbank and poked around until I found some lemongrass. I picked some young shoots and crushed them in my hands. I added a bit of water, and rubbed the citrus scent all over my body and head. My hair was slowly growing back, but it was still a very short brush-cut. I looked like a soldier. I smelled like a lemon.

When I approached Alexander's tent, the guards jumped up and looked uncomfortable.

'Alexander has instructed us to take you to your new quarters,' they said.

I hadn't been expecting this, but I was schooled in hiding my emotions. 'Thank you. Please do.'

Their smiles were relieved.

My tent was a small one, set up under a tall tree near Alexander's. It was nicely furnished, with a beautiful rug and a low, comfortable bed. I had a lamp too, and a bronze brazier. A young girl was sitting cross-legged on the rug, and as I approached she jumped up and made a bow.

'This is Chirpa, your slave,' said the captain.

'My slave?' I repeated blankly. 'There must be a mistake.'

'No mistake. Brazza too has been appointed to your service, and Nassar of course, although he is not a slave.' The captain knew everything that was happening in the camp.

I blinked. I'd take this up with Alexander, later. Chirpa gave me a shy glance and smiled. She looked about seven years old. I started to shiver, the events of the day catching up on me. I thought I'd probably faint again, which would please everyone. The soldiers bowed and left.

I sat on the bed, and noticed a lovely wooden chest.

'What's that?' I asked.

Chirpa ran over and opened it, showing me bolts of cloth. Another smaller box was inside, and from it, Chirpa extracted a round mirror made of polished bronze, a small flask of perfume, a comb, and some make-up – kohl for the eyes and carmine for the lips and cheeks.

The perfume smelled interesting, but not like anything I'd ever think of wearing and I didn't want to paint my face. The comb was useless, but the mirror was sweet. I looked into it.

My face had started to tan in the fierce sun. It made my eyes stand out, which didn't displease me. My cheekbones were a legacy from my Finnish grandmother – high, broad and sharp. My nose and chin came from my Russian father. My nose was narrow, my chin square, which gave me a haughty look. My hair was hoarfrost sparkling on my head. Strange. My mouth was wide and my lips curved naturally into a smile. It made me look almost friendly, until one saw my eyes. They had always frightened people away. They were the colour of glaciers, of polar icebergs, of pale aquamarines – of ice. They even made *me* shiver. There was no warmth in my gaze. I had tried for years to soften it, but I'd given up. Eyes were the mirrors of the soul, but mine were simply mirrors. They gave nothing away. Even the warm bronze couldn't thaw them. I sighed and put the mirror down.

I was melancholy and wandered around my tent for a long time, picking things up and putting them down. The wind increased and there was a hint of rain in the air. It made everything smell and I thought that I could do without one or two of the furs on my bed. Wrinkling my nose, I brought the offending bedcovers outside, hanging them to air in a tree. Chirpa offered to help, but I told her to go and amuse herself.

The soldiers sitting outside Alexander's tent were playing a game with pebbles. The sound of the stones clicking together was the only thing I could hear. The silence weighed upon the afternoon, unrelieved by small, playful gusts of wind. One gust blew the tent flap back, showing me the inside. Alexander was sitting motionless behind his table, his head in his hands. Nearchus was nowhere to be seen. Neither was Plexis.

I went back to my own tent and let my melancholy wash over me. However, it was only from solitude, and I'd suffered from that all my life.

Alexander came to see me that evening. He was announced as if I were royalty. I stood to receive him, draped in a transparent piece of muslin.

He saw my expression and his own eyes, usually

limpid, turned cloudy.

'Do you like it?' he asked, gesturing with his arm.

'I do, thank you.' I sat down gracefully. I had to rely on my finishing-school education now. Of all the people in the world, the powerful are the most ruthless. I'd learned how to meet them head-on. Alexander was the only person who could keep me alive now. To stay by his side, I had to prove myself useful.

'Do you know Lysimachus?' I asked.

'Lysimachus? The captain?' He looked perplexed.

'I had a dream about him. I dreamed he became a powerful Lieutenant. He served you well. I advise you to watch him carefully and when the time comes, don't hesitate to promote him.' I had to be careful, but I'd recognized Lysimachus's name from my history books and unless there were two Lysimachuses I wouldn't be changing history, much.

Alexander tilted his head to one side, considering. Then he smiled at me. 'Are you saying that as a goddess?'

'As a friend,' I said, and his smile broadened.

'Do you know what I did just before coming here?' he asked.

'You read your mail.'

'Yes. And I caught a pigeon.'

I was surprised. 'Already? What did she say?'

'She said congratulations. She's impatient to meet you.'

'Oh, well that will have to wait a while, won't it?' I asked. I wasn't looking forward to meeting Olympias, his formidable mother.

'In three weeks.'

'I thought we were going to Babylon?' I asked.

'We meet in Babylon. She's sailing down the Euphrates. We'll have our wedding feast there, at the same time as our victory feast.'

'So sure of yourself,' I said. 'Your mother isn't only coming for the wedding?'

'No, she's always wanted to rule Babylon. I shall put her in charge for a while.'

I nibbled the inside of my lip. Was history was following its normal course? I certainly hoped so. 'When shall we start packing?' I asked.

We went for our evening swim, and, to my relief, Nearchus and Plexis stayed away. I washed Alexander's hair for him while we floated in the shallow water. He was in a garrulous mood, and I took advantage of it to ask him questions.

'Are Plexis and Nearchus married men?' I asked.

'No, they're too young. Plexis studied with Aristotle too, and he's decided to follow his advice. Aristotle says men should marry at thirty-seven years of age and women at eighteen. How old were you when you married?'

I jumped. 'How did you know I was married?' I asked.

'You married Hades when he kidnapped you,' he said.

'Actually, my mother arranged the whole thing.'

Alexander sat up so quickly he smacked my nose with his head. I saw stars and blood splattered into the water. My nose was bleeding.

'I'm sorry!' He was contrite, dabbing at my nose with his linen tunic.

'That's all right, I always get bloody noses. It's nothing. It'll stop in a second.'

He stared first at my nose, and then down at his stained tunic. His brows drew together as he came to the logical conclusion. 'You're not actually a goddess,' he said.

'I never said I was.'

'No, you never said you were. Yet, I saw you under the tree, and you were starting to disappear. You were crowned in ice, and snow covered your body. You were held in the grip of a deathly blue light, and I could barely pry you away. When you broke loose, I heard the cries of the one I'd cheated.'

'I can't tell you who I am, because if I do, I will be destroyed. You must not ask any questions of me. I will do my best to help you, and I believe that I can. I'm not immortal. However, I will tell you this. When I was disappearing I was going to a place that is not on this earth at this time,' I said, 'and that is the truth.'

'I believe you.'

'Thank you.'

He dabbed once more at my nose, wiping off the last traces of blood, and then he grinned. 'O Ashley of the Sacred Sandals,' he said. 'Will you be my oracle, or, failing that, my talisman?'

'I'll be your oracle if I can, and your talisman if you wish. But above all,' I said, taking his chin in my hands and kissing him, 'I will be your lover, because I think that's what you need right now.'

'Right now at this minute, yes,' he said, his voice thick. 'But later I think I will need an oracle, because if we lose at Babylon, my mother will probably kill us both.'

'This is not,' I said firmly, 'the time to speak about your mother.'

Then we didn't talk for a while, and afterwards we went back to my tent, and we still didn't talk.

We went to Babylon on foot. Nearchus went by river, and to my relief, Plexis sailed with him.

The village held a feast for us the night before we left. I thought that was decent of them, considering Alexander had been camped on their land for nearly a month, and the army had eaten everything for miles around. But, as the village priest said, there were plenty more fish in the river. They even managed to catch enough to send us off in style.

Of course, the regular soldiers stuck to their diet of bread and garlic, onions and lentils. With the occasional crocodile thrown in.

Alexander gave a speech, and then we all ate. The soldiers didn't tell their usual dirty jokes; I supposed it was because the priest was there. We went to bed early. I didn't sleep in my tent; it had been packed up already.

In Alexander's tent there were Alexander and I, Chirpa, and Alexander's slaves, Brazza, Axiom and Usse. They slept behind curtains strung up for the night so that we could not see each other, although Axiom's snoring kept waking me up.

Travelling soon became routine. The slaves woke up before dawn and got the tent in order. Alexander woke up next, did his exercises before having a quick breakfast, and then, just as the sun came up, went out into the camp for inspection. I woke up a while later, when the sun had fully risen, and ate whatever Alexander had left me. Usually it was a few dried figs, some yoghurt and fresh goat cheese. Chirpa helped me dress, which meant draping a linen cape around my shoulders. Otherwise her tasks were limited to fetching water from the river and washing clothes. Clothes were rare and water only a few feet away so I didn't feel guilty about having her as my slave. I'd tried to talk to Alexander about setting her free, but all he would say was, 'Not now, not here.' I didn't press him. He had his own reasons.

Chirpa was Greek, from Athens, and I had no trouble communicating with her after I'd managed to convince her I was not going to turn her into an owl or a frog if she did anything wrong. She was about thirteen, but very small, which was why at first glance I'd taken her for a child of seven or eight. Her hair was reddish-gold; her eyes were large and grey in her heart-shaped face. I asked her about her childhood, and she told me her father had been a policeman. I was surprised.

'Wasn't he a slave?' I asked, not sure if I would hurt her feelings.

'Yes, he was a federal slave. There is a police corps in Athens made up of slaves. They are the only ones who can marry. My mother was a slave too; she worked in the public bathhouse. My parents sold me to pay for their freedom. Aristotle bought me, and then gave me to Iskander when I was ten years old.'

We chatted as we walked. The road was long, but the pace was leisurely. We walked well behind the army. By the time we caught up, they would already have made camp. Alexander had assigned four soldiers the task of holding the canopy over my head as I walked. The canopy was not heavy, and the soldiers didn't mind. I asked them to let me know when they were tired and they told me not to worry, so Chirpa and I strolled along in the shade. The only problem was the dust, but as we fell further and further behind, that ceased to be a bother.

'What did you do for Iskander when you were ten?' I asked.

She shrugged. 'Not much. I was taken into his household and his mother put me to work. I helped clean, and did the laundry. I learned how to style hair, so she asked me to do her hair sometimes. Iskander was gone most of the time.'

'But why are you here?'

'I became his poison taster.' She said it as if it were the most normal thing in the world.

'What?' I was shocked. 'How could he let you do that?'

She looked at me in puzzlement. 'He did not tell you? While I was in his household I went to the kitchen one day and noticed a strange odour. I followed my nose to a plate of sweets someone had left for Olympias. When the cook came in, she started to scold me, but I told her that they smelled odd. She didn't believe me; to her nothing seemed wrong. When I insisted, she gave a sweet to one of the dogs. The poor beast died. I have a talent, you see. I can smell poison. Not many people can. Olympias made me go with Alexander on his campaign. I don't mind. I like to travel. The work is easy.' She shrugged, twirling a lock of copper hair in her fingers.

I suddenly realized that Chirpa was the first person I'd met here who wasn't afraid of me. Everyone else was uneasy, most making the sign against evil behind their

91

backs when they spoke to me. Others were convinced I was a goddess, and would bow fervently whenever I crossed their paths. It rankled, and I found myself relaxing with Chirpa. It was nice, and I even surprised myself with a smile.

The camp was seething with activity as we arrived. Then, just as suddenly, all was calm. Soldiers built fires and ate their dinner. Music from flutes and smoke floated in the blue evening air. Alexander went to the pony lines to check on Bucephalus, and I went upriver and searched for a likely place to bathe.

It had to be upstream from the camp, and the banks had to be free from too many reeds and mud. I walked for a while before spotting a small, sandy beach. It was far from the camp, out of sight and sound of the soldiers. My modesty was preserved. Whistling cheerfully, I picked my way through waist-high grass, careful of snakes and crocodiles. I had just reached the water when strong arms seized me from behind.

My first reaction was to scream, which made my captor hit me sharply on the side of the head. I saw stars, and then my judo lessons came back to me. I leaned into him and hooked my leg behind his, reaching upwards and around in a smooth motion. I brought my knee up sharply and drove the base of my hand into his nose.

There was an explosion of movement then, as my attacker proved to be quicker than I was. He treated my moves as if they were in slow motion, blocking each one with an infuriating ease. My head was reeling from the blows I was receiving, but at least I'd broken free and was fighting back. I screamed once and then he hit me in the neck, bruising my larynx.

He was determined to capture me. He hadn't counted on my getting away, and it maddened him. However, every time he grabbed at me I managed to block him; I even threw him down once in a classic ippon, but there were no judges to stop the fight and declare me winner. Besides, I was losing miserably. My nose was bleeding again – the main reason I'd stopped judo – and my head was ringing. My wrist was certainly sprained and one finger felt broken.

My assailant had a swollen eye, a split lip, and limped from a bruised knee. Nevertheless, he hadn't given up. He seemed … I frowned and hesitated, suddenly unsure. He seemed to be waiting.

My impression was confirmed when a small boat grated up onto the beach and another man leapt out.

I redoubled my efforts and in a last, desperate effort to escape I darted into the tall grass, where the first man had been hiding. The chase was soon over. The men ran like wolves and within seconds they had me pinned to the ground. Without a single word to each other except guttural grunts, they tied my hands and feet and slung me into the boat. A gag was stuffed into my mouth, and a cloth was draped over my body, hiding and blinding me.

The boat moved in fits and starts as the men took turns rowing. I tried to determine if we were going upstream or downstream, but I gave up. I had no idea where I was being taken or what was going to happen to me.

I wished the men would talk, giving me a clue as to what this was all about, but they were silent. After a while I gave up struggling and simply shivered.

Whenever I get nervous, I tremble. My nerves twitch and jump, and my teeth chatter. I can't control it. I was shaking so badly it must have looked as if I were having a fit, because one of the men snatched the cover off me and grabbed my face, looking deeply into my eyes. I tried to talk but it just came out as 'Njggggmnnnjklg!'

He looked up at the sky and glanced nervously around, but then he put the cloth back over my head and it seemed to me that they redoubled their efforts to row even faster.

I'd seen fear in his eyes, and I hoped I knew why.

When at last we stopped, the men didn't untie me or take off my gag. They hid the boat in some rushes and made a fire behind a lean-to one of them built with reeds and palm tree branches. Then they ate some flat cakes, wrapped themselves up in scratchy woollen cloaks, and slept, with me firmly between them.

I had never had to learn how to sleep with my hands tied behind my back, or wedged between two perfect strangers who reeked of sweat and garlic. I lay awake for ages, shaking, uncomfortable, wondering if I would ever be rescued. The stars came out; I saw the constellations Alexander had shown me and started to cry. At that moment, I believed I would never see him again.

In the morning they untied my hands and gave me a piece of bread. They let me urinate, but I had to squat between them. I was mortified.

They tied my hands again and put me in the boat. As before, I was made to lie down and a cloth was thrown over my body, but I was no longer gagged and my head was uncovered. I contemplated screaming but was too frightened. They wouldn't answer when I spoke; they only tightened their lips. I gave up asking what they were going to do with me and simply watched the clouds drifting in the endless sky.

Chapter Five

After four days of travelling, we arrived at a temple where I was imprisoned for nearly a year. I was a captive, and the only people I saw were two priestesses and a deaf-mute eunuch who watched my every move.

My room was small and had no window. It was deep in a stone temple. I had a bed, a brazier, an oil lamp, a chamber pot and a rug. I can describe everything in the minutest detail because there was nothing else to contemplate except the cracks in the stone walls: no books, television, or music. A linen cloth the size of a bath towel was my only clothing –. it was also my bath towel. My bed was a wooden bench with a flat cushion stuffed with hay, and a woollen blanket. The cushion was itchy and lumpy, and the blanket was cream-coloured and scratchy. The rug was red and orange, with blue threads running through it horizontally. One of the blue threads was broken, and a green thread had been tied to it. The unexpected green line saved my sanity a few times when I thought I'd go mad with boredom. The chamber pot is probably in a museum somewhere now. It was a heavy earthenware affair with a beautiful deep red glaze.

I was taken outside twice a day, morning and afternoon, no matter what the weather. While I was outside, my room was cleaned, and a large basin of water for washing and a plate with my meal were set on the rug.

They took them away when I left in the afternoon, so I never saw who fed me. I ate once a day. It was enough. I didn't get much exercise. I started to get fat, which puzzled me, until one day I realized I was pregnant.

I was never very regular, and I had assumed that my lack of menstruation was due to stress and poor diet. I thought that well until my fourth month of pregnancy.

I had put my morning sickness down to nerves, and my sore breasts were because the bed was impossibly hard and lumpy.

When I finally realized the truth, I was stunned. Then I started to cry.

I'd never cried before, so the priestess who'd been tending the garden, hurried over. As usual, she was silent, only pointing to me with a worried look on her face. When I told her I was pregnant, her face turned as white as parchment, and that's how I found out she understood Greek.

I tried to strangle her. The eunuch pulled me off, but when he made to hit me, the priestess waved him away. I was trembling violently and I had to sit. I made my way to a bench beneath an apricot tree and sank upon it, hugging myself to keep from shaking. The woman sat beside me and I could feel her shaking too. Obviously something had gone wrong.

'Why didn't you tell me you spoke Greek?' I cried. 'Why don't you answer my questions? What's to become of me? What's to become of my baby? Where's Iskander? Does he know I'm here?' I gripped the edge of the stone bench. Otherwise, I would have attacked her again.

The priestess opened her mouth then snapped it shut.

Tears ran down her cheeks, but for what reason I didn't know. She had always treated me politely, although she'd never once spoken to me or answered any of my questions. Her homely face was kind, and I'd gotten used to her silent presence, much as I'd adapted to the eunuch who followed me around the vast, high-walled garden.

However, she didn't speak to me, and after a while she got up and left me alone in the garden. The eunuch stood by the far wall and stared at me with deep suspicion. I pried my fingers off the bench and stood unsteadily. The sun was bright and a bird sang in the apricot tree, but I was alone again.

I watched as the shadows lengthened and turned purple. I was always left in the garden until the sun set. As soon as the sun touched the horizon I was taken inside. Bells rang in the town and trumpets sounded. I couldn't see the town; we were high on a hill and it was beneath us. The walls were too high to see over. Mostly I wandered around.

After I discovered I was pregnant, I started talking endlessly to my baby. I didn't feel so lonesome any more. Soon I perceived the fluttery movement of the foetus and I would lie still, my hand over my belly, and try to imagine Alexander's baby floating dreamlike in my womb.

The flutter became a nudge, then a bump, and then a kick. My stomach swelled. My womb became an orange, a grapefruit, a melon, and then a basketball. I walked slowly, hands on the small of my back, and I grimaced when the baby rolled and stretched inside me. I became short of breath, and I received the first visit from a midwife.

I had long conversations with the baby. When the midwife came, I thought she would be as mute as the others were, so I described her entire visit to the baby; telling him exactly what she was doing, and, to entertain him, describing her thoroughly.

I got to the part where I was telling him how she was touching him to make sure he was in the right position to be born, when suddenly she rocked back on her heels. 'Does he understand you? Does he answer back?' she asked.

I had been so long without conversation that I didn't realize at first she'd actually spoken to me.

I gaped at her and she blushed.

'I'm sorry,' I said, when I'd gotten hold of myself. 'I think he understands some things I say. At any rate, he understands the tone, and I know he listens. When he's awake, he reacts to my voice. Sometimes he'll push a certain way and I know he's heard me.' My voice trembled and I took a deep breath. 'It's nice of you to talk to me,' I said. 'So nice.'

She nodded, evidently impressed. She was older than the two priestesses and her skin was darker. She looked as if she might be Egyptian. When I asked her she nodded. 'I'm from Egypt, yes,' she answered. 'But now I live here.'

'Where's here?' I asked, but she shook her head.

I was disappointed, but I didn't press her. I was too glad to hear her speak. 'When will he be born?' I asked.

'You're so sure it's a boy?

'Yes, I'm quite sure.' I smiled. 'I can't imagine anything else. I've even picked out a name, Paul. I was thinking about naming him after his father, but I decided not to. Things are complicated enough. Will you come back soon?'

She stood up, and I grabbed her robe. I was nearly in tears. 'Please don't go yet,' I begged.

'I must. I'll be back before the new moon. Most women birth at the full moon, but you will have your baby when the moon is like this,' and she made a thin crescent with her fingers. 'I will see you then.'

'Thank you,' I said.

She stopped at the door, her face reflecting her indecision. 'I know who they say you are,' she said. 'But I think you are even more.' And before I could reply to that she prostrated herself, touching her forehead to the floor.

'Don't do that!' I was shocked, but she got to her feet and, with a frightened look, left.

I was a prisoner in a room with no windows for nine months. I was treated with care. I had good food and was taken outside twice a day. The garden was enchanting, but empty. A mute slave watched me, not letting me near the walls or the multiple arched doorways. At first, he was very careful, following closely at my heels. However, as my pregnancy progressed he relaxed. I was not about to go hurling myself over a twenty-foot wall when I was eight months pregnant. I would often be left alone for the entire afternoon, and I would go to my favourite places in the garden and have long conversations with my unborn baby.

Some days I wondered if I could hit the eunuch over the head with a stick, stun him, then escape. But I didn't try. I was afraid my captors would hurt the baby or me.

No one spoke to me, and I didn't know where I was. I had no money, no clothes, and I wouldn't get very far. At least here I had a midwife and good food. I would just have to wait and see what happened.

The fact that I was treated well, and with deference, suggested they knew who I was reputed to be. I didn't try to flee, and then the baby was born.

It was easy, as far as first births go, I think. I've always been indifferent to pain. I didn't panic and I didn't scream until the very end, but it was more a scream of surprise than suffering. The midwife and the two priestesses assisted me and no one spoke, making the entire experience surrealistic, somewhere between a dream and a nightmare.

The baby was beautiful. I named him Paul, simply because I liked the name, and Alexander after his father. He was mine for ten days. Then three priestesses came and took him away. I can remember starting to scream, and think I went mad because I have no recollection of the weeks that followed. My sanity left me, and I plunged into a darkness that lasted until the temple was destroyed.

A noise woke me up. It was the deafening crack of rock as it fissured and rent, splitting apart. The sound was horrendous. It was accompanied by a peculiar undulating motion of the ground. It flung me through an opening that appeared in my cell. I slid outside on a wave of earth that picked me up and carried me right to the outside wall, where it gently deposited me. The wall collapsed, and I watched, stunned, as a city I'd never seen was obliterated. I was up on a hill, so the view was staggering.

In less than three minutes it was over and I was the

only one left standing. All sound ceased. In the strange quiet I heard a wail, and turned to see one of the priestesses who'd tended me crawling out of the ruins. I was about to run away, but then I remembered my baby.

I helped her to her feet, then in Greek I said, 'Where is my child? If you do not tell me I will destroy the world searching for him.'

She cowered from me and begged my pardon a thousand times, and then she wailed that the child had been taken to Babylon to be delivered to Marduk. That made no sense to me, but I knew I had to get to Babylon. Off I went in search of a horse, a chariot, or a boat to take me there.

It was not easy, in the massive confusion and despair, to find a horse and guide, but I had become as ruthless as the goddess whom I was reputed to be. I stole gold from the ruins of my temple prison. In the remains of the city, I bought a slave to guide me, and two horses for us to ride. Within three hours of the quake, we were on our way. My guide seemed glad to leave the city. He was a slave. I promised to free him if he got me to Babylon.

The horse I was riding was crazed with fear and I don't think I've ever galloped so fast. We streaked towards the setting sun. The horses needed no whips or spurs; we wrapped our hands in their manes and hung on. I soon found out why. Five miles out of the city an aftershock threw our horses to their knees, unseating us, and we watched, dazed, as a second earthquake levelled the few buildings left standing in the region.

We remounted and flew onwards. Our horses only stopped when they could not take another step.

That night we camped in a hollow surrounded by silver birch. I lay on the grass and watched the stars. They were the first I'd seen in nearly a year.

I wanted to know how much time had passed since my baby had been taken from me, but I didn't know how to ask. The calendar was not the same. I remembered something vague about the Attic calendar that Athenian Greeks used, but I didn't know what the Persians used to measure time. Days, yes. But how long was a week? Or a month, or a year? Was it the same? I put my head in my hands and keened. I didn't know if my baby had been taken from me a day ago, a week ago, or even a year ago. It was as if I'd woken from a coma; my mind was teeming with shadows and my head felt as if it were full of glass. I didn't dare fall asleep. I was afraid that if I did, I wouldn't wake up again, so I lay on the soft, sweet-scented grass and watched as the stars wheeled across the sky. I followed the planets as they danced: Mars, Venus, Jupiter, Mercury. They were all there.

I frowned. All the planets in the same hemisphere? Was that a sign? I thought of what the priestess had said to me. 'The baby is to be given to Marduk.' Shadows in my mind parted and the glass became clear crystal through which I looked. I could see the night sky; my eyes were open. But I could also see a temple. In the temple, a hungry God with its mouth all aflame devoured a baby. I screamed and the vision disappeared.

'How far are we from Babylon?' I asked my guide, shaking him awake.

He blinked and sat up, rubbing his eyes. 'Three, maybe four days.'

'We must go then, spare not the horses,' I said.

We mounted and rode on. The little horses were tough but we nearly killed them. When they couldn't carry us we led them, and when our legs gave out we mounted again and whipped the horses on. Twice we exchanged our mounts for new ones along the road. Each time my purse grew lighter, but I could think only of my baby and Marduk. If I had cut myself then, cold mercury would have flowed from my veins.

My guide finally fell off his horse from exhaustion. He lay on the road and stared at me. 'You go on,' he gasped, his breath whistling in his parched throat.

'No.' I dismounted and led our horses to the side of the road and let them graze. They were too tired to do more than sniff listlessly at the grass. Their eyes were dull. I stood and looked around. My body wasn't tired. It was full of a strange energy that seemed to get stronger the closer I was to Babylon. I was not hungry and I was not thirsty. I hardly blinked my eyes. When I did close them I saw strange visions. Visions that would haunt me. Blood fell like a shower of red rose petals. I didn't know if they were things to come, if they had already happened, or if they could be changed.

The road went straight on, disappearing in a bluish haze. A warm breeze raised whirling dust devils. On either side of the road dry plains seemed to stretch to infinity. The hills were to my left. They were low, rounded, and lavender in the opalescent air. I asked my guide how much further and he indicated the hills.

'On the other side is Babylon. On the banks of the Euphrates.'

'Marduk. When is his ceremony?'

'He is fed on the first day of autumn. Tomorrow,' said the man, sitting up. He fumbled at his belt for a drink, but his flask was empty. I handed him my waterskin. It was still full. He drank, and passed it to me. I took a sip, but it was like drinking sawdust.

Tomorrow. I went to get the horses and led them back to the road. 'Let's go,' I said.

We galloped until our horses staggered, then we trotted, and then we walked. The mountains drew nearer, but it was agonizingly slow. Around noon we came in sight of a long caravan. There were perhaps five hundred camels and as many donkeys, horses, and men on foot. We kicked our exhausted mounts into a shambling trot and caught up with them.

The caravan was made up of merchants who'd joined together for protection. They were coming to Babylon for the great ceremony. Hadn't we heard? Iskander's wedding and Marduk's sacrifices. Great trading opportunities. The only problem was they were late. They would have preferred to arrive early and maybe sell Iskander some gifts for his bride.

I asked to see some cloth. As we rode along, the traders jogged next to their camels, taking down bolts of cloth. I looked until I found two I wanted.

One was black silk, so dark it seemed to swallow the light, and one was a length of white silk. They were priceless, but the traders were late and sold them to me for their weight in gold.

I folded them reverently and put them in my saddle pack. Then I traded our tired horses for two fresh ones, and we galloped away.

I would have liked one of the haughty racing camels. The tall beasts were as slender as ballerinas and as fast as racehorses. However, they were too expensive and I'd already spent nearly all my gold. I might need some to bribe our way into the temple.

As we galloped, the words 'wedding, wedding, wedding' drummed in my head. I knew who he was marrying. The traders told us all the news. Darius had capitulated as soon as Alexander approached Babylon, and he'd offered his eldest daughter in marriage. Her name was Stateira; she was twenty-seven years old. She'd already been married, but her husband had been killed at Granicus, fighting against Alexander in the first of his skirmishes against Darius. I wondered how she would welcome being married to her husband's murderer. Remembering Alexander's formidable personality, I figured she'd certainly fall in love with him.

Thinking of Alexander's wedding was agonizing, but I was trying to keep a clear head. After all, I was the mistake here. I had no business in this world, but I was determined to save my son. Our son, Paul! I would get my baby back, and then I'd stop and figure out what to do. But first, my baby. Everything else paled into insignificance beside him.

I first saw Babylon in the late afternoon. The road dipped, curved, and the city sprang into view. The sun shone on the walls, and they glowed blue and gold. The bas-reliefs seemed to be alive; bulls, lions, and tigers walking majestically on fields of lapis lazuli.

The whole city was decked in blue and gold, and the

Ziggurat of Babylon soared above everything else. It was so massive it claimed the eye and subdued it. I bowed my head and let my tears fall in the dust. To look upon it was to perceive death. The city was beautiful, but damned. We got back on our horses and made our way towards the gates.

We entered the city through Ishtar's door; a huge gate made of bright blue enamelled bricks. Gold dragons and bulls adorned it. Gold lions guarded it. It was the most exquisite manmade object I'd ever seen. The whole city was dazzling, and I understood Alexander's impatience to rule it.

We entered the city, and I set about finding my infant. I thought about going directly to Alexander. I wanted to. However, the strange coldness in my head, that ice-crystal lens, showed me the path to take. I followed it as if I were being led. Perhaps, in some way, I was.

We wound through the streets until we arrived at the ziggurat. Next to it was a temple with a familiar carving over the door. I'd seen it twice a day for a year. It represented a winged dog, and it had been carved on the doorway of my prison. I hesitated, but my hand raised of its own accord and knocked six times, then six more times. That was the code I'd heard used in the temple. The door creaked open and a woman peered out. I recognized her as one of my former jailers. When she saw me, she gave a strangled cry, and fell backwards. It was all I needed. I pushed my way into the hallway.

My guide stayed in the street hanging onto the horses.

'Where is my baby?' I hissed, catching the woman by the arm before she could flee.

'How did you get here?' she moaned.

'An earthquake destroyed your city,' I snarled. 'And if you don't lead me to my child, I will destroy this city. Now, take me to him.'

'He's Marduk's,' she whispered.

'No, he's mine.' I stood up straight and threw off my dusty travelling cape. Torchlight shone off the pure white silk I'd donned, and my pale hair glittered.

The woman put her face in her hands and sobbed. 'We brought the baby here as the message insisted. But spies found out whose it was, and Darius has taken him to Persepolis. He left last night, before his daughter's wedding. He thought no one would expect him to leave before the ceremony. The baby is gone.'

Gone? Nausea twisted my gut, and I clutched at the doorway to stay upright. My baby was gone? Then I realized that he was in fact safe. He wouldn't be offered in sacrifice to a pagan god. I would go to Persepolis and get him back. Relief made me weak.

'What baby is to meet Marduk?' I asked, my knees trembling.

'A slave's child.'

'And my baby, how shall I know him? How old is he now?'

The woman glanced at me fearfully. 'The goddess's baby is three months old. He has hair like moonbeams, like yours, and his skin is fair as white coral. His eyes are silver stars. He has a scar, a crescent moon, on his right arm, here.' She pointed to her shoulder. 'No one dared to give him to Marduk. Marduk isn't his god. He would have killed us all. Now do you understand? But beware, the lady wants to destroy him.'

'Which lady?'

'The one who caused you to be brought to us. Ours was the Temple of Healing, under the order of Gulu. However, Gulu is an Assyrian goddess. She couldn't hold you or your son. We should never have accepted the gold.'

'Why did you?' I asked.

'Because we were told you were only Iskander's consort, and that you had no divine powers. We were ordered not to listen, which was why we assigned the deaf-mute to watch you. But you were well cared for. We didn't mean any harm!' She knelt on the floor and pressed her forehead against my feet. 'Your gods are stronger than ours. We have reached the end of the fourth kingdom! It is as Daniel said, "Strong as steel, fragile as the clay. Our city shall perish and shall leave no trace." It is written in the stars.' Her words ended in a high-pitched wail, and I had to bite my lip to keep from screaming at her. Then my childhood training took over. I pushed my emotions away and cleared my mind. I had to find a way to get my baby back and I would. After all, I was a child of adversity. Just getting to Babylon was a triumph.

'Where is Iskander? I must see him!'

'I will take you to him, but please, if the lady his mother sees you she will surely have me killed, and she will try and kill you too. This time she will not settle for kidnapping you.'

I cursed under my breath. How could I have been so blind? I had been so intent on getting Paul, I hadn't thought about asking who had kidnapped me. Olympias! I hissed her name and the woman at my feet wailed.

'Hush!' I commanded. 'Let me think. How can we get to Iskander without alerting his mother?'

'I don't know, I have never seen Iskander. I only know where his quarters are. His mother has spies everywhere.' She looked over her shoulder. 'I never know when they are listening.'

'Help me to understand. Olympias wanted me away from her son. She wants to give her own grandson to Marduk, and she doesn't know that Darius has taken the baby to Persepolis. Is that right?'

The woman nodded miserably. 'We were to have hidden you for ever in our temple.'

'It's destroyed now. I'm sorry,' I said.

She gaped at me. Minutes dragged by as we stared at each other. I felt the tingling of the nervous energy that had filled me ever since I'd woken up during the earthquake. She seemed to feel it too, because she covered her face.

'Don't be frightened. I need your help. I only want my son. Then I will go.'

I helped her to her feet, and she straightened her shoulders and took a shaky breath. 'Very well. We should hurry if you want to see Iskander. He is going to begin the purifying ceremony soon.'

I poked my head out of the door and gave half of the gold I had left to my guide. Then I told him to keep the horses and to consider himself freed.

He nodded. 'To free me you must take my contract to the court and have it stamped. Only then will I be a free man.'

I sighed. 'Well, try to find some lodgings. Meet me

tomorrow morning an hour after sunrise near Ishtar's gate, and we'll go to the courthouse.'

He left, leading the limping ponies.

The priestess took me into the temple and led me through the labyrinth beneath the ziggurat. We came out on the other side near the market square. It was teeming with people; the caravans had arrived, and the city was a bustling hive of activity. Stands were being set up. Merchants would trade through the night and the next day, up until the ceremony which took place at midday, when the sun was directly over the ziggurat. Camels and donkeys were being led to the stables just outside the city, and the streets were thronging with people and animals jostling one another.

We threaded our way through the crowd, heading towards the imperial palace. I wore my old cloak, so no one gave me a second glance. The priestess hurried, looking now and then over her shoulder at me. Her skin was white where it pressed against her bones. I hoped nobody would notice her fear. Just before we reached the palace I tugged on her sleeve. We ducked into a small recess in the wall. From there we could just see the palace gates.

'You look like death,' I snapped. 'Can't you put on a happier face?'

'I'm terrified,' she confessed.

'Where do you usually meet Olympias?'

'Shh! Don't say her name!' She twitched nervously. 'I send messages through a man. He comes to see me. I don't know his name. Iskander is here, in this building. His rooms are guarded.'

111

'Here's what you must do. Go to his captain. His name is Lysimachus. Say these words, "Ashley of the Sacred Sandals". Tell him I am here, and I want to see him. Then bring him to me.'

'Ashley of the Sacred Sandals.' She looked doubtful.

'It's important.'

She drew a deep breath and then vanished into the crowd. I saw her speaking to the guards at the gate, and they let her through. I hoped that Lysimachus was still guarding Alexander's door. If not, all my efforts would be in vain.

After what seemed a long time, I saw her coming back. At her heels was Lysimachus, and I nearly cried with relief. His face lit up when he saw me, and he prostrated himself. I reached down and yanked him to his feet.

'Not here!' I whispered. 'Too many eyes. I must see Iskander, but not in the palace. It's too dangerous for me.'

'It is you,' he whispered. 'We were told you'd been eaten by the crocodiles. We found signs of a struggle, and blood, and one of your leather sandals. There were traces of crocodile footprints in the sand. Huge ones. Iskander went mad with grief and cut all his hair off. He would have killed every crocodile in the river if Plexis hadn't stopped him.'

'Plexis?' I was surprised. 'Wasn't he with Nearchus?'

'He was, but he came back. He was there when you went missing.'

I thought about this for a minute, but I didn't see any link between him and Olympias. I turned to the priestess. 'Where can I hide until Iskander can come to me?'

'In the temple. If Iskander comes to pray, no one will

think it odd. He has gone to nearly all of the temples in the city. I will get you a robe like mine, and you can stay in my quarters.'

Lysimachus reached his hand out and touched my shoulder. He shook his head. 'You have come back from the dead,' he said. His face was pale beneath its tan.

'Just get Iskander to the temple as soon as you can,' I said, patting his arm. 'Don't worry about anything else.'

'I'm glad to see you,' he said, ducking his head.

'I'm happy to see you, too.' I'd only known him for a short time, nearly a year ago, but he was a familiar face in a strange city.

We looked at each other, then he said, 'You can count on me.'

'I know I can. Thank you.'

'Tell Iskander to ask for Nabonida,' the priestess told him.

We waded through the tightly packed crowd, and Nabonida led me to her quarters, taking the smaller passages to avoid being seen. Once in her room she asked me what I wanted, and without thinking I replied, 'A bath.'

She bowed and clapped her hands. A slave girl appeared, and Nabonida told her to bring a basin of water and some scented almond oil.

When I was clean, my body soft and fragrant, and my hair carefully dressed, I put my white robe back on. Then I sat by the window and waited for Alexander. The energy that had sustained me was still running like electricity through my body, making me quiver. It also gave me a strange radiance. My eyes glowed, and Nabonida covered her eyes with her hands when I looked towards her. We didn't speak. I had spent too much time in her presence wrapped in silence.

She straightened her meagre belongings, washed her robe and hung it to dry out a window, then mended a tear in one of her sheets. I watched her as she worked. I'd seen her every day for a year. She was familiar, yet alien. Why hadn't she ever spoken to me? Why help me now? Why was she here, and not in my temple prison? The questions stayed locked in my head. I simply watched as the woman, short, spare and homely, did the everyday chores of her existence. She seemed used to silence, and I began to wonder if I hadn't been in a sort of Carmelite convent, where speech was forbidden. Even while I'd been in the temple, I hadn't heard any voices. No babble, no murmur. I stirred myself and asked her if that was the case.

She looked confused. 'What's a Carmelite?'

'It's a person who's taken a vow to worship her God in silence,' I explained. 'Is that why no one spoke to me?'

She seemed to consider this. Then she nodded once, which meant no. 'The temple where you were kept was for the dying,' she explained. 'We keep silence out of respect. Gulu, our goddess, whispers only. If we talk we may not hear what she says. We have gotten into the habit of listening, not talking. But we didn't speak to you because we were afraid. Our goddess is not your mother.' She looked at me miserably. 'I'm not any good at explaining. I am unhappy about this whole affair. Please forgive me.'

'I only want my son back,' I said to her. 'There is nothing else to forgive. You looked after me well. For that

I thank you.' I saw a faint glimmer of surprise in her brown eyes and felt guilty for some reason.

I turned back to the window. The sun was setting, and orange shafts of light glittered off dust floating in the air, cloaking the city in a nimbus of gold. The priests in the fifty-three temples of the city blew their trumpets as soon as the sun disappeared below the horizon. My skin prickled. Trumpets filled the city with their brassy wails. The last notes died away. The air seemed to settle, and there was a silence.

In the quiet I heard his footsteps and rose to greet him.

He hesitated in the doorway. He had changed in one year. His face was harder, and he was thinner. His skin pressed against his cheekbones, and his eyes were greener. The jaguar stared out of them. His mouth had a different set to it, one I'd never seen. His hair was cut short and lifted off his temples and the back of his neck in fine curls. It was no longer gold; it had reverted to its normal colour, warm brown. It made his skin whiter. It turned whiter still when he saw me, and he stood quite still, not even breathing.

I froze. My breath caught in my throat. Then I felt the hot rush of blood in my cheeks and I swayed forward. 'Alex,' I breathed, and fainted.

He caught me before I hit the ground. He hadn't lost his extraordinary speed or grace. He picked me up and held me to his chest, calling my name until I opened my eyes.

'Is it really you? Are you back to stay?' he asked. He started to laugh, or maybe it was a sob. "Ashley of the Sacred Sandals" indeed. Your nose is bleeding again.'

I looked down and saw the scarlet splash of blood staining my robe. I put my hand up and stanched the flow. 'It's just nerves. I have so much to tell you, and we have no time.' I could hardly look at him; everything I'd lived through in the past year was like an explosion inside me that I had to defuse somehow. I took a deep breath to steady myself. 'We need to speak.'

'Nabonida?'

'We can talk in front of her. We may need her help, and she has something important to tell you.' I wiped my face with the hem of my robe.

Nabonida paled, but, to her credit, she didn't try and wriggle out of it. She told Alexander everything she knew. While she spoke she took my soiled robe and handed me a clean one. I put it on and turned to Alexander. He was looking at me with a queer expression.

'Your body?' he said falteringly. He raised his eyes to mine, and I read the unspoken question.

I told him about our son.

When he heard about the baby his face twisted and he buried his head in my chest. I held him. I could feel him shaking, but when I saw his eyes I realized it was from rage.

Afterwards, Nabonida and I sat while Alexander paced across the room. His fury was terrible, but mine was equal to his, and our eyes met with a clash that could practically be heard.

'I will kill her.' His voice was as bloodless as his face.

'No.' I stood up and levelled my gaze at him. 'No. You cannot kill your own mother. Send her back to her country.'

'To Macedonia?'

'No, to her own people. To Epirus.'

'Why can't I kill her now?'

I shuddered, imagining what the Time Senders would do if Alexander killed his mother. We'd all be erased, including Paul. 'Because the gods will take care of her. You have other things to do. We must go to Persepolis. We must get our son back. Please, Alex.' My voice broke. 'I want my baby.'

He gathered me in his arms again and I wept. The energy that had carried me for days across the burning plains was deserting me. I was simply a mother who wanted to find her child.

It was as if a dam burst inside me then. The pain I felt threatened to overwhelm me, and I sobbed until my throat was raw. Finally the storm within me ebbed. I looked up, and saw that Alexander had wept too. Tears still glittered on his cheeks. But he pulled himself together and smoothed the hair back from my hot face.

'What did you name him?' he asked me.

'Paul.'

'Paul?' His face fell. 'Not Iskander?'

'I called him Paul Alexander.'

He tried the name out a few times then nodded. 'I think I like it.'

I smiled. 'I think you'll like him, too.'

He bent over and kissed me gently on the lips, giving me gooseflesh. 'I love him already. We'll find him. I swear it. If I have to go to the ends of the earth, I will find Paul.'

'How?'

'We'll go after Darius. We'll leave as soon as the wedding is over.'

I thought of his army, camped just outside Babylon. Would they pack up and leave at a moment's notice? That hadn't been in their plans. Alexander must have sensed my doubts. He took my chin in his hands. 'I swear, we will leave tomorrow. As soon as I return to the palace, I will give orders to Lysimachus to start getting everything ready.'

'Will Darius fight?'

'He has his army. Other than that, I cannot say.' He rested his head against my shoulder, and I could feel his muscles quiver. Bells rang again, chiming softly in the dusk.

Nabonida stood, her hands clutching at her robe. 'The evening bells have rung. You should leave.'

He hesitated, but I nodded. 'Go now,' I said. 'Oh, I forgot, I have a gift for your bride.'

'For Stateira?'

'You must give her Chirpa. My slave girl. She'll need her. Make her understand how special she is. However, there is one condition. You must free her, and she must want to stay of her own free will. Do you promise?'

'Yes. Thank you on behalf of Stateira.'

'Is she nice? Is she beautiful?' I had to know.

He smiled and kissed me again. 'She's as sweet as an adder and as beautiful as a hippopotamus. I'm marrying her for politics. But as soon as the wedding is finished, I intend to go to Persepolis. Her father lied to me, and I won't let him off lightly. I gave him Persepolis in exchange for Babylon and the government here. Perhaps he thinks to hold my son ransom. I will leave within two days, with you at my side. I want to marry you. We will marry for love. I swear it. Wait for me here. Tomorrow I will be busy,' he grinned wryly. 'But at midnight I will knock on this door, and you must be ready to come with me.'

'I'll be ready.'

He kissed me again, gently, and then left. His eyes had been as hard as flint, and his mouth was drawn in a thin line of rage. I wouldn't want to be in Olympias's place that evening. I only prayed he didn't kill her.

I spent the night in Nabonida's room. When Alexander left to return to the palace, all the strength drained from my limbs and I collapsed. She laid me on her bed and gave me broth to drink. When my eyes grew heavy she drew the curtains and let me sleep. And when the dawn started to colour the sky she woke me and we crept out of her room and made our way to Ishtar's gate. I had to meet with the slave who'd brought me to Babylon.

His name was Seleucos, and he was twenty-four years old. During our journey he'd told me his life's story. He was a garrulous man, easy to listen to. He had been born in Pella, which was in Macedonia, but he'd been sold as a slave to a merchant from Athens, where he learned to speak Greek and Egyptian. When he was seventeen, his master died, and he was sold to a galley ship as a rower. The work didn't please him, so he asked to be sold again. A warehouse owner on the isle of Crete bought him. His aptitude with languages enabled him to work with the merchants at the docks. But one day pirates captured him and took him to Tyre. The pirates sold him to an Arab

119

merchant who had a caravan, and Seleucos helped him trade up and down the Euphrates River before finally coming to the city of Mazda. That was where the earthquake had destroyed my temple prison. In the aftermath of the earthquake his master had sold him to me, along with two horses, and he'd brought me to Babylon.

Mazda, the king of the Persian gods, was the protector of the city named after him. Gulu, the name of the temple in which I'd been a prisoner, was the goddess of healing. But neither had resisted the earth's shaking. Now Seleucos stood before me, waiting to see what I would do with him.

I freed him. We went to the courthouse facing the marketplace and I asked for a magistrate who could validate a franchise. The courthouse was interesting; it had no waiting room or desk. Clerks stood in a row by the door and welcomed the clients one after another. A very long table divided the room in half, and one wall had little cubbyholes where thousands of rolled-up scrolls were stored.

When I stated my business, the clerk called the proper magistrate. He asked Seleucos pertinent questions and examined the paper given to me by his last master. I ended up paying the court six didrachms – roughly a hundred and twenty-five dollars. Then I was instructed to shake hands with Seleucos and we had to exchange a ritual vow that separated us legally, but bound him to me for the rest of his days as a member of my family. In other words, I was his godmother, and responsible for his religious education.

I hadn't realized that by freeing a slave one adopted him, but that's how it was, and now I had a godson.

We celebrated. I bought drinks for Nabonida and Seleucos at a fruit stand. We sat in the shade of an awning, sipping our fresh orange juice while watching the crowd doing business in the market. We'd spent less than half an hour in the courthouse, and the morning was still fresh.

'What will you do now?' I asked Seleucos.

He shrugged. 'I don't know. I'd like to join Iskander's army. There's always a job for a soldier, and I enjoy travelling. His army is camped out on the plain. I thought I'd go there this morning, perhaps I'll get recruited.'

'Would you like that?' I asked.

'Very much.' He smiled crookedly, and two dimples danced on his cheeks. His brown hair was unruly and curly; his eyes were dark grey. He had an open face, which was why I'd insisted on buying him. However, there was something more in his eyes. I sensed quiet determination that hinted at huge ambition.

I drummed my fingers on my leg and said, 'I know someone who will help you. Go to the palace and ask for Lysimachus. Tell him Ashley of the Sacred Sandals sent you, and that you want to serve Iskander. He will find you a job. If not, leave a message with Nabonida, and I'll try something else.'

He thanked me, and I said, 'Don't forget, you have two horses. I gave you their ownership papers.'

His gratitude was embarrassing; I waved it away. I didn't need a slave, or horses, or anything but my son. When I thought of him, I ached. I would find him, if I had to go to the ends of the earth.

The ringing of bells startled me.

'What's happening?' I asked Nabonida.

'They are the bells for Iskander's wedding, they will ring until the sun sets.' Her eyes were huge and dark in her face. Will you come to the ceremony?'

The news about the wedding sent a fresh spasm of grief through me, but I quelled it and nodded at her. 'I will come to the ceremony of Marduk,' I said, 'because I must do something for the gods before I leave the city.' There was a note in my voice that made Nabonida look at me warily.

'Do you mean to save the child? It's not yours, you know.'

'It's still a child,' I said. 'And to kill it is an abomination.'

My two companions glanced at each other and then towards the market square where the bells were making conversation difficult. A scarlet flag unfurled over a market stand. A white camel walked by with a haughty swing of its long neck. Youths did handstands on the fountain wall and people pitched copper coins at them. Sunlight flashed on silver and bronze coins, glazed earthenware jars, and sparkled on the water of the fountain. Green and gold tiles gleamed.

The scents of garlic and jasmine, incense and fish, oranges, and sweat wafted in the air. A donkey lifted its tail and added to the odours, and one of the slaves who worked for the city drifted over and swept the manure into a wicker basket.

I finished my juice and handed the earthenware cup

back to the vendor.

'How will you do it?' Nabonida asked me after a while.

'I dreamt I was in the temple,' I said, 'and in my dream everything was very dark, as if night had fallen. In the darkness there moved a shadow, and the shadow took the baby from the jaws of Marduk and spirited him away. Marduk closed his mouth on emptiness and broke his jaws in rage. Then nothing else remained.'

'What does it mean?' asked Nabonida.

'It means I must be a shadow,' I said.

It was getting hot. People were leaving the marketplace to seek shade. Soon, in the temple of Hera, my lover would take his second wife. Then the procession would move to the ziggurat where Marduk awaited his worshippers. And I would become a shadow.

Before I left, I whispered into Seleucos's ear and told him what I needed him to do. He looked troubled but said he could be counted on.

Nabonida and I went back to her room, and I prepared myself. I washed the dust off my body with a sponge soaked in rose water, then I put on my black robe. The silk covered me entirely, and I could pull the cloth over my face as well. I was ready. The strange energy was back, but now it was a glacial calm. My hands didn't tremble when we took tapers and lit them from the brazier.

Nabonida led me through the ziggurat to the back rooms, the rooms where the priests would be, and I kissed her, told her to leave, and to forget she'd ever seen me. She prostrated herself at my feet. This time I let her. I needed her respect and fear now. I was still afraid she would betray me.

The morning dragged on. I wandered around the temple, keeping out of the way of the remaining priests. There weren't many; most had gone to Hera's temple for Alexander's wedding. Marduk's temple was vast, with narrow, winding corridors. The main room, where the sacrifices took place, looked like a theatre with a raised stage. A great, stone dragon crouched in the centre of it, staring out at the crowd of worshippers.

Marduk was a dragon god, with an appetite for human blood. Condemned criminals were his usual fare. They were led down a central aisle, past the rows of worshippers, and placed onto the altar. Marduk's head, a giant stone sculpture, opened huge, toothy jaws. Behind them was a table made of a slab of granite. The prisoner was forced to lie on the altar in front of the statue, and his head was pushed into its jaws. Then the altar was tilted upwards, so he slid into the gaping mouth of stone. A lever mechanism closed the jaws, triggered a guillotine, and the unfortunate victim was beheaded. To the watching public, it looked as if the monster had neatly nipped the sacrifice's head off.

A baby was too small for that method. Babies were not usually on Marduk's menu, so today something different was going to happen. The baby was to be laid on a large platter, exactly like a Thanksgiving turkey, and presented to the god. After the baby slid down the sloping altar, the priests waiting on the other side of the statue would whisk him away, as if the god had swallowed him. They would perform the sacrifice, then carry the body out front again and pour the blood into the ritual jar.

124

During the sacrifices, blood ran off grooves in the table into special bowls. It was collected and poured into a particular jar. I examined it. It was lined with hundreds of sponges to soak up the blood. Part of the ritual then, was to make the people believe that Marduk drank the blood from the jar. I wrinkled my nose in disgust, and then started to wonder how I could change the ceremony a bit. I listened for the sound of footsteps, but the novice priest in charge of sweeping the temple had finished and was now snoring loudly in his cell.

I took the sponges out of the jar and put them in the brazier. They burned badly and gave off a noxious smell, but with all the incense it was hardly noticeable. Then I looked around for something to replace the sponges. I found what I was looking for and grinned. Then I examined the levers and the gears that moved the great jaws, and I pushed on the stone head. It was absurdly heavy. The priests who worked the levers had to be powerful.

When the priests threw open the great, bronze doors to let the crowd in, I was hidden behind one of the long, heavy tapestries behind the statue. I peered out and watched as the crowd filed in silently. I saw Nearchus and the captain Lysimachus. However, I didn't see Plexis, and this worried me for some reason. I was also anxious to get a look at Alexander, his new wife, and Olympias.

They arrived last, accompanied by a blast of trumpets and a clash of cymbals. The people all bowed, pressing their foreheads to the floor. The priests did likewise. As Alexander and the two women walked down the central aisle, twelve priestesses strewed red rose petals over their heads. They were walking through a shower of blood. I shuddered.

Alexander wore his military regalia and a strange helmet made of silver-plated bronze. It had ram's horns springing from the temples. Red and orange tassels hung from the back, and an elephant's head, with its tusks sweeping forward, was carved on the front. Alexander's drawn face was clean-shaven and pale. Around his eyes, deep shadows looked like bruises. His mouth, usually so full and sensual, was a thin, hard line. His eyes glittered with a feral light.

Walking just behind him, with mincing steps, was his new bride, Stateira. She was a pudgy woman. Her expression was haughty, and her thick black eyebrows joined over the bridge of her nose. She tilted her head to gaze up at Alexander and her eyes, sharp and darting, softened. Her black hair was twined into braids intricately woven atop her head. She wore a gold necklace, set with the biggest blue star sapphire I'd ever seen. On either side of the sapphire were rubies as big as hen's eggs. She wore a crown of gold, and her arms were covered with chiselled gold bracelets. However, my eyes slid past her, as did everyone else's, to Olympias, mother of Alexander, daughter of a demigod, and concubine of Philip II who was supposedly the grandson of Zeus.

Olympias was dressed in white, which brought out her delicate colouring. Her hair was Venetian blonde, the colour of ripe apricots, and her eyes were as blue as the sapphire around Stateira's neck. Her pearly, translucent skin glowed in the penumbra. She wore a necklace of red coral beads and dangling pink coral earrings. Her hair was braided with golden beads. She had a long, straight nose, a full, sensual mouth, and her eyes were long and heavy-lidded like Alexander's. Her eyebrows were sweeping lines across a high forehead. She looked like a queen, or a goddess. I hated her. She was waiting for the ceremony to begin, so she could see her own grandson sacrificed to a pagan god. She would kill her own grandson as she'd killed her husband. He'd made the mistake of marrying a young, beautiful concubine. Olympias had murdered Philip, or had had him assassinated, and she'd had his new wife immolated on his funeral pyre. I'd heard the unfortunate bride had been forced to hold her newborn son in her arms as she burned.

She would try to kill her son-in-law, Cassander, but I knew from history books that he would have the last laugh. He would have her stoned to death. Knowing that, I was content to wait, while Alexander, Stateira, and Olympias moved to the front of the temple and were seated on a stone bench, practically at the feet of the statue.

A gong was struck, and the first prisoner was led to Marduk.

There were no windows in the temple and the flickering torches offered little light. In the dimness, the prisoners were all dressed in white to be better seen. They were drugged. Their pupils were dilated, and their mouths gaped in a parody of a grin. They were supposed to be happy, accepting the honour of being sacrificed to their god. They breathed in great, gulping gasps but didn't struggle when they were laid on the enormous stone altar and tilted into Marduk's mouth.

Three prisoners were executed, while I bit my knuckles to keep from screaming. Their blood was ceremoniously poured into the great jar, and then the gong reverberated again. A baby was carried down the aisle.

I saw Alexander blench and nearly rise off his seat. Olympia straightened and looked hard at the squalling infant. Her delicate brows drew together in a frown, and I wondered if she realized it wasn't Alexander's son.

The baby was wrapped in white linen and his head was crowned with jasmine. White rose petals were scattered over him, and the priests bowed when he was brought to the statue. The infant was placed on the altar, and there was a deep silence as he slid towards the great jaws of Marduk.

I pulled my hood over my head and stepped out of my hiding place. I snatched the baby away just as the jaws were about to close. I had rubbed black cinders on my face, hands and arms to hide them. To the onlookers, it must have seemed as though the baby had suddenly floated backwards off the altar and sailed into the air.

The gigantic stone jaws clashed together on nothing, and the priest who worked the lever was so surprised he let go of it too soon, causing the heavy stone to fall with a resounding crash. I held the baby high in the air and backed away. With a sound like a canon shot, the statue buckled and cracked. The bottom half of the jaws slewed sideways, catching the high priest on his chest. He was hurled backwards by five tons of carved granite, and when he hit the ground, he was dead.

The jar holding the blood tipped over and steaming blood poured out, sluicing over the floor and splattering priests and worshippers with blood mixed with the lamp oil I'd poured into the jar earlier. It made an extremely slick mess. I stepped carefully to the back of the room and ducked through the curtains. Guards, dispatched by frantic priests, slipped and fell when they stepped on the oily blood. People screamed and cried out in terror, but before I disappeared I turned and stared directly at Olympias. She looked like an alabaster statue, with a crimson stain down her robe where the blood had sprayed. Her eyes were fixed on the child I carried, but instead of the rage that I was sure I'd see, there was a cool, calculating look. I shivered. I hoped Alexander would succeed in sending her back to Epirus.

Alexander was no longer in his seat; he'd disappeared during the uproar.

Stateira was wailing, covering her face in her hands. Then I remembered: Marduk was her god.

Chapter Six

I met Seleucos outside the gate of Ishtar. I was dressed in my travelling cloak, and I'd wrapped the infant in a plain woollen shawl. Seleucos greeted me discreetly, and we ducked into a doorway to talk.

'I have done as you asked, and the child will be well cared for,' he told me.

'He won't be a slave, will he?' I was worried.

He shook his head. 'No. When I was with my master in the caravan I met many traders, and I know of one who will care for this child. I told him he was Marduk's sacrifice.'

'And that didn't frighten him?' I asked.

'No, he is a Jew, and he has no love for Marduk. Or even for Babylon. He comes to trade and leaves as quickly as he can. He will take care of the baby, never fear. He told me to tell you this; the baby's name will be Joseph, named after his foster-father. They live somewhere near Nazareth.'

I kissed the child on his soft cheek and hugged him. 'God bless you,' I whispered. Reluctantly, I handed him to Seleucos and watched as he disappeared into the teeming crowd. All around me I could hear the murmur of voices. The news from the ziggurat was spreading. The story would soon be all over the city. I hoped that the caravan would leave before they started searching for the babe.

The sun was setting. I felt light-headed and realized I hadn't eaten all day, so I went back towards the marketplace to try to find some food. Several stands had large barbecues next to them, and the smell of grilled meat and fish filled the evening air. I bought a lamb shish kebab, a slice of watermelon, and some unleavened bread. Sitting cross-legged next to the fire, I ate. The vendor had spread grass mats on the ground for his customers, and he had earthenware cups to scoop water out of the fountain. The cups were rented for half an obol. I paid for everything with obols, which were the lowest denomination of silver money, worth about twenty-five cents.

I returned the cup to the vendor and he sold me an orange for dessert. Then I wandered around the market, listening to the gossip. Of course, I could only understand Greek gossip, but most people spoke Greek. It was the language the merchants used, and almost everyone got by with it. Although there was some hushed gossip about the fiasco in the temple, there was nothing said about a missing baby, so I relaxed, knowing that little Joseph was free.

I threw my orange peel into a public trash basket and listened as two men talked about a scandal that had befallen Alexander while I was in my temple prison. It seemed that one of his officers, a certain Harpalus, had stolen five thousand gold talents. He had been assigned to guard the money and he'd taken it. He fled to Athens, where he was caught. The Athenians had wanted to return him to Alexander, but he'd escaped to Crete.

'Half the money was gone too,' chuckled one man,

'and the money certainly ended up "in the mouth" of the lawyer, Demosthenes, who had been in charge of the affair.'

At this moment in Athens, Demosthenes was being tried in his own court. I wondered what would happen to him. Five thousand gold talents was more than ten times the tribute paid to the city of Athens per year by the entire confederation. It represented an enormous sum. I wondered if Plexis, who'd invested his fortune, had had part of his money stolen. If so, he would certainly be interested in the outcome of the trial. Perhaps he'd gone back to Athens, and that was why he hadn't been at the ceremony.

When it was dark, I went back to the temple. Nabonida had given me her robe, so I put it on and slipped inside unnoticed. Everything was still chaotic. Guards had started to search the people leaving the city. Even in the temple people were being checked. I was glad of the robe: no one stopped me. Once in Nabonida's room I took it off. Then I went to the window and sat down to wait for Alexander.

I must have dozed off, because all at once, his arms were around me and his face was next to mine. His eyes were tender, his mouth even more so. I held on to his shoulders and he lifted me up and laid me on the bed. We made love with a fierce urgency. I wrapped my legs around his hips and met each thrust with a cry. I hadn't realized how much I'd missed him; how much I needed him until then. He bucked against me and then shuddered into me with a harsh groan. I held him within me and let my own orgasm sweep me away.

Afterwards, I watched his face as he slept. The moonlight cast deep shadows under his brows and his lashes swept his cheeks. He slept for perhaps an hour, while I looked on, jealously guarding his slumber. Then his eyes opened. He woke up, instantly alert. I felt a jolt of electricity and marvelled again at the incredible energy that he possessed. He kissed me, tenderly, and we dressed and left the temple. We hadn't spoken a word to each other. After a year of silence I'd gotten out of the habit of talking, and Alexander communicated with his eyes and his gestures better than any mime or actor. He used this talent to communicate with his soldiers from half a mile away, or through the babble of a banquet, or silently, just with me.

I wanted to say goodbye to Nabonida, but she was nowhere to be found. I never saw her again.

We left the city in disguise. Just outside the temple, Lysimachus was waiting with a camel laden with bundles of raw wool. Alexander, Lysimachus and I donned Arab robes, and I hid my face behind a veil, Arab-style. The guards searched us, looking for a blonde woman with a small baby. But I wore a wig of black hair that Lysimachus had procured for me, and no child was with us.

We left the city and went along the trading route, but once we'd gone five miles and were out of sight of the city, we cut across the fields. We changed our clothes along the way. Alexander became himself again, as did Lysimachus. I kept the black wig on and became a slave girl leading a pack-camel into Alexander's army encampment.

He had already given the order to move, and so, beneath the full moon, the army got under way. We moved quickly this time. Alexander was on his way to Persepolis, and it was a thousand kilometres away.

It took the army roughly a month. I lost track of time. Alexander's army, which was one of the most rapid ever known, moved more than fifty kilometres a day. He drove them ruthlessly; he drove them like I'd driven the ponies. We marched until we fell to our knees. We ate while we were marching and slept wrapped in our cloaks where we'd fallen. We hiked across plains, waded through marshes, crossed the Tigris River, and then we came to Susa. By then, we were exhausted. I don't recall much about the march until then. I was heartsick about my baby, and Alexander had much to do convincing his generals that the march to Persepolis was vital. The soldiers had been fighting and marching for over two years, and they needed a rest. But we couldn't stay long. In order to appease his men, Alexander decided to throw a party.

To reward his troops and to consolidate his victory over Babylon, Alexander decided to marry one thousand of his soldiers to Persian women. The wedding took place in Susa for two reasons: because we were halfway to Persepolis, and because the army was weak with exhaustion. Some of the soldiers had come down with malaria.

Alexander would have preferred crossing the swamps in winter, when there was less chance of sickness. We had left during a hot spell, a freak of the weather, and the swamps had been full of swarming mosquitoes.

Of course, they didn't know mosquitoes carried disease, but I did. The soldiers picked the lemon grass called citronella and rubbed it on their bodies. The sharp, citrus smell kept the mosquitoes at bay, and most of the army stayed healthy.

At Susa, we camped outside the city while Alexander organized the huge wedding. He ordered fifty cows and one hundred sheep to be slaughtered. Fires were lit before dawn, and the animals were blessed by the priests, slaughtered, and then cooked. The smell of roasting meat hung over the city, and the aroma raised the soldiers' spirits. Meat was a luxury at that time.

Although I was anxious to get moving again and catch Darius, I was happy to rest and took the time to seek out Nassar for a chat. Alexander was gone from before dawn until night, and I didn't get a moment alone with him. He had his tent set up in a vain effort to get some privacy, but all day a long line of people waited to see him – priests, satraps, magistrates, lawyers, merchants, and fathers of the girls to be wed to his soldiers.

Nassar was busy writing out marriage contracts, which was something rare, but Alexander had insisted. Fifty scribes worked unceasingly. They sat in a huge circle on reed mats. Slaves darted in and out, rolling up parchments, sealing them, and putting them in wicker baskets. Other slaves fanned the scribes to keep flies away, or gave them drinks of water. I watched them for a while, but the heat was making me wilt, so I walked back to Alexander's tent, determined to get some needed rest.

Lysimachus was in charge of taking the names of all the people waiting to see Alexander. I was pleased to see

Seleucos, my guide, helping him keep order. He saw me and nodded with deference. I didn't have to be shown in. The people parted as I arrived, most of them prostrating themselves, murmuring prayers. I was startled, until I remembered that they thought I was Demeter's daughter and therefore a goddess. I blushed and tried to look worthy of their attention, and then I ducked inside. The tent was cool and dark. Alexander was sitting behind his table with the beautiful glass lamp hanging over his head. It cast a wavering, blue-green light, making his face look as if he were underwater.

He looked up at me. He was immobile, and yet I had the impression I could feel his energy. His fey eyes glittered.

'I just want to lie down and sleep,' I said. 'I won't bother you.'

'We haven't had time to talk,' he said. 'I'm sorry.'

'We will, when we get to Persepolis,' I said, crawling into the soft bed and cuddling with the cushions. I was asleep before I heard his reply.

I woke up much later. The sun was nearing the horizon and I could see a bright red glow outside. The tent flap was up, letting in fresh air. There were no more people standing in line, and I realized I'd woken because the constant noise was gone. Everyone had spoken quietly, and the soft murmuring had lulled me to sleep. Now there were only two people talking. And one of them smelled foul. I opened my eyes and peered over to the other side of the tent.

Alexander was leaning over his table talking earnestly to a man dressed in a long white robe. The man had a beard, which wasn't considered chic then. He was elderly, and like most old people, didn't care about fashion. Or bathing, obviously. I wrinkled my nose.

He and Alexander stopped talking for a moment and then the man reached forward and moved something on the table. Alexander sat back and narrowed his eyes, and I realized they were playing chess. The old man chuckled and rubbed his hands together until Alexander leaned over and, with a decisive movement, swept the board clean with his arm.

'Oh, Iskander,' said the man in a stern voice. 'When will you ever learn to lose gracefully? You must learn this lesson!'

'I will not!' Alexander's eyes blazed.

Anyone else would have cowered, but the old man with the beard simply said, 'Tush!' and rapped his knuckles sharply on the now empty board. 'Iskander, stop acting like a spoiled brat.'

I sat up. I couldn't believe what I'd heard. 'Who are you?' I asked, before I realized how rude I sounded. I rubbed my eyes. 'Excuse me, I meant to say hello.'

'Isn't she lovely?' Alexander forgot his bad temper and came over, sitting on the bed next to me. 'I rescued her from Hades, and then my mother kidnapped her.'

The old man winced. 'Olympias always was a silly bitch. I'm pleased to meet you, my dear. I'm Aristotle. I came to Susa a month ago on business, and I had no idea my star pupil was dragging his entire army along behind me.'

'We're not following you,' Alexander said, 'I told you, we're pursuing Darius. He's got my son.'

'Well, Darius always was a hot-headed fool.'

I blinked. Hot-headed fool? A silly bitch? This was the world's greatest philosopher? I liked him already. 'My name's Ashley,' I said, getting up to greet him politely. 'I'm honoured to meet you. I've heard so much about you.'

His shrewd eyes twinkled. 'Oh? Have you? If Iskander told you about me, it certainly wasn't flattering.'

'Oh no, the only thing Iskander told me about you was that you hit him on the head with a big stick.'

'Well, that's all right, then. That's exactly what did happen. He was always touchy and he'd scream himself hoarse if he lost a game. I tried to teach him to lose with dignity, but as you can see, nothing I told him has sunk in. He's still as impossible as he was when his father brought him to me.'

Alexander scowled. 'The other boys called me a barbarian.'

'And you were, you were!' Aristotle laughed. 'But, dear boy, to Greeks, all non-Greeks are barbarians! You mustn't be so thin-skinned. You've done a marvellous job with your country, and with the army! You should be proud of yourself.'

Alexander beamed. 'Thank you, Master, I am. And I mean to do more. Your ideas about government – I mean to spread them all over Persia. Imagine! When Macedonia, Egypt, Greece, and Persia are all united under my rule, it will be the biggest democracy the world has ever seen. Why, Ashley, what's the matter. Are you choking?'

I fell off the bed and laughed until tears ran down my

face. When I finally stopped, Alexander looked at me in consternation.

'Are you better now?' Aristotle's mouth twitched, and I wondered if he felt like laughing.

'I'm fine, really.' I wiped away my tears and composed my face. 'It was nothing. A little giggle, that's all.' I bit my lip and buried my head in the pillow, my shoulders shaking. I couldn't help it. The laughter had eased the knots somewhat in my belly. I'd needed a good laugh, after the months of mourning and fretting over my baby. We were going to get him, though. I found myself starting to hope again.

Aristotle turned back to Alexander. 'I do think your idea to marry your soldiers to local girls is a good one. Although it goes against my ideas about marriage. You know how I feel about that.'

'Yes, but the soldiers I picked are all in their thirties and the girls are unmarried, so it should work out. They'll either stay in this region and settle, or they will go back to Greece or Macedonia.' Alexander ran a hand through his hair, making it stand on end. 'I'm tired, old man, why don't you let me sleep an hour, and we'll talk during the banquet tonight.'

'Very well, Iskander. I'll leave you two alone. Where's Chirpa, the slave girl I gave you?'

'I left her with Stateira, in Babylon. She will need her more than I do now. Stateira is pregnant, and the oracle said the babe was a boy. I've already named him after myself. Olympias wanted to stay and help Stateira rule Babylon, as you can imagine, but I sent her packing. She put up a fuss when I ordered her back to Macedonia.'

I was startled. 'You didn't tell her to go to Epirus?'

'I did, but she refused. Epirus is a small kingdom, full of barbarians. She went to Macedonia, but I'm having her watched. Never fear. I sent word to Nike that Mother was to be imprisoned when she arrives.'

'Will your sister do that?' I asked, worried.

'No, probably not, but her husband will. He doesn't trust Mother at all. He'll make sure she never leaves the palace.'

Aristotle shook his head. 'Your mother has longer arms than you think. Beware treachery. You should have had her killed, Iskander. She's a menace.'

'I couldn't. The gods were against the idea.' He looked at me gravely. 'Besides, I don't kill people in cold blood, and I don't destroy cities.'

Aristotle looked at him solemnly. 'You killed Cxious, Plexis's brother.'

Alexander met his gaze, although two bright red spots appeared on his cheeks. 'I lost my temper,' he said quietly. It was when his voice went quiet that I shivered.

Aristotle just puffed out his cheeks and blew a raspberry. 'Your problem, my boy, is threefold: you've always been in love with your treacherous mother, you can't control your temper, and you hate to lose.' Beside me, I could feel Alexander swelling like a storm cloud.

'No, Iskander!' Aristotle's voice, I realized, could be just as powerful as Alexander's. 'You will not throw away your future because you cannot control yourself. Remember, don't make vain promises, don't speak empty words, and damn it, boy! Control that TEMPER!' He shouted the last word at us, and then, remarkably, started

140

laughing and walked out of the tent.

Alexander recovered neatly. 'Go and take a bath before the ceremony, you old goat,' he yelled after him. 'You smell like you're wearing a stinky cheese around your neck!'

Aristotle poked his head back in the tent, his eyes bright. 'What do you think I've been living on all these months while travelling?' he asked. 'It's very good cheese; the barbarians from Gaul make it. It's called Camembertus, or something like that. And believe me, it keeps the mosquitoes away.' He grinned before he left.

'But it attracts flies,' muttered Alexander to the empty doorway. 'Why does he always get the last word?'

I pulled him down on top of me. 'Does it really matter who gets the last word?' I asked, nibbling on his earlobe. Then I remembered something Alexander had said. 'Stateira's pregnant?' I asked. 'How do you know?' Although jealousy pricked me sharply, I knew I couldn't interfere with his life. According to history books, he would have at least two legitimate sons, but they would both be murdered at an early age. Along with jealousy, I felt fierce pity.

Alexander caressed my back. 'The oracle said she would bear a son. We went to see the priestess right after the wedding ceremony, before we went to Marduk's temple.' He chuckled and nipped my shoulder. 'That was quite some trick you played at the temple. I left before the end; I wanted to get out of the crowd. Stateira came back to the palace with Mother, and they were so angry that they each flogged two slaves. Stateira has a terrible temper, I hope she learns to control it.' He spoke seriously.

I stroked his face. 'Alex,' I said. 'If I ask a favour, will you grant it?'

'Anything,' he said.

'When we find our baby, will you promise not to proclaim him your son?'

He was startled. 'Why? Don't you want him to rule?'

'We'll see afterwards.'

'After what?'

'Just promise me you'll wait.' I was still terrified the Time Senders would find out I married Alexander and had a son. If that ever happened, we'd both be erased. My panic must have showed, because he stroked my shoulders softly.

'Don't look so frightened. I promise I'll wait.' he looked dubious. 'You know, I'm terribly proud. I can't wait to see him. My first son!' He grabbed my arms and rolled over on me, his expression hard. Then his eyes softened, and he kissed me gently. 'I'll do as you wish, my Ice Queen. I nearly went mad when you disappeared. And that stupid Plexis, telling me that Hades had come back to get you. I nearly believed him. I suppose it was better than believing you'd been eaten by crocodiles. Lysimachus found the tracks, but he said they looked odd. I missed you so much. The weeks and months went by, and still I missed you. I missed you, and I've never felt that for anyone before. Not even my father, although I admired him. And now our baby is gone. We have to get him back. By your mother, Demeter, I swear I'll find him.' His voice broke. We made love slowly, gently, while he cried, his tears wetting my cheeks and neck.

When he fell asleep his face relaxed and lost its fierceness. His eyelids were lavender, and the skin over his cheekbones was translucent with fatigue. I wondered how he would convince his army to follow him to India after promising them a home here, in Persia. I lay still beside my sleeping lover and counted the years. It was the year 331 BC. In two months it would be 330 BC. Alexander's army took four years to march across the Middle East to the gates of Asia. He defeated the Indian army, but then he stopped at the banks of the Indus. It would take two years to get back to Babylon.

I brushed a strand of bright copper off his face and noticed his hair was made up of many colours; deep glossy brown, copper, glittering bronze, even gold. It was wavy and thick, growing in small curls on his temples and on the back of his neck. His sideburns were long, making his face appear narrower than it was. His chin was square and strong, his forehead wide. He got his pure brow and his long, Byzantine eyes from his mother. His colouring was his own, though, warm and vibrant, not the pale coldness of Olympias.

I closed my eyes. Seven more years of hard travel, then back to Babylon where Alexander would die. I shivered as if a wintry chill had touched my skin. He would die in Babylon, and his empire would be fought over like a piece of meat by a pack of hungry dogs. His wives and sons would be murdered, and his tomb lost for all time. But his name and his exploits would inspire men for thousands of years.

Why was I thinking of death? The delicate lamp swung ever so slightly in the breeze, and the flickering blue light made the inside of the tent seem unearthly. Shadows reared and subsided, the gold tips of the pens glittered, and the parchment rustled on the table. A cricket chirped, and the sun dipped below the horizon. Then the trumpets sounded, calling the men to the banquet and wedding ceremony.

Alexander sat up in bed, instantly awake, but for the first time I saw lines of worry on his face. He looked at me and said, 'I dreamt of our son.'

'How was he?'

'Peaceful. Darius dares not hurt him. I think he's well cared for, at least for now. I long to see him.' His eyes looked past me and he frowned, trying to bring the vision of his dream into focus. 'He was such a pale child, it was as if the moon had put her mark on him.'

I remembered the priestess telling me he had a crescent moon on his shoulder. My mouth trembled. Alexander gave me a quick, hard hug.

'If anyone can save him, I can,' he said, with his usual supreme confidence.

We dressed with care. Alexander put on his wedding outfit and I wore my white silk robe. He donned his helmet, and then took me in his arms.

'I have a surprise for you,' he whispered, his eyes dancing.

He would say no more, but left me with Aristotle while he went to get his horse.

Aristotle looked and smelled much better after his bath. He made room for me next to the satrap of Susa, an imposing man who was at least as wide as he was tall. We sat, with other dignitaries from the city, on a long bench covered with rich tapestries. All conversation hushed while the soldiers marched into the valley, Alexander riding in the lead. Then there was a complicated military manoeuvre, which the soldiers performed effortlessly. Bucephalus pranced and snorted, and Alexander rode the fiery stallion without any movement of arm or leg.

Soon his soldiers were standing in straight rows in the valley. Forty thousand strong, with the thousand grooms in front wearing scarlet sashes.

There was a clash of cymbals, and a thousand women filed into the valley. I have no idea where Alexander got them all. I think most of them were slave girls, and as marriage would free them, they were in high spirits. They were dressed in simple robes made of plain linen, but each wore a belt of bright yellow silk and had a crown of flowers in her hair.

They contrasted nicely with the stern soldiers as they chattered and laughed. They took time to look the soldiers up and down, and it seemed as if the woman did the choosing.

The men were not dressed for combat; they didn't have their shields or armour. Since most of them only owned two outfits, a linen tunic and a woollen cape, they were dressed as Greeks. They were wearing sandals and skirts, and that's about it. The women had the privilege of seeing exactly what they were getting. They laughed, talked, pointed, and argued when they wanted the same man.

After the women had decided, and were standing demurely next to their chosen mates, the priest came out of the temple and gave the ritual blessing. The women then took off their belts and bound their right wrists to their husbands' left wrists. Now married, the couples went to the campgrounds where fires were burning and the feast was ready.

Alexander and his officers had been standing on top of a hill overlooking the ceremony. Alexander, astride Bucephalus, looked majestic. When the ceremony was over, he raised his right arm in a salute and his men all raised their right arms. Then, as the newly married men took their wives to the feast, the rest of the army slowly parted, leaving a wide passage leading directly to me. I was with Aristotle and the village dignitaries. When Alexander came riding towards me, I was surprised. I was even more amazed when he stopped his horse and leaned down, holding his hand out to me.

'Come.'

Mesmerized, I obeyed. He swung me onto his horse's back. Bucephalus carried us towards the temple. The priest came out again, and spoke the ritual words. Afterwards Alexander took a golden bracelet out of his tunic and slid it on my arm.

The trumpets blared again, we kissed, and his men cheered. We were married. I had been married on a horse.

It was nothing like my first wedding. My wedding night had been a nightmare. I'd sworn never to marry again. Love had no place in my life. Somehow, Alexander had stripped my defences and had swept me along on his great adventure. He intoxicated me. And when we found our son, everything would be perfect.

I watched Alexander as he ate, drank and joked with his men, and I looked at the gold bracelet he'd given me. It was lovely, with figures of lions and griffins chiselled on it. I returned Alexander's smile, took some grilled mutton and wrapped it in a piece of flat bread. Our wedding night was filled with the music of a thousand musicians. Flutes, oboes, trumpets, drums, lyres and tambourines played until dawn. Women danced, men sang, the fires threw sparks into the night, and the moon hung fat and heavy in the sky. A good omen, said the priest, winking at us.

We had to wait until everyone left before we could go back to the tent. The sun was coming up by the time we crawled into Alexander's bed. I held him tightly and listened to the plaintive notes of the larks as they greeted the morning. Rays of warm sun crept into the tent and gilded our bodies as we lay entwined. Deep peace stole over the valley, and only the liquid notes of the songbirds disturbed it.

Chapter Seven

We stayed for one week in Susa. The thousand newly married soldiers had three choices: returning to Macedonia; staying with their brides in Susa; or continuing with Alexander's army. Roughly two-thirds of the soldiers stayed with the army.

Alexander spent three days sorting out the amount of drachmas he had to leave for the women, so they could start housekeeping. Most of them had families who would keep them until their husbands came back to claim them. Already I saw the results of the wedding. The Persians now treated the soldiers like family. They were no longer the conquering enemy; they were sons-in-law, fathers of their future generations. Even the Macedonian whom Alexander had chosen to replace the satrap, married a local girl before taking his post at the head of the city.

Aristotle watched it all with amusement. He ate with us every evening, trading the worst insults with Alexander, until I was choking with laughter and embarrassment.

Antipatros, an older man who had been one of Alexander's father's generals, dined with us as well. He was a silent man with a stern face, but he got on very well with Aristotle. The two men discussed religion most evenings, not war. I listened to their conversations with interest. Religion had all but disappeared in my time, so I was amazed that Antipatros could believe in a multitude of gods. Aristotle was more an atheist, but he was quite sure that if the people stopped worshipping the gods they would become depraved and debauched. It would be the end of the civilization as he knew it.

Aristotle shook his head. 'It's starting already, you mark my words,' he said darkly. For once his face was serious.

'What do you mean?' I asked.

He leaned towards me, and spoke in a low voice. 'You must watch out for Iskander. He has too much of his mother's character in him. Beware. He must not take the place of the gods in the minds of the people. In their hearts, perhaps. He cannot help but capture people's hearts. Look at him, the firelight shines less than his face, and his eyes are the stars in the sky. Everyone gravitates towards him and revolves around him, as the moon and other planets orbit the earth.'

'They orbit the sun,' I corrected him automatically.

'No, no. The Earth is the centre of the Universe.' He smiled at me kindly, and I smiled back.

'Well, at least you tried to tell Iskander the Earth was round,' I said. 'One out of two correct theories isn't bad.'

He looked at me doubtfully, and then assumed I was joking and chuckled. 'A sense of humour, good girl. I see why Iskander wants you near. But mark my words, and don't let him become deluded into thinking that he is a god himself.' He shook his head. 'If he does, he will topple, and drag the empire down with him. Do you know what they're saying in Alexandria now?'

I said that I did not. He said, 'They're saying he's the

god Amon himself.'

I looked blank. 'Who?'

'Amon!' He frowned. 'The king of the Egyptian gods.'

I took a deep breath. 'Oh, *that* Amon. I will try and keep Alexander's feet on the ground.'

'His feet on the ground?' Aristotle thought about that and then smiled. 'I like it, it's a good one.' We stared into the fire for a few minutes, and then Alexander said something witty to Lysimachus who laughed. The voices around us rose and fell, but Alexander was the pivot. He held the invisible strings that united us all. Our eyes were upon him. Our thoughts were about him. His smiles bound us to him for ever. He was the star we would follow to the ends of the earth.

Three hundred years later another star would rise. Another man would be born who would change the face of the world. The gods of Greece and Rome, depraved, debauched and stripped of their powers, would fall. A new God would take their place. His prophet would be a young man with magnetism and power that would rival Alexander's. He would die on the cross, at exactly the same age Alexander died.

Alexander would be called the son of the god Zeus-Amon, but malaria would strike him down three weeks before his thirty-fourth birthday. Jesus would claim to be the Son of God. We all know where that got him.

I saw the faces of the men as they watched Alexander. Their eyes devoured him. I turned to Aristotle.

'Some people burn too brightly for the rest of us common mortals,' I said. 'I don't think it's so much Iskander's fault as it is his followers. They are only following their instincts. Look at him. Can you truly say he's an ordinary man? When you see him, what do you think?'

Aristotle replied thoughtfully, 'I suppose what everyone else does. I think that he's magnificent. I think he's beautiful, and I want him to love me as I love him. I want him physically, spiritually, and mentally. I want to be his father, his mother, his brother, and his lover. When he was a child he was frightening in his intensity. He could make the other children do anything he wanted. And they adored him.

'Philip brought him to me when he was but ten years old. He was a beautiful boy, with those Byzantine eyes too big for his face and his hair like a golden helmet. He had a terrible temper, though. I tried and tried to teach him to control it, but he couldn't. And it ended tragically, as I knew it would.'

'What happened?'

'He killed his best friend's brother in a fit of rage.'

'I know that much, but how did it happen? Why?'

'Oh, love, I suppose. Love and jealousy and passion. All those things a boy feels so strongly when he's young. Cxious was a handsome youth. Handsome, sly, and unwise in love. Plexis looks a great deal like his brother and I imagine it's a knife in Iskander's heart when he sees him. Still, I warned him. He didn't listen, and now it's too late.' Aristotle sipped his wine and shook his head sadly, lost in thought. 'But it's all in the past now. And it's all in the hands of the gods. Where will he go from here? What will he do? Only the gods know.'

I laughed weakly. 'Well, I wouldn't say that, exactly.'

However, when he looked at me in puzzlement, I just smiled and said mysteriously, 'Only the Shadow knows.' Of course he didn't get that one either.

We marched on to Persepolis. The swamps gave way to low plains, then hills, and then mountains. Alexander strode at the head of his army. He didn't ride Bucephalus; horses were for battle. I rode the grey mare. I was always tired, my limbs felt leaden, and I slept, nodding on the pony's back as we jogged on, mile after mile.

The weather was on our side, neither too cold nor too hot. No big rainstorms, and game was plentiful. We camped after the sun set and broke camp before dawn. After nearly three weeks we arrived near Persepolis, and Alexander sent a messenger ahead, asking Darius to come meet him. In exchange, Alexander would spare the Persian army.

We made camp and waited uneasily, but the night passed without any news. In the morning, Alexander ordered his soldiers to rest – they would attack in two days. No one asked why, and Alexander said nothing about his son. I had wondered if his soldiers would follow his orders and leave Babylon without a fuss. Now, after being with him for nearly two months, I started to understand the formidable leader that was Alexander.

For now, the footsore soldiers were only too glad to set up their tents and sleep. Quiet settled over the encampment. The silence was unnerving. I had never been in the midst of men preparing for battle. They changed. Antipatros became even more stern. Lysimachus was all nerves. Seleucos, who had been promoted to sergeant, became withdrawn and snappish. Alexander seemed to grow, to expand. His presence could be felt all over the camp. His voice rang out; his eyes blazed. He didn't rest. He organized. He planned. He talked to his men, listened to them, and encouraged them. When the sun rose on the second day, to a man, his army was ready to fight and die for him.

Alexander's trumpeter blew the clarion and Bucephalus reared and whinnied. The men screamed in answer, giving me gooseflesh. I had stayed out of everyone's way, in particular Alexander's. I hadn't wanted to distract him. But while he thought of war, I thought of the baby Darius had stolen, and I trembled. I hoped my Paul was safe somewhere in the city.

I stood in front of the tent and watched the men file by. They were grim, holding their long spears and shields, wearing bronze helmets with white plumes. They had sandals and shin-guards made of stiff leather. Otherwise they were nude. This was the phalanx, their thirty-foot spears forming a nightmare porcupine. Following them were the infantry, armed with short swords and wearing skirts of leather to protect their thighs. Their arms were wrapped with leather thongs. After them trotted the cavalry. Their horses rolled wild eyes and snorted, anxious to gallop. I saw my grey mare and hoped she would be all right. The cavalrymen had long, bronze-tipped spears and short swords. Their legs were sheathed in leather, and they carried small, round shields. Their horses had wide leather bands across their chests and under their stomachs for protection. The *hipparchie*, a regiment of mounted archers with bows slung over their shoulders and clusters of sharp arrows in their quivers, came last.

Alexander paused in front of me. For a moment he didn't speak, and then he said in a low voice, 'Fear not for the child. I will get him back.'

I smiled then and didn't try to stop my tears. 'I know you will. Take care of yourself,' I told him, my voice shaking.

The men left the camp and rode toward the city. I stayed behind with the slaves and offered to help the doctors prepare for the wounded. I wanted to make myself useful, so I'd proposed my services to Usse, Alexander's physician. He'd accepted readily. In ancient Greece women were received into the medical corps without any problem.

There were about a hundred doctors in the camp; most were slaves trained for working in the army. The slaves were divided into groups, and tents were set up for the wounded. Usse, a tall, thin Arab, was in charge of the doctors. He supervised the fires and put irons in them to heat. I asked why, and he replied they were cauterizing irons for the wounds. I started a pot of water boiling for strips of linen. We'd need sterile cloths for bandages.

Usse was amused when I started boiling the bandages, so I tried to explain about microbes. He listened carefully. He had no idea what germs were, or why perfectly clean cloth had to be boiled. But he accepted my explanation, and even asked Axiom, Alexander's personal valet, to help me. We boiled bandages and hung them to dry. After that, I boiled surgical instruments. They were terrifying. Most were cauterizing irons, which Usse stuck like branding irons into white-hot embers. There were scalpels, as sharp as modern ones, clamps to remove arrows, and instruments I didn't recognize and hoped I wouldn't need to use. We also prepared splints and cataplasms. Usse prepared a malodorous potion that he told me could make people sleepy and would help in setting broken bones. I think there was opium in it, and something smelled suspiciously like hashish. Sheets were soaked in vinegar to help stop bleeding.

Afterwards everyone settled down to wait. I hated waiting. The army was out of sight but I thought that if I climbed the hill I could see what was happening. I started up the rocky slope, slipping on the frosty grass and wishing that I had something sturdier than sandals. Blades of grass stuck between my toes. A vulture wheeled overhead in the cloudless sky. I shaded my eyes to peer over the plain.

Persepolis was visible in the distance. An empty city built by Darius the Great for the master races, the Persians and the Medes. They used it for their spring rites and ceremonies. It was immense, with several palaces and temples set out in perfect harmony around a huge central square. From where I was, I could only see the stairs that led to the city's front gate. They were made of slabs of white marble, seven metres long and shallow enough to ride horses up, and flanked with walls carved with sacred beasts. I couldn't see the carvings from so far away, but I'd seen them before, in pictures. They had been ruins when I'd first seen them. I'd seen them as crumbling relics, and now they were shining before me in the bright sun. The temples, their roofs covered in gold-coloured tiles, were intact, not yet reduced to broken columns. I put my hands over my eyes and sat down, shaking. Living history backwards was a terrifying experience.

A cloud of dust billowed on the far side of the city. Darius had tried to defend the great eastern gate, but I knew that soon the city would fall to Alexander. Already I could see the first of the wounded limping toward the camp. Slaves ran out with stretchers, and I slipped and slithered down the hill. I would try to be useful. I only hoped I could do some good.

Later, I wiped sweat off my face and wished I had paid more attention during first aid class. I had no idea if what I was doing was helping. Usse set broken bones as fast as he could. He also received the wounded, putting them in one of three tents. One tent for those needing urgent help, one tent for those who could wait, and one for those who were dying. In the tent for the dying a brazier had been set up, and Usse put herbs upon the hot coals, making a thick, fragrant smoke. The smoke, Usse told me, helped the men's souls find the gods. I think it was mostly opium.

I was put to work cleaning and binding the wounds. As a woman, I was supposed to know how to do this. There were no sutures. Wounds were cauterized without anaesthesia using white-hot irons. Searing heat killed germs, so although the scars were horrendous, wounds usually healed cleanly.

Slaves held the men down. The screams of the wounded and the smell of scorching flesh permeated the camp.

Usse concocted a drink that he gave to the wounded. They calmed down and went into a trance. Their eyes glazed and they breathed through their mouths, making the ones with broken noses easier to treat. Broken noses were fairly common.

Alexander used a formation called a phalanx, which presented the enemy with a huge, prickly hedge of long spears. Rows and rows of soldiers with spears swept down upon the enemy, and the spears, thirty feet long, neatly shish-kebabbed those foolish enough to face them. However, the phalanx could be undone – with lobbed missiles, arrows, and enough victims to weigh down the spears and break them. Then the infantry fought hand to hand, with short, deadly swords and glaives. The wounded were dragged off the battlefield as fast as possible, while the remaining men slid and slipped on the blood and fought and cursed.

At that point Alexander swooped in with his cavalry, pulling the *hipparchie* behind him like a great curtain, sweeping into Darius's forces and finally annihilating them.

I wondered where the wounded enemies were taken but Usse told me, in a no-nonsense voice, that they were put to death. Alexander took no prisoners. Even when they did surrender they either joined Alexander's army or were sold into slavery. It depended on how the commanding officer was feeling that day. I swallowed hard. The Geneva Convention hadn't been put into effect yet.

I finished binding up a slashed arm and concentrated on my next victim, a young man with an arrow in his chest. He looked at me hopefully, and I smiled and cursed under my breath in English.

157

'Are you saying magic words?' he gasped.

'Yes, as a matter of fact I am.'

His face relaxed and he gave a huge sigh. 'You're a goddess, so I know that I will live,' he said confidently.

I studied the arrow and wished I felt as confident. Its feathered end was sticking out at an angle and the arrowhead was hidden by his armour, but judging from the amount of blood pooled his lap it must have struck something major. I undid his shoulder straps and carefully peeled his armour away. The arrow fell to the ground; it had simply been stuck between the leather and the brass plates. The blood was from someone else. There was no wound at all. I closed my eyes and clung to the edge of the table.

The man ran his hands up and down his chest, feeling frantically for the wound. 'It's a miracle,' he cried, 'a miracle!'

'No it's not,' I insisted. 'You weren't even hit, it was deflected by your armour.' However, he didn't believe me, and neither did anyone else. As a result, all the arrow wounds got sent to me.

I hate arrows. They usually kill outright, cutting arteries, severing veins, and the victim bleeds to death very quickly. But when nothing vital is hit, the arrow is stuck because of its shape and impossible to pull out. Then one has to either push it through, or cut it out using special clamps and spreaders invented for such occasions. Pushing it through is excruciating. The patient screams and tries to get away. Large slaves sit on them, and Usse gives a double dose of his potion.

I did my best. I had a working knowledge of anatomy

and that helped. More importantly, I was reputed to be a goddess and that helped most of all.

That day I discovered that men are both a lot tougher, and at the same time, more fragile than I thought. Wounds that I was sure were fatal were somehow healed because the man had decided he would live. And if a man thought he would die, he usually did, and there was nothing we could do to save him.

Most of the men didn't come to the hospital tents if they didn't feel the need and took care of their own wounds. I even noticed many soldiers cauterizing themselves, if they could reach the cut and it wasn't too serious. But the severely wounded were brought to us.

Usse could usually tell at a glance if a man was mortally wounded. If Usse nodded towards the third tent where the thick smoke made my head spin after only a minute, I knew the man was dying.

I tried not to think. I tried to make an empty place in my mind where I could work and not feel the suffering around me. Knowing that I had little knowledge of what I was doing distressed me. When I saw another man pierced with arrows being carried towards me I set my teeth and tried to stop my hands from shaking. The first thing I did was to smile at my patient, no matter what I thought. Then I gave liberal doses of Usse's medicine and did my best, for whatever it was worth. I tried my best with roughly fifty men. Some had sword cuts to the legs and arms, and broken noses, which never arrived on their own – they came with other wounds. A soldier would never come to the tent with just a broken nose. Nevertheless, if I found one I treated it. I liked to set them straight and splint them.

The first time Usse saw me do that he actually laughed. A slave trained as a doctor helped me, and he did most of the work. I was there more for moral support than anything else, but the soldiers sincerely believed I could help them.

Surgery was slated for the next morning, Usse told me, after the priests performed special rites and sacrifices were made to the gods. I told him to boil all his instruments and to sterilize the bandages and anything else that would come in contact with the wounds.

Usse listened gravely then asked me to explain once again about the minuscule creatures that caused infection. I was only too glad to comply; anything to get my mind off the horror of the wounded soldiers.

We talked as we made the rounds. Our group was composed of Usse, the twelve slaves who aided Usse, and myself. The wounded had stopped coming in, and a messenger came telling us that the battle was ended. Alexander had taken Persepolis. The battle had lasted all day. Alexander had forty thousand men. Roughly six hundred were injured, and one hundred and fifty of them died.

'It is over,' said Usse.

'Until next time,' I said. My voice sounded far away.

'Are you all right?'

I gave a wan smile. 'I'm just worried about the men. Where did you learn medicine?' I asked. I'd been curious about that all day.

'On the island of Cos there is a school. Antipatros, who used to be my master, sent me there.'

I was interested and wanted to ask him other questions

160

but my throat closed up and I found I couldn't speak. Instead I pointed mutely towards the tents where the wounded lay.

Usse looked at me. It was hard to tell what the tall man was thinking, but his eyes were always gentle. He wore his robes Arab-style and prayed to his own gods at his own times, which bothered no one in the camp. He came and went as he pleased, and although he slept in Alexander's tent each night I knew nothing about him. He rose each morning before Alexander, and was usually the last one to sleep. All the other slaves deferred to him, and even Alexander treated him with respect. While Aristotle had been with us, they had spent many hours talking together. Aristotle, who thought slaves were inferior, seemed to consider Usse an equal.

I was in awe of him, but then he smiled at me and put his hands on my shoulders. It was a gesture that no one else except Alexander would have dared, and it spoke volumes of this man. 'You did well,' he said to my infinite relief. I burst into tears.

I cried because never, in my sheltered life, had I come in contact with dying men. I cried for those I'd managed through sheer luck to save, and for the men who'd died. I cried with relief because it was all over, and because Alexander had won, and he was unhurt. I cried because Usse was looking at me with all the kindness in the world in his large, brown eyes. I cried because no one, ever, had looked upon me with such compassion. I was tired too. Even more exhausted than I'd been after giving birth. My whole body trembled, and I discovered that I couldn't move my feet. I swayed and nearly fell but Usse was

161

holding me firmly. He barked an order to one of the slaves, who came and carried me to Alexander's tent.

I wanted to wash, I wanted to run to Persepolis and find my baby, and I wanted to see Alexander. I ended up falling asleep on the rug, too tired to wash or crawl into bed.

I reeked of garlic and honey. I was spattered with blood and sticky with sweat. The honey was used as an antiseptic or an antibiotic. I didn't know, actually, why Usse slathered honey over some wounds, put garlic paste on others, and left some completely alone. There were tinctures made of sulphur and other elements. There were herbs as well; herbs I knew and some I didn't recognize. The soldiers carried a small pouch, and when they were marching they would sometimes stop and dig up a plant and stuff it in their bag. Usse opened their little pouches when the soldiers were carried in, and sometimes he used what he found. I would ask him about that … if I ever woke up again.

I slept until Alexander came back. Then I woke up as if swimming out of a deep pool. I tried to fight my way to consciousness but kept slipping back. I knew there was something I had to ask, something I had to know. Finally, I managed to open my eyes and sat up. My head spun and I ached all over, but I braced my hands on the floor and blinked until my vision cleared.

Alexander was sitting at his table. He'd bathed and he wore a fresh tunic. His hair was growing long again and was tied back with a thong. His eyes were fixed on the tablet in his hands. He put it down and faced me.

I could tell from his expression. He didn't have to say

a word.

'No!' I cried, and got to my feet. 'No!' My voice broke.

He sprang up and hugged me tightly to his chest. 'Shhh, it's not what you think. The babe lives. I swear it's true.'

'Where is he?' I whispered. I pulled away and looked at him.

His eyes were bleak. 'He was never in Persepolis. We'll go and see Darius tomorrow and I'll find out where he's been taken. Don't worry, I'll get him back.'

My knees gave out and I sagged against him. Tears scalded my cheeks as I choked back my disappointment.

'Don't cry, please don't cry. I'm sorry, I am disappointed too. But we'll find him. Don't you remember? I promised.' Alexander took my face in his hands and brushed away my tears with his thumbs. His face was drawn and pale, his eyes reddened from smoke and tears. He tried to smile, but it seemed an effort. 'Come. I have something for you.'

I followed him to the table. He lifted something sparkling off it and pressed it into my hand. It was a necklace with a chain of gold and silver. Of fine workmanship, it was perhaps the most delicate chain I'd ever seen. On it hung a white moonstone surrounded with tiny opals and rubies. The moonstone had a face carved on it. It was the face of Artemis, goddess of the hunt and of the moon, Alexander explained. He put the necklace around my neck. Then he led me outside.

'Hold the pendant towards the moon,' he ordered. I complied, and he said, 'Artemis, hear my plea. Take my son and keep him safe. You marked him as your own, and so we ask you to care for him until we find him.' He bent and kissed the moonstone then held it out to me.

I was surprised. I hadn't thought of him as being very religious, and pagan rites unnerved me. But Alexander's face was solemn. I kissed the pendant.

The moon turned the hillside to silver, and a strange calm had befallen the campsite. I saw Usse moving like a shadow among the wounded outside the tents and made a movement to join him, but Alexander stopped me. Instead, he led me back to his tent where Axiom had prepared a hot bath.

Alexander took off my dirty robe and bathed me tenderly. I stood in the basin and let the water sluice over my body. I had entered a monochrome world where sound was muted and sensation was dulled. I glanced at my pendant and gasped. The moonstone gave off an unearthly light.

Alexander filled the sponge with water and slowly squeezed it out onto my back. 'The pendant's name is Celine. The moon speaks to the moon's stone. Now, be calm.' He didn't sound amazed; his voice was level, deep, and soothing. I felt sleep claim me even as I stood. I closed my eyes and leaned my head against Alexander's shoulder. I wondered briefly if he were tired too. He didn't show it. Instead, he emanated the same glow as my pendant. An unearthly light.

Chapter Eight

Each spring, under the stern regard of the god Ahura-Mazda, and in the presence of the King of Kings, the great festival takes place in the city of Persepolis.

The master races, the Persians and the Medes, watch as all the other tribes parade before them to place their offerings at the foot of the throne.

The king sits on a raised dais directly in front of a passageway guarded by carvings of winged bulls who let no trespassers by. First the Medes and Persians parade with their chariots and warhorses. Then the Suzians present their lions. Armenians bring vases made of precious metals. Babylonians bring embroidered cloth and pure white bulls. Lydians bring gold. Sogdians bring sheep and fine wool. Phrygians bring splendid horses.

The parade stretches for miles across the plain and slowly files up the stone staircase, over the humped bridge, and into the vast central square. One by one, the people bow to the king and lay their offerings before him. As the day wears on, the square fills with gold and silver, bolts of shimmering cloth, pure white cows, gleaming horses, and enamelled vases glowing in every colour like jewels in the sunlight.

Afterwards, the king and his entourage retire to the royal palace where a sumptuous banquet awaits. They walk through the remarkable 'room of one hundred columns' and sit upon richly embroidered cushions in front of a long marble table. Musicians play oboes, while slaves serve food. Women chosen for their beauty dance, and a chorus of youths sing songs to the glory of spring, the gods, and to the king.

All this Alexander told me as he led me past the blinding white marble walls covered with bas-reliefs of life-size, fantastic animals.

The city was swarming with soldiers, but they weren't on parade. Alexander was systematically stripping every bit of treasure from the fabled city and was loading it on pack animals to take to Ecbatana, the seat of his treasury.

Antipatros and Alexander's second in command, Parmenion, and twenty other officers were sitting in the centre of the square surrounded by scribes and slaves. Over their heads, a blue and white striped canopy offered cool shade. They were taking an inventory of everything and writing it in triplicate on long scrolls. An incredible number of burdened camels and donkeys were being led from the city heading north towards Ecbatana.

Afterwards, I heard that it took ten thousand mules and five thousand camels to move the entire treasure. I didn't count it and didn't verify the scrolls. However, I do know that it took all winter. For three months the treasure was counted, wrapped up, and shipped out. And the soldiers worked non-stop.

With that money, Alexander built roads and developed a postal system. He built cities and seaports. He used the money to strengthen the governments in all the cities he conquered, creating a unified monetary system and founding schools where Greek culture was taught. He had the wisdom to let the people he conquered keep their religions and keep in place their existing administrators. He simply put his people in key positions.

While we walked through the echoing hallways towards Darius's palace, Alexander greeted everyone we met by name or rank. He smiled and asked them small questions and then listened carefully to the answers. Everyone received the same warm smile and genuine interest, whether they were general or simple soldier, cook or slave. To me they gave deep bows and fearful stares. I tried to look harmless, but my reputation as a *bona-fide* goddess made most people wary. They were sure that a wrong move would cause me to transform them into frogs.

I was nervous. We were on our way to see Darius, under house arrest in his own palace.

'Is he furious?' I asked.

'Furious?' Alexander frowned. 'I don't know if I'd say that. He doesn't realize what's happened yet. You know, he's a megalomaniac; he's certain he's a god.'

I looked at him sideways. 'Don't the Persians believe he's a god?'

'It's one thing for your followers to believe you're divine, but it's another thing if you believe it. The Persians think that their king is responsible for the rebirth of the world each new year. If the king doesn't make the proper sacrifices and follow the rituals, then the world will end. But that doesn't make him a god. Darius's problem is that he believes he is. Now that he's defeated, he's a dangerous man.'

'Will he tell us where Paul is?'

He paused. 'I don't know.' Those three words stabbed me in the heart, but I knew they had cost Alexander as well. He'd been so sure of finding Paul here.

We stopped in front of a massive door guarded by Lysimachus and Seleucos. I was glad to see that Seleucos had risen so quickly in Alexander's army. He now held the rank of captain of the cavalry. They stood at attention. No sitting on mats and throwing dice here.

'How is he?' asked Alexander.

'Quiet. We searched his rooms for poison. We found none.'

'He won't kill himself,' said Alexander. 'Open the door and announce me.'

Lysimachus obeyed, and we walked through the doorway to find Darius sitting pensively on his throne.

He was taller than I'd expected. Most of the people I'd met were of medium height. Darius, when he stood up to greet us, towered over me. He was nude, except for a golden chain around his neck. Nudity was so common that I'd ceased to be aware of it. The soldiers went around unclothed and, in the villages, children were nude. Persian men wore very brief loincloths. Women wore robes or belted a cloth around their waists, although slave women were often naked. Alexander chose the Greek mode, which meant he wore a pleated tunic or slung a short cape over his shoulders. Today he wore his tunic.

Darius's hair was long, black, and wavy, brushed back from his high forehead. He was clean-shaven; the beard he wore on ceremonial occasions was in his hand. It was made of finely knotted black silk. He looked at his beard and then placed it gently on the seat of the throne.

'It's yours now,' were his first words to Alexander.

'You can keep it.' Alexander's voice was neutral. It almost sounded like pity, and I looked at him sharply. So did Darius. For a second his eyes flashed, and I saw a glimpse of the king he'd been.

'Thank you.' His voice was careful too. They talked about the battle, verbally dancing around each other like fencers. Neither gave the other any advantage, but there was an undercurrent of sadness in Alexander that I could not fathom. Darius was puzzled as well, because, after an awkward silence, he motioned toward the table where a tray of fruit sat. 'Would you like some figs? They're fresh. I imagine you've been living off dried ones during the march.'

Alexander said, 'No thank you.'

Darius nodded. 'Ah well. How's Stateira?' It was almost an afterthought.

'She's well. She's ruling Babylon.'

He looked surprised. 'Oh? And your mother?'

'I sent her back to her own people. It was either that, or kill her.'

Darius froze. I held my breath. He turned his head very slowly and looked at me for the first time. He had long-lashed, honey-brown eyes. Vanity prompted him to line them with kohl, making them appear even larger and more brilliant. His face was dark and his eyes were lighter than his skin, like a lion's eyes. And like a lion he blinked and looked away from my gaze. 'So you knew,' he said.

'Why did you think I came after you?' Alexander's voice rose, a note of anger in it.

'Oh, I suppose I'd guessed.' Darius shrugged and took

a plump fig. He squeezed it appraisingly and then put it back in the bowl. 'You want the babe.'

'Where is he?'

'Is it true she's a goddess?' He wouldn't look me in the face and I found that disturbing.

'It is.' I was startled by Alexander's answer, but even more startled at Darius's next question.

'Tell me when and how I shall die, Goddess.' He was staring out the window, bracing his hands against the sill. His body was all flowing lines and muscle. I couldn't help admiring his physique.

I looked at Alexander who nodded once.

I drew a deep breath. 'You'll be killed by someone you trust before the summer ends.'

A shudder ran through his body. When he spoke his voice was broken. 'The child is in the hands of a Bactrian satrap. I gave him to a caravan going east. He'll be in Bactria in the spring. The babe is marked by the goddess. He'll come to no harm.'

I put my hand on Alexander's arm to steady myself. 'Why?' I whispered.

'Because of the oracle,' said Darius. He sighed and then looked at me at last. 'When Olympias came to the city she had the babe brought to the temple of Marduk. She was going to sacrifice him. An oracle told her that the babe would be her downfall. In a way, I suppose it was true.

'However, my astrologer said that if the babe died I would lose everything that was dear to me. I love my daughter Stateira more than all the gold in this city. And I love her more than my own life. How long do you think she would have lived if you had found out that your child had been sacrificed on the altar of Babylon's god? Now she is the Queen of Babylon. The babe is safe, but the prophecy said one more thing, Iskander, about you.'

'What did it say about me?' asked Alexander.

'It said to ask her.' He pointed at me. 'The oracle said, "All Iskander's questions can be answered by the child's mother." It claimed she knows all.' Then he turned to the window again. 'Ask if you dare, Iskander. I did.' His voice was almost inaudible.

I would have run out of the room, but Alexander caught my wrist. He bowed to Darius, and made me bow too, although Darius had his back to us and was staring out the window. Alexander knocked on the door, and Lysimachus let us out.

'He can see anyone he chooses,' said Alexander.

'Anyone?' Lysimachus looked surprised.

'Anyone. He'll be trusting no one now.' He looked at me with flinty eyes as he said this, and I quailed.

I wanted to beg Alexander to go after our child right away. I had no idea exactly where Bactria could be. But common sense told me I had to curb my impatience. The army had just fought a bloody battle, and Alexander had to settle things here. I trusted him to find Paul, so I stayed silent and clung to the faint hope that was left to me.

When I got outside the palace, I gulped the air. The atmosphere had been suffocating. Darius was doomed.

I had hated Persepolis from the moment I'd entered it. Perhaps it was the emptiness of the city. No one had ever lived there. There were no women, no children, only Darius and the soldiers. Or maybe it was the pall of smoke

171

that hung low in the sky. Thousands of men were clearing the bodies from the battlefield. The dead soldiers were being cremated, and the smell was ghastly. Darius had lost nearly half his army. Thirty thousand men had died five miles from the city, and the stench of blood was in the air. The rest of Darius's men had either been absorbed into Alexander's army, or, if they wouldn't swear allegiance, sent to the mines as slaves.

Alexander brooded as we walked. Several times he made as if to speak, but each time he fell silent. At first, I wondered if he were thinking about the men he'd lost, and their families' grief when the news arrived. Then I saw him looking at me out of the corners of his eyes, and I realized he was thinking about what Darius had said.

I reached out and touched his arm lightly, meaning to comfort him, but he flinched.

'All right, that does it!' I stopped in the middle of the path and folded my arms across my chest. 'We have to talk about this. It will do no good for you to go on sulking.'

He spun around and faced me, his eyes blazing. 'Sulking? Sulking, am I?'

'Yes.' I glared back at him, but I couldn't stay angry long. 'Oh, Alex, I'm sorry. I never should have said anything to Darius. It was a mistake, I admit. I regret it and I wish you had never made me do it.'

'Made you do it? I made you do it?' His anger was terrible to behold. 'I told you not to!'

'You nodded!' I was furious. 'You nodded your head like this!'

'That means "no"!' he sputtered. 'Everyone knows

that!'

'I forgot,' I said miserably. 'I'm sorry. Where I come from that means "yes".'

'Where *do* you come from?'

I shook my head. 'That means "no", where I come from. And I can't tell you.'

We stared at each other. Alexander's face was paler than usual, his forehead damp. 'The gods are playing with us,' he said slowly.

'Perhaps it's true.' I couldn't face him any more and I turned my head.

'Oh, no, you don't.' He took my chin and made me look into his eyes. 'How do you know he will die by the hand of someone he trusts?'

I shivered. I would have to tell him, and by doing so change the course of history. A sharp pain was starting in my toes and I wondered if it was the erasure that was beginning. In a moment I would disappear. Probably writhing in horrible pain. I glanced down, expecting to see my feet disappearing but no, it was just Alexander, standing on my foot. 'You're on my foot,' I said, pointing.

He cursed and stepped backwards. 'I need to know. Are you really an oracle?'

I shook my head. 'No, I'm not. I've never even seen an oracle, and I don't know what they do, or how they act. When I was in the palace, all I could think of was my baby, and that Darius had kidnapped him. I was angry. I said something I regret. If it turns out to be true, we'll talk about it then. Right now I'm just glad to be out of there and away from him.'

'He was a great man,' said Alexander.

'But you're a greater one.' I touched his face and then pulled him towards me and kissed him. 'And you're the best kisser in the world. Who taught you?'

He opened his mouth to speak then snapped it shut. 'My mother was right. All women are sorceresses.'

My mouth twitched. 'For once, she was probably right.' I linked my arm through his, and he didn't pull away. He was not convinced and was still angry, I could tell. He hadn't forgiven me, and I knew it was only a matter of time before I'd have some serious explaining to do. Bleakly, I wondered what I could invent.

Back at the camp, I went to help Usse in the three hospital tents. My patients were doing better than I'd hoped. So far, none of then had developed a fever. Usse had prepared fresh bandages, and we changed them each day. We kept water boiling to sterilize the bandages. Usse had accepted what I'd said about germs.

Later that evening, Alexander joined us, visiting with the wounded soldiers. He followed at our heels, talking, soothing, encouraging and praising his men. When he arrived, their cheeks flushed as if they'd just received a transfusion. When Alexander left us to go into the third tent, I scratched my head and turned to Usse.

'I will never understand how he does it,' I said, a hint of peevishness in my voice.

Usse was thoughtful for a moment, while we strolled out of the tent and stood in the cool dusk. Then he said, 'He attracts people. He has a magnetism that is given once every three or four centuries. It is written in our book of prophecies. He will change the world, and one cannot help but feel drawn to him. We are as helpless as moths before a flame.'

I grimaced. 'Well, I wouldn't mind a dose of his magnetism. I was never any good at making friends.'

He didn't smile back, and for the first time his dark eyes were sad as he looked at me. 'Iskander has no friends,' he said, in a low voice. 'Only followers.'

I shook my head. 'You're wrong. You're his friend and so is Aristotle, and myself, and Lysimachus, Nearchus ...' I was counting on my fingers but he stopped me.

'A friend is someone special. I am his slave and his doctor. Aristotle is his teacher. You are his wife. The soldiers, captains and generals are men who fight for him. All the love we feel for Iskander touches him not. That's what I'm trying to say. To be a friend one has to give and receive. Iskander receives our love and devotion, but it is like candlelight to the sun. His brilliance outshines us. He gives equally to each and every man, but as unconsciously as the sun gives off heat. He is above us, whether we like it or not. The gods placed him there, and it is both an honour and a curse. He is not a common mortal.' His face was earnest. 'You, of all people, should know this.'

'Me? Why me?'

He shook his head. 'Because you don't belong here. I don't know where you come from, but I feel this.' He reached out and nearly touched my arm. 'There is a space around you that nobody else has. Perhaps someday you'll explain. Until then, I will be your friend.'

Usse observed me, his brown eyes full of kindness. It took me a moment to gather my thoughts. No one had ever wanted to be my friend. I stammered, 'Thank you,

Usse.' My throat closed up, and I could say no more.

Usse smiled at me and then entered the third tent. I braced myself before following. In the first two tents, the sick were slowly healing, but in this tent the men were dying. Here, I stood back and watched Usse and Alexander. The tent was dim and silent. Braziers smoked; rich fumes calmed the agonies of the thirty soldiers lying on pallets.

Alexander knelt beside each man and took his hand. If they were conscious he spoke to them, his voice a low murmur. Slowly he went from one to another. They were all so young, ranging from around sixteen to forty, with the majority in their early twenties.

The youngest, a boy of sixteen, was unconscious but his eyelids fluttered when Alexander spoke to him. The youth was suffering from a head wound, and Usse said he would die within the hour. Alexander sat with him, holding his hand until the young man drew his last breath. Then he gently touched the boy's face.

He held the hands of the men as they lay dying, and I stood behind him and watched as his presence eased their passage from this world to the next. It was almost as if they were waiting for his touch. Some died watching him, and Alexander met their stares, never blinking or lowering his eyes.

I saw one of my patients with an arrow stuck in his chest. I couldn't remove the arrow without killing him outright. The arrow wavered with each heartbeat. He was still alive, though barely. Usse had insisted on leaving the arrow. Now I found out why. Alexander sat next to the man and they spoke. The patient was conscious, and his voice was clear. After they had talked nearly an hour, the man nodded to Alexander. 'It's time,' he said. Alexander took a firm grip on the arrow and drew it out. Blood gushed over his hands but he didn't move. Soon the man died with a deep sigh, but his face stayed peaceful.

Alexander turned to a slave carrying a basin of water and rinsed his hands. Then he dried them on a towel and went to the next man. His face looked so hard it could have been marble.

Usse and I stood silently behind him. Once he murmured that I didn't have to stay. I don't know where Alexander got the strength to help the dying. Wherever he got it, I admired him. I stayed.

The three of us left the tent together. Usse and Alexander talked in low voices. I walked in a daze. I had thought that after the battle I had become immune to death, but I hadn't. It frightened me.

In the dusk, the campsite was peaceful. Orange campfires flickered. Tents looked fluorescent in the purple air. Smoke was pale blue, and Alexander's white skirt seemed to float in front of me. I blinked my eyes but the dark kept closing in, and soon all I could see was a spot of white.

Alexander turned because some sixth sense told him I was falling. He caught me before I hit the ground. He moved faster than anyone should be able to move. I knew it was he, I knew his hands, his scent, his voice. But I didn't know why I'd fainted until Usse examined me and pronounced me pregnant again.

'A baby?' I was stunned.

Usse smiled and sat back on his heels, his dark eyes

twinkling. 'A baby. In seven months.'

'So that's why I'm so tired,' I said. Lately I'd felt as if I were dragging around a heavy weight. Paul would be six months old, and I was two months pregnant. I worried about that. Was it too early? I'd gotten pregnant only four months after my baby's birth.

Usse told me that it was normal; I'd stopped nursing and my milk had dried up early. 'When the milk dries up then the woman gets pregnant again.' He said this with a shrug. 'That's nature's way.' I supposed that was why so many women kept breastfeeding their children until they were nearly three years old.

Alexander was delighted. He gave me Brazza, his eunuch, to take care of me. I accepted, upon one condition: that Alexander free Brazza and tell him that whenever he wanted he could leave. He was to be paid a real salary, not just given room and board. I insisted on the same treatment for Usse and Axiom, Alexander's other slaves. Alexander accepted. He told me he'd give me whatever I wanted. It was traditional for a husband to give in to his pregnant wife's wishes. The slaves we freed were officially adopted into our family, as was required by Athenian law. We celebrated by having a ceremonial dinner. Alexander had a goat slaughtered, and we managed to get some fresh fruit, although that must have cost Alexander an exorbitant amount of money in the dead of winter. I didn't think he'd mind. He had more than enough, with all the gold he was taking out of Persepolis.

Now Axiom, Usse, and Brazza were our godchildren, which is the closest description I can give to their relationship to us. They were also free to go. None of them left.

After the ceremony I wondered if their attitude would change, but I saw not the slightest difference. They had always been kind, polite, and a bit distant. I knew that the distance was because of my own personality, and nothing could be done about it. The invisible space around me that Usse felt was felt by all. They loved Alexander but were in awe of me. Nothing I could ever do or say would change this.

Usse was the closest to me. We would often talk for hours. But I had to be careful what I said; I still had the threat of being erased if I changed history. For days I fretted about that. When I'd healed the wounded soldiers was I changing history? Then I thought about it differently. Usse had given me the soldiers who were the least likely to die. I was no doctor, and so in all likelihood the men I'd treated would have lived anyway.

Usse sensed my restraint but didn't press me, and I, strange as it may seem, felt no wish to confide in anyone as to my secret. I had grown up as an only child, never having the luxury of a friend. The idea of having a confidant was alien to me, and that probably saved my life.

Chapter Nine

For weeks after the battle, I saw little of Alexander. I was asleep when he came back to the camp after spending most of the day at Persepolis. He woke up before dawn, so there was no way I could see him unless I got up as early as he did.

I started waking up with Alexander. That way we shared breakfast and did our exercises together. However, the intimacy lasted but a quarter of an hour before he was obliged to leave again. He had to organize everything, and there were not enough hours in a day for all he had to do. He had to oversee the departure of the treasure. He had to liaise with all the dignitaries of the surrounding villages and make arrangements to feed his army for the winter. He had to take care of Darius, and that, I think, drained his energy more than any other chore.

He also had to stay in touch with the cities he'd already conquered. And he had to deal with things like the Harpalus scandal. His lawyers actually came to Persepolis for him to sign papers. Harpalus had fled to Crete, and someone had assassinated him there. Meanwhile, half the treasure he'd stolen had disappeared. Demosthenes, the magistrate who'd been in charge of sequestrating the money when it arrived in Athens, had already been accused.

Alexander made a face as he told me this. He ran his

hands through his hair, yawned, and then scratched himself. Brazza brought us our breakfast and I picked up a dried fig.

'What will Demosthenes do? Wasn't he a friend of yours?' I asked Alexander.

'He's no friend of mine, he hates everything non-Greek. He's a lawyer and an orator – one of the best. I imagine he'll defend himself and the jury will free him.' He grinned. 'He could probably talk himself out of Hades' realm if he tried. I doubt anything will happen to him. He's as sly as Hermes himself.' He took a sip of yoghurt then put the dish down. His face had gone sombre.

'What's the matter?' I asked, when I saw he wasn't going to speak.

He looked at me and his eyes were bleak. 'I've thought about what Darius said for more than a week now.'

'You mean about the oracle?' I'd been wondering when he'd get around to that. I could tell it had been on his mind. Sometimes he could be remarkably transparent.

'Yes, about the oracle. What did Darius mean? Do you really know everything I want to know? And dare I ask?' he added, almost to himself.

'All I know for certain is that I want to find our son.'

'No,' he said, and his voice was sad. 'No, don't lie to me. I can feel it. So can Usse. And everyone around you. The soldiers you treated, they felt it too. I heard about the miracle of the arrow. From "Ashley of the Sacred Sandals" you've become "Ashley of the Arrow Miracle".'

'It wasn't a miracle. It was stuck in his armour and he was too shocked to realize it. Even I was fooled. When I took off his armour and it fell on the floor, I was as

181

surprised as anyone else. Honest.'

Alexander sighed and nibbled on a piece of bread, but I could tell he was distracted. Finally he squared his shoulders and looked at me. 'Do you still love me?'

The question surprised me. 'Of course! Why do you ask?'

'Because of me, you were kidnapped. You had a baby, and he was taken away from you because he was mine. I was the one who brought you back from the cold realm of Hades, but it was against your will. You fought me while I was trying to rescue you. Everything bad that's happened to you has been caused by me. I haven't even been able to find our son. And so I wondered how you could still love me.'

I got up, walked around the tray, and sat on his lap, pulling his head onto my shoulder and putting my arms around him. 'I love you more than anyone I've ever known. I love you more than I love myself.' I hugged him tightly, willing him to believe me. 'I can't help it if I seem cold and distant. I was brought up to hide my feelings, I told you that. I don't know how to deal with emotion. I had the worst time with the wounded men. I never saw anyone die before, and it terrified me. I couldn't bear it. You're so much stronger than I am. You're not afraid of anything.'

He put his arms around me and held me. 'I'm afraid,' he whispered. 'I'm afraid that you'll leave me. I'm afraid of losing you. You heard Aristotle – if there's one thing I can't stand it's losing.' He laughed softly. 'Do you remember when I asked you to be my oracle?'

'I remember.' I felt ill.

'Then tell me. I am as brave as Darius, and he is a very brave man. So tell me. Will I see the edge of the earth?'

I smiled through my tears. 'Look at me, Alex,' I said. He did, and I picked up an orange. 'This is what the earth is like. It is as round as this orange. You can walk from one side to the other, but there is no edge. Therefore, I can answer your question. No, the edge of the earth you will never see.'

'So why are you crying?' he asked.

'Because I don't want to be your oracle. I want to be your friend. I'm already your wife and your lover, but what I want most of all is to be your friend. And I'm afraid Usse is right, I'm afraid it's impossible.'

His mouth twisted and he cursed softly under his breath. 'I had a friend once,' he said, 'and I killed him. I'm afraid I'm not very good at friendship.'

'What happened?' I asked, turning his face towards me.

He wouldn't look at me. 'I thought I was as brave as Darius, but now I'm not so sure.' He paused and laughed shakily. 'I'm afraid to tell you.'

'Don't be. Please.'

'Maybe someday. When things have calmed down a bit. Right now I have too much to do. Nearchus has sent word. He and Plexis will be here within two weeks.'

He left right after that, leaving me to draw my own conclusions about what he'd said. I realized that he was hurting. Hurting because he hadn't gotten our son back, because I couldn't express my feelings for him, or for anyone, and because he wanted to leave and find Paul. But he was trapped here. He had to wait for Nearchus to arrive.

I shivered. I'd managed to feel safe for a while but Nearchus worried me. He'd shown up a year ago and I'd been kidnapped. Even though Olympias had been behind it, she had to be working with someone. I thought that someone was probably Alexander's general, Nearchus. For some reason, he wanted me out of the way. And this time, it might be for good.

Chapter Ten

I spent my mornings helping Usse. He told me that there was less infection than usual, and he attributed it to the boiling of the bandages. He had accepted the existence of tiny, invisible creatures. He now waged a pitiless war against them, boiling all his instruments then peering closely at them, trying to catch a glimpse of the micro monsters.

In the afternoon, I walked for miles each day to go to the village near Persepolis. I could have cut my walk in half if I'd gone through the fabled city, but I couldn't. It gave me the creeps. It made me think of a huge, empty tomb. The ghosts of the soldiers who died defending it lived there. I walked around the city and avoided the battlefield, which had so much blood steeped into it.

The way to the village was pretty. It wound past two small hills and crossed a shallow creek. There was no bridge but large, flat stones had been placed in a straight line. The water didn't cover them entirely; they formed stepping-stones from one side to the other. Alexander had given me a white donkey to ride, but I preferred the exercise, so I led the donkey and used her to carry provisions back to the tent.

Alexander's army was staying in the area over the winter, and in the spring we would head north towards Bactria, to try to find our son. The weather in Bactria was much cooler than in Persia and I was afraid the soldiers, half-naked and used to a warmer climate, would suffer. I decided to see what I could find to keep them warm. In the marketplace I found a merchant selling wool flannel. I bought a few yards and took it to my tent to talk to Axiom about it. He was Alexander's valet. Perhaps he could help me.

Back at the camp there was an unfamiliar bustle around Alexander's tent and, with trepidation, I recognized Plexis standing under the fig tree, speaking seriously to Antipatros.

I wondered at my reaction. Why didn't I like Plexis? He was a handsome man; perhaps that was part of the problem. He was even better looking than Alexander because he was smoother; there were no rough edges. He was refined, whereas Alexander still had some of the barbarian left in him. Plexis was Athenian – everyone else was beneath him. It was the city dweller's snobbery. He looked down his perfect nose at the country bumpkins. The fact that Alexander was his king didn't change anything. Athens was a democracy. Plexis couldn't care less about kings. And he didn't care for women. Athenian women were the unhappiest women in the entire federation. They would have preferred to live on Lesbos, an island in the Aegean populated almost entirely by women. It had schools for girls. – something unheard of in Athens where women were expected to stay home cooking, cleaning, sewing, weaving, and doing all those fascinating things men would rather die than do. Plexis wasn't a bad man, he was simply a product of his city and times, and I would cheerfully have pushed his head in the

186

latrine.

Especially after his greeting – he saw me and scowled.

I'd stabled my donkey and washed my hands and face in one of the large pots of water heating near the bathhouse, so I was clean. Rosewater scented my skin, and I'd run a comb through my hair, which was the wonder of the camp. No one had such pale hair and most people marvelled at it.

I was looking quite presentable, but Plexis still scowled as I approached.

I decided to charm him. I put on my brightest smile.

'Hello, Hephaestion – or do you prefer Plexis? Won't you come in the tent and get out of the hot sun? I'll ask Brazza to bring us some fruit juice, unless you'd rather have wine?' I smiled and put my hand on his arm, which was a polite sign of greeting in Athens.

He looked at my hand as if it were a new type of bloodsucking insect he'd just discovered crawling up his arm. 'Yes, I prefer Plexis. No, I'm not thirsty. When will Iskander be back?'

I snatched my hand away. 'Fine, I'll just leave you here for now. Iskander, as you probably know, is in Persepolis taking care of several tons of treasure.' I smiled sweetly. It was when I smiled sweetly that I was the most awful. 'Don't you think it's wonderful? I mean, about all that treasure. Speaking of treasure, I do hope Alexander sorts out that dreadful story about Harpalus. Was he a friend of yours? I heard he was from Athens, and Athens is such a small village, I'm sure you know everyone.' Calling Athens a village was possibly the worst affront I could give it.

187

He blinked. 'Are you from Sparta?' he asked coldly, giving me the most terrible insult he could imagine.

I batted my eyelashes. 'Sparta? No, I never had the pleasure to visit that city.'

'And I suppose you've been to Athens?' His voice was freezing.

Freezing voices had sung me to sleep. 'Many times,' I waved my hand dismissively. The ruins of the Acropolis had been crawling with tourists and covered with graffiti when I'd seen it last. 'It's quaint.'

'Quaint?' he choked.

'Well, you know, charming. Will you be coming to Bactria with us? I do hope so. It's a wild country, but beautiful. And I know how much you Athenians love beauty.'

He had most likely never talked to a woman about his plans for the future, and he was certainly not going to start with me. He turned toward the fig tree as if looking for some ripe figs. Perfectly ridiculous, they wouldn't be ripe for another six months. I decided to needle him just a touch more.

'Is Iskander really your king?'

'Yes, of course. He's a great king.' He frowned at the tree.

'And what about his wives? Are they queens?'

'Technically, yes.' There were no ripe figs, so he plucked a leaf and rolled it up tightly.

'Ah. That's nice to know. So, technically I'm your queen.' I smiled.

He turned green.

I went into the tent humming. I couldn't give a fig

about him.

I remembered belatedly what Aristotle had said. Alexander had killed his best friend, and it had been Plexis's brother. Abruptly I felt remorseful. I didn't want him as an enemy. I went back outside where I saw Plexis still standing in the shade. He hadn't moved, but the leaf had fallen from his hand and lay in the dust.

'Plexis?'

My voice startled him, or perhaps it was the tone. 'Yes?' he was wary.

'Please come inside. I have some lovely wine and I want to ask your advice about something. I'm sorry I was such a bitch. Can we start over?'

He hesitated, then nodded. 'Very well. I think wine is just what I need.'

Once inside the tent he was awkward again, refusing to sit on the rug next to me. Instead he paced back and forth until Brazza bought us the wine. I had fruit juice.

Plexis stared suspiciously at the wine and I uttered an exclamation of impatience. 'Give me that.' I took a healthy swig and gave the glass back to him. 'See, no poison. Sit down, Plexis. We definitely have to talk.'

He stared at me in surprise. 'About what?' he asked.

'Why are you here?' I thought it was best to remain direct.

Plexis sipped his wine and thought a moment. Finally, he said, in a normal voice, 'What is your name, if I may ask?'

'You may. My name is Ashley. Iskander married me in Susa so I'm legally his third wife. You and I met once before near Arbela, when you came upriver with

Nearchus.'

'I remember. You disappeared while we were marching toward Babylon. What happened? We thought you'd been eaten by a crocodile.'

'No such luck,' I said flippantly. 'I was taken to Mazda. I spent a year there at the temple of Gulu.'

He nodded. 'Ah, so you went to study healing to help in Iskander's army. I admire your devotion.'

'No. I was a prisoner. Olympias decided she wanted me out of the way. Some silly misunderstanding about an oracle.'

He raised his eyebrows. 'So that's why she was so angry. I saw her in Athens, she passed through on her way to Pella.'

I studied his face. He looked back at me. He had long eyelashes and they made it hard to judge his expression. He was one of the few people who met my gaze without blinking.

'Your eyes are so cold,' he said, looking at me from beneath his lashes.

'I always thought that the eyes were the mirror of the soul,' I answered, piqued.

'A philosopher. Iskander is lucky indeed.'

'Thank you.' I finished my fruit juice and wondered how much I should tell him, and how much he would tell me. 'Are you staying long?'

'I may. I haven't made up my mind. Nearchus is coming in a few days.'

'Actually, I thought you were together.'

'No, he's overseeing construction of the port in Alexandria.'

'How nice. Have they started building the great library yet?' I had spoken without thinking.

'How could you know about the library? It was supposed to be my surprise for Iskander!' He was startled out of his composure.

'I won't say anything, honest.'

'Answer my question, woman, how did you know?' He leaned toward me, a fierce gleam in his eyes.

'I just guessed, all cities have libraries, don't they? You're hurting me!'

He was gripping my wrist. 'I spoke to Olympias. There was no mistake. The oracle said that you would bring about her ruin, and you did, didn't you? She said something else, do you want to …'

Things might have gotten out of hand, but luckily, at that moment, Alexander decided to make his entrance. He ducked into the tent and stopped. No one had told him Plexis was here in his tent, bending my arm.

'Plexis!' The word cracked through the air.

He let me go, sulkily, and turned away from me. 'Iskander, my king.'

'Do you really believe that?' he sounded curious. He squatted down next to me and examined my wrist. It was sore, but not bruised. 'The next time you hurt my wife I may lose my temper, Plexis.'

'Is that a warning?' he snarled.

'I would take it as one,' said Alexander, looking into my eyes. 'Are you all right?'

'I'm fine. Actually, it was my fault. I frightened him. I'm sorry. I seem to be good at that.'

'Yes, you are. I think you should be careful whom you

frighten in the future. A caged king is one thing, but a free Athenian is quite another.'

I grinned. 'I'll remember that.'

'Good.' He stood up and faced his guest. 'Can I get you anything to drink, Plexis?'

'Like hemlock,' I muttered.

Plexis gave a startled laugh. There had been real fear in his eyes when Alexander had come in. 'No, thank you, your wife has already taken care of that.' He looked at me again, his eyes hooded. 'I beg your pardon, Lady. I didn't mean to hurt you. What you said was true. You did frighten me.' He turned to Alexander. 'I meant it to be a surprise, but I will tell you now. I'm building a monument in your honour in Alexandria. It will be the largest library in the world, and it will stand on a hill near the city's entrance.'

Alexander looked pleased. 'Thank you, that's wonderful news. When will Nearchus arrive?'

'In a day or so. I got word just before I left Athens.'

'How goes the trial?'

'It hasn't started yet. I shouldn't worry. Harpalus is dead, by the way. I don't know if you'd heard.'

'I heard.' Alexander was grim. 'Who killed him?'

'Don't you mean who had him killed? I don't know. There are rumours, of course. Olympias, your mother, thinks he was killed by yours truly,' he bowed. 'But I was nowhere near Crete.'

'You saw my mother?' Alexander asked darkly, pouring himself a cup of fruit juice from an earthenware pitcher.

'The beautiful Olympias. Incredible how well she

looks. Did you know she went to see Barsine?'

Alexander dropped his drink. Juice spilled all over the rug, and his cup bounced twice before rolling under the table. I grabbed a linen towel and sopped up the mess. 'Who's Barsine?' I asked.

'Wife number three, meet wife number one,' said Plexis sweetly. I'd met my match.

'The barbarian? Barsine is her name?'

Alexander looked pained. 'Why did my mother go to see Barsine?'

'Oh, hadn't you heard?' Plexis looked like a cat tasting cream on his whiskers. 'Barsine's planning on joining you. She heard you were camping here all winter, and she wants to see you. I think,' he paused and looked at me slyly, 'I think she wants to have a baby. That's how women are. They want little ones to cuddle and tickle. Sweet babies. Olympias convinced Barsine that now is the time to see you, before you leave for Zeus-knows-where.'

We stared at him. Plexis smiled broadly and swept out of the tent. I sat on the bed. I had to think.

Alexander paced aimlessly, picking things up and putting them down. He took his ceremonial helmet and looked at it, smoothing the tassels in the back. Then he unfolded his tunic and fingered the stiff pleats. He touched the blue glass lamp, making it swing. Finally he sat down next to me on the bed and said, 'You know, I really should have had her killed.'

I laughed nervously. 'No, you were right to let your mother go. She's just trying to help, I'm sure. From what I understand she went to see an oracle and this person put some wild ideas in her head. It's not your mother's fault.'

'But Barsine! Why?'

'She's a woman, she wants a baby. It would make her happy.' I shuddered, though. If the history books were correct, Olympias would kidnap one of Alexander's wives and her child. They would all be killed by Cassander. Was it Barsine? Stateira? I wished I could remember more details. What would happen if I told Alexander? If I warned him, what would happen then? I put my face in my hands. What could I do? When Alexander died I would be alone here, and I would have a hard enough time keeping out of the murderous fray that followed his death. If I had my own baby back, my Paul, I would have to find a way to care for him. I bit my fingernails, distressed. I couldn't risk being erased; no one would take care of Paul. Or would he disappear too? I got up and paced back and forth.

'What are you doing?' Alexander was staring at me.

'I'm thinking.'

'I see that. If you're so upset about Barsine I can intercept her cortège and send her back.'

'No, don't do that. I'd like to meet her. Really, I would,' I insisted, seeing the doubt in his eyes.

'Why do you look so, so …'

'Upset?' I tried to smile, failed, and sat down again. 'Oh, Alex, it's nothing. You know how pregnant women get, all emotional and silly. I'm sure Aristotle must have said something about that.'

'Some women, maybe, but not you. You don't ever let your emotions show. You keep everything hidden behind that icy gaze. Do you know what they say about you?'

'You mean besides saying I'm a goddess and an

oracle?'

'They say you spent too much time in the kingdom of the dead, and that your heart is frozen.'

I was startled. 'But why?'

'When the wounded soldiers came in you would smile at them, as if you didn't care.'

I gasped. 'But I thought that it would comfort them! I didn't want them to see how worried I was!'

'But they knew how grievous their wounds were. My soldiers are all professionals. They don't need you to hide your feelings from them. They want honesty. It's a sign of respect in this world. To them you were making light of their wounds.'

'Do you believe that?' I asked, hurt.

'No, of course not, nor does Usse. But you have to stop hiding your feelings and saying things with two meanings. Perhaps in the world of the gods it is different, although you claim to be a mortal. For a mortal, you act remarkably like a god. We're used to their duplicity, but not yours.'

I couldn't meet his eyes. He was too earnest and each word was painful. 'I didn't realize that,' I whispered.

'I think that if you cannot tell the truth, perhaps it would be better to say nothing.' Alexander's voice was gentle, as if talking to a small child. I felt my cheeks get hot and I knew that my nose would start bleeding. I pinched the bridge of my nose hard to try and stop it, but it was too late. Blood spattered on my lap, staining my robe.

'Oh no,' I moaned, grabbing a towel. I pressed it to my face and used it to hide my angry tears. Did he think it was easy for me? I lowered the towel and narrowed my eyes. No one understood me. I was stuck here. There was nowhere I could go. I could never return to my own time. I was pregnant, and the only man I'd ever loved was criticizing me – and his first wife was arriving in a matter of days. A shudder ran through me.

Alexander took the towel from my numb hands and gently wiped my face, pausing now and then to kiss me. I pushed him away, but he persisted. I turned my back to him, and he ran his hands down my spine, rubbing his thumbs into my muscles, kneading my back and ending up with his hands encircling my shoulders. Then he started to massage my neck, tickling my cheeks, and leaning down to nibble on my earlobe and lips. I ended up kissing him back. I put my arms around his neck and pulled him down on the bed. When he was near me, touching me, his mouth on mine, his hands roaming over my body, I simply couldn't imagine life without him.

His eyes, so large, long, and fierce, saw right through me. His body was an electric charge. His personality was a drug. I was completely addicted to him. I fastened my mouth on his neck like a vampire, and gave him a love bite. He growled and bit my shoulder. Our lovemaking degenerated into a wrestling match. He was a pro at wrestling; I suppose he learned at school in Greece.

I had been on a wrestling team in my all-girls school. It was one way of getting our frustrations to a manageable level. I had some terrific memories of those games, legs sliding against legs, backs arching, bellies and hips touching. In a moment I would dissolve into a boneless shiver of desire. I threw myself sideways and then twisted around, straddling his back. I flung my arm around his neck in a half nelson and tried to throw him. He just gave a deep chuckle and slid out from beneath me with a movement like silk. I gasped and then moaned as he pulled me to him from behind. I don't think I had ever been as excited.

However, I was strong and lithe, and he hadn't won quite yet. I scissored my legs and grabbed him around the torso. Using my body as a lever, I managed to throw him down. He was a bit hampered by his erection, but he easily avoided being pinned and slipped away again, his eyes dancing.

My breath was coming in short gasps, and I decided that the best way to finish this game would be to surrender. So I did by grabbing him around the neck and dragging him down on top of me. I arched my back and met him halfway.

In the end, I'm not sure who won. I woke up on the floor. Alexander's body seemed to be braided with mine and with all the covers on the bed that we'd dragged down on the floor with us. He had fallen soundly asleep, as he usually did after a bout of lovemaking. I had slept too. I wondered what had woken me and then I heard a small cough.

I turned my head, not an easy feat with all the covers and one of Alexander's arms around me, and looked.

Axiom was standing in the tent's entrance. He looked decidedly uncomfortable. I tried to help him. 'Yes, Axiom, what can I do for you?'

'It's just that someone has arrived, my lady, someone for Iskander.'

Alexander stirred and raised his head. His hair fell into his eyes, making him look like a dissolute lion. 'What is it?' he groaned, getting to his knees and pushing his hair back.

'It's your first wife, sir. It's Barsine. She's come early.'

Chapter Eleven

Axiom, bless him, managed to get Barsine settled in another tent while Alexander and I rushed around looking for clothes and combing our hair. I braided his hair, although my hands were shaking. I tied a ribbon on it and tried to make it as neat as possible. Then I found a clean linen robe and threw it at him, while I dug through the bedcovers looking for my robe. I found it, but when I held it up, I saw the stains and remembered my nosebleed.

Swearing, I took one of the new bolts of cloth and draped it around me. I was going to meet Alexander's first wife dressed in woollen flannel. There was rather more cloth than I needed, so I asked Alexander to cut it in half with his sword.

'My sword is for killing enemies,' he said, 'not for cutting cloth.'

'Please!' I cried, 'I'll look ridiculous!'

He snorted, grabbed the cloth from me, and ripped it straight down the middle. 'Is this all right?' he asked.

'Fine, fine. Thanks.' I draped it Greek style, which meant I had to keep my arms down or my breasts would be bared.

I shouldn't have worried.

When we entered the tent, Barsine stood up. And up, and up, and up. She must have been at least seven feet tall. She had a round, open face and a short thatch of fiery red hair. Her eyes were bright blue and crinkled at the edges when she smiled, which she did non-stop. She was … I searched for the perfect description, and came up with a jolly giant. She was dressed in a pleated, un-dyed linen skirt, and her breasts were bare. She wore a wide leather belt, with one of the biggest swords I'd ever seen stuck into it. Her hair had been cut using a bowl, I think. It stuck out raggedly on either side of her head. She had long, curly red hair on her legs and under her arms. I was fascinated. She was not badly built at all. Junoesque, perhaps, would describe it. Her shoulders were wider than Alexander's, and her breasts large and round. Her legs were long and shapely, although a bit muscular, and her arms … well, Hercules, watch out!

I was getting a serious case of the giggles. Part of it was Barsine's own good humour. Another part was her accent. She sounded like a Swedish comedian speaking Greek.

Alexander bowed. She gave him a big bear hug, and I was worried when he turned blue, but she let go before he suffocated. I was more prudent; I put out my hand. She only bruised three bones.

I liked her right away. I'd been feeling like a giant for so long, towering over most men and all the women, it was refreshing to stand next to someone who made me feel petite. She told me that she was the smallest in her family, and that her family was one of the smallest in her tribe. I stared at Alexander. Now I knew why he insisted on marrying her. Get these people on your side and you'll never lose a battle.

Plexis was in the tent, looking smug. Alexander said to

him, 'Why didn't you tell me Barsine was coming so soon?'

'I did tell you she was coming; did I forget to mention when? How silly of me!' Alexander was getting a look on his face that I recognized, and I didn't want him to lose his temper in front of Barsine.

'No harm done,' I said hurriedly, taking Plexis by the arm and leading him out of the tent. 'Why don't we leave Alexander and Barsine alone, they haven't seen each other in so long. I'll show you my new donkey.'

'Your new what?' Plexis balked. He seemed to want to stay in the tent, but I knew that Alexander was angry with him, and that staying was not wise. Luckily, Brazza was on my side. He took Plexis by the other arm, and we escorted him out of the tent. Once in the sunlight he turned to face us, furious, but Brazza put his finger to his lips and jerked his head sideways.

We looked. A wall of massive barbarians was standing between the tent and the stables. There must have been three hundred of them. Plexis opened his mouth like a fish, then snapped it shut.

'Shall we go and see my donkey?' I asked, sweetly.

He just gaped.

Once in the stables, and out of earshot of the redwood forest of Barsine's kinsmen, Plexis calmed down a bit. I was afraid he'd be angry, but he wasn't. Something had gone wrong. I thought I knew what it was: Barsine hadn't decided to have me put to death on sight. However, something had obviously gone right, and he seemed pleased. Of course, he wouldn't tell me what it was. He was a difficult person.

To tease him, I had my donkey led out and I trotted her up and down before him, asking him what he thought. He thought I was expendable, but he had resigned himself to waiting for another moment.

'Isn't she adorable?' I asked. 'I've named her Penelope. Don't you think that's a good name for a donkey?'

'Penelope was my mother's name,' he said, between clenched teeth.

I was disconcerted. He looked truly chagrined. 'I'm so sorry! I'll change it right away.' I thought quickly. I couldn't name her after a goddess; it would be a frightful affront. I needed something innocuous. 'How about *White Beauty*?' I asked brightly. 'She's white, isn't she?'

He didn't deign to answer, absorbed in examining an invisible spot on his tunic. I sighed and put my donkey back in her stall. Out of habit, I glanced over at Bucephalus's stall, intending to give him a pat on the nose, but he wasn't there. *Strange*, I thought. Maybe he was out in the pasture. I looked at Plexis, standing near the stone wall. I was going to have to make friends with this prickly person, and I hadn't the faintest idea where to start.

When I emerged from the stables, I noticed a long column of soldiers forming lines on either side of the road at the far end of the camp.

'What's going on?' I asked, pointing.

Plexis looked up and shrugged. 'Oh that. They're sending the dead soldiers to their villages for burial.'

I shuddered. 'Poor men. What will happen to their families?'

'What do you mean?'

'I mean, what will happen to their wives if they had them, or their children? Will they be taken care of?'

He looked shocked. 'Of course. What kind of a question is that?'

'Well, I don't know,' I said crossly. 'How *are* they taken care of?'

Plexis frowned. 'Well, it depends which tribe they belong to; the funeral rites are different all over. But most will be cremated with full honours, and their names will be marked on their graves.'

'I meant, how are the families taken care of.'

Plexis gave a look that plainly said he thought I was retarded, but he answered me civilly enough. 'Soldiers' orphans are taken care of by the state until they are grown. When they reach their sixteenth birthday, the boys are taken to the theatre and presented to the public with these words: 'We the people raised these children, whose fathers died valiantly in the war. We give them arms and armour, so that they may go out into the world and fight their own battles.' Then they are invited to sit in the front row of the theatre. It is all very ceremonial and touching,' Plexis said, warming to his task as teacher. 'The wives get a pension, of course. As for the soldiers wounded in battle who can no longer fight or work, they are fed and clothed by the state until the end of their days. Does this answer your question?'

'You didn't mention the soldier's daughters,' I said. 'If they don't get arms and armour to fight with, do they at least get to go to the theatre?'

Plexis heaved an enormous sigh. 'Girls usually find a

husband, and of course they get to go to the theatre. Now, are you satisfied? What are you staring at?'

I was staring at the long line of wagons getting ready to leave the camp. Usse was supervising. The dead soldiers were carefully rolled up in their own capes, placed in a narrow coffin made of freshly cut wood, and loaded onto a wagon. As each wagon was filled, it moved off slowly.

The soldiers standing in line saluted. A grim quiet had fallen over the camp that I hadn't heard since the men were getting ready for battle.

I turned towards Plexis. 'Shouldn't Iskander be here?'

He pointed, and I saw the flash of sunlight on gold. Alexander had left the campsite and was mounted on Bucephalus. Dressed in full regalia, he walked his horse slowly to the head of the line of soldiers and then someone started blowing a trumpet. Three notes, over and over again, the first note being taken up only when the last note had completely died away. My skin prickled. It went on for an hour. Plexis and I joined the very end of the line and stood in silence, watching the coffins being loaded and the horses being hitched to the wagons.

As the wagons left, the soldiers all raised their right hands in a silent farewell. Only Alexander sat motionless on the back of his gleaming pony. Without thinking I turned, buried my face in Plexis's chest, and sobbed. He recoiled, and then his arms came up around me. He didn't say a word. He just held me.

Two hundred soldiers left the camp that evening in wooden boxes.

I couldn't eat dinner. I sat next to Barsine and watched

as she devoured a whole kid goat practically by herself, but I couldn't touch a thing. My stomach was clenched tight with grief. I kept seeing the faces of the dying soldiers. Those I'd spoken to, those I'd tried to comfort, and those Alexander had held while they died.

Alexander moved the food around on his plate, but didn't eat much either.

'When did you get married?' Barsine asked me, polite interest on her round face.

'Two months ago, in Susa,' I replied. I tried to smile, but my face hurt. The funeral procession had overwhelmed me. 'Was your trip difficult?'

'No.' Barsine speared another piece of meat with her dagger and ate it as if it were a large lollipop. 'My horses are strong.'

I nodded. They would have to be.

Her tribesmen were outside; only two of them had joined us for dinner. I was surprised that we were eating in our tent. Usually we ate dinner outside with the men. The two men eating with us resembled big, hairy mountains. They ate silently and voraciously. I wondered how long they were planning to stay, because if there were three hundred appetites like that outside, I was worried about our livestock.

I was about to ask, when Alexander stood up to make a toast. He raised his golden cup to his first wife and said, 'Barsine, my queen, I am honoured by your visit. Let us drink to your health.'

We drank. Brazza and Axiom poured us all more wine.

'I would like to welcome your kinsmen into my army. They will be an important part of my cavalry. I thank you for this precious gift. We drink to their health.'

One of the 'precious gifts' burped loudly, shaking the tent, and we all drained our glasses again. Brazza and Axiom poured us more wine.

'I hope your visit will be a long one, and that when you return to your people you will bring back gifts to show my thanks.' His voice was careful now. Not quite slurred, but not exactly clear.

We drained our cups. The tent was slowly spinning around and around. I hadn't eaten anything, and the wine was unwatered for once, as sweet and strong as sloe gin.

I have no idea how I got to bed. One minute I was sitting next to Barsine and the next minute I was lying across her lap snoring. I was aware of the murmur of voices, warm laughter, and then someone picked me up and put me in bed. I think it was Brazza. Then I fell asleep and dreamed of giant bears that growled and roared all night long.

The early light of morning is very dazzling. It spears the eyeballs and makes the head scream. Especially if one has a monster hangover. I groaned in pain, but my groan was lost in the rumbling growl of a bear. I froze. I was awake, my dream was over. Carefully, I raised my head. Slowly, so my eyeballs wouldn't fall out of their sockets, I peered over the great mound of covers on the bed next to me. Barsine was spread over the bed, naked except for her leather belt, and she was snoring loudly.

Loudly? It was deafening! I had no idea how I could have slept all night with that noise next to my head. Alexander was on the far side of the bed; his head was under one of Barsine's arms, his nude buttocks sticking out of the covers, one leg hanging off the bed. His snores were muffled.

I wondered where Plexis was and nearly giggled, but my head hurt too much. Slowly, painfully, I stood up. The ground tilted and I fell to my hands and knees, my head swimming. I felt seasick. I knew I was going to vomit. I moaned and looked for something to throw up in. The closest thing was Alexander's helmet, but I thought he'd probably kill me if I used that, so I managed to stagger outside and made it as far as a clump of grass. Then I barfed all over.

'Lovely morning, isn't it?'

I raised my head. Usse was standing not far away, hands clasped behind his back, a wide smile on his bony face. He waited until I was finished, and handed me a linen towel. I wiped my face, then realized I was naked.

'Do you have anything for a headache?' I asked him. 'If you do, will you please get it, and stop shouting at me?' I winced as my own voice seemed to boom in my head. I stood up on wobbly legs and wrapped the towel around me. 'I'll be in the bathhouse.' I said with great dignity.

He nodded and left, his shoulders shaking with what looked suspiciously like laughter.

The bathhouse was empty. The soldiers bathed in the evenings. A huge cauldron of water heated outside. I filled a pail and ducked into the little stone house. It was rather like a Swedish sauna. Hot rocks were in one corner, and I threw water on them to make steam. I poured the rest of the water over my head, and then scrubbed with a handful of soft 'soap'.

The soap was Usse's invention. It was actually a bucket filled with crushed plants and smooth clay. Soap did not exist in Grecian times. The soldiers often scrubbed themselves with sand mixed with oil, then scraped it off with a long, dull knife before entering the bathhouse.

The clay cleaned well, and the plants made it smell minty. It was important to rinse thoroughly. Otherwise, the clay hardened as it dried and could get extremely uncomfortable.

I filled the brick bathtub and lowered myself into the steaming water. The soldiers didn't use the tub; most of them thought that hot water would weaken them.

After bathing I felt better. Usse gave me a bitter drink that made my headache go away. He told me it was boiled willow bark. Then I hunted down Brazza and asked him to find me a new tent. I'd decided to leave Alexander and Barsine together. There was no way I was going to share a room with Barsine, nice as she was. It was still early morning. My head felt much better, and I thought I'd get my things out of Alexander's tent.

I ducked under the tent flap and saw everyone was still asleep. As my eyes adjusted to the dimness, I saw Barsine, all seven feet of her, splayed on the covers. Half-hidden next to her was Alexander. I started to smile but it froze on my face. Underneath Alexander was Plexis. I hadn't seen him earlier. Otherwise I probably would have vomited on him.

It was hard enough having to share my husband with his first and second wives, but sharing him with that insufferable Plexis was unthinkable. I narrowed my eyes.

Alexander was still half-hidden beneath Barsine's arm, but I could see the curve of his cheek, pale next to Barsine's tan. His face was turned towards Plexis, who was sleeping soundly with his head on Alexander's shoulder. Their hair was tangled together, dark and golden curls. Plexis's shoulder was wedged beneath Alexander's and their legs were entwined. Actually it was oddly sweet, and the scene would have been almost erotic if it weren't for the giantess spread-eagled and snoring on top of everyone. *And* if it weren't my husband. I shook my head. This would never do. I bent to pick up my things. There weren't many. A small gilded box with my comb and my jewellery, two halves of wool flannel material, a linen towel, my silk robes, and a pair of sandals. All these fit into a plain sandalwood box I tucked under my arm.

I moved everything to the new tent Brazza set up for me near the fig tree. It was about thirty feet away from Alexander's tent. I told Brazza, with my awkward hand signs, that he was welcome to sleep in mine. The floor was covered in woven grass mats, and I had a small bed and a small rug. Brazza, Axiom and Usse each had a mattress to sleep on, and I had given them each a woollen blanket. The night air was cold in the winter.

Brazza seemed to consider, then his hands flew as he explained that he couldn't leave Alexander alone. He had to protect him.

I was piqued; after all, I was sure Barsine was more than a match for anyone who'd want to tackle Alexander, but I knew how devoted Brazza was, so I just shrugged. My hangover was making it hard for me to hide my feelings though, because Brazza peered at me in surprise.

He mimed sadness and pointed to me.

I hesitated, then nodded.

He smiled and startled me with a hug. 'Oh, stop it,' I said, pushing him away. But I was pleased just the same. We grinned at each other shyly. It was a start.

I pointed to Alexander's tent and mimed Barsine, then mimed snoring, plugging my ears and grimacing to show him that the noise was horrendous. He was deaf, so he didn't hear anything. He laughed and pointed to Axiom, sitting on a mat not far away mending one of Alexander's dress outfits. Axiom looked exhausted. He probably hadn't gotten any sleep. I nodded. Brazza was telling me to ask Axiom to stay in my tent.

I was starting to thaw out at last, and it was both an uncomfortable and exhilarating feeling. To let people know how I was feeling about them, or what my feelings were, was so difficult that when I did, it surprised me as much as it surprised the others.

Chapter Twelve

Barsine had no such reservations about letting her feelings show. I was lying on a fragrant grass mat in a patch of pale, morning sun, drying my hair, when I heard a lion's roar. I jerked upright, my thoughts scattering all over, unable to figure out what was happening.

The next instant there was a frightened scream from Alexander's tent. Axiom's head whipped around and he grabbed Brazza by the arm. They both bolted towards the tent. They hadn't made it halfway there, when they were suddenly met by a flying man. Plexis sailed out of the tent, accompanied by the raging bellows of a furious barbarian.

Barsine strode out of the tent and stood, legs spread, hands on her hips, red hair standing straight up on her head, blue eyes throwing sparks. She was naked, except for the sword belt – thankfully empty, or Plexis would have been skewered – and she looked like one of the old gods you read about in Celtic myths or Nordic legends. She had presence, and I could imagine her as an opera diva captivating an entire audience.

Plexis obviously didn't know what had happened. I thought that if he felt even half as bad as I'd felt upon waking, it was criminal to shout at him the way Barsine was. He sat in the dust gathering his wits. His wits were scattered all over, and he was having trouble finding them.

He blinked and tried to stand up. That didn't work, so he sat very still and put his hands over his ears. It took a couple of tries to find his ears. When tears of pain started leaking from his eyes, I decided he'd had enough.

A good-sized crowd was presently gathered around the tent, so I had no trouble finding Usse.

'Can you make some willow-bark tea for Plexis?' I asked him. Then I put on an engaging smile and went to stand in front of Barsine.

'Good morning,' I said. 'Did you sleep well?'

She blinked at me owlishly, then her usual good humour asserted itself. 'Oh yes, very well. Thank you.'

'So, what's the trouble?' I asked, surreptitiously motioning to Brazza to take Plexis away to the bathhouse.

Her face darkened. 'I don't hold with the ideas of the Greeks,' she stormed.

'Which ideas?' I thought I knew, but I thought I'd give Plexis time to make his escape, and Barsine a chance to vent her anger to someone neutral.

'The idea that real love is friendship between men, and that women are just for procreation. I don't hold with that. If the Greek women want to act like silly, downtrodden geese, that's fine with me. But no homosexual Athenian is going to fornicate with my husband while I'm around.' Her face was like a thundercloud, and I hoped Plexis was out of earshot. Her language was crude and loud, and I wondered if it was a good idea to go on shouting like that in front of the soldiers. They had started to mutter, and I was unsure what their personal opinions were. If they were Greek, they would side with Plexis. The barbarians would side with their princess. I didn't want the camp to

212

start fighting. I wondered what was taking Alexander so long to wake up.

'I'm sure he wasn't doing what you're thinking,' I said desperately. 'Come, why don't we go into my tent. I'd love to show you the present I picked out for you. I didn't have the chance to give it to you last night.'

She calmed down and followed me like a tame bear. In the confined space of my tent, she was overwhelming. She sat on the rug and watched as I opened my gilded box. I had asked Alexander to give me something I could offer to the barbarian princess, and he'd obliged me by finding a necklace. It was made of large squares of gold, hammered flat and carved with lions. In the centre of each square was a ruby. I thought it was magnificent, and luckily so did Barsine.

She put it on and asked for a mirror. She admired it for a few minutes then her smile faded and she sighed deeply. 'It's very pretty, to be sure. Thank you.'

'Don't be sad,' I said, troubled by her expression. 'Iskander was so glad when he heard you were coming.'

'Was he?' She brightened a minute. 'That's good.' However, her happiness didn't last. 'Why did he have to be taught by an Athenian? That stupid father of his, infatuated with Athens, infatuated with Greek culture. Why didn't he stay in Macedonia?' She glared at her reflection. 'It's the fault of the Greeks..'

I was shocked. 'Surely you don't mean that!'

She looked at me in surprise. 'Where did you come from? Don't you know anything about the sort of education they get?'

I shook my head. 'No, all I know is that Aristotle

taught Iskander.'

'Well, he's not too bad,' she admitted. 'Most of the time the boys are taught that friendship is the highest form of love. It's supposed to be pure and noble. In principle, there is nothing physical between men and boys, and there are rules forbidding it. In Greece, love is reserved for men, between men. It doesn't usually exist between a man and woman, unless the woman is particularly beautiful and cultivated, which is rare since in Greece the women aren't educated. However, in Athens the youths run around naked while the girls and women are secluded in their households.

'The Greeks admire beauty above all else. I know that I'm not the Greek ideal for beauty. Perhaps you think I don't realize that, but I do. In my tribe we don't care. So I don't mind, except with Iskander.' She shook her head and fingered her necklace. 'When I saw Iskander, I finally realized what beauty was. We don't worship it as the Greeks do, but I fell in love with him. In our tribe the women choose their husbands and we love them well. Usually, we don't share.' Here, she looked at me and smiled to take the sting out of her words.

'I'm sorry.' I knew how she felt.

'When Alexander was a youth, he studied in Greece. Because he was a barbarian, he wanted very much to become Greek. His father was enamoured of all things Greek. But Philip never slept with men. Philip loved women – beautiful women – like Olympias. And there's another problem,' grumbled Barsine. 'The army. In the army, there are no women. Oh, I know there are whores, slaves and a few wives tagging along, but there certainly aren't enough to go around, so they fall in love with each other. Luckily Alexander's army isn't all Thracian.'

'What about the Thracians?'

Barsine rolled her eyes. 'While they're in the army, Thracians form couples who care for each other and share a tent. They fight side by side in battle, and if one is killed, often the other will commit suicide.'

'It's not like that between Alexander and Plexis!'

'But still I have to get rid of Plexis. I knew last night when I saw him there'd be trouble. I'll chop his head off. Or maybe just his penis.' She leaned forward. 'What do you think?'

My head was still aching from my hangover, and Barsine's information about Greek education hadn't helped. 'Listen, Barsine. I don't think you have to worry about Alex. He loves you very much.'

'Alex? You mean Iskander.'

I massaged my temples. I was having a hard time concentrating. 'That's right. He loves you. His problem is that everyone loves him. When you saw him, you realized what beauty was. Everyone has the same reaction. We all want to love him and want him to love us, whether we're women or men. Don't worry, Iskander still thinks like a Macedonian. He may have been educated in Greece, but he's thoroughly barbarian, believe me. Why don't you go back to his tent and get dressed? Then, if you want, I'll show you my new donkey.'

Barsine seemed to think about this. 'So you don't want me to kill Plexis?'

'Well, I didn't actually say that.' I grinned. 'No, I don't want you to kill him. I'll make sure he doesn't bother you any more, how's that? Now, why don't you go back and see Iskander?'

'All right, I will. He should be regaining consciousness about now.'

'Regaining what?'

'Consciousness. I knocked him out when I woke up and found him fooling around with Plexis.'

I winced. His hangover was going to beat all of ours.

Luckily for Barsine, and the history books, Alexander didn't remember a thing when he woke up the next morning. His wife had hit him so hard he was unconscious a full twenty-four hours. No one contradicted him when he woke up thinking it was still the morning after Barsine's arrival. He lost a day out of his life and never knew it. Barsine had calmed down by then. The soldiers had settled down, and Plexis was in his own tent.

The barbarian princess was easy to get along with. I wondered if I would have liked her as much if she'd been a raving beauty, like Olympias. However, if she had been, her personality would have been different. There was something touching in the way she saw herself. She was proud of her prowess in throwing spears and shooting arrows. Hardly a day went by she didn't organize a contest that she invariably won, to her immense delight. At the same time, she knew she wasn't the Greek's ideal for beauty, and it rankled. It rankled the same way it would annoy you if you were a stocky, dark-haired woman in a culture that worshipped willowy blondes. It was, I reflected sourly, the Barbie-doll syndrome fifteen centuries too early. However, Barsine refused to change the slightest thing about her dress, her hair, or her way of thinking, even though she knew Alexander had been brought up by a father enamoured of everything Greek.

Alexander had suffered from being called a barbarian when he was young, and he'd done everything possible to become fully Greek – to the point where he would spread Greek culture all across the Middle East. However, Alexander, to give him credit, was innocent. He saw Greek culture through the eyes of his father, who, as Barsine had so pointedly said, never slept with a man. He saw its culture through the eyes of Aristotle, who gave little thought to love, be it for women or men, and instead concentrated on the deeper questions of philosophy and science. Finally, he saw its culture through the eyes of his people who looked at the Greeks with envy, admired their art and way of life, and wanted to be thought of as Greeks, not as barbarians.

Barsine didn't understand that. She saw all the negative aspects of Greek culture, and she also foresaw the form its downfall would take. In some ways, she was ahead of her time.

I told her that as we walked towards the village. We had taken my little white donkey and were going to shop in the market.

'Is that so? You think I'm clever?' She was pleased with the compliment.

'Yes, I enjoy talking to you, and I think you're absolutely right. The Greeks don't have much time left if they keep on like they are. Even now the population has dropped by half, and it can only get worse. The army calls itself Greek, but most of the soldiers in Iskander's army aren't Greek. They come from Macedonia, or from places

Iskander has already conquered.'

Barsine patted *White Beauty* absently and then sighed. For a barbarian she seemed to sigh a lot. 'It's a pity Iskander had to go to Athens.'

'It made him what he is.' I wished she wouldn't mope; it made me uncomfortable. I hadn't seen Plexis since he'd been ejected from Alexander's tent, though I knew he was still around waiting for Nearchus. I was worried about Barsine's reaction to Nearchus. While I couldn't fathom Alexander's love-hate relationship with Plexis, I knew the bond Alexander had with Nearchus was very strong. Nearchus was Alexander's admiral, and, I suspected, his lover as well.

Barsine loved sports and competition, so she started a regular Olympics in the camp. With more than forty thousand superbly conditioned soldiers, there was more than enough material for games.

Soccer was a big favourite. Not the soccer I knew from my time, but close. Rugby was also played, and Usse was kept busy the week that tournament started. Alexander had spectators' stands set up on a vast field, and every day there was some sort of competition.

It was funny watching Barsine's kinsmen playing rugby. They took the stuffed goatskin and trotted it to their goals. Thirty men couldn't stop one of them. They were like bulldozers.

The Greek soldiers loved wrestling. They mud-wrestled. A large pit was dug and filled with clay and some water. The men slipped and slid and wrestled in it, and I could see why Barsine would tighten her lips and refuse to let Alexander take part in the competition. Even I turned bright red and nearly got a nosebleed when I watched a game. The Thracians were the worst.

Spartans never took part in the games. The reason was simple; they were terrible losers. They absolutely refused to admit they were beaten, and the words 'I give up' were not in their vocabulary. The first and only time a Spartan soldier was persuaded to wrestle with one of the barbarians, he ended up dead. The silly goose wouldn't give up. His heart gave up for him. Usse shook his head and steered the Spartan warriors towards the horse games where they made excellent polo players. I started calling them 'The Brash and the Brainless'.

There were archery competitions, marathons, spear-throwing, different sorts of ballgames, field hockey, gymnastics, and shows of strength. The preliminaries were held in the morning, and the finals took place in the afternoon.

Alexander took part in some competitions, but Barsine wouldn't let him do anything too physical, so he was banned from wrestling, rugby, and soccer. The soccer was more like rugby, the rugby was more like a free-for-all, and each sport saw half its players in the infirmary after the games.

Alexander particularly loved polo, even though it was dangerous. There were roughly six men to a side, though this number varied from game to game and could go from four to ten. The field was larger than the ones I had seen. There was no referee for any game except wrestling, and half the time the referee was there to make sure it didn't degenerate into a melee. Polo was as hard on the horses as it was on the men, but it was the oldest sport and the most ceremonial. Trumpeters and drummers lined both sides of the field. The horses were decked out in gold and silks, and the players sported brightly coloured, padded jackets, and wore turbans to protect their heads. I thought they wore more protection for polo games than for battles. The game was incredibly violent. Anything went. The fist-sized wooden ball was hit with a whippy bamboo mallet, but they could scoop the ball up and carry it, throw it, or kick it in the air. One could hit the ball with his mallet, or hit the opposing players, although hitting the ponies was considered bad sportsmanship. The players rammed into each other, trying to unseat their adversaries. Half the time, everyone ended up in a pile on the ground, ponies thrashing wildly, players shouting and swearing, trumpets blaring, and the spectators screaming. The ponies weren't shod, which was lucky, considering the number of kicks the players received. Only half trained, the horses would often rear or buck just as a player was leaning out to hit the ball.

Bucephalus was a great polo pony. Tough and quick, his stocky strength was an advantage in a melee. Plexis played in every game, riding like a centaur on his black pony.

I was persuaded to play a ceremonial game with Barsine and Alexander one night. We didn't play a regular game, although women did play polo, I was told. Their games weren't as rough and crazy as the men's games, but I was pregnant. I didn't want to take any chances. We rode sedately, hitting the ball to each other, torches showing the goal posts. The ball was ingeniously made of silver filigree with a gyroscope inside of it. It held rags soaked in oil, burning brightly to make a glowing ball. In the darkness, we could see the sparkling light, flying like a tame comet around the field.

Barsine insisted on dragging me out to the archery field one morning. I liked archery, but I wasn't familiar with antique bows. The string took half the skin off my arm when I released the arrow. I'd forgotten to secure my arm guard.

I was happiest just sitting in the stands under an awning held up by four soldiers. Usse sometimes sat with me, when he wasn't binding someone up or setting bones. Barsine could usually be seen in the very middle of the field. Plexis took part in most equestrian competitions. But Alexander was busy elsewhere. Alexander did play some games, but aside from polo, he didn't shine at contests. He was too serious for the frivolity of sport. He was made by the gods to lead an army and to found a kingdom, not to run foot races or shoot at targets. Besides, as Aristotle wryly said, he hated to lose. Alexander, dressed in his finest, came to watch the games. He handed out prizes, congratulated the winners, and comforted the losers, but mostly he held himself aloof. On most days he was in Persepolis, sorting out the treasure, writing letters, giving orders, making plans, visiting Darius – and waiting for Nearchus.

Chapter Thirteen

Alexander had already decided to go to Bactria to recover our son, but he hadn't told anyone. Even the soldiers didn't know.

'They think they'll be heading back to Babylon in the spring,' Alexander told me, handing me a bowl of steaming tea and perching on the side of my bed. He came to my tent and spoke to me every morning after he inspected his troops. I looked forward to these visits; they were the only times we had to be alone all day.

'I hope they won't be disappointed,' I said, sipping my hot tea. I was aching to be on the road to fetch back Paul, but my pregnancy was making me tired, and in the morning I always felt nauseated. Alexander had started bringing me herbal tea in the morning. Usse made it, and Alexander would fetch it in the cook's tent before coming to see me.

Alexander shook his head. 'They'll be thrilled, I promise. I'm saving the news as a sort of surprise.'

I hoped the surprise would be well received. I also hoped Nearchus would agree, and wondered what Alexander would do if he did not. Alexander looked out the tent flap and sighed. It was getting late, and the myriad of things he had to do wouldn't wait. He kissed me tenderly on the lips, and left.

At night I lay in my tent and watched the stars through

a hole. I could hear Barsine's snoring, and the snoring of all her tribesmen. It sounded like a bestiary. Barsine said that her tribe's ancestors had used snoring to deter enemies. I could imagine how reluctant any enemy would be to attack a village apparently full of savage animals.

Axiom stayed with me, but he slept in a small tent next to mine. He explained now that he was a free man, it wouldn't be correct for him to be alone with me. Usse usually slept in the infirmary – to escape the sound of snoring – and Brazza refused to leave Alexander's side. So I was by myself. I hated it. It reminded me of my prison and the isolation I'd suffered in the temple of Gulu.

A cloud scudded across the sky, hiding the stars. I closed my eyes, but sleep eluded me. Pregnancy was making me tired, yet I suffered from insomnia. I wondered if Usse could give me some herbal potion for sleep. I decided to ask him the next morning and was just about to pull the covers over my head in a vain attempt at sleep, when I heard a faint noise.

Silently, I got up and pulled my tent flap aside. A man was sitting under the fig tree. In the starlight, I saw him pluck a leaf and roll it tightly. It was Plexis.

Axiom was asleep in his tiny tent, the tips of his feet just poking out. He didn't stir.

My tent was nearest the hillside. Then came the fig tree, Alexander's tent, and an open space leading towards the stables and the bathhouse. Beyond that, the white, dusty road to Persepolis reflected the moonlight.

We were above the field where the infantry camped, and thousands of tents stretched out beneath me. Lamps were lit inside a few of the tents, making them glow like

Japanese lanterns. Guards stood in the flickering light of campfires or sat on grass mats, quietly playing dice. Behind me, the hillside was covered in long grass and stubby bushes. A rocky path led to the top, its white quartz stones gleaming faintly.

Plexis didn't move, so after a few moments I tiptoed over to the fig tree.

'Can't you sleep either?' I whispered.

'You make more noise than a charging hippo,' he replied, not turning his head.

'Come, we can't stay here. Let's go up on the hill. I bet the view is lovely from there.'

He sighed and tossed the leaf away, following me across the clearing and then up the path marked with bits of quartz. When we reached the top, we sat on a large, flat rock that had kept the heat of the sun. It was still pleasantly warm.

'Why can't you sleep?' I asked him, after we'd sat in silence for nearly half an hour.

He looked at me. In the starlight, his eyes were black holes. 'Why can't *you* sleep?' he countered.

I sighed. It was so difficult to talk to him, yet I decided to be frank. 'When I was captured, a year ago, I was taken to Mazda and put in the temple of Gulu. I was kept in a room with no windows, and only taken out twice a day for exercise. I was pregnant, had a baby, and no one spoke to me.'

'No one?' he sounded sceptical.

'One day a midwife came and she talked to me. She said three sentences, I think, and then she left. That was it. A deaf-mute watched me while I was in the garden. Two priestesses were in charge of me, but they never said a word. When my baby was born, he was born in silence. Even now, sometimes, I think he was a dream, or part of one.'

'A child?' Plexis suddenly realized what I'd been saying. 'You had a child? When? Was it Iskander's? Where is it now?' His voice was oddly tense.

'Weren't you listening? I had a baby. Six months ago, I think. I've lost track of time. Of course it was Iskander's. When he was ten days old he was taken away from me. I haven't seen him since.' I felt my eyes brimming with tears and my cheeks grew hot. Why was I talking about Paul to this horrible person?

'Where is he? Did the babe die?'

'I don't know.' I was crying and my damn nose was bleeding again. I dabbed at it furiously with my tunic and cursed.

Plexis stared at me. I couldn't read his expression. He opened his mouth, then frowned and shut it again. 'I didn't know that,' he said finally, almost angrily.

'I'm so sorry I didn't tell you,' I said, not hiding my sarcasm. 'You have to understand. First Olympias kidnaps him, then Darius, and now he's disappeared. I didn't particularly feel like trusting anyone.'

'Does your nose bleed often?' Plexis's voice held a note I hadn't yet heard from him.

'No. Only when I get upset, embarrassed, go from hot to cold too quickly, or get banged on the nose. When I was little, I had to learn to control my emotions because of my stupid nose. OK? Are you happy?'

'What does oh-kay mean?'

My mouth twitched. 'It means all right.'

'Most people think it's a sign.'

'My nosebleeds?'

'Yes. Oracles often get them.'

'Well, for me it's just a sign that I'm upset, or that I've just gotten hit on the nose,' I snapped. I looked at my tunic, decided my nose wasn't bleeding any more and sniffed loudly.

He drew his legs up and folded his arms across the tops of his knees. 'You have been honest with me, so I will be honest with you. I can't sleep because Iskander is so near. He's in his tent, right down there. I can hear him breathe if I listen. But he might as well be on the other side of the earth.' Plexis laughed mirthlessly. 'I made the mistake of falling in love with the Sun God.'

I was startled. 'But didn't he kill your brother? Don't you hate him for that?'

'I thought I did. Cxious was my older brother. He was a bit like Iskander. He caught the eye and held it. He was dark-haired like me, strong and well built, with a talent for making friends and for making people laugh. When he was thirteen, my mother sent him to study with Aristotle. That's where he met Iskander. I was there already; I'd been sent away by my mother when I was ten.

'Iskander and I were best friends. When Iskander tamed Bucephalus, I had the first ride. He even invited me to his home in Macedonia during the holidays. And then we turned fourteen.' His voice had become crystalline. I shivered.

'If you don't want to tell me about it, you don't have to,' I said. But he didn't seem to hear me.

'A man named Agathon took a fancy to my brother. Although Aristotle told him to beware, Cxious started to go to this man's house and follow him everywhere. Agathon was a well-known playwright, and he wrote several plays especially for Cxious. My brother loved attention and this turned his head. He was invited to all the banquets Agathon gave, and he became a sort of celebrity within the theatre society. He even had small parts in the plays.

'We thought Cxious was wonderful – he was older than we were and he lorded over us. Iskander didn't mind. I think he was amused at first. We were all were still the best of friends. But then Agathon seduced Cxious. He opened up a new world for him. The world of pleasure. For a sixteen-year-old, it was too much to handle. Cxious lost his head. He insisted on initiating Iskander. And Iskander fell in love. It was unfortunate, because as friends they could survive. As lovers they burnt each other out.

'Agathon was insanely jealous, and plotted to turn Cxious away from Iskander. He wrote a play portraying a young, licentious barbarian who seduces a noble Athenian, then breaks his heart and kills him. He managed to convince Cxious that Iskander was playing him false. There was a huge row one evening after the theatre. Iskander wasn't stupid, he recognized himself in Agathon's play. It was a terrible blow to his ego. The boys had been drinking, and Agathon and his cronies egged them on. It started out as a simple wrestling match, but Cxious ended up dead.

'The older men would sometimes organize these

matches. The things they made the boys do were against the law, but the pleasures of the flesh, and the beauty so worshipped by the Athenians, made it seem "oh-kay" as you put it. Only it wasn't.' Plexis stopped and drew a ragged breath. 'In the end Iskander rose above it. Aristotle helped – after all, he is a philosopher and he loves Iskander, as do we all. Agathon was ruined and his friends disgraced. And I was left to pick up the pieces.'

'Why you?' I asked gently.

'I had lived in Athens longer than Iskander or Cxious. I was the one who introduced Cxious to Agathon. I was one of the boys who would wrestle at night at the banquets to entertain the playwright's friends. At the time, I only thought about the enjoyment. What mattered was the physical pleasure and the admiration that was showered upon me.' He shook his head. 'I never thought about love. It was only when Iskander's heart broke that I started to see how wrong I'd been. You see, of the three of us, only Iskander really loved. That's why he's still intact.'

'You were too young to know what you were doing,' I protested. 'Those men were adults, they should have been punished! They had no right influencing young people like that. Why, it could happen to anyone. What happened was awful, but it wasn't your fault. It was the fault of your hormones. When you're that age you are ruled by hormones, you're incapable of thinking clearly. Adults should be there to help you, not pervert you. I'm so sorry your brother died.'

There was a long silence while he digested this. 'I don't know what you're talking about,' he admitted finally. 'Hormones don't rule us, we elect our own leaders in Athens. What do they have to do with perversion? Are hormones kings who pervert children?'

We stared at each other. He had such a perplexed look on his face that I giggled. It began as a nervous little hiccup that I tried to smother, but it turned into a snort. I started laughing, and then couldn't stop. I laughed hysterically. Plexis smiled, uncertainly, then started chortling. It was contagious. We dissolved into gales of laughter, holding on to each other, tears running down our faces. Every time I stopped laughing, his chuckles would start me up again. We whooped, choked, howled and cried with laughter. Finally we stopped and lay still, gasping for breath. My stomach was sore. I wiped tears off my face, sitting up stiffly.

Plexis rubbed his eyes, and sat cross-legged in front of me. His handsome face was open for once, and I thought I could almost get to like him.

'You're not what I expected,' he said, after he'd gotten his breath back.

'What *did* you expect?'

'The goddess's daughter. Lysimachus calls you "Ashley of the Sacred Sandals", and the soldiers claim you wrought a miracle with an arrow. I heard about what you said to Darius. You frightened me, but I was wrong to think of you as a goddess. Obviously you're not Greek. You're not a barbarian. I don't know where you're from, but you're different.'

'After what you told me, I'm not sure I'd like to be Greek,' I said.

'No. You're right, it's up to the adults to channel youth. But if the adults are dissolute, they will pervert.'

'I don't mean to imply that you're a pervert,' I said.

'I know the difference.' He looked down the hill towards Alexander's tent and his face softened. 'I love him.'

I nodded and put my arm across his shoulders. 'It is the difference. And he loves you, too.' I smiled, remembering Usse's words. 'He loves everyone, perhaps that's his problem.'

'Perhaps.' He didn't shrug away from me, but he held himself perfectly still.

'Do I make you uncomfortable?' I asked, withdrawing my arm.

'I don't understand you,' he admitted. 'You are like a shadow without form or substance. You profess to love Iskander but you make no claim upon him. You bore his child and have another in your womb, but it seems to touch you not. Neither the bearing nor the losing. I can't explain it. You make me uncomfortable. I think it's because you seem to be looking at us the same way Aristotle looked at his collection of sea-creatures. He would study them for hours, making notes and observing, watching and trying to understand. That's the impression you give me. I'm sorry if I hurt you, but I am trying to be honest.'

'I'm sorry, too.' I wiped away a stray tear and tilted my face to the stars. 'I do love Iskander. More than I love myself.'

'It is your selfless love that I understand the least and admire the most,' he admitted.

I took a deep, shaky breath. 'It's not easy. But you have to understand, Iskander has things to do, important things. The gods put him here for a reason, and it's not me, or a baby, or anyone else that will stop him. You knew Iskander as a boy, so you don't see him the way I do. I knew him as a legend.' I frowned, was that giving too much away?

'A legend?' He was serious again. 'Where are you from, Ashley of the Sacred Sandals?' His voice wavered, as if he were afraid of the answer.

'I can't tell you.'

'Why not?'

'Because if I do I will die.' He looked confused, but I'd learned by now the Greeks believed in anything connected to oracles, so I explained further. 'An oracle told me never to reveal my secret.'

He accepted that, and we sat on the flat rock in a silence that was almost companionable. I leaned against his shoulder, and he didn't pull away. Just before the sun came up he asked me, 'Aren't you afraid Barsine will bear a son? And that she will take your place in Iskander's heart?'

'If I could make one wish tonight,' I said softly. 'I would wish that Barsine's son would be the light of Iskander's life, and that they would grow old together. I would wish that all of us would grow old together.'

Plexis shivered. 'I hate it when you talk like that,' he said. Then we were quiet as the first songbirds announced the dawn.

Chapter Fourteen

Nearchus arrived with the sound of clashing cymbals and blaring trumpets. A long line of dusty horses and tired soldiers filed into the camp.

As before, we had to do the whole welcoming ceremony, complete with priest, sacrificed goat and the reading of the entrails. Yuck.

The entrails were pronounced auspicious. Nearchus strutted about with his regalia. Barsine played the part of the first lady. Alexander gave a speech. Plexis and I waited in the wings.

We had become uneasy allies. Uneasy, because Plexis considered I knew too much about him, and he knew far too little about me.

Barsine was glowing. After two weeks with Alexander she was sure she was pregnant, and she slathered ritual red mud on her belly and thighs and walked around scaring Nearchus's soldiers who hadn't quite gotten used to her yet.

She didn't let a little thing like a baby get in the way of sports and she continued to hurl javelins, ride, and shoot arrows all day long. I worried until Usse told me he didn't think it would hurt her, so I relaxed. I wanted everything to go well for the cheerful princess.

I went to find Lysimachus on his day off and told him that the name 'Ashley of the Sacred Sandals' was just a joke between Iskander and me. I begged him not to go around repeating it to everyone. He agreed, and in the same breath asked me to tell his fortune. The soldiers were very superstitious; they would spend ridiculous amounts of money on oracles and priestesses to try and divine the future. Perhaps the fact that their job was so dangerous had something to do with it. In a time where a simple cut could get septic and kill within days, being a soldier was risky indeed. I sighed.

'Lysimachus, I don't tell fortunes. You can't look into the future. There's no such thing as fate!' I tried to talk common sense to him, but it was hopeless.

'Please, we'll pay you! Look, my friends and I have sixteen obols, and we'll throw in a white chicken. You can sacrifice the chicken and tell us our fortunes with the entrails. Please?'

'Aren't you afraid of what I might say?'

'Of course, who wouldn't be? We know you're a real oracle. Please? The one in the village is so old, we can't understand a thing she says.'

I pursed my lips. This oracle business was starting to get on my nerves, yet it intrigued me at the same time. 'On one condition.'

'What's that?'

'First, you take me to see the oracle in the village.' I wanted to see the old lady and find out what all the fuss was about.

Barsine insisted on coming with us. Even she believed in oracles. Alexander was in Persepolis with Nearchus. Otherwise, I don't know what he would have thought about this outing. Plexis joined our troop. He said he wouldn't miss it for the world. Usse watched us leave with a faint line of worry between his brows.

I rode my white donkey, but everyone else walked. We sang and joked as we went toward the town. For me, the whole thing was a lark; a sightseeing trip for a tourist from the future. I didn't believe in gods, oracles or fortune-tellers, but for the people walking along beside me, the gods were real. For the Greeks, the only difference between the gods and men, was that the gods were immortal and could change form. The gods had the same emotions and frailties as men, and loved to meddle in human affairs – they would often come to earth from their home on Mount Olympus and walk among the unsuspecting humans.

My little donkey picked her way delicately over the stepping-stones in the stream, crossing to the other side without a stumble. Plexis wasn't so lucky. His foot slipped, and he fell with a mighty splash in the middle of the creek. He stood. The icy water was only waist deep but he was shivering. The soldiers and Barsine all screamed with laughter; decidedly the trip was getting better and better. But I frowned.

'You should go back and get some warm clothes,' I said. 'You'll catch cold if you don't.'

Plexis shook his head stubbornly. 'No, I've been sitting around the camp doing nothing. I want to do something interesting. Why, if I were in Athens right now we'd be celebrating the fête of Demeter, and the biggest festival in Athens, the festival of Zeus, is in seven days. I don't suppose we'll do anything wonderful here.' He voice was mournful. Obviously he missed his busy party life in Athens. He took off his sopping wet cloak, wrung it out, and hung it on a branch to collect on the way back. Then he walked along behind us, naked. I knew that as an authentic Athenian he wouldn't like to go about with no clothes. The soldiers didn't mind, but they were soldiers.

I had a skirt and a long tunic, so I took off my skirt and gave it to him. 'Here, wear this.'

He seemed pleased. My skirt was very fine linen with small, even pleats. He wrapped it around his slender waist and tied a jaunty bow at the side. 'Thank you, my lady,' he said with a low bow.

We all laughed at him, and the soldiers teased him until we got into sight of the village. Then my companions fell silent. Now I can say it was the silence Catholics get when they go to communion, but at the time it just seemed as if the sun had gone behind a cloud, and I shivered.

The oracle, or *pythia* as she was sometimes called, was an old woman living on the outskirts of the village. Her cottage was surrounded by a hedge of fragrant thyme and lavender. Several white goats and chickens were in a small paddock in the back.

Her house was actually a temple. It had an open courtyard with a large stone altar under an olive tree. When we arrived, the old woman was outside sitting in the sun, her face hidden in the shadow of a large-brimmed straw hat. She wore a white robe, Greek style. When she stood to greet us, I saw she was almost as tall as I.

She might have looked old but her voice was authoritative. 'Bring the donkey to the altar,' she ordered.

'Why?' I asked, getting off *White Beauty*'s back and

patting her affectionately.

'For the sacrifice. You've brought her for the oracle, have you not? Do you want to consult Apollo? Have you the *pelanos*?' This was the fee paid to the oracle.

'The donkey is mine,' I cried. 'She's not to be killed!' I got back on, intending to ride away.

One of the soldiers caught her bridle. 'The oracle has spoken,' he said. 'The donkey will be sacrificed.'

'No!' I kicked at him with my foot, trying to wrench the donkey's head away. But she was too docile and just stood calmly while the soldiers pulled me off the poor creature and led her to the altar. I screamed, 'Barsine! Plexis! Lysimachus! Do something!'

But Barsine wore an expression of pity and disgust, as if I were committing a heinous crime. Plexis grabbed my arm and squeezed it so hard he bruised it. 'Don't say another word!' he hissed. 'What do you think you're doing? It's an honour for your donkey.'

'You're just mad because I named her Penelope,' I sobbed. 'Lysimachus, don't let her do that!'

Lysimachus's face was twisted with pity, and he tried to calm me with gentle words. 'Why do you protest? You wanted to see the oracle. Don't worry, we'll let you go first, and Apollo will speak directly to you.'

While he spoke, the old woman took off her hat and washed her hands in a small spring next to the altar. Then she reached up into the branches of the olive tree and took down a sharp knife. *White Beauty* didn't even blink when the woman seized her under the chin and lifted her head up. With a deft movement, she cut the donkey's throat. I saw a red line bloom in her snowy coat, and then I fainted.

236

Barsine shook me awake. She was holding me up, and my head lolled against her arm. 'Wake up! Wake up! It's done.'

I opened my eyes and saw the old woman take a pitcher and fill it in the spring. Then she dashed cold water onto the body of my poor donkey, whose nerves were still twitching, making her look as if she were trying to get up. I gave a sharp cry, and then my nose bled all over Barsine and my tunic.

Blood splattered everywhere. The soldiers were most impressed. They leapt backwards and stared at me and at the dead donkey. The old woman had disembowelled the carcass and was busy spreading the intestines and liver onto the altar. She looked up and saw me, and her eyes widened.

'A good omen!' she cried, pointing at me with the bloody knife. 'A good omen indeed!'

The soldiers cheered and Barsine beamed, and then Plexis took off his skirt and held it to my nose, begging me in a low voice to control myself, or I'd ruin everything.

I was not used to having a naked stranger standing so close to me, especially one as good looking as Plexis. His thighs brushed against mine and I could feel the heat of his body. My nose bled even more. I closed my eyes and said in a strangled voice, 'Plexis, will you please get away from me? And put some clothes on, you're making it worse!' He stopped touching me and jumped back as if he'd been scalded. 'I don't believe this,' I said, my eyes still closed. I sat down and used my tunic to staunch the blood.

237

The old woman's yard looked like a battlefield. Most of us were covered with blood, either *White Beauty*'s or mine. The intestines and liver were examined and pronounced 'most auspicious'. Apparently, all our dreams would come true. I kept my eyes closed as much as possible. For me this day was rapidly turning into a nightmare.

It wasn't over. The woman washed in the spring and bade us wash too. Then she led us into the temple where a fire smouldered in a bronze brazier. She threw handfuls of leaves and herbs on the fire, and stinging smoke filled the room. I choked and my eyes started watering. Strangely enough, no one else seemed affected. The woman sat with her head right in the smoke for a while, and then she disappeared down a staircase that led to a cellar. We followed her, and found ourselves in a small square room hewn out of the bedrock. The room was lit by a single torch, and there were benches all around the walls. Everyone sat as if they were in a doctor's waiting room. Barsine pulled me down beside her and held my hand. I was still crying. Plexis wouldn't look at me, Lysimachus looked apprehensive, and the soldiers all seemed in high spirits.

The woman went into another room and drew a heavy curtain behind her. After a few moments she called out in a strange voice muffled by the curtain, 'Who asks Apollo first?'

Barsine dug her elbow into my ribs, but I shook my head. 'You go first,' I sobbed.

She stood up and with a shy smile asked, 'Will I have Iskander's son, O Mighty One?'

The old woman answered, still in her weird voice, 'Yes. You will have a son in nine moons' time.'

Barsine gave me a radiant smile and sat down.

After looking at me for a minute, Lysimachus stood up. 'Is my fortune to be made?' he asked.

'Your fortune will be made at the end of the king's reign. But beware; in the end, a new acquaintance will be stronger than you.' The voice was sly.

Plexis was next. He cleared his throat. 'Will I find the answers I seek?'

The woman cackled. 'Most handsome one, listen well. You shall go east and east again. You will see the twelve pillars and the sacred river. However, the answers you look for will only be revealed on your deathbed. Don't seek them too soon.'

Plexis turned white and sat down rather suddenly.

The three soldiers looked at me uncertainly; then they stood up and asked their questions, one after another. The voice told them they would go further than they'd ever dreamed, and that they would all found large, prosperous families. This seemed to satisfy them. They sat down, and then everyone looked at me. I didn't move, tears running down my face. For this nonsense, my beloved donkey had been killed?

'I see a stranger in our midst,' the voice came from behind the curtain. 'Stand! So that I may see you.'

Barsine pushed me roughly to my feet.

'Will you not ask a question of me?' asked the mocking voice.

'No. I don't believe in you.'

There was a collective gasp from my companions, and

Plexis drew in his breath with a hiss.

'To believe or not to believe, that is not the question.' The voice was sly again, and teasing. 'You have come from farther than anyone here can imagine, and you will have the chance to return. However, to return you must sacrifice a human life: one living man. A donkey is just an animal with no soul, but you must kill a man with a soul. I see past the ice in your heart. Didn't you know?' There was a dry chuckle. 'Here is a riddle for the Ice Queen. The king is dead, long live the king.' A silence greeted these words. We all looked at each other, perplexed.

'I don't like riddles,' I snapped, more angry and miserable than confused.

'I'd love to stay and chat,' said the voice, with something very like regret in it. 'I too have questions to ask that only you may answer. Grant me one, just one, and I will tell you about your son.'

The blood drained from my face and my heart thumped painfully. 'What do you want to know?'

'Will my name be remembered? Is my name still on people's lips?'

'What do you mean?' I was confused. What was the old woman's name anyway? 'What name?'

'Apollo. I am here, and I want to know. Answer me, child of the future. Answer me now, for soon I will vanish and the centuries will bury me in their dust.'

At first I thought the woman was talking about herself, but a shiver run down my spine. My head tingled. 'It can't be ...'

'There are things you will never be able to explain. Just answer me, if you will. Do you know the name

Apollo? Have you heard of me once before, perhaps as a whisper? Perhaps in some long, lost song? Do they still sing about me? Answer me … please.'

The voice was plaintive, and for some reason I saw Darius's tragic face in my mind. The deposed king, a fallen angel. I thought of the Apollo space programme. Tears pricked my eyes. 'Yes,' I whispered. 'Your name is spoken all the way to the moon, but it has nothing to do with you any more.'

There was a deep silence while my words were considered, and then the voice came again, calm and oddly quiet. 'Well. I suppose I had to ask. Do you see how similar we are? The gods and men.'

'My baby,' I breathed. 'You promised.'

'You shall find him in the sacred valley. Guard him well. He will find the lost soul.'

After that, there was no more sound, except for harsh breathing coming from behind the curtain. I was shaking uncontrollably, but no one would look at me or touch me.

'Apollo asked you a question!' Lysimachus shook his head in awe.

'Don't ever speak to me about it again,' I said fiercely.

We left in silence. The carefree group that had crossed the stream was now dirty, bloodstained, and weary. I walked behind everyone else. I was angry at the old woman, angry with Lysimachus, and most of all, angry at myself.

We passed the bush where Plexis had hung his cloak to dry. He took it and draped it over my shoulders, leaving his arm over them.

I buried my head on his shoulder and sobbed bitterly.

All the tears in the world wouldn't bring back my donkey or stop the slow, inexorable march of time. The king is dead. Long live the king.

'You seem to like crying on me,' said Plexis, and he almost sounded pleased.

I raised my face. 'I was so foolish. I thought that I could be happy here, but I can't. I have to leave. Will you help me?'

'What do you mean?' He took a corner of my tunic and wiped my face.

'You were right the other night. I can't stay here. I'm a stranger and will never understand your customs. I'll just be in the way.'

'You're married to Iskander,' he said. 'You're my queen. You have to go where Iskander tells you to go, and stay if he asks you to stay.'

'And what about you?'

He looked amused. 'Didn't you hear the oracle? I will go east with Iskander to the sacred river, wherever that is.'

'But you love him. Won't it tear you apart, being near him?'

'No. No, I don't think so. I think that just loving him and being near him is enough for me. If you can do it, so can I.'

'But we're not at all alike,' I said. 'Iskander won't mind if I leave. He hardly notices me any more.'

He smiled. 'I think you're wrong about that, and I think you're wrong about Iskander. He's more than you think.'

'He's more than anyone thinks,' I said.

We joined the others, waiting beneath the shade of a

242

tree. The afternoon was getting very hot, and my stomach growled. 'What's for lunch?' I asked Barsine. I noticed the soldiers gathering wood to light a fire.

'We're going to cook your donkey,' she said, matter-of-factly.

She wasn't being callous. She honestly thought it had been a great honour for my poor little donkey to be sacrificed to Apollo.

I sat some distance away, watching as the soldiers grilled steaks and served them on fresh leaves in the guise of plates. I shook my head and refused to eat, but my ire had gone. I felt empty, depressed, and even a bit frightened. How had the old woman known my nickname, the Ice Queen? How had she known about the baby? And why call me a child from the future?

My head ached, and I rested it against my arms. I wished I'd never gone to that place. I tried to forget, but the words 'human sacrifice' played themselves over and over. I could return, she had said. Return to my own time? How was it possible? Whom would I have to sacrifice? Why? What did she mean when she said my son could find a lost soul? Where was the sacred valley? And why hadn't she spoken of the child I carried? I was sitting in the sun but I couldn't get warm. Was it really Apollo who'd spoken to me? How was it possible? The questions jumbled and clashed in my aching head. I put my hands on my temples and pressed hard, willing the pain away. Where was Usse when I needed him?

I got to my feet and stumbled down the road, determined to find Usse and ask for something to make my migraine go away.

I hadn't gone far, before Plexis fell in step next to me. He held a bit of meat in his hands and gnawed on it as we walked along.

'Why are you following me?' I asked after a while.

'I couldn't let you go back on your own. Look at yourself.'

I glanced down. I was wearing Plexis's cape, so most of the bloody tunic was hidden, but my hands and arms were still stained with ribbons of dried blood, and I guessed my face must have been just as dirty. My eyes were probably red from crying, and swollen. I sighed, and turned to Plexis. 'What do you suggest?'

'Come to the creek and I'll help you wash. Then we'll all go back together. If Iskander sees you coming back like that, he'll kill us all. You don't know his temper.'

I tried to smile. 'No, I don't.'

We left the road and walked to a clump of trees on the side of a small stream. Once in the shade, I dipped my hands in the cool water and washed my face and arms. My feet were blistered, so I took off my sandals and dabbled my feet in the water. I thought of my donkey.

Plexis looked at me worriedly. 'What is the matter?' he asked. 'The oracle was most auspicious and for once very clear. It's rare that the questions are answered so directly. Have you seen Barsine? She's positively glowing. She asked if she would have Iskander's son, and the oracle actually replied "yes", clearly. It's rare, it's unique!' He peered at me. 'Do you understand? Why are you crying again? Aren't you happy for Barsine? If I remember, the other night you said that you wished that she had a baby, and she will! A boy! Won't Iskander be pleased? He's

244

always wanted a son. He'll be a wonderful father. I'm sure …'

'I know what I wished,' I said. 'Just shut up! I think I liked you better when you ignored me!'

He stepped backwards as if I'd hit him. His face hardened. 'I don't understand you,' he said. 'Not at all.'

'You can never understand me,' I cried. 'No one can.'

We faced each other uncertainly. He was angry, I could tell, but something kept him in front of me. 'What about Iskander?' he asked.

'Perhaps Iskander least of all,' I said, my voice breaking. I stared at the horizon. 'It will all be for nothing,' I shouted towards the uncaring mountains. 'Nothing! Do you hear me! Nothing! All this! All his effort, all his dreams, all his children, everything, gone!' I shook my fist at the empty sky and screamed. 'Damn you! Damn …' I got no further. Plexis leapt forward and grabbed my arm.

'Stop it!' He pulled me to him and held me immobile. 'Don't do that,' he begged. 'You don't know what you're saying.'

'I do know, that's the problem,' I said, struggling against him.

'If the others see you, or hear you, they'll think you're mad!' His body was tense, a coiled spring.

In the struggle I'd lost his cape and my tunic had fallen off my shoulders. Our naked bodies were pressed together, chest to chest, thigh to thigh. I was shivering, I was afraid my nose would betray me again, and I'd already lost too much blood. I was feeling light-headed.

Or maybe it was Plexis. I had gone too long without a

lover. My body hated solitude, it wanted to be touched, held, and possessed. With a groan, I wrapped my arms around his neck and dragged him to the ground on top of me. I arched my back, feeling his penis pressed to my belly. I found his hand and guided it between my legs. He touched me and I moaned. I kissed his chin, his neck and then his mouth, wanting him, needing him. He responded with passion. Then he pushed me away and started to get up. I grabbed him and pulled him back on top of me. He struggled, but he was aroused, and although his head might have been saying 'no', his body betrayed him. I managed to get him inside me, but he thrust only once before pulling away again.

'No!' I cried, panting. I grabbed him and rolled him over, straddling him, intending to rape him. But then I got a look at his face. It was terrified.

'Damn you, Plexis,' I cried. 'Damn you, then, and your big brown eyes. Oh … damn!'

He uttered a startled laugh. 'Do you want to have me killed?' he asked. 'What price do you think will be on my head if Iskander knows I've touched you?'

'Is that the only reason?'

He blushed. 'No, of course not, but I won't play games with you. I said I'd never understand you, and I won't. But I respect you.'

'Oh, God.' I rolled over on the ground and stared up at the sky. 'The man I just tried to rape says he respects me.'

My body was burning with lust. That's the only thing I could feel at the moment. I closed my eyes. It was torture. I was surrounded by half-naked or fully naked men, and my husband had been sleeping with his first wife for over three weeks now.

I felt a gentle touch between my legs, and I moaned. 'Don't do that unless you plan to finish what you start,' I growled.

'The oracle said I'd go east and see the sacred river. This is west, and this stream isn't sacred, so I suppose I won't die this afternoon.' Plexis lowered himself onto me and took possession of my body. I wrapped my legs around him and pulled him in deeper. We said nothing for a long time. He moved slowly, thoughtfully, while I came, and came, and came again. All the tension left my body, all the frustration I'd been feeling. My headache disappeared completely. I hadn't realized just how tightly I'd been strung. His movements accelerated, and his breath came in short gasps. I rolled over and pushed him back to the ground, holding his shoulders, grinding my hips into his until he gave a hoarse cry and spent himself inside me.

We lay near the stream, watching the water flow, not talking. Actually, I had no idea what to say. Maybe he respected me before, but now? I wasn't sure I respected myself. I was supposed to be madly in love with my husband. I wondered if I should cry or something.

'How do you feel?' he asked me, after a long silence.

'I feel peaceful,' I said, propping myself up on my elbows and looking at him.

He opened his eyes and smiled at me. He was lying exactly how I'd left him. His body was dappled in the shade, his arms and legs akimbo, his hair tousled, his penis lying sweetly in its curly nest. 'I do too,' he said. 'But how long that will last I don't know. Probably until I see Iskander.'

'Probably. Do you love me?' I asked, curious.

'Love? By the gods, I don't know. I like you. I think you just needed a man, don't fool yourself. I'm familiar with that feeling. Remember, I was perverted when I was young.' He grinned.

I couldn't tell if he was being serious or not.

I was getting cold in the water so I got out and draped his cloak around me and put on my sandals. He picked up my tunic and my skirt. We walked together out of the grove and towards the road.

When we got back to the camp we went to our separate tents. I took off Plexis's cloak and spread it on my bed, and then I lay down on it and buried my face in it. Plexis was both wrong and right. Alexander had hurt me more than I would admit. I knew he didn't love Barsine. I knew that he'd married her for politics, but he shared his body with her, and it tormented me. I felt shut out and alone. I knew he'd come back to me after she left, and I even thought he might love me. I was afraid, because I'd never really loved anyone in my life as much as I loved Alexander. I realized I was changing – that the shell around my heart was cracking open, and it frightened me so much I felt paralyzed. The sorrow I'd felt when I'd lost my son had nearly destroyed me. When he'd been snatched from my arms, I'd lost my mind and blanked out whole months of my existence. The thought of that happening again terrified me. Alexander had made the first crack in my defences, and now I was afraid that the whole dam I'd been so careful to build was about to burst, and I would be swept away. I thought if I could just love

Plexis a little, it would save me.

I hugged his cloak to me and closed my eyes. I was ashamed again. I wondered if I'd ever make a right decision in my life. I could hear my mother's voice, mocking. 'So, Ashley. In trouble again, I see. First you run away, then you divorce. Now what? A baby out of wedlock? A lover? Don't you have enough problems?' I put my hands over my ears and tried to shut out her voice. 'Oh, Ashley, don't try and hide. Stand up straight. Stop snivelling. Don't embarrass me. Grow up. You should be ashamed.' I was. I wasn't surprised to find my nose bleeding. As usual, I'd goofed up. A prisoner in a time not my own, alone, misunderstood, frightened, and desperately in love with a legend.

Someone called my name, softly. I opened my eyes. Plexis was sitting next to me, his face next to mine.

'Why did you come here?' I asked. Then, 'I'm so sorry. I wish we'd never met.'

'Do you really? I hope you're not telling the truth.' His breath was warm on my cheek. 'I came back to get my cloak, and to say thank you.'

I rolled over and sat up. 'Why?'

'Because you gave me something special. I may not be an expert on women, but I'm starting to become an expert on you.' His mouth covered mine, and then his body. He pressed me back onto my bed and we made love again.

'I wanted to show you that it wasn't a mistake,' he said when it was over. 'I wanted to show you that we could do it, and that it wouldn't matter, and it wouldn't change anything. If Iskander can do it, so can we.'

'Are we doing it out of revenge?'

'I don't think so. I think we're doing it because we need each other. You don't know any other way to bind a man to you. Your land must be a very difficult one in which to live. I will be your friend and, if you choose, your lover. I've shown you that I want you.'

'Thank you,' I said. I stretched. My body felt languorous and relaxed. 'But isn't it dangerous here?'

'No. Axiom is with Iskander in Persepolis, Brazza is at the river with Usse helping him gather clay, and there are no soldiers around. Barsine is in the tent snoring. She wouldn't mind anyway.'

I took his face in my hands and kissed him. We became lovers, Plexis and I. Lovers, despite our love for Alexander. Or maybe our love for Alexander was the foundation upon which we stood. I didn't know, but I began to wake up in the morning with a light heart. I was no longer alone.

When Barsine was sure she was pregnant, she decided to return to her people. I was upset. She was the first girlfriend I'd ever had, even though she treated me like a slightly retarded little sister. She spoke slowly and clearly to me –which made her sound even more comical – giving me advice about spear-chucking, arrow-shooting, feeding an army, and giving me little gifts. My favourite present was a short lance made for a woman, with a bronze spearhead. She had been determined to teach me to wield the lance from horseback, and we'd spent hours on the playing field, riding full tilt at a small ring hung from a string. I was supposed to poke the lance through the ring. When I finally did it she slapped me so hard on the back I thought she'd broken some ribs. Then she announced she was leaving, and I burst into tears and embarrassed her by crying on her shoulder.

'I have to leave before the snows block the pass,' she said apologetically. 'My baby will be born into my tribe. It's only right. Why don't you come back with me? Iskander can come in the spring and we can show him his children.'

I dried my tears and sniffed. 'I would love that, but I can't. I don't mean to sound ungrateful, but I don't want to leave Alexander.'

She shrugged. 'I understand, but I'll miss you. I hope we'll see each other soon.'

'I hope so too,' I said sadly. I knew that neither Alexander nor I would ever see the jolly princess again. Her life would most likely end in a siege in Macedonia, prisoner of Olympias, victim of the insane scramble for Alexander's kingdom after his death. I tried to smile bravely, but knowing what the future held for Barsine was too depressing for me. Forty, fifty, a hundred times I nearly opened my mouth to put her on guard against Olympias, but each time the words died in my throat. How could I warn her without changing the future? How could I save Barsine and the baby she carried? Even if I did warn her it would do no good. Once I was erased, the timeline would just continue as if I'd never been there.

At least that's what I'd been told.

People had already tried to fiddle with time.

In school we studied the more famous attempts. The one that tried to save Martin Luther King, the one that tried to save the Archduke Ferdinand, or the one that was

251

supposed to bring back Steven Hawking. Every one had failed miserably. After the debacle of 2089, when the whole world teetered on the brink of disaster after a time-travelling journalist killed Hitler and someone even more diabolical took his place, the time-senders perfected the system of erasure. The undertaking was enormous and cost an astronomical sum. Erasing history meant going to the point where the change occurred and taking out a chunk of time. It's the last resort. Don't ask me how it's done, it's used only in dire need. Mostly, they use correctors to set time right.

When a journalist is sent back in time, he – or she – is left there for exactly twenty hours and then brought back with the molecular magnetic beam to fame and fortune. When a corrector is sent back in time to correct a mistake, he's left there to fend for himself for ever. The job is not coveted. Usually the 'volunteer' is taken out of a prison programme.

How could anyone know if time had actually been changed? If you changed the past, you automatically changed the future, right? Wrong. Well, almost wrong. Most of the butterfly theory is correct. Little things can have enormous consequences. However, big things, things you assume would alter history, are usually swallowed up in what scientists call the 'Molasses Theory of Time'. Time follows its schedule like inertia, starting slowly and then flowing like a bottle of molasses tipped over on a table. The molasses is thick and torpid, but it flows. To stop it one must be very quick. Otherwise, the sluggish, sticky stuff will ooze all over the table. It follows its own schedule, just as time does.

To make sure time isn't changed in any irrevocable way, scientists placed a detailed history book in a permanent molecular magnetic beam located in the exact centre of the magnetic pole of the earth. The beam doesn't send the book anywhere, but it does keep it from becoming altered in any way – no matter what happens when someone goes into the past and modifies time from there. A replica of the book is kept in another room, in a normal environment. After each time trip, the books are compared. The differences show up within a day. Any discrepancies are fed into a computer and the results analyzed.

If there is no danger of time moving from its flow, then the book is closed and everything continues blithely on its way. If, however, the changes are major and cause the flow of time to deviate, then something is done to put it right. Within a year, a 'volunteer' corrector is found and trained and sent to live and die farther away from home than most people ever imagine. A year to train a corrector and pray the mission is a success. After that, the possibility of correcting time becomes improbable and likely to influence the present in calamitous ways. Or so it's theorized. It's never been allowed to go that far. The TCF always erases it.

Because of the high cost, little alterations to the continuum are ignored, and time, like thick molasses, keeps flowing, as it should. Those changes never affect our present because the flow of time tends to glide over flaws without a bubble in its surface. Nor does the history book have the name and date of birth of every human being who ever lived on earth. The faceless mass remains anonymous. A person could go back in time and fade into the background, and no one would ever be the wiser if they did their job well.

At any rate, time-travelling journalists are painstakingly trained to stay neutral and as far removed emotionally from their jobs as possible. The time spent in the past is reduced to a strict minimum, and measures taken to ensure that nothing interferes with the smooth passage of time gone by.

To the time-senders, I had disappeared into the mists of time. After twenty-two hours, finding someone again was nearly impossible. As long as I did nothing to interfere, they wouldn't waste the enormous amount of energy it took to erase me. For as long as I could remember, no one had been erased; it took the equivalent of an act of war to do so. The energy used was extravagant. Erasure was a story I'd heard about, but it hadn't taken place in my lifetime.

I walked an emotional and mental tightrope, loving a man who would die in a few years, knowing the fate that would befall most of my friends. Unable to utter a warning.

I sought out Plexis and walked with him to the top of the hill. We watched the stars shift and blaze in the heavens. We watched the bonfires burning in the camp. We made love on the soft grass and held each other, and sometimes we'd cry.

It's nice crying with someone when you're both crying for completely different reasons. Plexis, because he was so desperately in love with the man who'd killed his own brother, and I, because I was in love with a man whose death was already written in the stars.

Alexander gave a great feast for Barsine the night before she left. Darius came as a guest of honour. It was not the first time Barsine had seen Darius. She had been presented to him shortly after her arrival, and she had gone several times to Persepolis to see him. She treated him with great deference.

Darius bowed to me and I bowed back, but we didn't speak. He was wearing a bright yellow linen robe and his beautiful silk beard, made of thousands of intricate knots. He looked very impressive. He sat between Alexander and Barsine. I was sitting several places away, next to Plexis.

In public, Plexis and I were quite formal. He was polite, but distant. Alexander had even reproached him, telling him to be nicer to me. I wished he'd tell Nearchus, but Nearchus acted the perfect gentleman when Alexander was around. It was when Alexander was not there, that Nearchus let his true feelings show.

That evening I was determined to have a good time. Winter was drawing to a close. Soon Alexander's army would be on the march again and I would start an incredible journey across the Middle East. I was looking forward to it. First, we'd head north to Bactria to seek Paul, and then we would go towards India. I'd always wanted to go to India.

Alexander wanted to see elephants.

He'd seen his first elephant when he'd fought against Darius in Gaugamela. Now his conversations with Darius were filled with questions about what to feed them, how to capture one, and what happened when they stepped on someone.

Darius's elephants were both killed during the battle at Gaugamela, which had saddened him more than losing the battle – so it seemed to me. They had been named Vasi and Kish, and were Indian elephants, captured from a marauder on the very borders of his kingdom in the east. Alexander couldn't wait to go and see one for himself. He was as enthusiastic as a boy, jumping up to mime the lumbering walk of the beasts, or imitating their trumpeting bellows.

Even Darius forgot his customary frown and laughed at Alexander's clowning. He had taken the silken beard off to eat, but it was never out of his reach – always on his lap, or held in his hands and stroked like a cat. He laughed, but then his golden eyes grew sad again, and he sat still, staring into the firelight, his fingers twisting themselves into the glossy silk of his beard. Alexander sat down again and picked up his golden cup. It was a lovely object, shaped like a griffin. The beast's wings held onto the cup while its paws served to hold the cup upright. Darius had offered him the cup when they'd met in Babylon.

'Would you like to come with me to Bactria?' Alexander asked him.

He'd asked in a low voice, but his words carried over to me.

'No, I think I'll stay here, in Persepolis, if you don't mind,' Darius said reflectively.

'As you like. You can visit Stateira in Babylon, if you want,' Alexander offered.

Darius smiled briefly. 'Thank you. Maybe I will. I will give it some thought.' He looked at Barsine and asked,

'Did you have a good visit, my queen?'

She smiled broadly and began to talk about her stay, telling him in great detail about all the sporting events she'd organized and the results of each. He started getting a glazed expression after an hour.

Alexander was talking to a man on his left, a satrap from the village. They had been chatting idly mostly about the crops and the hunting in the region, when suddenly the man said something that made my skin prickle.

'Our oracle died last night,' he said, taking a piece of flat bread and scooping up a helping of lentils with it.

'Oh?' Alexander raised his eyebrows. 'Was it sudden?'

'No, no, she was very old, but we'll have to find a new one. It's a bother. She could have waited until after the spring ceremonies. Now we'll have to get another one quickly, so that the village can organize the sacrifices and festivals. You wouldn't happen to be sending a messenger to Babylon?' This was said in a hopeful tone of voice.

'I do, often.' Alexander was just a shade evasive about his messenger service. He didn't seem to care about spies, but he took extreme care when sending messages. 'What do you want me to say?'

The short, plump man's shoulders slumped in relief. 'Oh, if you could send a message to the syndicate, and tell them we need an oracle right away. If they could possibly get one here before the festival of Apollo, we'd be so grateful. Our village needs to be purified.'

'Purified?' Now Alexander looked interested. 'Why?'

'Just before she died, our oracle said that a stranger had profaned our temple. She wouldn't say any more, but

257

she insisted that the village be purified during the festival of Apollo, or else our harvest would fail.' He shrugged. 'It all depends on whether you believe in that or not. As you can see, our village adopted Greek customs. Our oracle was Greek.' He said that with more than a trace of pride.

'You don't worship the Persian gods?' Alexander asked.

'Some do, still, in the temple of Mazda. But most of us worship Zeus now.' The satrap blushed. 'We wanted to worship the strongest gods, you understand.'

Alexander smiled. 'Well, it's always nice to talk to someone with such a liberal viewpoint. I'll do my best to send a messenger. I hope the new oracle will arrive before Thargelion.' That was May, month of Apollo.

I remembered the dark room under the temple, full of stinging smoke, with the distorted voice of the old woman coming from behind the heavy curtain. I shivered. She was dead now, and with her gods.

I stared at the satrap, who was busy stuffing his mouth with food. He seemed like a nice fellow. Modern, forward-looking, willing to change gods if some proved stronger than others. Well, why not? We traded in our cars. We dumped our computers for newer, more powerful models. We changed husbands and wives, tossing the old ones away, getting different, more interesting ones. If we found another god who was stronger, better, more merciful than our god, mightn't we change too? I nibbled on a crust of bread and wondered.

Darius was looking at me. I saw a flash of gold. His yellow eyes reflected the firelight. I smiled, but he turned his head. He still hadn't forgiven me. I couldn't blame him.

Barsine and Alexander left before anyone else. They went back to his tent to spend their last night together. Plexis caught me staring after them, but his startled glance showed he had never expected me to be watching them with so much pity. I smiled quickly, but he didn't answer. His eyes were searching, worried. I gave his hand a squeeze and went back to watching the sparks fly upwards from the fire.

The party ended after that. Like most parties when the host leaves early, it fell apart. Some die-hards insisted on playing flutes and drums until dawn, but most people left right after Alexander, fading into the night, shadows walking back towards the village or the camp.

Darius left, surrounded by his honour guard; three of his generals he'd chosen to accompany him into exile. He bowed to Nearchus, and Plexis, but didn't even glance at me. Plexis looked startled; after all, I was Alexander's wife, but Nearchus's face was expressionless. Lately, Nearchus had been watching me closely. Perhaps he was wondering what would happen when Barsine left. He never tried to hide from me the fact that he was attracted to Alexander. Barsine had been very nice to Plexis after throwing him out of the tent. I guessed Alexander had something to do with that. But she had been fooled by Nearchus, who had the sense to make his advances to Alexander well out of her sight. However, I had seen them embracing. Nearchus's face had been intense, but Alexander's had been inscrutable. I couldn't tell what Alexander was feeling. Nearchus was a Greek admiral, and Alexander admired him greatly. He also knew he needed him, and Alexander, as I was discovering, could be absolutely ruthless.

Barsine left early the next morning. Trumpets blowing, seashell sky above, spring grass pale green on the fields, and the horizon blue as an opal. I waved until she was out of sight. Thirty of her giant tribesmen accompanied her on her journey. The rest were assimilated into Alexander's army.

The day passed quietly. The soldiers cleaned up the remains of the banquet. Alexander went to Persepolis to see Darius. Usse went to gather herbs, and I wandered around the hillside wondering if now Alexander would ask me to rejoin him in his tent, or if he'd leave me in my own tent. Sunlight sparkled on white quartz, and I amused myself searching for the prettiest pieces. I also picked some spring flowers, watched as two snails made love to themselves, and wondered what to do about Nearchus. He was standing guard in front of Alexander's tent, probably waiting for me to make my move.

I was waiting for Alexander. I had no idea what he was feeling about me. He had given himself wholly to Barsine, and I had faded into the background like a good little ghost. Now she was gone, and I was sitting on a gentle slope, wondering if I should start watching out for poison.

A cloud of dust appeared on the road leading to Persepolis. Someone was fast approaching. I could make out shrill cries now. The air was so fresh and still, sound travelled through it like water. I stood up and shaded my eyes. It was one of Alexander's messengers, the one jokingly called 'Hermes' because of his incredible swiftness. He was small and light, a consummate rider. He was the equivalent of a Pony Express rider, and he boasted he could go as many as four days without sleep.

I scrambled down the hill. Whatever had happened must be important. Soldiers were jogging towards the rider.

I reached the bottom of the hill just as Hermes flung himself off his steaming pony. Nearchus waved everyone back and said, 'What is it?'

Hermes paused to gasp for breath and cried, 'Darius has escaped! He left this morning with one of his generals. Iskander has decided to raze the city. All the soldiers are to join him there. He has given me messages to send to Babylon, Athens, and Ecbatana. Where's the scribe?'

Nassar stepped forward and bowed, his narrow face stern. 'I am here. We can begin.' Since being appointed my translator and camp scribe, he had become important. Alexander now trusted him with messages he sent all the way to Athens. He even wrote in hieroglyphics, sending notes to Egypt and Alexandria.

Hermes and Nassar went into Alexander's tent to write the letters, while Nearchus rapidly gathered the army together and marched towards Persepolis. They were about to destroy the fabulous city.

I shuddered. Whatever had happened, Alexander must be enraged to want to do that. He'd told me: 'I do not destroy cities, I build them.' What could have made him so angry? I stood in the shade of the fig tree, undecided. Should I go or should I stay here? Finally, curiosity overcame caution. I put a bridle on the grey mare and cantered off towards Persepolis.

I caught up with the army as they came into sight of Persepolis. The city was empty of all its treasure; the endless caravan of heavily laden camels and donkeys leaving the city had ceased. Now the gates stood open, and a strange wailing was heard. I wondered what it was. Was it some sort of weird, warning trumpet? Whatever it was, it made the hair on the back of my neck stand up. I stayed well back, letting the soldiers file into the city and line up on the immense plaza. Then I rode my mare slowly up the stairs, her hoofs echoing on the stone.

When I arrived at the plaza, I saw what had been making the sound. Two men were hanging by their wrists from a pole suspended over the king's throne. They had been stripped of their clothes and were now being stripped of their skin. Bit by bit. Three soldiers with thin knives were carving them up, alive.

Darius sat on the king's throne.

I gasped. He was supposed to be gone!

Nearchus had seen me coming, and he stalked to my horse and grasped her bridle.

'Come,' he said harshly. The soldiers parted as he led me towards the gruesome scene.

I sat very still on my mare's back. As we got closer, I saw that it was not Darius, but a man who looked like him. He was tightly tied to the throne, his head held upright with rope. He was dressed in ceremonial robes and wore the beautiful silk beard. On his head was a golden crown. His eyes were open, staring up at the men writhing and shrieking above him. Blood dripped down and spattered his face. He didn't move and I wondered at his stillness. Then I saw the crimson stain beneath the beard. The beard didn't quite hide it. His throat had been cut.

'Who was he?' I whispered.

'One of Darius's slaves. He took his master's place while Darius escaped.'

'But … but …' I faltered, at loss for words. 'Who are the men being punished?'

'The satraps who helped Darius,' said Nearchus. 'They are being executed.'

I didn't move. Nearchus held my horse's bridle. I sat frozen in horror. Something warm fell on my hands and I knew it was blood. It fell from my nose in a crimson cascade, staining my robe, my hands, and the horse beneath me. The sun in the plaza was dazzling on white marble. Everything was white, bone-white and scarlet. The men's screams were dwindling.

I lifted my arms towards Alexander. He was standing behind the slave, his face as empty as the dead man's, watching me, his eyes blazing with something like hatred. 'I had nothing to do with this!' I cried, then there was a roaring in my ears and I lost consciousness.

Nearchus managed to hold me on the horse. As soon as my head cleared, I rode back to the camp. I left to the sounds of the city being smashed to pieces and the wails of the dying satraps. The dead slave sat and watched, impassive. After the city was ruined he was the only thing left, sitting on his throne in the midst of a shattered palace. They left the dead satraps hanging.

I didn't turn back once. The sound of shattering marble was like the breaking of bones.

That evening Alexander held a meeting with his generals. He was grim and pale beneath the dust and smoke stains. He ordered everyone to be ready to march at first light. We were going after Darius, who was headed for Ecbatana, the city where the treasure of Persepolis was waiting.

Chapter Fifteen

I had thought myself in disgrace but it wasn't so. After his speech, Alexander came to my tent. I had been packing, and now everything was neatly arranged in my small sandalwood box. I had bathed and my hair was still damp.

Alexander paused for a moment at the threshold of my tent, then stepped in. His presence filled it, making it seem tiny. Before, I had thought it too large and empty. Now it was full of a man whose body seemed to burn hotter than anyone else's. My back was to him, but I could feel him as if he'd touched me.

'Ashley?'

I turned. 'Alex!' I held my arms out again, but this time he came to me. I put my head on his shoulder. Everything was all right. 'I missed you.'

'I missed you, too. I'm sorry.' He held me lightly.

'About what?'

'About today. About our son. About Barsine. About everything. Plexis told me about your donkey.'

I stiffened at the mention of Plexis, then relaxed. It didn't matter. Alexander was here, in my arms, and I was happy. 'I didn't know Darius was going to flee,' I said.

'No one did. How could they? He went to join his family, did you know that?'

'His family?'

'Yes, he has a wife, children, and a mother, like most

265

people.' He chuckled, stepping back and holding me at arm's length. 'His mother is a wonderful lady, you'll like her. She's nothing like Olympias. She's, well, motherly.'

'I'm going to meet Darius's mother?'

'Of course. I wouldn't drag you all the way to Ecbatana and not present you.'

'Alexander, what about Paul?' I managed to keep my voice level. 'I thought we were going after our baby.'

'We are.' He pulled me into a tight embrace, then stepped back. 'We'll be going in the right direction. At Ecbatana, we'll get fresh supplies and rest the army.' He paused. 'I didn't tell you because I didn't want to worry you, but Bactria is enemy territory. We'll have to pass through Barsine's father's territory. She is carrying messages for me. They should let us through, but he's allied with Darius. We have to get to Ecbatana as fast as possible.'

I listened to him, the implications of what he'd said sinking in slowly. I'd been living in a daydream where Alexander's army could just sweep into some satrap's territory and demand his child back. 'I'm sorry,' I whispered. He'd never planned to go so far. He should be back in Babylon ruling Persia. Instead, he was spurring his army into battles, and I'd seen how many men were wounded and died. Were all their deaths my fault? I must have blanched, because he grabbed my arms.

'You'll love Ecbatana. And Darius's family is very kind. His wife is believed to be the most beautiful woman since Helen of Troy. You must tell me if it's true.'

I managed to speak in a normal voice. 'Why? You've never seen her?'

'No, in Persia the women live in separate palaces. There's the men's palace, and the women's palace,' he explained, as if I hadn't caught on.

I made a face. 'And in Ecbatana I'm supposed to stay in the women's palace, right?'

He smiled brilliantly. 'Right.'

'I thought you were on my side,' I said.

'You know what I miss,' he said suddenly. 'I miss swimming with you in the evenings, talking, floating on our backs in the warm water, watching the stars, and fighting crocodiles.'

I looked at him sharply, but the fun had gone out of his face. 'I miss that too,' I admitted. 'But it seems so far away now.'

'The army gets bigger every day,' he continued. 'More and more people following me. The other day the scribes counted thirty new families. Families! Men, women and children! Do you think I should allow it?'

I wondered about that. History books had alternately described Alexander's army as 'a lean, mean, killing machine,' and as 'an unwieldy Dionysiac procession of soldiers, fortune-tellers and whores.' Which was the true description? Perhaps somewhere between the two. I had seen from experience that some people attached themselves to the army for the space of a journey. They wanted to go in the same direction as the army, and they tagged along for protection, food, and company. When they arrived at their destination, they fell off like ticks from a dog. I saw nothing alarming about several families going to Ecbatana, and joining the army to do so. The soldiers had wives, the wives had children, and they tagged along at the rear of the army, camping a few kilometres away. The soldiers went to the 'family camp' when they were off-duty. When Darius had been at war, he had hauled his entire household along; Plexis had told me all about that. However, Darius had been in his own kingdom, and his army had been going from one residence to another. Alexander was going into hostile territory.

'I don't know what to tell you,' I said. 'It's probably not important. They might just want to go along with you north to Ecbatana. Who knows?'

Alexander looked uncertain. He had chosen a seat on the floor, on a small grass mat, and he was plucking at it, pulling pieces of grass out and then shredding them. I cleared my throat. 'Is anything else worrying you?' I asked. He didn't look quite like the confident king I'd been used to seeing.

'I had a strange dream last night,' he said. 'And I wanted to tell you about it. But I'm not sure how to start.'

'At the beginning,' I said gently.

He smiled faintly but his voice was strained. 'I saw a swallow flying in a clear sky. It was so happy, so free, just soaring through the air. I watched it for the longest time. It seemed as if my heart were flying also, and I was filled with a wild joy. Then someone called my name. I looked down and I saw I was in the middle of a raging battle. Men were fighting and falling all around me, while I had been staring at the bird in the sky! My friends were all dead. While I had been watching the sky, they had been killed! Everyone was waiting for me to give orders, to tell them what to do, and I had been looking at a bird. The swallow swooped down from the sky and landed right on my helmet. And then I woke up.'

He was staring at me with a frightened expression so I hastened to reassure him. 'It was only a dream,' I said. 'Don't worry.'

'I wrote to Aristotle about it. I wonder what he will say.'

'He'll say, "Don't worry, it was only a dream." I think it means you feel that you have too much responsibility, and you believe your men cannot function without you. Why don't you give more duties to your generals and try and relax a bit. The world will still turn when you're gone, you know.' I had meant it as a joke but Alexander took it seriously.

'You're right,' he said. 'The world will turn whether I exist or not. I must stop trying to do everything myself.' He heaved a sigh and leaned back on his elbows, his handsome face in shadow. I had to lean to get a good look at him.

'What else is there?'

'Oh, nothing. Rumours, things I hear. Don't worry. You're right. I have to start to let the world turn without my trying to push it along.' He pulled me down on top of him. 'I couldn't do this with Barsine.'

I giggled. 'You're not supposed to talk about another woman when you're with me.'

'No? And just what am I supposed to talk about?'

'About how much you love me, and how you can't do without me, and how we'll always be together.'

'Mmmm, that's a nice thing to say,' he murmured into my ear. 'And do you feel the same about me?'

'You know I do,' I whispered.

'Then tell me, please?' His eyes were huge, the little boy staring out of them. A king on the surface, a child beneath, trying to hide a keen need for love and approval.

'I love you, I love you, I love you, Alexander, and I'll never leave you, and I can't live without you.' My lips found his and we kissed. His kisses were long, languorous, and sweet, and I felt my body dissolving into his. I was in love with the sun god, with a shooting star, with a legend, with Alexander.

Later, much, much later, we lay on our backs and Alexander pointed to the constellations and told me stories about them. I was fascinated, but my thoughts slowed and swirled around as sleep claimed me. I fell into a deep slumber that lasted until the trumpets blew just before dawn.

Alexander had gone, but Brazza was there. He busied himself rolling up my rugs and putting my bedding in a large bundle. There was a donkey tethered outside my tent; its large, furry ears pricked forward, its soft eyes questioning. It was a pale grey donkey, not as white as *White Beauty* had been, but nearly. She had a red tassel hanging from her bridle, and Brazza motioned with his hands, telling me she was a gift from Alexander. And I was not to bring her to visit any oracles. I smiled, a lump in my throat. We loaded my baggage onto the donkey. It consisted of one small sandalwood box, a rug to sit on, and an extra cloak in case it rained.

The sun was just starting to colour the sky pink. While Brazza took my tent down and put it on a packhorse, I went towards a large campfire. I smelled breakfast cooking, and because I'd missed dinner, my stomach was growling. An endless line of soldiers was waiting to get bread. Cooks were busily knocking the loaves out of the clay pots in which they were cooked, Egyptian-style, and handing them out. The cooks usually worked all night, making enough loaves to feed the army. There were also large baskets full of onions and garlic for the soldiers. Another kettle held cold lentil stew. The soldiers folded this into flat bread and placed it carefully into their pouches. The men were ready. They had their breakfast, lunch, and dinner and they would line up again tomorrow morning. Their diet was basically the same, with fresh fruit when the season permitted, honey sometimes, and meat when there was a ceremony or sacrifice. I hadn't seen any dried or salted meat, although salt fish was sometimes to be found.

Usse was standing next to the fire, watching the soldiers as they filed by. If he spotted someone who looked ill he would pull him out of line and examine him. There were a few infected sores, some fevers, broken teeth, and one broken nose. Usse treated most of them on the spot. Broken teeth were the most common. The grain from which the bread was made was stone-ground, and bits of stone were often left in the dough. The result was a cracked molar. Usse knocked the broken teeth out with a wooden hammer and chisel. Often they were replaced with false teeth carved from ivory, and the soldiers often had one or two in reserve. I chewed everything very carefully.

After breakfast, everyone found his place in the long

line and the march began. Alexander was always at the head of his troops, and he set a rapid pace. All morning long, the camp emptied itself out. I stayed until last. I wasn't in any particular hurry. I knew I'd catch up as soon as the army stopped for the night.

When the sun was fully risen, the last soldiers had left. The priests, women, children, and families were loaded into their wagons and left soon after the soldiers. The pack animals with all the tents and food were led off. The bathhouse was dismantled and packed up. Everything was gone. I went back to the empty place where my tent had stood, and picked up a piece of white quartz. It made me think of Plexis, and I slipped it into my pouch.

I saw the first of the villagers appear on the road, eager to see what had been left behind. They would glean whatever they could.

I untied my donkey and started down the road. The dust had settled somewhat, and I slowed my pace. I had no wish to catch up with the army yet. By early afternoon it was getting hot, and I had developed three new blisters on my feet. I picked some reeds and long grass from the banks of a stream to plait a makeshift hat. It kept the sun off my head, and I made one for my new donkey as well.

She plodded along at my side, content to walk when I walked and stop when I stopped. We ate lunch in the shade of a large locust tree. A shallow brook bubbled merrily. I took off my sandals and dabbled my sore feet in the cool water. My donkey was grazing nearby. I rested my head against the tree and closed my eyes. It was so peaceful. The only sounds I could hear were the bees buzzing in the tree, and the water gurgling over smooth stones – and the sound of hoofbeats.

Hoofbeats? I sat up and peered down the road. In the shimmering heat, it was hard to make out details. A horseman was hurrying toward me. I stood, unsure of what I should do. Hide? Run? Wave?

The horse drew to a walk, and then pulled up. Plexis got off and shook the dust out of his cloak and hair. He didn't speak, but came and sat by my side, splashing water from the brook over his face and arms, drinking deeply. He smelled like hot grass, sun and dry dust. His face was sunburned, making his eyes brighter. I cleared my throat, suddenly shy with him.

'Why did you come back?' I asked, when it seemed clear he wouldn't speak first.

He frowned and looked at his hands, and I realized that he was feeling just as awkward as I was. 'I was sent here to make sure you were all right. Iskander was worried.'

I smiled then. I had to smile. I couldn't help it. Plexis was next to me. He'd come back, and I knew that as much as I loved Alexander, I loved Plexis. 'Ah, then, that's OK.' I looked sideways at him. I couldn't stop grinning. 'I'm glad you came.'

He was still staring down at his feet, two spots of red on his cheeks. 'Oh? Why?'

'Because I'm in love with you, Plexis, that's why.'

'You can't be. You love Iskander.'

'I know. It seems impossible, doesn't it? Iskander is so, so ... I don't know. He's the king. I love him because of who he is, but I love you for what you are. Oh, I give up. I can't explain. But I'm glad to see you.' I leaned over and kissed his cheek.

273

'I'm glad, too. But I don't know why.' He groaned and flopped backwards, lying on the grass, his arms over his head, his eyes closed. 'I think maybe we're both mad.'

'I don't think so. I'm not, anyway. I just think you're nice and I like being with you. If I weren't married to Iskander, I'd marry you.'

'But you *are* married, and that's the problem.'

'No it isn't.' My voice was gentle. 'You love Iskander more than you love me, and I think you're jealous of me. But I also think you love me a little, and I'll always be happy with that.'

'That's what I was going to say to you,' he said, but then he didn't say any more and we sat holding hands under the locust tree while the bees droned in the fragrant blossoms.

He put his hand on my belly and felt the slight roundness. 'It's getting bigger,' he said.

'Mmm. It's growing. Soon I'll have a bump, and then I'll start to look like a hippo with hormone problems.'

'There you go again with hormones. What are they? Can you tell me? Do they always cause problems in your land? Are they like criminals?'

I chuckled. 'Hormones are things that control your body. They convey messages from different parts of your body. When you're growing they say "Make hair here! Make these breasts grow!" They also make milk when you have a baby. When you're a teenager they go crazy, your whole body is changing, and they make you go a bit mad too. That's why you were so eager to make love when you were a teenager. Your hormones were going full-tilt. Everything is emotion; the brain goes down the drain when you're a teenager. You felt everything more strongly. Love, hate, sorrow, joy ... all because of hormones.'

Plexis made a wry face. 'But what do these hormones look like? I've never seen any! Aristotle never taught us about them. Are they just in women, perhaps? Aristotle doesn't know much about women, he'll be the first to tell you that.'

'No, they're not just in women. Men too, and animals have them. Like a stallion prancing in front of a mare – it's hormones. They take a little boy and make him into a man. When a woman menstruates, it's hormones.'

'Where did you learn all this? Was your teacher a great philosopher? Did he write a thesis on these hormones? Can I read it?' His interest was real. He had a quick mind, eager to learn and open to new ideas.

I sighed. 'No, no writings exist right now for this. It's not philosophy, it's science. Or biology, I suppose.' I made a face. 'I wish I could tell you more, but I didn't like science class. The only subjects I appreciated were the dead languages like Latin and Greek. They seemed romantic to me ...' I broke off, embarrassed. When my guard was down I talked too much.

'Dead languages?' Plexis looked confused.

'Nothing. Forget it.' I got to my feet and made a great show of brushing off my cloak and putting on my grass hat. 'We'd better go, it's getting late.'

Plexis obliged me by forgetting what I'd said about the dead languages.

We talked while we meandered toward the encampment. Plexis wanted to know all about hormones, although I wondered if he believed me. He looked sceptical, but asked pertinent questions. I tried to remember all my biology. I wished I'd read more science books. Plexis, like Usse, believed right away in the presence of germs. Aristotle had started teaching about an invisible world, a world he had just started to discover. He did all sorts of experiments with mould and fruit flies. Plexis was fascinated by all that.

However, he firmly believed the earth was flat.

He and I walked along, our feet stirring up little puffs of dust. I tried to convince him the world was round, but he wouldn't listen. Then I told him I didn't believe in fate.

He stared at me, shocked. 'How can you not believe in fate?' he asked, with worry in his eyes. 'It's like saying you don't believe in the gods themselves! Or in the spirits that live in the trees and water!'

'I suppose it is,' I said wryly.

He gaped at me. 'I've heard tell that the gods always dissemble themselves when they come to visit with us mortals, so *are* you a goddess in disguise?'

'No, don't be silly. You know I'm not.' I sighed. 'What I want to say is, I believe that you can make what you wish of your own life. I don't believe that my life is already traced out and everything I do is already written.'

'And yet it is,' Plexis said gently. He took my hand. 'It is already written, and nothing you can do will change it. The gods have decided our lives, and we can do nothing about it but bend to their wishes.'

'Or caprices.' I was ironic but he didn't seem to notice.

'Or caprices. We are all part of the grand design. Everything that has been and will be is written in the stars or hidden in our very bodies. That's why the oracles study the heavens and examine the entrails and blood of sacrifices. They do it so we may see what will be.'

'Aren't you afraid to know?' I asked.

'Of course, but the future is told to us in riddles, and it is up to us to seek the truth behind the answers.'

'But why should the gods play games with us? If you believe in fate, how can you go on living, knowing that you have no choice in life? If I thought that my whole life was already decided for me, I would feel as helpless as a paper boat in a raging river. Can you understand?'

'I do.' He smiled. In the half-light of the evening his teeth gleamed. 'I understand exactly what you mean. I feel as if I am a paper boat, and Iskander is the river who is carrying us in his raging torrent.'

'As long as we both agree,' I said a little shakily.

At the encampment we parted without a word or a gesture.

Nearchus stood in the shadow of Alexander's tent and greeted me as I walked over. Brazza took my donkey and led her away. I lifted my sandalwood box off her back and ducked into Alexander's tent. He was not there. The long march to Ecbatana had started, and he would be submerged by generals, priests, soldiers, scribes, and all the people following in his wake; a flotilla of tiny paper boats.

I ate dinner in the tent with Brazza, Axiom and Usse. We were all tired after our first day of marching. I was emotionally drained as well. The talk about fate had shaken my belief in myself. I almost felt as if I could believe that everything that had happened was preordained. But that would mean that I had no choices, or rather, that my choices had already been made. It gave me vertigo.

I was also feeling confused about love. My feelings for Plexis were complex. I couldn't understand how I could love him when I loved Alexander. I wondered if I were a product of my civilization, or if the people in Alexander's time felt the same.

I nibbled on my bread, a frown on my face, trying to sort out my thoughts. Usse, always perceptive, spoke first. 'What is bothering you, my lady?'

I looked up quickly. My first instinct was to lie, of course, and say, 'Nothing,' but Usse was a friend now, and I couldn't do that. I took a deep breath. 'Do you think it's possible to love more than one person at a time?'

'Like Iskander loving Barsine and you?'

'Something like that.' I smiled weakly.

Usse tilted his head to the side. 'When I was in school, we had long debates about many things. Eros, or love, was a common subject. Some men said women were incapable of love, and that it was only real if it were pure, as between friends and equals. If that is true, then of course it is possible to love more than one person, because one usually has more than one friend.'

'What about a mother's love for her children?' I asked.

Usse smiled. 'That was my argument during these discussions. I said that a mother's love was the strongest, and the fact that a woman loved all her children seemed to suggest that love was not exclusive.'

'I don't know – some mothers have favourites and some mothers don't seem to love their children at all. I doubt Olympias really loves Iskander.'

'She is a witch.' It was Axiom. He listened to our conversations, but rarely joined in. He had been with Alexander since he was a boy, so perhaps he knew more than we did about Olympias.

'What do you mean?' I asked.

'She raised Iskander to be her consort, not her son. She always treated him as a lover, not as a child.' He spat angrily out the tent door and Usse and I raised our eyebrows in surprise. 'She's no natural mother, she's evil,' he said darkly.

'Oh!' I was shocked. I hadn't known about that. 'But, if that's true, does it mean Iskander is depraved?'

'No,' said Axiom, and he sounded sad. 'But it means that all your talk is for naught. Iskander doesn't know what love is. Here's what I believe. Love is something you have to learn, like language. Some people speak well, and some don't know all the words or grammar because they weren't taught. Love is like that. Love is learned. Your mother is your first teacher. From her, you learn that you are worth loving. First, you must learn to love yourself. Your friends teach you about loving others, and sharing. Your lovers teach you about physical love. Then you marry, and you put all of that together. Finally, you have children, and you learn what it is to love selflessly. When you know all that, you are ready for the lesson of God's love. God's love is all, and all is one, and all is love.'

I was startled. 'God? Then, you believe in just one god?'

Axiom nodded. 'I do. I was brought up by a Jew

279

before being sold to Philip of Macedonia. I still worship the one God.'

'So, do you think it's possible for me to love more than one man at a time?' I asked, forgetting to dissemble.

'More than one? Of course, it's possible. If you truly love one person then you love all mankind,' said Axiom gently. 'You cannot love only one person. It goes against the nature of love.'

I looked at Usse. 'What do you think?'

He smiled. 'I think I agree with Axiom.'

'And what about Iskander, if his mother did, uh, did what you said, how does that affect him?'

Axiom shrugged. 'I don't know. He learned about love backwards. His mother taught him all about hate and jealousy, his father taught him about power and might. He learned the pleasures of the flesh before his mind learned to love himself. He fell in love with his friend and then he killed him. What can he have learned? I don't know. Perhaps Iskander himself doesn't know. He is touched by God's grace, though. You have only to see him to know that.'

'Perhaps he is a god,' said Usse pensively. 'That's what I've heard.'

'Why? Because of the temple in the desert?' Axiom sounded angry.

'Yes. They have started calling him the son of Amon.'

'His mother's work,' Axiom snarled. 'When Philip married Cleopatra, Olympias started spreading rumours that Iskander wasn't really his son. She told stories about being visited by a serpent, and that the snake was the god Zeus-Amon. The boy, Alexander, believed her. She turned him against his own father.'

'Well, she'll come to no good,' I said.

'May God hear you,' said Axiom.

I nearly laughed, then grew sombre again. My question hadn't been answered the way I'd hoped.

Yet, when Alexander joined me late that night, slipping into bed beside me, and taking me in his arms, my heart was filled with joy.

The next day was like the one before. The army lined up before daybreak in front of the bonfires and took their rations. Everyone marched towards Ecbatana, and Plexis and I walked slowly behind the cortège.

'Do you believe in one god or many?' I asked him.

'Why, many, of course. Don't you?' He was amused, as if my question was of no importance.

'And what if I told you I didn't know what I believed in? I was raised to believe in one god, but now I'm not so sure. I mean, I don't even know if I believe in any god.'

He looked at me, his face twisted in disbelief. 'You don't mean what you're saying, surely!'

I didn't reply, because I had no answers.

The road was long, and it took us nearly a month to reach Ecbatana. I stopped walking and rode on my little donkey, *Sibyl*, because I felt ill. I had odd pains, and Usse told me I should rest as much as possible.

I didn't want to tell Alexander; as we approached Ecbatana he had practically stopped sleeping. I had no idea how anyone could go so long without sleep, but he seemed driven. Meetings with his generals lasted late into the night, and I discovered he had already started making plans to head north to Bactria. One night I managed to

281

stay awake and wait for him. As he slid into bed and curled up around me, I whispered, 'Is everything all right?'

He laughed sleepily. 'Yes, and it will get better and better. Soon we'll be in Ecbatana, and we'll stay there until the babe is born.' He cupped his hands around my tummy. 'And as soon as you can travel, we'll go after our first son.'

'How will we find him?' I asked, worried.

'Darius's mother will make him talk. I know her. When she hears what he's done, she will be so angry even the gods will tremble.' He nuzzled the back of my neck. 'You smell so nice, like spring flowers.'

'Thank you,' I said, turning around and cupping his face in my hands. I looked into his eyes. Ever since Axiom had told me about his childhood, I'd felt a deep pity for him. Though my mother had been cold and unfeeling, she hadn't done as much damage to me as Alexander's mother had to him. She had nearly crippled him in ways I couldn't begin to fathom. Yet, he had risen above it. I kissed him. 'I love you, and I think you're wonderful,' I said.

'Do you trust me?' he asked softly.

'With my life.'

'I believe you,' he said, and with something like a sob, gave himself to me.

He didn't fall asleep afterwards, but sat and stared at the doorway. I sat up too, and for the first time I was conscious of Axiom, Usse and Brazza in the tent with us. The curtains were hung and the darkness hid everyone from view, but the night was so still that I could hear their soft breathing. Outside, were the night-time sounds of the camp; the faint jingle of metal, the guards whispering, a baby crying, and someone cursing. There was always someone cursing. I nearly smiled.

'What's the matter?' I asked, stroking his back.

He turned his head, showing me his pure profile. I loved the shape of his nose and his chin. His throat was long and strong, his body made of flowing lines. I wanted him to live for ever. I suppose, in a way, he would.

'I was thinking,' he said quietly, 'of all the different kinds of love.'

'Oh. Did you hear us speaking, then?' In the darkness, I thought I detected a slight pause in the breathing around us.

'I did.'

The air held its breath.

'What do you think, then?' I asked.

'I don't know. I wish I had some sort of conviction, like Usse or Axiom, but I don't. Do you?'

'No. I think it's too complicated. And at the same time, ridiculously simple.' I took a deep breath. 'When you see Paul, I think it will all become clear. It did for me. Since he was taken away I have been living in shadow.'

'I'm sorry,' he said, putting his hand on mine. In the dark, something glittered on his face.

'I'm sorry too.' I knew he was talking about us, though, not Paul. 'Someday we'll have time to swim in the evening again. Things will get easier, and we'll be together, you, and me, and the children. Barsine will be there, she'll organize their games, and Aristotle will teach them.'

He lay down beside me and let my voice lull him to sleep. I talked about where we would go, what his babies would look like, and the games we'd all play together. His body relaxed, his breathing deepened, and all around me the men slept. I thought maybe Axiom was right after all, if you loved one person then you loved everyone.

Chapter Sixteen

The next day we rode into Ecbatana. I was riding next to Alexander. The generals were right behind us, and the whole army stretched into the distance. The gates of the city were flung open to welcome us. Fifty girls dressed in white robes ran ahead and flung rose petals at our feet as we rode through the city toward the palace. Alexander didn't seem to notice them. He gazed straight ahead, his face stern. He didn't acknowledge the people lined up along the road crying his name, waving, and throwing flowers. I was riding the grey mare, and she, being a battle horse, was used to noise and fuss. She didn't even toss her head when flowers hit her.

Bucephalus loved the attention. He arched his massive neck and pranced. The people screamed his name nearly as much as his master's. But nothing moved Alexander until we came in sight of the palace. Then his cheeks lost all their colour and I nearly grabbed his arm, so sure was I that he would faint.

Antipatros was on his right, and he looked at me sharply. I licked dry lips and nodded. I understood his look. It was a warning. Let Iskander handle this. We were riding into Darius's city and we didn't know what he had prepared for us. The fact that Alexander had put me in front with him was a sign. He was coming unarmed. I looked at him again. His face was as white as the egret plume nodding on his golden helmet.

The palace steps were full of brightly dressed people. I wondered where Darius was; I didn't see him.

On the top step was a short, plump woman. She had grey hair, dressed in a chignon. Her robes were of deep purple, edged with gold and green embroidery. Gold chains gleamed in her hair and around her neck, and her arms were heavy with bracelets.

As we rode up she raised one arm and said clearly, 'Hail, Iskander! We welcome our king.'

Alexander let his breath out. Then, with a wide smile, he turned and greeted the crowd on either side of us. There was an eruption of cheers, and two slaves hurried forward to take our horses. Alexander swung off Bucephalus and carefully lifted me to the ground. My legs were numb but I braced myself against him and stood straight. I felt the weight of everyone's gaze upon me, and it nearly crushed me. I wondered how Alexander could survive day after day of this, and decided that he must be superhuman.

We walked up the stairs to the little woman dressed in purple. Then, to my amazement, and to the amazement of all those watching, Alexander knelt and pressed his head to the ground. There was a gasp from the crowd.

'Get up, you silly boy,' she said, but her voice was fond, and her eyes glittered with tears. She pulled him to his feet and hugged him.

'I'm so glad to see you,' he said, his own voice thick with emotion.

They held each other at arms' length and stared. Alexander venerated this woman, and I could do no less than bow before her.

I was glad I'd worn my silk robe. Everyone on the steps was dressed in the most fabulous garments. Gold, green, blue and red glowed in silks and satins. Precious jewels were encrusted in sashes and collars, and flashed in the sunlight. It was overwhelming.

The palace steps were made of pink marble, and the doors were gilded in pure gold. Palm trees grew in huge pots next to each door, and flocks of colourful parrots were chained to their branches. Screeching noisily, they added their raucous cries to the sounds of the crowd. The noise was numbing, battering, and made coherent thought impossible.

As we entered the palace, the heavy doors shut behind us. Sudden quiet made me stagger. Alexander caught my arm and held me close. We stood in a half-circle: Alexander and I, the plump woman, Antipatros and Nearchus, and several of Alexander's generals. For a moment we said nothing, savouring the silence. In the gloom of the palace I noticed many ornately carved screens. Behind them were people. I could see their eyes glisten through the latticework. They stayed hidden, making me nervous.

Alexander presented me to the plump woman – Darius's mother, Sisygambis. Everyone called her 'Sis,' which suited her. She was a comfortable, motherly sort of woman, who nonetheless commanded respect and attention. Her voice was nearly as deep as a man's, and her eyes were a remarkable gold, like Darius's.

She took my arm and led me through the palace to the woman's quarters, chatting in a friendly fashion all the way. I barely had time to look around.

On the steps there had been no young women, and Sisygambis told me, when I asked her about this, that women stayed in their quarters from the time they started menstruating until they reached menopause. Before and afterwards, they could go where they pleased and do as they liked. Older women often studied and were awarded high positions in the government. However, younger women were expected to stay in the *gynecie* and bear children. It was just as well, I thought with a trace of sarcasm. Hormones did tend to get in the way of clear judgment.

Young men were expected to join the army or to farm. Older men could do as they pleased, as long as they had children to support them. Sis talked non-stop, waving her hands to illustrate what she was saying.

We arrived at a dead-end hallway. Two rather fat men with smooth cheeks stood in front of the largest doors I'd ever seen. The doors must have been twenty feet high, and at least as wide. The guards were dressed in red silk robes and carried huge, curved scimitars.

Sisygambis clapped her hands sharply, and the eunuchs opened the doors. Behind them was a garden paradise the size of a football stadium. Full-size trees spread their branches above our heads, and in their branches were more raucous parrots. I could hear water splashing in fountains, and a white jasmine vine twined itself around the arched doorway, welcoming us with its heady perfume. However, after spending a year as a prisoner in one of these paradises, I was suspicious. Sis had to tug my arm before I would enter. With a nervous glance at the armed eunuchs, I crossed the threshold.

She led me down a smooth marble path winding between flowering shrubs and sparkling pools of water, where goldfish glinted and opulent water lilies floated. Over our heads, flowering vines had been trained on arched trellises, forming an exotic canopy of purple, green and white. Perfume filled the air, as well as glittering, jewel-like humming birds, and huge, metallic, blue and green butterflies. In a clearing, sitting on white marble benches, were twenty young women dressed in silks of all the colours of the rainbow.

In their midst was a sloe-eyed beauty with hair as black as the midnight sky and skin like warm amber. She stood up, and I saw she was as tall as I, slender and graceful. She held out her hands and greeted me in perfect Greek. 'Welcome, sister, to our pleasant garden. May you be happy here, each moment of your stay.'

I took her hands and kissed her formally on each cheek. 'I'm honoured by your welcome,' I said. 'My name is Ashley, and I cannot help but be happy here, surrounded by such grace, beauty and kindness.'

Silvery laughs rang out, and a clear voice chided, 'She has a honeyed tongue, Dora. You must try and do better next time!'

This was my introduction to Darius's family. His mother, Sis, presented his wife, Dora, the gentle beauty. His sister was Didtra, a stout woman with the family's light-brown eyes. She was the one with the clear voice. Ithaca and Drypetis were Darius's teenage daughters, tall, willowy girls with black hair and creamy skin. Thanis was Darius's daughter-in-law, a very young girl with a pale face and bright, copper hair. Her eyes were grey-green and very serious. She smiled shyly.

The other women were slave girls. They stood back and bowed but weren't introduced by name. Everyone made me feel welcome, and soon we were sitting in the garden while servants brought us honeyed almonds and cups of cool water on silver trays.

I was glad to rest after my voyage. My back and legs were aching and my bladder was full. I looked for a chamber pot. I wasn't sure how to ask for a bathroom, and I didn't want to sound rude.

Sis perceived my discomfort and pointed out bathrooms behind an ivory screen. I went, and discovered a small room paved in green tiles. There was a marble 'toilet' and a hand basin full of rose-scented water. After travelling with the army so long, and using portable chamber pots or ditches, this was a welcome respite. I washed my hands and face and straightened my robe. I wanted to give a good impression; after all, I represented Alexander. I wondered how long we would stay in this palace. Would Darius meet Alexander here? I hadn't seen him anywhere and didn't dare ask his mother where he was.

I rejoined the women and spent the rest of the afternoon resting in the garden. When the sun started to set, Sis stood up and clapped her hands, giving a signal. Slaves appeared from all sides, and each woman left with her slave. Sis waited until everyone had departed, then she took me by the hand.

'Come, child, I will show you your quarters. Did you bring your slave?'

'No, I don't have one.'

Sis looked taken aback. 'No? How strange. Well, I will give you three slaves for your stay.' She clapped again, and more slaves appeared. They were all either women or eunuchs. 'Hester, Pyron, Millis,' she said, pointing to two women and a stunningly handsome eunuch. 'These are your slaves. Come,' she said to them, and they fell in line behind us. I was uncomfortable, as usual, with slaves. Why couldn't I just pretend they were maids and valets? However, I couldn't. I wondered how to tell Sis I didn't want them, but thought I would probably offend everyone if I did that.

My quarters consisted of three rooms: a spacious bedroom with screened doors opening onto a marble terrace, a dressing room – with my sandalwood box sitting on a low table and looking positively lonely – and a tiled bathroom. There was a sunken bathtub full of hot water and rose petals. 'Oh! This is incredible! Thank you!' My reaction was genuine and Sis looked pleased.

'We dine in two hours. I took the liberty of sending for some robes. They will arrive shortly. Choose what you wish. Hester is a wonderful seamstress – she will alter anything to fit you. Pyron will fix your hair. Send Millis for anything else you need. He is mute, but not deaf.' She kissed me and left. I sat down on a wooden bench and stared at my slaves who were standing in an expectant row. I cleared my throat.

Hester was a woman around fifty. She had iron-grey hair and dark grey eyes. She stood straight, with her hands folded in front of her ample bosom. She was dressed in Persian robes. Pyron was a younger woman, very thin and dark-skinned, with large doe eyes and soft black hair. She wore a short dress of brick red cotton with white stitching along the hem.

Millis was something else. I had rarely seen such a beautiful man. He was tall and broad-shouldered, with dark-brown hair cut short around his well-shaped head. His eyes were honey coloured. I wondered, for a second, if he were related to Darius; he had the same look about him. His mouth was sensuous, his cheeks as smooth as a girl's. The way he was looking at me made the blood rush to my cheeks.

'Um, my name is Ashley. You may call me Ashley. I mean, please do.' I blushed. This wasn't going right. The slaves were looking at me with wide eyes. They hadn't moved. 'What shall I do now?' I asked finally. 'I'm sorry, you're going to have to help me, I'm not used to having slaves.'

Hester stepped forward. She was the oldest, and obviously the one in charge. She bowed. 'Would you care to bathe? Your bath is ready, and the water will not stay warm for long. While Millis helps you wash, I will take your robe and clean it.'

'Thank you, Hester,' I said.

Millis stood in the middle of the bathroom, staring at me, waiting for orders. I sighed. 'Millis?' He blinked quickly, looking at me questioningly. 'Would you mind very much not watching me while I bathe? I'm sorry, but I get embarrassed when men watch me undress. I don't think I need three slaves. You may leave.' I said it gently, but I wasn't prepared for his reaction.

A slow red blush spread up his neck and stained his

cheeks. His eyes actually filled with tears. I turned to Hester. 'What did I say?'

She shook her head, her expression shocked. 'Millis isn't a man. He's a eunuch. You mustn't send him away; he's been given to you. You insulted him by asking him to leave.' Her expression softened when she saw my distress. 'He's an excellent masseur. You'll see. He'll make you feel as if you just slept twelve hours instead of riding all day. Now, don't get upset. Come and take a bath. Here, give me your robe. That's a good girl.'

I handed her my robe and climbed into the warm bath. I was embarrassed and tired, and I didn't feel well. My nose was going to start bleeding again if I didn't get hold of myself, so I took a deep breath and closed my eyes. Warm hands started kneading my shoulders, and I tried to relax. After all, I was surrounded by hundreds of fragrant, pink petals in a white marble bath with a gorgeous man, no, sorry, eunuch, sitting behind me in the water rubbing my back. I felt as if my bones were turning into light feathers, and my muscles loosened like warm taffy. I floated in water scented with roses and kept my eyes squeezed shut.

When he finished with my neck and back, he started on my buttocks and I was helpless to stop him. Then he turned me over, resting my head on a pillow on the edge of the tub. He massaged my feet, my legs, my belly, my hands, and my arms, and soon I had no more strength left. I couldn't even make the effort to open my eyelids.

Millis got to his feet and lifted me out of the bath. He laid me on my bed and dried me off. Then he pulled the soft linen covers over my body and kissed both my eyelids. I was asleep before he kissed the second one.

Chapter Seventeen

I didn't miss supper. I woke up an hour later feeling like a new person. I stretched and yawned. If I were a cat, I would have purred. I sat up in bed and saw I was alone. My outfit had been put on a chair, an ice-blue silk dress that matched my eyes.

I swung my legs over the side of the bed and almost stepped on Millis. He was curled up on a mat. He sat up at once and bowed. I sighed.

'Millis, you can't sleep on the floor. You'll have to find somewhere else to sleep.' He nodded his head, but I put my hand on his chin and held it. 'No, Millis. You don't understand. I won't have it. It's an order. I won't be able to sleep a wink with you lying on the floor. You're a human being, not a pet.'

He looked into my eyes with confusion mixed with fear. His lashes were very long and dark. His eyes were gold and green with metallic glints in them. I touched his smooth cheeks. He took my hand and pressed it to his mouth.

'I want to thank you,' I said softly. 'You are a very talented masseur, and I feel much better now. I hope we'll be friends, but I don't want you sleeping on the floor next to my bed. I don't want to hurt your feelings, do you understand me?'

He nodded briefly, his eyes bright. Cross-legged, he sat

on the floor and put his chin on his hands, studying me. I felt my resolve begin to weaken. Then he leaned back and peered at me. What he saw must have pleased him, because he grinned. I shook my head. This was going to be tricky. I would have to talk to Alexander about it.

I didn't see Alexander. The woman dined in one room, the men in another. Sis told me I would see Alexander when he sent for me. First, he would be expected to meet the satraps, see about organizing the government, and get the city in order.

'Everything is a total mess,' she confessed, her cheeks bright with emotion. 'Darius is a fool. I told him, time and time again. After Granicus I told him. "You silly fool," I said. "You've lost your son, two of your sons-in-law, and your brother. Why not give in to Iskander now? Especially since you know him so well. He'll never give up. Give in now, and he'll let you rule Persia in his stead." Oh, I admit, it wasn't quite the right thing to say. The words 'in his stead' stuck in his throat. He was too proud, and now look where it has gotten him.'

'But where has it gotten him? I mean, I haven't seen him here. Where is he?' I hoped I hadn't heard correctly. Alexander had killed her son, her grandson, and two of her sons-in-law? No, I must have misunderstood. I concentrated on her next words.

'He's fled to Bactria. The silly fool. With Bessus, the satrap of Bactria. And I wish him well. Bessus is a scheming man. They certainly have something planned, but he wouldn't tell me what. He only said, "Mother, Iskander killed my son, and now I have the chance to do the same." But I just laughed; Iskander has no son. Why, child! What's the matter? Millis! Come quick! Carry her to her quarters! Call a doctor! Oh dear, what did I say?'

My nose was gushing blood, and I was half-choking. I flailed my arms, screaming, 'Alexander!' and tried to struggle, but darkness came upon me like a heavy curtain. I must have called for Usse, though, because when I awoke he was kneeling beside me, his kind face drawn in lines of worry.

'Usse,' I cried, 'Oh, Usse, he's gone to kill my son, you must tell Iskander; he's gone to kill my baby,' and then I started crying again, harsh sobs that hurt my throat.

'Hush, hush. Iskander will come shortly. Sisygambis is nearly mad with worry. I told her you were prone to fits of divination, and now she thinks her son is in danger. The whole gynecie is in an uproar.'

'Usse, listen to me. I had a baby. You know that.'

'I know that, yes. The boy Olympias stole from you.'

'Darius kidnapped him, and gave him to someone in Bactria. Now do you understand? Sis told me that Darius left with someone named Bessus and swore to kill Iskander's son, because Alexander killed his son. Is that true?' I asked worriedly. '*Did* he kill Darius's son, his sons-in-law, and his brother?'

Usse bit his lip. 'In a way, it's true. You are surrounded by women who have been widowed or lost sons or brothers to Iskander in battle. Yet they love him still, and you can trust them, I think.'

'You think?'

'Iskander and Darius have known each other since childhood. As children, they played together in the palace. Iskander and Philip were frequent visitors.' He shook his head. 'No one blames Iskander; Persia attacked Greece, not the other way around. Darius is a fool, but Iskander loves him. Now you say he means to kill the babe?' He shook his head. 'Surely he won't do that. He knows that will bring the gods' wrath upon him. It is an abomination to kill an innocent child.'

'Please, you must tell Iskander,' I said. 'They won't let me out of here. I feel like I'm in prison.'

He stroked my forehead. 'You must try to rest. You will lose your child if you lose any more blood. You are far too pale. Drink this and sleep.'

'Usse?' I asked, after I'd drunk a bitter potion and started to feel as if I were floating several inches above my bed.

'Yes?'

'What is this thing with the eunuchs here? Are they allowed to sleep with the women? What is the custom?' I giggled. I didn't know what was in the potion but whatever it was, it was making me awfully indiscreet.

He looked interested. 'The eunuchs? They are the sons of the slave girls who live in the men's quarters. They are often kept as slaves after they've been castrated. The women can sleep with them if they wish. Why?'

'Is Millis related to Darius, do you think?' Millis was standing near the doorway, watching us.

'Probably. Hush, don't worry about it. The slave girls often bear the babes of kings. Millis does look like Darius.'

'And will Iskander have a baby with a slave girl?' I asked, troubled.

'Who can know? Why, is it important?'

'Yes,' I whispered. 'If he does, and it's a boy, you must make sure he's never castrated and never a slave. You tell Sis that I said so as an oracle. Make her scared,' I said, and giggled again. 'Please, Usse, it's important.'

'You love him so much?' he asked.

'More than you think,' I said, 'much more.' I closed my eyes. The potion was making me sleepier and sleepier but I had to know something. 'Usse?'

'I'm here.'

'If Iskander makes love to a slave girl, does it mean he doesn't love me?'

He chuckled. 'No, child, he will always love you. Now sleep.'

I fell asleep to the sound of his warm voice, holding tightly to his hand. But when I woke the next morning, I was holding Alexander's hand. He was kneeling next to me, his face drawn with sleeplessness and worry.

'Alex,' I said, and smiled.

'You know about Darius,' he said simply.

It all rushed back and I blanched. 'How can we stay here?' I asked. 'You killed his whole family! Why did you bring me here?'

'Hush,' his voice was strained. 'You don't know what you're saying. Sis loves me, she will protect you. Darius is a fool.'

'Everyone seems to agree about that,' I said. 'But I don't want to stay here. I want to go after my son.' I closed my eyes. 'What will happen to Paul if we don't catch Darius?'

'No harm will come to him, you must believe me.' Alexander looked at the floor and bit his lip. 'Darius has taken his army with him, and I heard that Barsine's father has joined him. They mean to make war against me, and they're counting on Bessus to rally Bactria around them.'

'How do you know all this?' I asked, licking my dry lips.

'Ptolemy told me. He's been here for months now, keeping Sis safe.'

'Who's Ptolemy?' A nagging pain had started in my back, but I ignored it. It turned into a deep cramp, making sweat stand out on my forehead.

'He's my half-brother.' Alexander cocked his head. 'Are you all right? You look pale.'

'I'm fine. You have a brother?'

'Well, two actually. Ptolemy is the youngest. He's in my army. And then I have another half-brother.' His face darkened. 'He's an idiot, a curse upon the family.'

'What?' I tried to sit up but there was a sharp pain in my abdomen and I gasped. The pain grew and grew, swallowing me. I felt as if my body were a glove being pulled inside out. My stomach cramped and I felt a gush of warmth between my legs. I knew I had lost my baby. 'Get Usse,' I gasped. Alexander leapt to his feet. His voice cracked like a whip, and the slaves near the door disappeared.

'Ashley! Are you all right? Answer me!' He bent over me, shaking my shoulder.

I wished I could faint when I really needed to. Waves of pain carried me along, and all I could do was clench my teeth and try not to scream. I had already given birth, so the pains were not unfamiliar, but they were sharper, more tearing. I tried to speak calmly. 'I'll be all right.' A new pain made me gasp. 'Where is Usse?'

Usse came in with a rush. He took one look at me and his shoulders sagged.

'Don't feel bad,' I said.

He pulled the covers back, and Alexander gave a hoarse cry. The bed was soaked with blood. Usse shook his head sadly. He gave me some of his 'magic potion' and then waited until I'd drifted off. Then he made sure everything was finished. His hands were deft and gentle, and I felt practically nothing. Afterwards he supervised Pyron as she cleaned me and changed my bed linens. I slept then, until the next morning.

In three days, I was better. Alexander wouldn't leave me alone and I had a constant stream of visitors, a thing unheard of in the gynecie. Sis was torn between shock and awe. I didn't know why she was so deferential, until I found out that Plexis had told her I was Demeter's daughter, Persephone.

'Why on earth did you say that?' I asked, angrily. 'Usse already told her I was prone to fits and told the future. Now you go telling her I'm some sort of goddess! It's absurd!'

Plexis bowed his head and looked at his hands, clasped in his lap. 'I was afraid for you,' he said simply. 'When the slaves came searching for Usse, they were panic-stricken. They said you'd been poisoned.' His face twisted. 'I wanted to put the fear of the gods into them. Sis would rather die herself than let anything happen to you now. I had to tell them, don't be angry, please. I'm so sorry about the babe,' he finished, and he turned away so I wouldn't see the pain in his eyes.

However, I had seen it, so I pulled him down, holding him to my chest. I told him that he was the best friend I'd ever had, and that I loved him, and that I would never forget how good he was to me. He put his face into the crook of my neck and his warm breath tickled my skin. I felt at peace. But it didn't last. When Plexis left, a tall dark-skinned man walked in the room. He was escorted by two slaves and Sis.

Sis hardly dared look at me any more, so I wondered who this person could be. He bowed, touching his forehead to the floor. The slaves stood back with wide, spooked eyes, staring at me as if I'd turn into a monster. When I smiled at them they jumped. I sighed.

'O daughter of Demeter,' the man said in a rich, low voice. 'Please grant us this interview. We need your advice.'

I sat up and reached for my robe. I was tired of lying around in bed anyhow, and since I was better, I might as well get up. 'Who are you, if I may ask?'

'Ptolemy.'

I raised my eyebrows. Was this Alexander's half-brother? I smiled and tried to look harmless. 'I'm pleased to meet you, I've heard such nice things about you. Iskander said you were his brother.'

Ptolemy gaped. He looked like a fish gulping for air. Then he recovered. 'No, my lady. I am Ptolemy, son of Lagos. Iskander's brother is also called Ptolemy.'

'Oh.' I blinked. 'I'm sorry. All right.' I put a robe over my shift and tied a silk belt around my waist. 'What can I do for you?' I asked while I laced up my shoes and looked for my sandalwood box.

'Please tell us what to do. We wish to know whether Darius is in danger or not, and if we should stay and fight the Persian army here, or go into Bactria. Perhaps you have heard that Bessus plans to make war on Iskander if he goes into his territory.'

'He'll probably make war on Iskander whether he goes or not,' I said shortly. 'If Darius went with Bessus, then they're most likely plotting together.' I eyed him appraisingly. 'Does Iskander know you're here now?' I asked him.

He paled. 'No, he does not. I thought only to ask your opinion.'

I tipped my head to one side, considering. 'And you didn't know whether you should follow him or not? Is that it?'

He looked miserably at Sis, and she shrugged as if to say 'I told you so.'

'I will listen to you,' he said.

I wasn't sure if this Ptolemy was important or not. I did know that a certain Ptolemy would found a dynasty in Egypt, but I had no idea if it was this man. Ptolemy was a common name here. I'd already met five, actually. But I couldn't afford to make a mistake. I tried to look mysterious. 'Do as Iskander commands,' I said in a deep voice, praying that was good advice, and wouldn't change the history books.

Ptolemy swallowed hard and nodded. 'Very well, I will ride with Iskander to Bactria. I will lead the Macedonians. We will fight.'

Eyes closed tightly, expecting to be erased, I held my breath waiting for some sort of sign. I don't know who

303

was more nervous – me, Sis, or Ptolemy. Then I opened my eyes and saw them both staring at me, leaning forward on the balls of their feet. If I had said 'Boo!' they would have fallen right over.

Nothing happened. History was still on the right track. I grinned feebly. 'Let's go.'

'Now?' he choked.

'Now.'

I packed my things and hugged the women of the gynecie goodbye. If everything went according to the scant history I knew, I would see most of these women again in four years. I hoped I'd have a little boy with me. My eyes brimmed with tears. He was alive. I knew he was. And we were going after him.

Chapter Eighteen

The army moved out, but this time it was organized differently. The cavalry were all mounted. The infantry followed, and the engineers with the phalanx brought up the rear. Alexander was sure they would be attacked from behind. He wanted to go as fast as he could to catch Darius. The rest of the army would have to catch up with him.

For weeks we sped across the mountains and plains of northern Iraq. The horses were pushed to their limits, and I wondered how the army would keep up, but there were rarely more than twenty miles separating the cavalry and the army.

News came to us in fits and starts. First it seemed that Darius would turn and fight. Then it was rumoured that Barsine's father had decided to join Darius, and that they had gone to rally the tribes of Bactria. Then news came that Darius had lost his crown to Bessus. It came one perfect summer morning.

We were just breaking camp. Alexander and I were watching a hawk wheeling in the sky. Alexander was telling me he wished he could fly. He was wondering if he could make some papyrus wings strong enough to hold his weight, when the hawk suddenly folded its wings and plummeted towards the ground. There was a soft thud and a spurt of grey feathers. Alexander shouted and bounded towards the hawk sitting on the ground, a pigeon in its talons. The hawk screeched defiantly at the man leaping over the rocks, then abandoned its prey, flapping away with a last, frustrated scream.

Alexander paid it no heed. He knelt by the pigeon and carefully peeled a thin paper from around its leg. He unrolled it and held it smooth against his thigh. After a moment he raised his head, and I saw his face was bleak.

'What is it?' I cried. 'Bad news? Whose pigeon was that anyway?'

'It was one of Bessus's. We were lucky to have intercepted it. The message says the Persian army is on our heels. It also says he's claimed the crown of Darius, and that Darius is now his prisoner.'

'How far away are they?' I gasped.

'Not far, perhaps twenty miles.' He stood up and I saw the king had taken control.

He mounted Bucephalus and ordered one thousand of his best cavalry men to accompany him. Within the hour they had set out to save Darius. The ground shook as the horsemen galloped away at full speed, and the dust they raised was like a sandstorm in the desert.

He forbade me to follow, but I threw a dusty cloak over my bright hair and mounted the grey mare. Drumming my heels into her flanks, I galloped after the cavalry, deaf to the cries of Plexis and Usse behind me.

I followed the sandstorm. It was easy enough at first, but hour after hour Alexander kept the gruelling pace. My mare was covered with foam, and her sweat soaked through the sheepskin blanket and thick felt pad saddle. The reins were slippery with sweat, and my hands grew covered with blisters. I stopped the mare when she could go no further, and I saw that Alexander had slowed as well. The great cloud of dust was settling. I hardly had time to get my breath and take a sip of water from my flask, when they started again. I jumped onto the mare's back and galloped after them.

They had stopped at a water hole. They had only paused long enough to give the horses a drink and then leave. The water was muddied and churned from a thousand horsemen, but my mare was thirsty and drank deeply. I didn't let her drink much. When she lifted her dripping muzzle to take a breath, I pulled her away. Then we galloped after Alexander.

An hour later, I was still galloping. We started to catch up with Alexander, so I slowed and saw he'd started alternating bouts of trotting and galloping. We continued like this until it was too dark to see.

In the dark, I stumbled into the army and was immediately captured by the sentinels.

'Halt! Who goes there?'

It was Seleucos. I nearly cried with relief. 'It's me, Ashley,' I said weakly.

'Ashley?' His voice climbed into the stratosphere after the first syllable.

'Don't tell Iskander I'm here, all right?'

'What? Don't be ridiculous!'

'He'll just send me back – please!'

'But we're going to move out as soon as the horses are rested. There's a spring a few hundred feet over there, let me water your mare.'

'No, you're supposed to be on guard. I'll go.' I got off

my horse and fell on my face – my legs had forgotten how to hold me. 'Damn. Did you see which way she went?' My horse had disappeared.

'She went toward the water. Don't worry, I'll go get her.'

'No, no. I'll get up in a second. I just felt like resting, that's all.' I grinned at Seleucos. In the dark, I could see the flash of his white teeth as he grinned back at me. 'It's just like old times, huh?' I asked.

'Oh, yes. When we galloped to Babylon.' He laughed. 'But it was I who lay on the ground then, not you.'

'Now I know how you felt,' I said. 'Well, I think I'll go see about finding my horse. Don't tell Iskander. Please?'

'All right.' He sounded doubtful.

In that moonless night it was hard to see. I staggered over to the water and found my horse standing knee-deep in the spring, drinking. When she finished, I took off her saddle and rubbed her down, then I hobbled her and took her bridle off so she could graze. Horses milled about; every one tied to its rider so they couldn't wander off. Mine was easy to spot; her pale coat made her look like a ghost.

I washed in the spring. I drank the water, although it was silty and tasted as though a thousand horses and their riders had already waded in it. I was too thirsty and dusty to care. I was just getting out of the water when I heard someone whisper my name.

'Ashley?'

'Who's there?' I asked, peering through the inky darkness.

'It's me, Plexis.'

'What on earth are you doing here?' I was cross.

'I followed you, what do you think?' He sounded just as angry as I did. 'And if you imagine I ...'

There was a short blast from a bugle and the night was suddenly full of movement and the sound of horses whinnying. Plexis cursed.

'What's that?' I asked.

'They're moving out.'

'Already? But I can't see a thing!'

'The horses see well enough in the dark.' He grabbed my arm when I tried to get by him. 'Wait. Wait until they've left. It's dangerous to be in the middle. If you fall asleep and fall off your horse you could get trampled.'

'Fall asleep on a horse? I never heard of that!' I said in disbelief.

'You've never been in a real cavalry unit, have you?' he asked dryly.

We waited until the last horses were gone, and then we mounted and rode after them. In the dark, on his black horse, Plexis looked as if he were floating in air. He rode behind me. 'To pick up the pieces', he told me when I asked him why. I set my teeth and wrapped my hands in my horse's mane. The pieces indeed!

I fell off twice that night. Once when my horse stumbled and tossed me over her head, and once when I fell asleep.

Each time Plexis was there to pick me up and brush me off.

He didn't seem to need sleep. My own eyes were burning with fatigue and my eyelids weighed a ton. It was awful. When dawn came we were still going, though by now the horses moved at a shuffling trot. We went on and on. The sun climbed into the sky, and we started passing the men who'd fallen off, or whose horses had died beneath them.

Some men had broken arms or legs and were turning back towards camp. Some were on foot. They were carrying their bridles and weapons. Tears ran down their cheeks as they told of horses foundering and falling, blood frothing from their nostrils as their lungs literally exploded with the effort of galloping all day and all night. As the sun climbed higher, its heat was like brass cymbals clashing overhead, blinding and suffocating us.

Still we went on.

Bessus fled before us. We came across the first victims of his flight on the afternoon of the second day. We had stopped to rest our horses. Far across the plain was the cloud of dust that marked Alexander's cavalry. We'd fallen behind, but we weren't too far, Plexis assured me. We weren't alone. Seleucos had come back to find me. He told me he was worried. When he saw Plexis he grinned and saluted. 'Hail, General.'

I raised my eyebrows. 'General?'

Plexis nodded, his eyes on the horizon. 'Yes, I was promoted in Ecbatana.'

'Congratulations,' I said.

'Well, it won't last. When Iskander finds out I've followed him, I'll be demoted to assistant cook.' He grinned tiredly.

'I hope you like peeling potatoes,' I joked.

'What's a potato?' they both asked at once.

After a few more miles, we saw the bodies of four men. I didn't recognize their outfits, and Plexis told me they were from Bessus's army. We were catching up.

That evening, we reached a village in the foothills of the mountains. It was a wretched place. All the people who lived there were sitting on their doorsteps as if they had been watching a parade go by, and I suppose they had. First Bessus and his army, then Alexander and his cavalry, and now us.

Plexis rode up to an old woman standing at the steps of a small temple and said, 'Hail, Grandmother. What can you tell us?'

'Tell you?' She spat reflectively in the dust, making my horse jump. 'I can tell you this. First we saw a group of five horsemen riding at full speed across the plains. They entered our village shouting that we should get out of the streets because the army was coming through. Behind them, was a team of six horses pulling a wagon. In the wagon was a giant. He was tied hand and foot, and he sat so still some of us thought he was dead.'

'A giant?' I asked.

'A tall man,' whispered Plexis. 'Go on, Grandmother.'

'He had black hair and he was naked, but I could tell he'd once been a king.'

'Ha!' Seleucos jeered. 'And how could you tell that, Grandmother?'

'Because I saw the ghost of a crown over his head. But his eyes were empty.' Her voice became shrill and I felt the hair on the back of my neck stand up. 'His eyes were empty pools of gold,' she said, in her weird voice. 'Hail to the king, the king has come and gone! Twice today have I

311

seen a king! Behind the empty-eyed king came an army, and after them came the new king. Bright he was and shining like the sun! In his eyes were the twin kingdoms of heaven and earth, and I knew him for the eternal one! Hail to the new king! His kingdom shall be like a path of shining stars on the face of the earth. A column of fire shall rise to the sky, and he will unite the past and the present in the future!' Her voice rose to a shriek and she fell to the ground, frothing at the mouth, blood pouring from her nose.

'Ashley!' cried Plexis, and he took my chin in his hands.

I stared at him, uncomprehendingly, until he held up his hands and I saw they were red. A few scarlet drops landed on my lap, but it was simply a nosebleed. It stopped right away, as usual, but the old woman still lay on the ground. I wheeled my mare around with an oath, and dug my heels into her belly. I wanted to get out of that village. I didn't stop until my mare was so lathered and gasping for breath that Plexis leaned over and pulled on my reins.

'It's behind us,' he said, and there was a strange pity in his voice.

'We have to catch up to them now,' I said.

He just nodded. We kept our horses moving, and we caught up with Alexander just as the sun set on the second day.

He didn't seem surprised to see me, and I glared at Seleucos. He tried to look very interested in a grasshopper sitting on his horse's ear.

'When will we catch up with them?' I asked.

Alexander shook his head. 'I don't know. They've started splitting into groups. How many dead did you count?' he asked Plexis.

'Thirty-four of Bessus's. One of ours.'

'And how many of ours have dropped behind?'

Plexis frowned. 'Twelve or thirteen, and five horses dead.'

'Tomorrow it will be much worse,' said Alexander. His voice was sad.

We slept for an hour, watered our horses, and then set off at a gallop. We galloped until the dark forced us to slow down. I rode in the back with Plexis and Seleucos. I had learned my lesson. During the night, three men were trampled to death.

In the morning we had slowed to a walk. My horse walked as if she were drunk. Her feet dragged, and her head hung to her knees. We stopped at a spring and rested for an hour. Alexander came to find me and held me tightly in his arms. I felt him quiver. The skin on his face was drawn over his bones and his magnificent eyes were shadowed.

'Ashley, I need you to see for me,' he said quietly. I flinched. 'Please. Tell me. Should I continue? I am responsible for these men. If we continue like this, there will only be half of us left after today, and then half again tomorrow. I need to know, Ashley, is it all in vain?' My mouth was set in a stubborn line and my eyes were pleading. He lifted my chin and kissed me ever so softly on the lips. 'Listen. When we were in the village, the old woman said she saw Darius in a cart, naked, bound and tied. He's been humiliated. It's true I killed his son and

313

his brother. Sis should hate me, but she doesn't. She's always loved me – she was the mother I should have had. How can I look her in the eyes if I don't try and rescue Darius?'

'He's a fool,' I said, my voice a harsh whisper.

'He's a fool but I love him.'

I took a deep breath and let it shudder out. His arms tightened around me. 'You've just answered your own question,' I said.

I looked at him he gazed back at me, his eyes wide and guileless. What had the old woman said? 'The king, with the twin kingdoms of heaven and earth in his eyes'? One eye was the cool of the morning sky; the other held the warmth of the earth. At times I was almost afraid to touch him.

We rode through the furnace of the third day. Before us, Bessus fled. The bodies of his men and horses lay in our path, and we lost ground when our own horses had to leap or swerve to avoid the dead.

Behind us, our men fell. That afternoon, five hundred horses perished. By evening, there were only four hundred left of the thousand men who'd followed Alexander in his mad chase after Darius.

We didn't stop. Alexander had answered his own question. Now he would go on until he caught up with Darius, no matter what the consequences.

That night we kept going, though we mostly walked our horses, trudging beside them. I copied the cavalrymen, tying my arm over my mare's withers, so that I wouldn't go down when I fell asleep while walking. One time I woke up, my feet dragging along the ground, my arm half-pulled out of its socket.

My hands were bloody, and my lips were cracked and bleeding. My eyes stung with sweat and dust. I had great, raw patches where the skin had rubbed off my legs and buttocks, but I followed Alexander. My mare was valiant and she bowed her head into the night and plodded onwards. We ate nothing and we drank only when we crossed streams or met springs head on. We didn't deviate from our route. Like bloodhounds that scent when their prey is just within reach, new energy carried us towards the mountains. We mounted and urged our horses onwards, kicking them into a shambling trot.

The dawn coloured the sky crimson, and Plexis cursed once when his steed pitched forward and threw him. His black horse got back to his feet and stood unsteadily, then it seemed to lose control of its limbs. It collapsed, pink froth pouring from its nostrils.

'No!' Plexis's cry was torn out of him. He knelt by his horse and held its head. 'No, no, no!' he sobbed.

But there was no help for it. The horse died and afterwards Plexis stood with his head down, breathing harshly.

'Take mine,' I said, getting off my mare and holding out her reins, but Plexis shook his head.

'No, go with Iskander. I'll follow on foot, don't worry about me.' His face was white with shock and fatigue. 'I was a foot soldier before I joined the cavalry, and there are a few hundred men behind me.' This was true, most of the horses had died but the men walked on, stoic.

I got back on my horse and galloped after Alexander.

The hours were measured in hoofbeats and they

dragged out for ever. The sun rose, and I followed Alexander's shadow as he galloped across the rocky terrain.

There were sixty of us left when we caught sight of Bessus's army in the distance.

Sixty of us were facing the rest of the Persian army and the army Bessus had managed to raise against Alexander by claiming Darius's crown. Perhaps thirty thousand men were in front of us, so I would have understood had Alexander hesitated.

He didn't.

He raised his clarion and blew blast after blast. The men who had horns blew them, the rest of us screamed into the empty sky. Our horses were trained for battle, and they whinnied piercingly. Alexander raised his glittering shield, the shield he always carried into battle, and we charged.

We were spread out, riding abreast, but even sixty men abreast is a tiny thing compared to an army.

The sun glinted off the men's shields, their spear tips and off my pale hair as we galloped towards an army in a halo of light, in a nimbus of dust illuminated by the sun. There was certainly a phenomenon of mirage, the blinding sun and the flat plain making our meagre force appear like ten thousand men; our dark shadows an army behind us.

Bessus's army turned and saw us, and they ran.

They panicked, because they thought that Alexander's army was sweeping down upon them, and they knew they were lost. They flung down all their weapons, and heedless of Bessus's screams, they galloped madly away, abandoning him and Darius. They galloped as fast as they

316

could, or ran, or crawled away, because they knew how merciless Alexander was. They knew that they would be cut to ribbons, and so they scattered and didn't look back.

We arrived in the valley on horses that were staggering instead of walking. Even Bucephalus, proud and mighty Bucephalus, could carry his master no further. He sank to his knees, his great head bowed as if in prayer.

Alexander leapt off his groaning horse and ran towards a wagon standing off to one side. The horses had been unhitched, and it was a forlorn thing with splintered wooden wheels and its wooden sides stained with blood.

It was Darius's. He lay in the wagon in a pool of blood. His chest was nothing but a mass of wounds with his ribs showing through, white and broken. His face was devoid of all expression except, perhaps, surprise. His golden eyes were empty, as the old woman had said, staring at the sky.

Alexander let out a hoarse yell and jumped into the wagon. He gathered Darius into his arms and held him like a little child, and then, incredibly, Darius smiled.

I swear he did. He didn't say anything as he died in Alexander's arms, but he died smiling while Alexander kissed him and called his name in a voice that made my bones shake.

I sat down in the shade cast by the wagon. I didn't take my eyes off Alexander, who had curled up in a ball, still clutching Darius.

The men who had managed to stay with Alexander, cared for their horses and for Bucephalus. They led them to the shade of a nearby grove of trees, watered them, and rubbed them down.

An hour went by, then two. The sun dipped below the horizon and the sky turned a violent orange-red. Storm clouds gathered in the distance, and green lightning flashed beneath them. It seemed as if the sky were mourning as well. In front of us were the mountains, behind us were the plains and the passage known as the Caspian Gate. We had passed through it, and now Alexander was master of all of Persia, and he held the king he'd dethroned in his arms as the variegated sky above him turned red, violet and black. Thunder growled across the plains, stars blazed in the clear sky above the mountains, and Alexander raised his head and turned his haggard face to the night.

'I didn't want him to die!' he cried at the uncaring heavens. 'I never wanted him to die! He was the king! He was the king ... and he was my friend. Oh, Darius, why were you such a fool?'

I went to him and he stared at me. 'Do you know what day it is?' he asked in a whisper.

'No,' I said, reaching over and gently pulling his hand off Darius's arm. I took one hand, then the other, and I got him to his feet and led him towards the fire the men had built. Despite the evening's heat, he was shaking and his teeth chattered.

He sat down slowly, like an old man. I gave him a drink of water and he drank deeply, pausing only to gasp for breath. Then he turned towards me and buried his face in the crook of my neck. I felt hot tears on my skin and they burned like acid.

'It's my birthday,' he said.

And I realized with a shock that he was right.

Chapter Nineteen

We waited for the rest of the army. Darius was taken out of the wagon, bathed, and wrapped in Alexander's cloak. We spoke little, ate what the fleeing army had left behind, and slept uneasily wrapped in our cloaks underneath an olive tree. In the morning, my arms were covered with dew. I was so thirsty I licked it all off.

Alexander was staring at me with a rapt expression.

'I love how you do that,' he said.

'It takes a few years of practice.'

'Can I do it?'

'You can try,' I smiled at him and licked some more. I was filthy. The dew was mixed with sweat and blood but the salt tasted good. I was burned by the sun, dehydrated, my skin was rubbed raw from riding, and I thought I wouldn't be able to sit down for a month. What's more, I didn't want to hear the word 'horse' ever again.

'Ashley ...' His voice was tentative.

'What is it?' I tried to sit up, figured it hurt too much to be worth the effort, and lay back down. 'Are you going to say you're sorry? Because if you are, I don't want to hear it.'

'How did you know what I was going to say?' He looked surprised.

'Because I haven't forgotten Paul either,' I said gently. 'But it's not your fault. Don't worry. I'm sure you'll find him. I have faith in you.'

'Thank you, Ashley of the Sacred Sandals.' He leaned over and kissed me, which he did very well, and my arms were just creeping around his neck, when the sentry posted near the horses suddenly leapt to his feet and cried out, 'I see men coming!'

'Who is it?' Alexander stood, all the feline grace back in his stance.

'Artabazus!' cried the sentry.

'Who?' I asked, still flat on my back and incapable of movement.

'Barsine's father,' said Alexander, frowning down at me. 'Can't you get up?'

'No, I hurt too much. I hope he has news of Barsine, I miss her.'

Alexander grinned. 'So does the sports committee. But I do hope that Artabazus has decided to change sides.'

'Change sides? Why?'

'He was fighting with Bessus as of yesterday,' he said dryly. 'And as there's only sixty of us left, I'd hate to have to fight just now.'

'And you can count me out. I can just barely move my mouth to talk.'

Alexander looked interested. 'Just your mouth? Not your tongue or anything else?'

I stuck my tongue out. 'Plexis will be here soon. He was on foot, but not too far behind.'

'Sixty of us plus Plexis, minus you, still leaves a lot less than Artabazus has with him.'

'You're turning chicken. Why, yesterday you faced down thirty thousand armed men. People will be writing

320

songs about that for centuries. I bet it will become some sort of a legend.'

'I bet you're right.' He looked immensely pleased with himself. 'I did do something rather amazing, didn't I? I'll wager that when Artabazus hears about that, he'll want me to marry all his daughters.'

'And why not the wife as well?' came a booming voice from behind us. Alexander whirled around.

'Artabazus! I didn't hear you coming!' Alexander drew his sword and held it, a bit nervously I thought.

'I'm waiting for an answer. Will you take the wife as well? Because she's starting to wear me out.'

Barsine took after her father. He was huge; a giant with a red beard down to his waist and blue eyes like chips of turquoise in his wind-burned face. His hair, liberally streaked with grey, was a fiery blaze around his head. He stood with his hands crossed over his massive chest and didn't even glance at the sword.

'Artabazus! What are you telling the boy?' A woman appeared. At least, I think it was a woman. She was as tall as Artabazus and wore a bronze breastplate that would have made my horse's knees buckle. 'Iskander! Is it true about Darius? Artabazus came to get us two nights ago. We rode as fast as we could. Is he still with Bessus?'

'No,' Alexander replied shortly.

'Oh, that's a relief! When Artabazus told me that scoundrel Bessus had taken the crown and was going to turn against Darius my ...' Her voice died away when she saw Alexander's expression. 'Oh, no, oh no.' She shook her head, swinging her braids from side to side. 'Poor foolish man. Where is he?'

Alexander pointed to the still form wrapped in his cloak lying in the deep shade. His expression was stony.

I was still on my back, in the dappled half-light beneath an olive tree. I couldn't see what was happening, but by the way the ground shook, I thought it was either an earthquake or Alexander's entire army arriving. But it was just Artabazus's tribe, filing by to pay their last respects to Darius.

We camped with them that evening.

They had come down out of the mountains to fight with Darius one last, glorious time against the young king. But Darius had been betrayed by Bessus, and Artabazus had gone to rally his own troops to try and save Darius, alas, too late.

The huge barbarian chieftain sat before the fire gnawing on half a goat. His eyes were sorrowful, and he put the goat down on his lap and leaned towards Alexander. ''Twasn't because I had anything against you personally,' he said seriously, 'but you understand. My land is caught between that of Darius and that of Bessus. My tribe has guarded the Caspian Gates for generations.'

'Thank you for letting me pass,' said Alexander, a real smile on his face.

'You didn't think I would stop you, did you?' Artabazus was amazed. 'My own daughter's husband.' He shook his head. 'No, 'twas going to be the best of fights, I'm sure. Darius had it all planned out. Your army caught between two forces, one behind and one in front. But he didn't plan on treachery.' His face darkened. 'Bessus!' He spat and the men around him all spat as well and growled like savage animals.

'To be sure, I wasn't too keen on fighting you myself, seeing as half my tribe stayed with you, but we would have worked something out.'

'Maybe some games?' suggested Alexander, his tone sly.

Artabazus laughed like a volcano erupting. 'Exactly! Oh, we could have played some good ones.' He wiped his eyes, serious again. 'Poor Darius. A good man, to be sure, but a foolish one.' He shook his head. 'Always spoiling for a fight, then running away just when things got tough.'

'I chased him across half the world,' said Alexander dreamily.

Another tree trunk was tossed on the fire by a hulking tribesman, and red sparks flew into the air. Artabazus finished his goat and reached for another. His wife smiled at him tenderly, and he grinned back, goat sticking out of his teeth.

I lay back, comfortably propped against Alexander's chest, sipped my hot broth, and blinked like a sleepy cat at the firelight.

We were surrounded by friendly giants. The shortest fellow was seven feet tall. They wore leather clothes that smelled like the animals they'd belonged to first, and they didn't believe in washing their hair. But they were jolly and good-natured, loud talkers and hearty eaters. They had invited us to their campground, and they had sworn to replace the nine hundred horses Alexander had lost in the four-day chase. I liked them immensely, and I was sad that Barsine had chosen to stay at home, a place far in the north.

While we were sitting around the fire, a shadow

appeared. It was small, compared to the barbarians, and it wobbled somewhat as it walked. The sentries didn't spot it, but Alexander did. He leapt to his feet.

It was Plexis. Footsore and exhausted, he appeared among us like a spectre, his eyes two black holes in his white face. He saw Alexander and his smile was blinding. 'Iskander!'

They fell into each other's arms. Whatever differences there had been in the past were over. There was no more hesitation, no doubts. Plexis buried his face in Alexander's neck and sobbed.

'Hephaestion.' His voice was tender. I'd never heard him call Plexis by his full name.

'My horse died and I think I broke my collarbone,' Plexis said, when he got his breath back.

'I know, I'm sorry. I'll give you another horse. You can have first pick when Artabazus brings the herds down from the pastures.' He led Plexis to the fire and made him sit. Then he gave him soup from his own bowl and wine from his golden cup. When Plexis fell asleep, slumping over as suddenly as a child, Alexander wrapped a blanket around him and made the men around the fire hush.

Our eyes met across his sleeping form. It was like a play of four mirrors.

We all slept right there around the fire. Throughout the night, I was woken by terrible growls and roars, but it was just the fearsome barbarians snoring. Every time the fire showed any signs of dying down, a brawny arm would stretch out, grab a branch the size of a small tree, and toss it onto the fire. A shower of sparks would fountain up to rival the stars, and there would be a chorus of thumps as everyone beat out the embers that had landed on them. Then we would fall asleep again.

When day broke, everyone awoke, stretching, yawning and scratching. I managed to get to my feet and tottered off in search of a stream in which to bathe.

I had long ago lost any notion of modesty, so I squatted in the deep ditch that served as a latrine next to several other men and women doing their business. Afterwards, I found the stream and I shucked off my robes and started to wash. I must admit that I was so sore, and my skin so raw, that I didn't bother scrubbing with handfuls of sand. I simply sat in the stream and let the running water clean my body. Then I turned and lay down on my belly. The stream was only about a foot deep, so I had to duck my whole head underwater to wash my hair.

I grabbed a couple of rocks and ducked under, letting the current wash my hair for me. When I came up for breath, I saw about fifty men on the banks of the stream, on their knees, watching me.

'Hail, daughter of Demeter, water nymph, goddess of the stream,' they intoned. 'We ask your permission to drink.'

I was used to this by now. Plexis was in the camp and he was up to his old tricks. I searched for him and saw him, standing under the birch trees, trying to hide his grin, his arm in a sling.

'By all means, drink,' I said, getting to my feet and trying to salvage some dignity. Not easy to do when you're naked and you recognize the fellow who'd been in the latrine next to you. 'Would you please hand me my robe?'

It was sopping; someone had washed it for me. I sighed and draped wet wool over my shoulders, then I waded out of the stream. 'I suppose this means you won't be an assistant cook?' I asked Plexis.

He smiled. He'd never looked so happy. His collarbone was badly broken, his face was drawn, and huge violet bruises surrounded his eyes, but they were clear as rainwater. I sat under the tree on a patch of soft moss, and started to comb out my hair with my fingers. He sat with me, sighing, and leaned against the white trunk.

'Do you *have* to tell people that I'm a goddess?' I asked.

He leaned forward and caught me with his good arm, giving me a huge hug. 'I'm so happy this morning,' he said, letting go of me and sitting back again. 'Look at that view, there's not a cloud in the sky, the mountaintops seem just within reach. Why, I feel as if I could run to the top, scoop up some snow, and run back down before it melted.'

I sighed. 'Plexis?'

'Hmmm?'

'Oh, nothing. Here's Iskander.'

Alexander had been gone when I woke up, but now he wandered over, holding a short spear. He planted it in the ground beside me and sat down. He was wearing a clean tunic and he smelled good, as if he'd just rolled in freshly cut grass.

'I want to thank you, Plexis, for watching out for my wife.' He spoke formally, and I heard Plexis take a sharp breath.

'He tried to stop me,' I said, 'but I wouldn't listen. I'm sorry, I had to come.'

'I know, but I was worried just the same. Did you think I hadn't heard about the army closing in behind us? I knew we were caught in the jaws of a trap. We were lucky Bessus is a greater fool than Darius. His treachery lost Persia to me.'

'I'm sorry about Darius,' I said. I held out my arms and he came to me, laying his head on my shoulder. He was terribly thin, I realized suddenly. So thin I could feel every rib.

Plexis cleared his throat. 'I wanted to give you something for your birthday,' he said. He reached into his pouch and drew out a tightly rolled parchment. 'Here, I've carried it since Persepolis.'

Alexander took it and carefully unwrapped it. 'Oh!' he breathed.

'What is it?' I craned my head around his shoulder to look. All I saw was an old, worn scroll wrapped around two ebony sticks.

Alexander didn't answer right away. He seemed suddenly very concerned with a speck of dust on his skirt. Then he cleared his throat and said, 'It's the *Iliad*. A poem by Homer. It's a very old copy, do you think it could be one of his?'

Plexis grinned. 'No, it's not possible. It can't be more than a hundred years old, not five centuries. It's a good copy, though. I found it in the library in Persepolis. I knew you'd like it. You never used to go to sleep at night before reading at least one verse.'

Alexander raised his head. 'Thank you,' he said, his

voice raw. 'Have you forgiven me, then?'

'Do you really need ask?' Plexis shook his head. 'You're my best friend, Iskander, and nothing will ever change that.'

'Ahem,' I coughed. 'Well, what a nice birthday surprise. We'll organize a party this evening, and I'll bake a birthday cake with candles. Whom shall we invite? Artabazus? His wife? His army? That will be about ten thousand, so I'd better get cooking.' I got up, intending to leave them alone, but Alexander pulled me down on his lap.

'What are you babbling about?' he asked, amused.

He held me in his arms so I propped my chin on his shoulder and blew softly in his ear, making him laugh. He had been swimming; his hair was wet and hung in light brown ringlets, lifting off his temples and forehead. His skin was very white behind his neck. I glanced at Plexis. His amber eyes were very bright.

It is rather confusing to love your husband and a man who loves your husband. Especially if you truly love your husband. However, everyone loved my husband. He was the king, he was young, he was handsome, he was dashing and intelligent. Who could resist him? I only wished he were *more* resistible.

Alexander took my face in his hands. He tipped my head slightly, catching the sun in my eyes. 'Such frost in the heart of summer,' he said, and his voice had lost its lightness.

'Why do you say that?'

'Oh, no reason. The new horses are coming; I feel the ground vibrating. Tomorrow morning the rest of the army will catch up with us, and we will head over the mountains. I've always wanted to go to the other side of the world. Ashley?'

'Yes?'

'If you're not a goddess, then, please tell me, who or what are you? Are you a nymph?'

'No,' I shrugged.

'Are you a dryad then?' Plexis asked.

'A dryad?' I echoed. 'What's that?'

'You've never heard of a dryad?' It was Alexander, his expression shocked.

'Well, no. I can't say I have. Is it that serious?'

'And you don't know about nymphs.' Plexis spoke heavily.

I looked from one man to the other. 'So?'

'Ashley.' Alexander took my hand and held it gingerly. 'Everyone learns about nymphs and dryads from their parents in our world. Everyone knows about the naiads, sprites, sylphs, oreads, undines, fauns, and fates. Do you know who Lachesis is?' I shook my head. 'Clotho? No? Atropos? The Muses? Do you know anything?' He sounded as if he were in real pain.

I looked at Plexis. He was staring at me, and on his face was the strangest expression. I tried to laugh but the sound stuck in my throat. 'I'm sorry,' I whispered, 'I didn't learn about any of that.'

'But you said you went to school. You had teachers, you knew about Plato and Homer, you even spoke to Aristotle about the world being round. And that's a new idea.' He shook his head. 'I just don't understand.'

'I'm sorry.' I blinked. I wasn't used to anyone paying

so much attention to me. It was unnerving. 'I don't know what to say.'

'But where were you educated?' Alexander asked me. 'Even the barbarians know about dryads!'

'I can't tell you,' I said, shaking my head.

'Why not? I just don't understand you, Ashley.' There was such pain in his voice that I felt awful.

'I'm sorry,' I whispered, 'but I can't.'

'Perhaps it's just as well you don't say anything,' said Plexis. 'This is what the oracle meant, wasn't it? I'll find out on my deathbed, after we've reached the sacred river and after I've seen the twelve pillars.'

'What's that?' Alexander said, attentive.

'An oracle's riddle.' Plexis shrugged. 'I don't know where the sacred river is, perhaps in India, I heard of one that flowed there. But I know not where the twelve pillars are.'

I stared at Plexis, he looked at me and then his face softened. He smiled. 'Don't cry. Why, thanks to you I'm probably the only person in the whole world to look forward to my own death.'

'Don't say that.' Shivering, Alexander put his hand across Plexis's mouth.

Plexis took it and kissed it, drawing it across his cheek. He looked at it a moment, turned it over, and traced a faint scar on the thumb. Their fingers entwined. Then Plexis placed Alexander's hand on my leg. 'You're going to have your hands full teaching your wife everything she needs to know before we get back to civilization,' he said in a light voice.

Alexander didn't say anything, but I felt his sorrow

keenly.

'Is it because of me?' I asked Plexis.

He shook his head, mute.

'I won't stand in your way,' I said to Alexander. 'If you love him I won't stand in your way.'

'There's nothing in our way,' said Alexander quietly, 'except ourselves.' His fey eyes were filled with something like joy.

Plexis shook his head. 'Ah, Iskander. There was never anything between us except friendship. Cxious tried to change all that, but you were right all along. Sometimes the difference between love and need is as thin and transparent as spring ice.'

'And the difference between love and need is like the difference between ice and water.' Alexander spoke automatically.

'I see you haven't forgotten your lessons.' Plexis smiled. 'Aristotle should be proud.'

'No, I never forget my lessons,' he said.

'May the gods hear you.' Plexis winced as he levered himself from the ground. 'I think I'll go find Usse and beg some of his sleeping draught. My shoulder pains me. Perhaps I was hasty, moving about so soon.' He turned and left, but not before I saw something shine on his cheeks.

'Oh. Alex,' I said, laying my head on his chest. 'I'm so sorry.'

'Don't be.' His heartbeat was slow and regular. 'I have all I need.'

'And what about what you want?' I asked.

'You asked me that question long ago, if I remember

331

well. It's easy to answer. I want to find my son. I want to avenge Darius. And I want to make Alexandria the most beautiful city on earth. I want to grow old with you by my side, our children playing at our feet. I want the stars and the moon.' He paused and kissed my nose. 'I want to rule the world and the heavens. So, tell me. Tell me, my oracle, my love. Will I get what I want?'

I gave him the sweetest smile I could muster, and I said, 'Alex, you're standing on thin ice.'

He sputtered, then laughed. 'I *would* be married to the only oracle in the world with a sense of humour!'

We sat in the fragrant grass watching as the horses came down the mountainside. The breeze was redolent of freshly cut hay and summer flowers. Dust sparkled in the air and butterflies darted about. White clouds looked like fat sheep grazing on an endless blue plain above us. The campsite was set up on the flank of the mountain, amongst the trees. Men came and went, fetching wood, forage, water, and meat. All around us there was bustle and the sound of men laughing, arguing, and singing.

We sat on the mossy bank of a silvery stream in a grove of white birch trees, surrounded by a sort of quiet grace.

I looked at the man I had read about three thousand years in the future, the man who would be known as Alexander the Great, and he smiled at me.

Chapter Twenty

Darius was sent back to Ecbatana to be buried. We lined up to watch the funeral cortège leave the camp. Alexander's soldiers and Artabazus's tribesmen lined each side of the road to salute him. With sixty thousand men lined up along the road, the farewell salute was fifty kilometres long. Alexander rode at the head of the funeral procession until he reached the end of the line of men. Then he stopped and let the wagon go by. He stood until it had disappeared, then he rode silently back to the camp.

We waited until the army caught up to us and then we headed across the Elburz Mountains towards the Caspian Sea.

The cavalry had new horses, courtesy of Artabazus and his mountain tribes.

The Caspian Sea was covered with whitecaps when I first saw it. We came down a winding mountain pass through a small pine forest. The air was full of the spicy scent of pine and the salty odour of the sea. I closed my eyes and breathed deeply. The pines were balsamic and the fragrance was divine.

The wind hit us when we left the cover of the trees, and I caught my first glimpse of the huge salt-water lake called the Caspian Sea. It was grey-green, streaked with foam. Two white seagulls flew above us, calling to each other in their mournful voices. Alexander seemed to think this was an excellent omen, and he burst into a marching song, thankfully drowned out by soldiers with better ears for music.

I'd noticed Alexander's mood could be influenced by such banal things as birds and dreams; he put great store in omens. It made me laugh sometimes and I'd tease him about it, but he saw nothing strange in his attitude. Rather, he tried to teach me all the things he thought a 'normal' person should know.

I spent most days being tutored in the major and minor deities, gods and demigods, and of course, the heroes. Alexander had been modelled by his mother into a sort of hero himself. He'd been raised believing his mother and father were both descended directly from the gods, and that the great hero Achilles was, in fact, his grandfather.

'Do you really believe this?' I asked one night as I lay in his arms.

'Of course.' He frowned. In the moonlight, his skin was as white as milk, and his eyes became even more strange. His full mouth curved in a smile. 'Mother always told me, "You have the blood of heroes in your veins." She meant Achilles and Heracles. Oh, by the way, Artabazus told me that Barsine had decided to name her babe Heracles if it's a boy, and Persephone, after you, if it's a girl.'

'How sweet,' I said, grinning at his expression.

I had figured out that Heracles was in fact Hercules.

Names were quite fluid at this time. For example, Hephaestion was Plexis, and sometimes he was called Chytroy, which was a big pot, because when he was little he got stuck in a chamber pot. Nicknames were common, and Iskander even had a few, but he wouldn't translate some of them.

Nearchus was sometimes called Cretos, because he

334

was born in Crete, and Baldy, as a joke, because of his beautiful blond hair of which he was inordinately proud. He was called Blondie for the same reason.

Ptolemy Lagos was sometimes referred to as Baldy too, because he *was* bald, and Sotar, which was what his nurse had called him. One got a nickname and it stuck until a new one came along, which drove the scribes and the historians crazy, especially the ones who were supposed to be writing Alexander's journal.

We had historians with us. They wrote about our journey, copied Alexander's speeches, and described everything in great detail. One was very nice, he was actually related to Aristotle – his nephew, I believe. His name was Callisthenes, and Alexander put him in charge of my education. There was also Aristobulus, an engineer, who would come into Alexander's tent at night and interview him, writing everything on a long roll of papyrus.

Ptolemy Lagos was also a writer. He was using Nassar to record his memoirs, which Nassar told me were quite interesting, being the description of all the battles he'd fought, both with Philip of Macedonia and with Alexander.

Alexander's half-brother was also named Ptolemy, but Alexander referred to him as Pylos – bathtub – for two reasons: he was rather tubby, inheriting none of his famous brother's good looks; and he hardly ever washed. I avoided him. I much preferred Ptolemy Lagos, who'd come to see me in Ecbatana with Sis. He was a quiet man, with dark, piercing eyes and a keen wit. There was something about him that I didn't quite trust, though.

Perhaps I sensed his immense ambition, carefully hidden, like a shark beneath the surface of the sea.

Another man often visited Alexander in our tent. He had also joined us in Ecbatana, and his name was Cleitus. His nickname was 'Blackie,' another joke, for he was as blond as Nearchus, and his candid eyes were blue. He was also referred to by his father's name sometimes, Dropides, and I liked him very much. He was of royal blood: he told me that each time I saw him. He wasn't too bright, but he was of royal blood. He commanded all the Macedonian soldiers who came from royalty, and his squadron was called 'The Royal Guards'. I got a case of the giggles every time I saw them. He adored Alexander, though. He honestly loved him. He didn't expect anything in return. He was ' as proud as a peacock to be able to follow my king and serve him, as my father served Philip, and as my sons will serve Alexander's sons'. – his words exactly.

He was also a heavy drinker, and he would sometimes be seen weaving through the camp, his tunic on backwards, his sandals around his neck, singing love-songs at the top of his lungs. Then he would stop a few minutes in front of Alexander's tent and serenade us. He would sing a garbled song about valiant soldiers and beautiful women, devious gods and goddesses, and then he'd hiccup loudly and bid us sweet dreams. When he did this, he would inevitably wake us up. Ignoring Alexander's bellows that he shut up and let us sleep, he'd bow gracefully and roar, 'Long live the King!'

Alexander loved when I sang. He adored rock and roll songs, soft ballads, and opera arias. The music they played in Alexander's time was heavy on percussion, strings, woodwinds and brass. Choruses were popular, and the music would give me shivers. It could be amazing, especially when all the trumpets blew together. I loved the sweet music of the harps and flutes and there were reed instruments, like oboes, included at every banquet. However, music was also an everyday thing, with the soldiers singing as they marched or worked. People sang as they went about their everyday business. And children were taught with songs, as I found out when Callisthenes came for my first lesson.

We had stopped for the night on the shores of the Caspian Sea. The wind was making the tent lean in a way that frightened me, but Alexander assured me there was no danger. I expected to be blown away any second, but the tent held. Callisthenes came by after dinner. I was lying on the bed, and Alexander was at his table going over the day's journal with Ptolemy Lagos and Nearchus. Plexis was being treated by Usse – his collarbone still hurt – and I was playing a game of checkers with Axiom.

I was winning, for once, so I was cross when Alexander ordered Axiom to fold up the game, and told me to go sit in the corner with Callisthenes for my first lesson. I made a face, but obeyed. Besides, I was curious. What would I learn?

Callisthenes took a small harp out of his robes and proceeded to sing a very cute song about nine women called 'muses' who lived on an island somewhere, and did all sorts of artistic things. Their names were lovely in themselves, and the song had three verses, with a chorus that went like this:

"We are the muses, all standing in line,
Nine sisters, nine inspirations divine,
We sing, dance, tell stories and give you stimulation
For all your artistic inspiration."

Well, it loses something in the translation. However, it was the first little song a child learned. It told him about the nine subjects he would study: epic poetry; history; lyric poetry and hymns; music; tragedy; mime; dance; comedy; and astronomy. Those would be my lessons, and since each subject belonged to a muse, that's where we started.

I went around humming about Clio and Calliope, Urania and all the other sisters until my next lesson.

The evenings were spent learning, but the days were spent walking. We marched around the shore, passing through many modest villages, all of which swore allegiance to Alexander. In each village he sacrificed a goat to the local gods, and met with the chieftain. It took us three days to reach the largest village on the shores of the sea, where we met the high chief of the Tapures, the tribe living in that region. The high chief laid down his arms without fighting, and Alexander rewarded him with the title of Satrap.

We travelled through his territory and then penetrated into the Hyrcania region, where we spent two weeks in Zadracarta, the capital. The people there, called the Madrians, submitted themselves to Alexander without a fight, and we were received with many banquets and feasts.

We stayed long for several reasons. Alexander was

heading toward hostile territories. Bessus was still in front of us and was rallying the Bactrians against us. Alexander wanted to make sure of his allegiances, so he would never have to worry about being attacked from behind. It was his worst nightmare, the thing he worked the hardest to avoid. He would spend sleepless nights with his generals, working out the various things that could go wrong. He approached fighting exactly as if he were playing a gigantic chess game. He had to make sure he could plan every one of his opponent's moves before he himself decided what to do. Afterwards, he would often sleep twenty hours to recuperate. He used up more energy planning than he did fighting.

He told me fighting was a relief to him. Planning was torture.

I'm sure that most of the cities' names have been changed since I was in Iran. My journalist instincts made me ask for names and explanations everywhere we went. Sometimes they were hard to understand. A place could be named after a tribe or the tribe's chief, or it could be the name of the river it was on, or a landmark, or even something that had happened there, as the place called, 'Orian's Big Trip'. I inquired after that name. Orian was a man who'd stumbled on a rock, and fallen off the cliff overlooking the village. Nearly all the villages we passed were named after the Caspian Sea. We passed through – rough translations – three 'Lake Views,' five 'Lakesides,' one 'Saltwater Town,' a 'Lots of Fish Place,' – I liked that one – and a 'Deep Water, No Wading'. It seemed the smaller the village, the more picturesque the name.

Plexis was bucked off his new horse, and his arm got

worse. I was worried, but Usse wasn't. He told me that two weeks' rest would help put things right, and so, when we got to Zadracarta, I made Alexander forbid Plexis to ride.

Plexis took a great interest in my education, and he would often sit with Callisthenes while he gave me my lessons. He and Callisthenes would usually end up in a lively discussion about philosophy, literature or science. Alexander would join in if he had finished working, and I would take Callisthenes's harp and try to play a few of the songs I knew on it.

They were all impressed by rock music; it sounded like great incantations to them, and they thought I was talking directly to the gods.

Callisthenes had a remarkable voice, so I taught him some of the songs I knew, and we would sing harmony for Alexander. He loved music; it brought tears to his eyes. He would insist on singing along, which brought tears to our eyes; I have never heard anyone with a worse singing voice.

340

Chapter Twenty-one

Autumn was coming, the autumn of 330 BC. We headed due east and arrived in Arie, a large country in what is known now as Turkmenistan. Here Alexander founded another great city, Alexandria Arian, or Alexandropolis, as it was also called.

Whenever he founded a city, he made it completely independent; that is to say, it had its own government and didn't have anything to do with the surrounding kingdoms. Alexander left Macedonians in charge most of the time, promoting them to governor, and giving them the freedom to control the city and the immediate countryside. The result of this manoeuvre was threefold. First, it meant that the cities would not be swallowed up in the local customs; on the contrary, they would be islands of pure Greek culture, where schools were set up and artists and poets would express themselves in what would be known as Hellenistic Art. Secondly, these cities would be democracies, able to decide their own governments, separating them from the satraps who ruled the great expanses of land around them. Thirdly and lastly, this meant that after Alexander's death, when his kingdom splintered into many different parts, these cities stayed exactly as he'd planned. They continued to be landmarks of Greek culture, inspirational landmarks that would continue to thrive centuries later. They would be a wonder unto themselves and would carry forward the legend of Alexander. While the world around them changed, they remained the same.

We followed a river east, then climbed over a small mountain range to a large plateau. We'd come to a place called Phradra, a windy plain, where we decided to spend the week to rest the horses. It was a natural pastureland, with tall, waving grass like some vast, whispering, green sea. The tents were set up, the horses were corralled, and Alexander sent his best scouts to find out where Bessus had gone.

That night, while we slept, a young soldier crept into our tent and woke Alexander.

I heard them whispering together. Somehow, he'd gotten past the guards, and even past Axiom, who slept in front of our bed, and was the lightest sleeper I knew.

The young soldier was kneeling next to the bed, whispering into Alexander's ear. His face was not familiar to me. He had the smooth, round cheeks of a teenager, and his beard was sparse. His eyes were red from weeping, and he clutched Alexander's arm so hard his fingers were white.

'What is it?' I murmured sleepily, rolling over in the bed and putting my chin on Alexander's hip.

The youth gaped at me.

'Don't be frightened,' Alexander was using his most gentle voice, the one I'd heard just once before when he was in the tent with the dying soldiers, right before he plucked the arrow from the man's chest.

'I swear by Zeus and all the gods that it's true,' the soldier said, and he collapsed into tears.

That woke Axiom, of course, and he poked his head up and asked Alexander if everything was as it should be.

Alexander said "no", it was not as it should be, and he got out of bed, standing in a pool of silver moonlight, his head tilted to the side, considering. His eyes were wells of sorrow.

'You said that you told Parmenion, and he did nothing? Three times you told him?'

'But what could he do?' The boy's voice was pleading. 'It is his son.'

'But Parmenion is my general,' said Alexander still with that gentle voice. 'He should have told me.' To Axiom he said, 'Wake Hephaestion, tell him to bring Parmenion to me.'

'I can get him,' said Axiom, looking over at Plexis, sleeping deeply on the far side of the tent.

'No, this is between generals,' said Alexander. His voice was giving me the shivers. I dived back under the covers and found my shift. Alexander could parade about naked and look like a king, but I needed clothes if the tent was going to fill with men in the middle of the night.

Alexander stood while Axiom roused Plexis. When he realized what Alexander wanted him to do, he was wide-awake in an instant. His face was pale, and his eyes very wide. 'I'll get Parmenion,' he said, throwing his cloak over his shoulders. He left silently; I never knew anyone who could walk as quietly as Plexis.

The young soldier knelt near the bed and said nothing. Tears ran down his face, and his mouth trembled. Axiom looked grave. He set about lighting the lamp and making hot tea.

Brazza woke when the lamp was lit. He was deaf, not blind, and the light made him sit up and blink. He didn't move, though. He saw Alexander and his face became troubled. He stayed where he was, but his hands twisted together, reminding me of Lady Macbeth. When I think back on that night, I always see Brazza's hands, wringing and twisting in his lap.

After a minute, Axiom draped a cloak over Alexander's shoulders. Alexander looked at the fine wool as if he'd never seen it before. His face was drawn in thin lines. I noticed his hands were shaking. What was going on?

Plexis stepped into the tent and formally announced General Parmenion.

The man ducked under the tent flap, and I recognized him at once. He was an older man, one of Antipatros's cronies, and they often rode or played dice together. He always had a smile for me, and I leaned forward, a smile on my face, ready to greet him.

He didn't see me. His expression of desolation mirrored Alexander's countenance.

'Why didn't you tell me?' were Alexander's first words to the old soldier.

He flinched. 'I didn't believe it,' he said slowly. 'How could I? My own son, accused of treason? It isn't possible.'

Treason? My skin prickled. So that was it.

Plexis stepped into the tent, his face impassive. 'My king, we've found Philotas.' There was something in his voice that made Alexander look up sharply.

'And?'

'He was with Lycenus.'

'Where is Lycenus?'

'He cut his own throat when he saw us coming.'

The words fell like missiles among us. I gasped, Alexander straightened, and Parmenion sank to his knees as if a huge weight had just fallen on his shoulders.

'It was meant to happen tonight,' said Alexander, and each time he drew a breath, it seemed to hurt.

The young soldier put his face in his hands. Alexander placed a light hand on his shoulder. 'Go back to your tent now and try to sleep. I can never thank you enough. Come to see me in two days' time, I will speak to you then.'

The boy got to his feet, and left without a glance at the old man kneeling on the floor, his head bowed against his chest.

There was a silence in the tent after he'd left. It was an awful silence, as if everyone were holding his breath. Then the generals filed in, without speaking: Leonnatos Pella; Nearchus; Antipatros; Cleitus; Craterus; Plexis; and Ptolemy Lagos.

Afterwards came Philotas, accompanied by Seleucos and Pharnabazus, Artabazus's son.

Everyone stood in the tent, and no one seemed to know what to say, or where to start. Alexander wouldn't look at anyone. He stood with his hands shaking, and looked at a corner of the tent where a patch of moonlight made a milky stain on the floor.

Finally Philotas threw himself on his knees, next to his father, and started to sob. His father put his arm around his son's shoulders.

'What have you done?' asked the old man.

'It was Antigone,' sobbed Philotas, 'She told me we would never see Macedonia again if Iskander lived to see the dawn. She said that we would all be lost in the wilds of Bactria, and that the barbarians would slaughter us all. She said that if Iskander died, you would be king. You are second in command, are you not?'

'Antigone?' The old general's voice rose several octaves and he rocked back on his heels, away from his son. 'You listened to your mistress?' His face was twisted in disbelief and pain. 'Have you lost your senses, boy? I am second in command of Iskander's army, not to rule. How could you plot to kill your own king?'

'He's not my king!' Philotas shouted harshly. 'Philip was, and he never named his successor! Iskander's an imposter! He killed his own father. I won't be led by a bastard who committed patricide!'

His words were greeted by silence. Alexander's skin shivered like a horse with flies, but otherwise he was still. His hands had stopped moving. 'Is that what they say?' he asked, when the silence, stretched as tight as a rubber band, finally snapped.

'I was there, did you forget?' hissed Philotas. 'I was there! Your father wanted to marry your brother Arrhidaeus to Pixodaros's daughter. You sent that actor to his court to show what Arrhidaeus was like so you could marry the girl. You were so afraid your father would declare Arrhidaeus his heir! Have you forgotten?'

'He's not my brother,' retorted Alexander, 'he's an abomination of nature.'

'Because your mother poisoned him when he was a babe!' shouted Philotas. 'The abomination is you! How

346

many of your half-brothers and sisters did your mother kill when they were still sucking at their mothers' breasts? Infanticide! A witch, and the son of a witch, that's what I was plotting to kill.'

Alexander's face turned ashen. My own nose started bleeding, and yet I couldn't move, frozen in place by the terrible look on Alexander's face and on the faces of his generals.

I don't know if what Philotas said was true, or if Alexander had ever heard the slightest rumour about it. It seemed that he was innocent of the murders attributed to his mother, whom he 'hated and loved'. I shuddered.

'Iskander.' It was Plexis, stepping forward.

'No, don't touch me.' His whisper was hoarse. He stared at Philotas without blinking. His face was awful to look at. It seemed that his flesh had contracted around his skull. 'We vote,' he said, 'as an assembly.'

The generals didn't move. No one even breathed.

'All those who think Philotas guilty raise their right hand,' said Alexander. 'All those who think him innocent raise their left hand.'

There was no hesitation. All present lifted their right hands, including the boy's father, Parmenion.

'Father!' Philotas's voice was ragged.

Parmenion got to his feet and walked across the tent to Alexander. He stood straight; no sign of sorrow was in his voice. 'I only ask one favour of you,' he said clearly.

'I will grant you whatever you wish, old friend,' said Alexander, putting his hand on Parmenion's shoulder.

'Is that a promise?'

'Yes.'

347

'Then grant me this wish. You must kill me before you kill my son. I won't watch my own son being executed, and I won't live knowing that I was warned of the plot and did nothing to prevent it.'

Alexander's hand slipped off Parmenion's shoulder and he staggered. 'No!'

'You swore.' The old general's voice was gentle. 'And now you must.'

Alexander's eyes glittered with tears. 'I cannot kill you,' he said.

'And yet you must.' Parmenion smiled kindly. 'I will die gladly by your sword, my king.'

Philotas was sobbing now, his face buried in his hands, but no one looked at him.

'You were not tried by the assembly,' said Alexander, searching for words.

'I will be ready when the sun rises,' said Parmenion. 'I will need a scribe until then.'

'Take Nassar,' said Ptolemy, snapping his fingers at Axiom, who bowed and ran from the tent.

'Will you tell me just one thing?' asked Alexander, drawing deep breaths like a man who is drowning. 'Will you tell me if you believe what your son said, about me killing my father, and about my mother. Do you think it is true? Will you tell me? Will you …' He broke off and gasped, his face turning grey.

The old man's face crumpled, and he took Alexander in his arms, holding him tightly, patting his back gently. 'By Zeus and by Amon, I swear to you, I never believed you killed Philip. You loved your father, and he loved you. He was proud of everything you did, and he would

348

be even more proud of you now. You're a good boy, Iskander, a good boy. Now, let me go. I must prepare myself. But I promise, by all the gods in Olympus, I love you still, Iskander, and I'm proud to die by your hand.'

He turned and left the tent, with only a brief glance at his son, prostrate on the floor.

The generals took Philotas to a tent and stood guard around it. He had a scribe assigned to him, but he spent the rest of the night screaming. His voice scraped and battered against the night until the sun rose, and the noise of the camp finally drowned his cries.

Alexander spent the night standing in the middle of the tent, silent and unmoving. Only now and then, his whole body would convulse. Once he vomited, but he would allow no one to touch him.

Brazza cleaned up the vomit. Axiom took Alexander's ceremonial robes out of the large cedar chest at the foot of the bed, and got them ready. I started to cry, and finally Brazza crawled into bed with me and held me. I couldn't stop crying, and it was good of him to hug me. I wanted to comfort Alexander, but he would not allow it. Plexis had gone to stay with Philotas, he didn't return until the next morning.

Towards dawn, Philotas's voice gave out. I laid my head on Brazza's chest, and his heartbeat lulled me to sleep.

I woke, and there was still no change. Philotas had started screaming again. Alexander stood while Axiom dressed him and shaved him. Brazza brought breakfast but none of us touched it.

Plexis came in and put on his finest tunic, and I put on

my black silk. We didn't speak, but waited until the sun no longer touched the horizon. Then Alexander took a deep breath. His colour was still bad, but at least he could breathe more easily.

In the centre of the camp was a large empty space where the sacrifices were carried out or meetings were held. The entire army gathered around. Word had travelled fast. Everyone was standing mutely, feet shifting, eyes worried, hands twisting.

Treason was the worst thing, perhaps, that could befall a king. What's more, Alexander had been betrayed by a childhood friend. A Macedonian no less, whose father happened to be second in command. Rumour swept the camp that both men were to die, but that the father had not had a trial.

Parmenion walked out of the tent where he'd spent the night dictating his memoirs to Nassar. He had dressed in his military finest. He walked with his back straight, and his step was as light as if he were going for a quick stroll. The murmur in the crowd grew, but it hushed when Parmenion stopped in front of Alexander and knelt. Alexander wouldn't look at him. He looked over all our heads into the distance. Parmenion got to his feet and embraced Alexander, who simply stood there, his arms by his sides. Then slowly, slowly, his arms crept up, and he hugged the old general. His composure shattered. Tears spilled down his cheeks.

Suddenly, he stepped backwards and seemed to dance once in and out, his hand a dazzling blur. Parmenion staggered, but before he fell Alexander caught him, and a knife dropped to the ground. A fountain of scarlet blood drenched both men as they sank to their knees. For a split second, I didn't understand what had happened. Then I saw Alexander's face, and I knew he'd killed a man he loved, and he would never be the same.

The ground drank the general's blood as if it were a thirsty beast, while Alexander held him and begged him over and over to forgive him. Afterwards, he laid the old man on the ground and folded his arms over his chest. A single wound showed where the knife had entered his chest and severed his aorta.

I didn't faint, and my nose didn't bleed, but beside me Plexis hit the ground, hard. I heard a distinct crack, and I realized his collarbone, not quite healed, had broken again. Usse, standing not far away, groaned.

I made it to the tent before I collapsed, and then lay on the bed and wished myself somewhere else. I didn't watch Philotas's execution, carried out by another soldier. I was seriously considering packing up and returning to Ecbatana, where I thought I could stay with Sisygambis.

Plexis was carried into the tent. He lay on his pallet, moaning, until Usse gave him a sleeping draught and reset his collarbone. Then Plexis dropped off to sleep.

I thought Alexander would want to avoid us, but soon afterwards he came into the tent and crawled into the bed next to me. He was covered with blood, and I nearly pushed him away, but then I saw his face. It was as if he didn't even know I was there. He lay in the bed and shivered. I started to peel off his clothes and shouted for Usse and Axiom.

'Usse!' I said urgently, 'I think he's in shock! Help me elevate his legs and pull these covers over him.'

351

We worked quickly. Axiom took the bloody clothes away, and Usse brought me a small pot of honey. I dipped my finger in it and tried to put it in Alexander's mouth. I didn't know if that would help, but Usse seemed to think so.

Alexander was unconscious, so I had to rub my finger along his gums, waiting for the honey to melt before putting some more in his mouth. After nearly an hour, his eyelashes fluttered and he awoke. He still had that frightening blank look in his eyes though.

'Alex, please, speak to me, are you all right?'

He closed his eyes and squeezed them shut.

'Answer me, we're so worried about you, please, Alex!'

'Leave me alone.' Each word was as clear as cut glass and separated by a harsh breath.

I pinched my lips, but I'd had time to think. 'I will never leave you, Alexander,' I said. 'I love you, I want you, and I need you. You are the only reason I came to your world, and you are the only reason I stay. I will not leave you, ever.'

A faint smile stirred his lips. 'All right. Leave me alone for a little while, then.' His voice was still faltering, but no longer tortured. It was all he said, but it was enough. My shoulders sagged, and I took a deep breath. I turned to Usse, who stepped backward and smiled. 'He'll be all right,' I said. Then I left the tent. I wanted to be alone.

Chapter Twenty-two

I went to the stables and found my grey mare. She was happy to see me. I spoiled her terribly. I fed her the morsel of stale bread I'd kept aside for her and put her bridle on. With all the tragedy in the camp this morning, hardly anyone was about. They'd gathered into tight groups and were discussing the events. I noticed Ptolemy Lagos stalking around; his face was tight with anger, and I wondered what else was going on. Cleitus and Nearchus were trailing after him, but none of them noticed me leaving. I rode along the path towards the village in the distance. I'd put some coins in my pouch, and I was thinking of buying some warm cloth. We were climbing higher and higher, and I knew that soon we would reach the Hindu-Kush Mountains. Alexander had discovered that Bessus had headed that way and was intent on catching him.

He was also drawing plans for new cities; I'd seen them on his desk. They were all based on the plans of Greek cities, with a square market place, gymnasium, government centre, baths, and temples. Everything that a Greek-style metropolis had, was transplanted into Alexander's plans. It was so typical of him. He didn't once think of asking anyone else what they wanted. What he wanted was obviously the best for everyone. That was his philosophy. Yet, he wasn't a tyrant. He surrounded himself with intelligent men, and he was open to their ideas, but after hearing them he made his own decisions, and everyone was expected to follow. I wondered what would happen if his generals all revolted, if they just suddenly became fed up with Alexander. Why should they follow him? What made them walk across Asia Minor in his footsteps? Land? They had too much of it. Fortune? The treasure at Persepolis was the most they'd ever see. Power? They held as much as they would ever get, as long as Alexander lived. So what was it? Was it a kind of love? Awe, perhaps? Or did they share the same urge to go forward into new territories? An ancient saying came to my mind: '... to go where none have gone before, to explore new worlds ...' Was that it?

I patted my little mare on the neck and wondered. It was as if Alexander had put an enchantment on his men. Then I shivered. If Philotas had been considering treason, it meant that others could be thinking about it too. The magic was wearing thin. Yet, we were only on the first part of our journey. We still had six more years to go before we turned back to Persia. Would the army last that long?

In the village, I bought some thick felt for a jacket and some leather boots. I would show Alexander my new outfit and suggest he give one to each soldier. Climbing snow-covered peaks in flimsy sandals and linen skirts would definitely make the men regret following him.

Back at camp, I saw that we were getting ready to march again. I had no time to pack – Brazza had done it for me. When I arrived in the tent, Alexander was up and pacing.

354

'Where were you?' he asked, before I could greet him.

'In the village.' I frowned. I'd only been gone four hours. 'Where are we going?'

'South. We're going to consolidate the territories in the south before heading east again.' His voice was curt.

I nodded. 'Fine, let's go south. I was worried about spending the winter in the mountains anyway.'

His mouth twitched. 'Well, that's another reason we're going.'

'Fine. Did you tell your men?' I asked sarcastically, 'or did you just say "march south", as if they were a gaggle of geese?'

'A gaggle of geese?' His eyebrows raised. 'I don't think my men think of themselves as geese.'

'Oh? Well, excuse me. It's a just silly impression I got, that's all.'

'Explain.' It was an order.

'Did you tell them why you did it?' I asked, getting angry now. 'Did you bother to explain? Do you know what they're saying?'

'About what?'

'You know damn well about what. I'll tell you what they're saying. They're saying that Parmenion had no trial. They're saying you were the judge, the jury and the executioner, and that you did it out of sheer fury! That's what they're saying.'

'Where did you hear this?' His eyes were blazing.

'In the stables, the grooms are talking. Alex, you have to do something. You can't just expect your men to read your mind and follow you blindly. They deserve your trust.'

355

'Oh? They do? What about Philotas?'

'I think he was an exception,' I said levelly. 'But if you go on pretending to be God, he'll become the rule.'

'Pretending to be God?' Alexander sat heavily on the bed and stared up at me. 'You, of all people, telling me that? I see you're blushing. Good, so you do see the irony of your statement.'

'I only meant that you could maybe do a bit of explaining. Call your men together and give one of your speeches, you do that so well. They want to see you; they love you and want to follow you. But if you close yourself off from them, they will be hurt, then angry, and then they will refuse to follow.' I looked at him pleadingly.

He studied my face for a few minutes, then looked down at his feet. He wiggled his toes. 'They really love me?' he asked, looking up again.

'What do you think?'

'I wasn't sure, you know, after last night. It came as such a shock.'

'I know.' I sat next to him and touched his shoulder. 'I'm sorry.'

'Well, if it makes you feel any better, I've already written a speech, and I was going to give it before we broke camp.' His mobile mouth twitched.

'You did?'

'Yes, I wasn't just going to drag my men around after me like an old sack. Or a gag of geese.'

'A gaggle.'

'Yes, nice word. I think you worry too much, Ashley of the Sacred Sandals. You worry and fret like an old mother hen.' He took my hand and pulled me down on the bed next to him. He started to take off my tunic, not heeding Brazza who was packing the rug, or Axiom who was taking down the lamp.

He bared my breasts and then took one in his mouth, sucking on it hard, teasing it with his tongue. I tried to push him away but he was much stronger than I. He took off his own clothes while holding me on the bed. I squeaked, 'But Alex! We're not alone!'

'We will be,' he said, slipping his hand between my legs. 'I need you and I want you, Ashley of the Sacred Sandals and Ashley of the Arrow Miracle. You told me that this morning, and you made me want to go on. So now it's my turn. I can tell you, and I can show you.' He reared up above me and I saw that what he said was true. His body was ready to take mine for its own. 'Will you let me?' he asked softly, and I nodded.

Brazza and Axiom had left, closing the tent flap behind them. Not that it would have mattered. My body reacted to Alexander's caresses, and my hips lifted up to meet him.

He smiled as we came together.

His speech was beautiful. Nassar wrote it down, and I have a copy of it somewhere. I don't need to read it though; I can remember the gist of it.

He gave a great banquet the next night, and the whole camp received meat. Fires burned, and the smell of roasting lamb and oxen filled the air. The men came to the banquet rather silently. They were confused and apprehensive. Rumours were circulating. Alexander waited until everyone had started eating, and then he stood. The cliff behind him amplified his words so that everyone could hear. The speech was long and it went something like this:

'Hail Iskander's army! Hail Macedonians, Greeks, Thracians, Persians, Madrians, Ariaspians, Uxions, Cosseens, Egyptians, Phoenicians, Thessalians, Corinthians –*etc., etc., etc.* I greet you. May your lives be long and all your endeavours crowned with success.'

(Polite applause made by snapping fingers, slapping thighs, clapping or hooting, depending upon the tribe.)

'I am speaking to you as your king, your commander, and also as your friend. We have gone through much together. You are more my family now than my mother or my father. You *are* my family, and as such I love and venerate you all.'

(Sounds of approval from the crowd.)

'We have travelled far, and yet I still have places to go. Faraway places. I hope you will all come with me. But I have not brought you here to talk about that just yet. Rather, I would like to say a few words about what happened yesterday.'

The crowd grew very still.

'Parmenion was a friend of my father's. He served him, and he served me. He was like a father to me, and I admired him. He loved me well; I was like a son to him. However, his true son, Philotas, was plotting to kill me. Three times did Liddexis come to tell Parmenion of the plot, and three times did Parmenion ignore him. Finally, out of desperation, Liddexis came into my tent at night, wakened me, and warned me of the plot.

'Philotas, his mistress Antigone, and his co-conspirator

Lycenus, were confronted. Lycenus cut his own throat. Antigone drank poison.

'Parmenion was a loyal general, and he venerated me. He also loved his son. He had already lost two sons in battles against the Persians. Perhaps you all remember them? Philotas was his last son, and Parmenion could not bear to outlive them all. He made me swear to grant him a wish, and then he asked me to kill him. He said he would be honoured to die by my hand.

'I did not want to kill him. I swear by Athena, I did not. However, I had sworn to grant his wish. All I could do was make sure he did not suffer. I promise you, he did not suffer.

'But *I* did. I had to kill a man I loved because of treason. Therefore I ask all of you now. Before thinking of treason, come and speak with me. Philotas thought, wrongly, that if I were killed, his father would reign and he could return home.

'Perhaps you want to go back home. I am saying right now, if any soldier wants to leave and return to his home, he may do so immediately. There will be no shame for him. I will understand, and he will be fully paid. I want you all to reflect upon this.

'Now, while the night is still young, let us dedicate this feast to Parmenion, to Zeus our father, and to Dionysus who gave us wine.' He raised his golden cup and drank deeply. His soldiers did the same with their cups, and the feast began in earnest.

He'd spoken simply, yet his voice had trembled with intense emotion. I was sitting close to him and I saw the effort he had to make to stand still. His whole body was vibrating with nerves. He was not a man who liked to explain himself. He expected those around him to share his viewpoints and agree with him, but he was an excellent orator when he had to be. He could rouse his men to absolute fever pitch when he needed. Tonight, when he wanted to calm and reassure, he was perfect. He ended on a happy note, with the mention of home and pay. The soldiers nodded sagely, and raised their glasses to him. If they hadn't understood the part about Parmenion and treason, they understood the notion of rewards and family. Smiles replaced frowns, and the atmosphere cleared even as the clouds moved aside. The stars shone upon us.

Now the crowd was lively and talk was loose and relaxed. Nervous tension had completely disappeared. Laughter ran around the edges of the camp, and the fires gaily threw their sparks into the air.

Alexander sat down beside me and took my hand in his.

'I meant what I said,' he told me. 'If you ever want to leave I will understand.'

'I will never leave you,' I said, kissing him softly. 'I may be on thin ice, but I need you, I love you, and I want you.' I slipped my hand under his tunic and tweaked his penis.

He jumped. 'Hey!'

'And I'm awfully proud of you,' I whispered in his ear. Alexander actually blushed.

Chapter Twenty-three

Alexander needed reassurance as much as anyone I'd ever known. Perhaps more than others. After the incident with Philotas something in him broke, and he was never the same. But the thing that broke was one of the fragile barriers that separated him from the rest of mankind, and suddenly he opened up. For the first time since I'd met him, he really talked to me.

We'd been travelling steadily for three weeks. The pace he set was gruelling, but the men were used to it and never complained. When we marched, the days all blended into each other so it was hard for me to keep track of time. Days flowed into weeks, and most of the time I had no idea what day it was.

I had always tried to keep track of time by my own calendar with names of the months and days I knew, but it was impossible, and so I drifted gradually into keeping time the Greek way.

Alexander kept all the major celebrations and made numerous sacrifices to the gods. His relationship with them was coloured with ambiguity. The Greeks believed in many gods, and, as I was learning, hundreds of spirits, sprites and nymphs. But for the past hundred years or so, philosophers had been challenging the old beliefs and trying to change them.

The gods were omnipresent and could be swayed by

words or sacrifices. Every morning the sun was greeted with a salute. After all, it was Helios, in his golden chariot, and his sister Eos was the dawn. Rain was not rain, but a gift, and the Greeks didn't say, 'It's raining,' they said, 'Zeus rains,' or 'Zeus thunders.' Bread was not baked without a prayer of thanks to Demeter, goddess of the harvest. The fire in the fireplace was not lit, water was not fetched, grass was not cut without asking permission of one of the gods. If misfortune followed, it was because the gods were not pleased.

By the time Alexander was educated, there was an important shift in the way people thought about gods. Some people were even professing themselves atheists. Alexander was caught in a time where the changes were not fully developed. The ideas were there, but they were superimposed on the old customs. It was a time of fluid uncertainties, and Alexander hesitated between wanting to appease the gods and wanting to defy them.

He wanted to defy them, because he was sure that his cause was divine in itself. Wasn't he bringing Greek civilization to the far corners of the world? How could they not appreciate him? Who were they anyway, to meddle in his business? Didn't Aristotle teach him that the gods were not concerned with human affairs? However, his mother had been a priestess in the temple with the sacred fire, and she believed otherwise. Olympias didn't take a step in the morning without consulting the oracles.

So who was right?

Deep down, Alexander was an atheist; his only god was himself. But he had been raised by a hysterical woman who thought she had conceived Alexander while visited by the god Zeus. It was flattering, somehow, for him to think he descended directly from a god, especially when there were great heroes in his family. He was torn between pride in himself, for what he had achieved, and pride in the idea he was partly divine. The two thoughts were diametrically opposed, and yet he held tightly to both ideas, somehow forcing them together and combining them in his 'self'. He loved the sacrifices more for their celebration than for their reasons. He was born in the month of Hekatombaion, late July. He claimed to be the sign of the Lion, 'The first day of the Lion,' as he'd say proudly. He was born in the middle of a raging storm, full of the thunder of Zeus and the rain of Zeus, which made it doubly auspicious.

'And do you know what else?' he asked me. We were both riding, which we didn't do very often, but I had a stomach ache so had been lagging behind, and he'd felt the urge to ride Bucephalus. He'd gone galloping around all morning, and now he was cooling his stallion off. He joined me at the end of the line, where I was plodding along on my little grey mare.

'No, what?' I tried to put polite interest into my voice, but I was in a terrible mood. My period had come, and with it cramps and irritability. Because of my miscarriage, and the fact I was so thin, I hadn't had my period in over six months, so I hadn't been expecting it and didn't know how to cope with it. I was in a land with no tampons or feminine hygiene napkins, and since I lived in a tent with only men, I was embarrassed about asking them what to do. It made me grumpy.

'While my mother was writhing in labour, trying to

363

expel me from her womb, you'll never guess what flew into the temple to take shelter.'

'What did?'

'Come on, take a guess!'

There's nothing worse than someone cheerful when you're in a bad mood. You just want to push them off their clouds. I pretended to think. 'Bats?'

'Bats! No, something incredible. Something that made my mother and the priests say, "This baby is going to be something special!".'

'Let's see. Something that flies at night, but wasn't a bat.'

'There were two of them,' he reminded me.

'Moths? Two big moths?'

He snorted. 'No! You're not being serious. What's so special about moths?'

'What's so special about you?' I asked, making a face as another cramp twisted my stomach. 'Being born in a rainstorm? Having things come inside to get out of the rain? Having a crazy mother?'

He was speechless, staring at me. His face fell. His bubble had burst, and I felt awful. I reined in my pony.

'I'm sorry, I'm being terrible. Will you sit here with me for a while? My back aches, my legs are sore, and I want a drink. There's a stream over there, and a shady tree. Let's rest, and you can tell me about the eagles.'

'You knew about the eagles?' He sounded unsure of himself.

'Of course, everyone does.' I smiled, trying to appease him. 'It was an amazing sign. Naturally, everyone was impressed.'

364

We took our horses' bridles off and hobbled them, then sat side by side on a fallen log. I was thirsty, so I filled my water flask with fresh water from the stream and sipped it. 'Do you want some?'

'Why do you never thank the nymph of the stream, or ask to take her water?' he asked me.

'Does one have to speak aloud?' I countered. 'Don't you think that, if there is a divinity here, and she's watching me, she'll see how much I appreciate the water? She should be able to read my thoughts and hear my silent thanks.'

'Sarcasm displeases the gods,' he said.

'Sarcasm displeases people who take themselves too seriously,' I quipped.

His fingers were laced over his knees, his parti-coloured eyes staring into mine. I was suddenly shocked to see tears. He didn't move, didn't try to hide. He sat there, and looked at me and cried. My own bubble burst with a whoosh.

'Please don't look at me like that,' I said miserably. 'It makes me feel like I've kicked a puppy.'

'What gives you the right to act so high and mighty?' he asked suddenly. 'What gives you the right to pass judgment? Who are you? How can you say my mother is crazy?'

'Ah, the crux of the matter,' I murmured.

He looked startled then bit his lip, frowning. 'Yes, the crux of the matter.'

'I'm sorry, I didn't mean to hurt you. I take it back about your mother.'

'Don't you think I knew about all that?' he asked. He

looked bleakly at the swift stream. 'Don't you think I heard the rumours growing up? I was there. I was there and saw everything. My mother never hid anything from me, even though sometimes I would have given my right arm to be blind and deaf.'

He looked up at me, his face desolate. 'When I was a little boy I believed she was the Goddess of Love. She used to laugh when I called her that, but she didn't contradict me. Later, when the priest taught me about Aphrodite, I was whipped because I dared say I saw her every day. I was five years old, and I didn't quite understand.

'At first my father and my mother loved each other well. Everything was as it should be. Then he married another woman, and my mother told me she feared for her life. She fled to Epirus with me. I spent three years with my mother's family in Epirus, then, when I was ten, my father sent for me. I went back and was educated in Macedonia, and then Greece. My mother came every now and then to make sure I was being raised properly, and I know that each time she caused trouble in the court.

'She was so lovely. How could my father resist her? But he did. He was terrified of her. He would leave to go to war, then she would visit, and my new brother or sister would mysteriously die. I was twelve years old when I realized she was actually killing the babes. Do you think I liked that? Knowing she was mad? Yet with me she was sweetness and light, all the good things possible, and she let me touch her, and she showed me how to pleasure her and myself.' He shuddered to a halt, breathing hard.

I just opened my flask and closed it, turning it in my

hands, watching the tiny minnows in the stream. The silence dragged on. I said nothing. There was nothing to say.

'I loved her and hated her. I think that the reason I'm who I am is only because of her. I'm doing everything I can to get as far away from her as possible. I'm trying to amass more power than she, a goddess, can ever have. To avenge each babe I must kill a hundred thousand enemies. To honour each brother and sister I never had, I must build great cities. For my father, I can never do enough.' His voice was a hard whisper. He was having trouble breathing again; his face was congested, and I wondered if he were asthmatic.

'Alex?' I put my hand on his arm and squeezed. 'None of that is your fault. You were caught between your parents, but that doesn't mean you are like them. It was just circumstances, and you must try not to let them ruin your life. You're a good person, a great person. Why, you're Alexander the Great, don't you know?'

The look on his face was so terrible. It was like that of a dying man. 'I *don't* know,' he said slowly, taking time to draw each breath. 'And I don't know who you are. Will you tell me, Ashley? Please?'

I closed my eyes. It was taking all my willpower not to break down and tell him, but how could I? If I loved him at all, I couldn't tell him. I shook my head dumbly.

He stood up and untied his horse. Without a word or a glance, he left. He was nearly purple with the effort of breathing. I knew Usse would give him something to ease him, but nothing Usse had could ease my pain. I curled up under the tree next to the brook. I decided to stay there, under the tree, for ever. I would just let myself die. It would be easier than seeing Alexander tearing himself apart.

What I'd seen in Alexander's face was the knowledge that he was mortal, the knowledge that he was going to have to pay for the sins of his fathers, and the realization that he was nothing. Nothing but dust upon the face of the earth.

Chapter Twenty-four

Plexis came back for me. He would always come back for me. He had been watching Alexander, as he always watched him. He watched him leave in high spirits and come back suicidal. He divined some sort of problem with me, since I was nowhere to be seen, and once he'd made sure Alexander was all right, he rode back to find me.

He never would have seen me but for the grey mare, grazing nearby. He parted the branches of the willow tree and saw me, huddled in the grass. He was used to misery so he sat on the log and rolled up a few willow leaves. It was a habit he had. Soon I was surrounded by little coils of leaves. I watched as they slowly unwound themselves. One landed on my cheek.

'Why didn't you leave me behind?' I asked.

'Did you want me to?' He sounded sincerely hurt, and I rolled over and sat up.

'No, I suppose not.'

'You made Iskander very unhappy.'

'I'm sorry, but the worst part is, I didn't make him unhappy. He was already unhappy, and he just let some of it out. That's all. He told me about his mother.'

Plexis raised one eyebrow. 'Oh.'

'But I *was* mean to him. Oh, Plexis, I'm such a horrible person! I teased him about the eagles.'

His mouth twitched, but he didn't quite smile. 'He

doesn't have too much to be proud of in his childhood, except those eagles.'

'I realize that now,' I said heavily. 'It just seemed so ridiculous to me at the time. He has so very much to be proud of, and yet he doesn't seem to know it.'

'Why don't you tell him, then?' The tone was still gentle, making me feel even worse.

'I will.' I sighed and got to my feet. The fact that there were no decent feminine hygiene products became evident the minute I stood. Blood ran down my legs. I started crying.

'Hormones?' Plexis's voice was sympathetic.

I was laughing and crying at the same time. Plexis did that to me. He led me to the stream and I sat in it. He washed me with his one good arm quite clinically. He washed my body, and my face, and even my hair, which always got horribly greasy when I got my period. He washed me off and dried me with his cloak. He held me tightly, and let me cry on his unbroken shoulder until I felt better.

'I'm sorry,' I said again. 'It's just my period. I'll be all right. If only there were something I could wear that would help.'

'Your mother didn't show you?' he asked cautiously. He didn't like getting onto the subject of my family. I shook my head. He sighed. 'Ah, well. I think you'd better come with me. I'm sure Usse will find you something.'

We rode slowly after the army and arrived when everyone had settled, and dusk was making it hard to see the road. The fires looked inviting, but before I could go into the tent I took care of my pony, and then went into

370

the bathhouse to clean off again. It was dreadful not having tampons.

Usse gave me a few linen bandages and I made bulky napkins. I tied them around my waist and between my legs with more linen strips. It looked awful and felt worse, and I spent three days being absolutely miserable to everyone. They learned from Plexis that I had some dreadful affliction called 'hormones'. Axiom was very impressed, Usse warily sympathetic, Callisthenes bore the brunt of my bad humour, with his silly harp and silly baby songs, and Alexander stayed as far away from me as possible.

I think Plexis explained things to him though, because after a few days he joined me at the back of the line again. I was feeling better; I'd found a stream, bathed with some of Usse's 'soap' and felt almost human again.

Alexander and I looked sideways at each other. He'd been coming to bed very late each night, after making sure I was asleep. And I'd lain as still as possible so he'd think I was asleep. Everyone in the tent was pretending to be asleep, and the result was no one slept, and we were all getting terribly tired and cranky.

'I'm sorry, can I explain?' We both spoke at once. I blushed and Alexander grinned. We pulled the horses up, leaned over and kissed. I slid off my mare's back, and we walked a little way until we came to a pretty meadow.

I bent to pick a flower, and then, mindful of my mistake with the stream, I asked, 'O flower, do you mind if I pick you?'

'What are you doing?' Alexander was staring at me, perplexed.

'Asking permission of the flower nymph.' I was proud of myself; I'd remembered something.

'Flowers have no nymphs,' he said, frowning. 'They last but a few days. Streams, trees, springs, lakes; these things have nymphs.'

'Oh.' I looked at the flower and then at the meadow. 'It's an easy mistake for a beginner,' I said, smiling.

'Ashley,' he said, 'sit here next to me.'

We walked to a little hollow surrounded by tall, yellow golden-rod. Alexander spread his cloak on the ground, and we sat on it. The bees were buzzing around us, and the air was scented with honey and dried grass. There was an autumn smell in the air. I was feeling melancholy; the season did that to me. I sighed deeply.

'It has come to my attention that you've been crying a lot lately,' he said, plucking some daisies and starting a daisy chain. 'I want to know why you're so unhappy. Will you tell me that at least?'

'Well, yes, if I could. I think it's just an autumn thing, you know, leaves falling, flowers dying, and winter coming. I get melancholy around this time. I love this season, but it's a sad time of year. It's like nature's in mourning, and I get depressed easily.'

'I see.' He held up the daisy chain and looked at it critically. 'So, it has nothing to do with me?'

'No, nothing to do with you.' I lay down and put my head on his lap, so I could look up at him. The sun was behind him, making a corona around his head. He'd started dying his hair again, brassy yellow, but it suited him. I smiled. 'You're so handsome,' I said. I reached up and stroked his cheek. It was softly scratchy with whiskers and there were scars on his chin. I twisted around a bit and examined his leg. A scar climbed up his thigh, and another scar made a 'V' on his shoulder. I traced it with my finger. 'What was that?' I asked.

'A lance.' He sounded tired.

'Did it hurt?'

'Of course. Are you just going to say inane things? Or do you really want to talk?'

I tried to look as if what he'd said didn't hurt, but it was impossible. I'd started wearing my emotions close to the skin and I was hypersensitive now. My mouth trembled. He leaned over and pressed his lips to mine. They were warm and firm. I pulled his head down further and kissed him hard.

'Can we talk now?' he asked. His eyes were pleading, one blue, one brown, both colours sad today.

I closed my eyes. If I were erased, so be it. I couldn't hurt Alexander any more. He took my silence for a reproach. His childhood had been so dreadful that he couldn't stand rejection. When I was erased, Paul would vanish too. It broke my heart, but we had no place here anyway.

'I will tell you everything you want to know,' I said.

'I don't want you to tell me what I want to know.' He was infuriating. 'I want you to tell me what is bothering you. Don't you care about me any more?'

'Of course I do!'

'How can you care for me and not tell me about yourself? How you grew up, where you lived, what you did as a child? How can you keep such things secret?'

'Don't *you* have secrets?' I asked. 'You never told me

about Cxious, for example.'

He blanched. 'I only wanted to hear a little about your childhood,' he said. 'Perhaps some good memories you could share with me.' He said this heavily, shredding the daisy chain into little pieces.

I took his hands. 'I said I would tell you everything, and I will, despite the consequences. I love you. I don't care about Cxious, or your mother, or your father, or even your other wives. I care about you.' I stopped and searched for the words I needed. 'What I tell you must stay a secret between us. No one else can ever know.'

'Except Plexis when he dies.' It was said without the faintest trace of humour.

'If I'm there to tell him.'

I thought that when I told Alexander I came from the future, I'd disappear in the seconds that followed, but I was ready. Perhaps it was the season. I was surrounded by autumn.

I sat up and hugged Alexander tightly. Then my hands moved down his body. I closed my eyes. I wanted to memorize each and every inch of him. I wanted to imprint his body into my being. I loved the way his stomach contracted when I stroked his groin. I loved the wiry hair on his belly and the smoothness of his sex. I stoked it and felt the velvet softness become a shivering hardness. My heart echoed in Alexander's harsh breathing. I looked up at him. 'May I make love to you?'

He nodded, and I saw the muscles work in his neck as he swallowed.

I pushed him down, and I made love to him. I wouldn't let him move. Each time he tried to, I held him still. I had never made love to him before, he had always made love to me, and I had accepted it. Now I took my time, and I took his body and made it mine.

He was not used to staying motionless. I sat on him, looking down at him, and I moved my hips gently. I closed my eyes and held myself very still, to feel the beating of his heart within the very depths of me. Then I opened my eyes wide and stared into his face. He was concentrating on not moving. Sweat pearled on his brow; his hair touched the moisture and curled, lifting off his forehead and temples. I pressed my lips to his, then moved to his eyes, his temples, and down to his neck. I kept on going downwards, tickling with my tongue until I found him, and then I took him in my mouth.

He jerked like a fish on a line, but I put my hands firmly on his hips and held him. My hair was a silvery curtain, hiding my face. He was breathing in great gasps, with a soft moan in between. I tickled him with my fingers and my hair, but I wouldn't let him finish. I would start a rhythm and then change it. Each time I brought him to the brink, and then I pushed him away. I wanted it to last for ever. It was the last chance I'd get.

I sat up again and straddled him, gently guiding him inside me. I made him arch his back up towards me and rode him like a horse, sliding back and forth until suddenly the breath caught in my throat, and the throbbing in my belly exploded throughout my body. With a cry, I flung myself onto him and rolled over, pulling him on top of me. I urged him on with my hands and my hips. I whispered all the things I loved the most about his body, while he shivered and shuddered against me, finally losing himself with a hoarse cry that seemed to shake the ground beneath us.

We quivered, our bodies trembling against each other's. I held on to Alexander while my body convulsed. It seemed that it would never be still. Each time I moved and felt his body, his arm, his leg, or his chest, it would start again. The throbbing would shake me, and I would moan into Alexander's neck.

He held me until the tremors ceased and I relaxed. He rolled away from me. He face was drained of all emotion. It was as if he'd woken up after a long sleep. He looked over at me. I was still lying on my back, incapable of moving anything.

'I can see why you don't do that at night in the tent,' he said, when he got his breath back.

'It would wake up most of the camp,' I agreed, smiling wanly, my chest heaving.

'But I think I could get used to it, you know, every once a year or so.' He cleared his throat. 'It was very nice.'

'Thank you.'

'Thank you.' He pursed his lips. His eyes were dreamy.

I cleared my throat. 'I was born in the future. It won't mean anything to you to know the date, but it will make sense if I say that it's more than three thousand years from now.' I glanced at him to see how he was taking this, but he hadn't moved and his face hadn't changed. 'I was born to elderly people who were profoundly embarrassed by my arrival. I was unwanted, and was sent away to school as soon as possible. I grew up surrounded by tutors of every kind, but had no friends at all. My father died when I was ten. When I was sixteen I was married to a much older man. The marriage was a disaster, and I divorced soon after.

'I enrolled in journalism school, because I'd always wanted to, and because I'd always been good with languages. I was especially gifted in the dead languages, Ancient Greek and Latin, so I specialized in a programme called Time-Journalism. Five years later, I won a prestigious award and I was chosen to travel in time. I decided to interview you, and the rest is, as they say, "history".'

I laughed nervously and looked down at my feet. For some reason, I was sure that the erasure would start at my toes and then work its way up, rather like the Cheshire Cat in *Alice in Wonderland*. Perhaps my smile would float in the air a bit before I disappeared completely. I hoped my teeth were clean. I wanted to leave a good impression.

My toes were still there. I wiggled one. Yes, it still worked. I frowned. How odd.

'You came from the future?' Alexander's face was very white.

I nodded, not sure what he'd understood.

'You came from more than three thousand years in the future,' he breathed. His eyes started to glow, as what I'd told him sank in. 'And more than three thousand years from now people still know of me?' His face broke into one, huge, gigantic grin.

'Listen to me,' I said sternly. 'I will not tell you anything about your own future, is that clear? I told you I'd talk about me, not about you.'

377

He laughed and rubbed his chin. He shook his head and looked at his own toes, flexing his feet. 'Three thousand years.' He put his hand on my arm. 'So the people of your world travel through time as easily as we sail down a river?'

'No, it's not easy at all. It takes so much energy that the voyage is limited. Only one person a year can travel, and can stay but twenty hours.'

'Amazing. Amazing.' He kept shaking his head, an idiotic grin on his face. 'And how does it work? I mean, I can't imagine,' he spread his hands, 'three thousand years. It seems so … so immense.'

'It is immense,' I said sadly.

'I want to understand,' he said, getting excited, 'I want to know everything. What do the people eat, how do they live …' He broke off suddenly, his eyes growing wide. 'There are no gods in your time!' he whispered.

I shook my head. 'Not exactly; not the ones you know.'

His mouth twisted and he shivered. 'Are there any kings?'

I shook my head. 'Not in the sense you know.'

'Is there anything I know?' he asked forlornly.

I smiled. 'Democracy. The system has lasted and prospered. Philosophy, art, Hellenistic art, the kind you love so well, is highly appreciated still. Music and wine, we love these things. We still hate lawyers,' I grinned.

'Ah well, Demosthenes *was* a bad precursor.' He grinned back, but it was strained.

'We have no slaves. We live in huge cities, bigger even than Babylon. We don't use horses any more. We use

378

electric cars and fly in gravity planes. Centuries ago our world discovered fossil fuel, and we had cars and planes, but they caused too much pollution, and the world nearly ended. Since then we've been more careful.'

He shook his head. 'I know not what you mean.'

'I mean mankind nearly destroyed the earth in the name of progress.'

'Progress is bad, then?'

'No, but it has to be controlled. Unfortunately, we are not good at controlling ourselves.'

'You use words that have no meaning to me,' he said, bewildered. 'Fossil fuel, pollution, electric cars, gravity planes. They mean nothing.'

His memory was phenomenal. He'd recited the words without a fault, but I hated his forlorn look.

'I'll explain everything slowly, each time we're alone. But never, ever, tell anyone else.'

'I swore – does that mean nothing to you?'

'I'm sorry. That's another thing. In my time people say things they don't mean all the time.'

'A whole society of lawyers,' he said, smiling through his tears.

I hugged him. 'Oh, Alexander, I love you so much.'

'I love you too.' He sounded surprised. He tipped my head back and kissed me. 'What made you choose to come to me?'

'I'm not sure,' I said. 'I think I was in love with you the moment I heard about you.'

'Three thousand years from now, people will hear about me?'

'Yes.'

'Amazing.' He shook his head again. 'I can't take it all in. It's too strange.' He thought for a while, a frown on his face, then he said, 'And you were only supposed to stay a very short time. Is that what you said? Only a day?'

'That's right.'

'And when I saved you I was actually condemning you to live for ever in my time?'

'Yes, that's right.' I looked at my toes again.

'And you don't hate me for it?'

I looked up at him quickly. 'Oh no! I don't hate you at all!'

'Are you sure?'

'Yes. I swear, I swear by all your gods and mine, the ones I know about, anyway. I'll always be happy, if you just let me stay with you. So please, promise you'll always let me.'

His smile was blinding. 'Oh, Ashley. Of course you will stay with me.' He gathered me in his arms. 'And we'll find our son and live in Alexandria, and I'll be king and I'll make you my queen and ...'

'Alex,' I put my hand on his arm. 'Listen to me. Listen carefully. I must never become your queen. I must never appear in the history books. If I change history the slightest bit, I will ...' I searched for an appropriate word. 'I'll vanish. I'll be undone. I don't want to disappear. I want to stay here with you. Do you understand my predicament?'

He was silent a long time, pondering my words. Then he shuddered, once, very hard. 'Have you heard about the sword of Damocles?' he asked.

I nodded, my skin prickling.

'That is what is hanging over your head. I understand now.'

'Thank you,' I whispered. 'It means so much to me to be able to talk about it.'

'I'm sure it does,' he said. 'And you must feel free to tell me whatever you want me to know. I will never ask of you anything that may bring the sword down upon your head. And if you see that I am deviating from the history books because of you, you must tell me what to do to save you.'

I was crying now, as was he. I simply nodded, incapable of talking. We sobbed in each other's arms, and then Alexander said, 'I'm so glad I decided to cheer you up.'

I wiped my nose with the back of my hand and sniffed. 'I was thinking that I spent too much time crying.'

'You were right,' he said, and we burst into tears again. That's how Plexis found us.

He rode up, swinging off his horse when he heard us crying. 'Iskander! Ashley! What is it? What happened?'

'Nothing,' Alexander wiped his tears away and tried to grin at his friend.

'But didn't you tell me that you were going to find Ashley to cheer her up?' Plexis was confused.

'I did,' said Alexander.

'He did,' I echoed, wiping away my tears.

'Oh, well, I'm glad to see that you're both joyful now,' he said, looking back and forth at us. 'So, what was the problem?' he asked, poking a toe at Alexander's cloak.

Alexander smiled at me. 'Ashley wanted to make me scream with pleasure,' he said, 'and she didn't want to do it in the tent, because she didn't want to wake everyone up.'

'Oh?' Plexis looked really interested now. He pursed his lips, and I realized he and Alexander shared many of the same expressions. He cocked his head. 'Will you let *me* comfort Ashley next time, then?' he asked. He dodged a well-thrown rock and got back on his horse. 'It's not fair,' he called back over his shoulder, 'I was the one who told you she needed cheering up. You get all the fun.'

He rode away, and I lay back on the ground. Alexander lay next to me and we watched the sun setting. 'I know about you and Plexis,' he said at last.

I froze, then blushed. His voice held no clue as to what he was thinking. 'Are you angry?'

'I was at first. But I love you both so well, I could not stay angry for long.'

I heaved a sigh. Sighing and crying, two things I'd never done in my time. 'I promise I will never be unfaithful to you again,' I said, taking his face in my hands.

'Whatever you do,' he said seriously, 'do not make vain promises. If by chance you and Plexis make love again, I will probably kill you both.'

I swallowed. 'I understand,' I said in a tiny voice.

He raised his eyebrows. 'Really? Are people in your time so concerned with faithfulness? I would never kill you or Plexis for that. I would be frightfully jealous, I already was. But I figured you were mad about Barsine, and Plexis always was a horny bastard.'

'So why did you say it, then?' I asked.

He shrugged. 'To frighten you. I suppose, for a second

at least. When I thought you didn't love me any more, I was frightened. My mother taught me a great deal about revenge.'

'It would be best if you forgot most of it,' I said.

'Doubtless.' He grinned.

'So, can I show Plexis how I made you scream?' I said teasingly.

'Yes, with me. If you really want to, we can show him.' His smile showed how well he knew me.

I drew my finger down his forehead, over his nose and across his beautiful mouth. I cupped his face in my hands and I drank his kisses. We made love again as the sky turned violet and gold and the stars started to twinkle above us.

'There are so many things I want to ask you,' he said dreamily, 'so many things, I don't know where to start.'

'Start with the stars then,' I said softly.

'Are they really suns and planets?'

'Yes, and further away than you can imagine.'

He propped himself up on his elbow and looked down at me. 'My imagination knows no limits,' he said. 'Absolutely none at all.'

This, I thought, was perhaps the secret behind his success. He knew no limits, and he made everyone around him believe in the impossible.

'How many people would believe me?' I asked, kissing him again. 'Hardly anyone, and even if they did, they would be incapable of understanding me. They would think of me as a goddess. They would strip me of my humanity. You are the only one who could actually comprehend the distance that separates us and still believe we can love each other.'

'Maybe it's because nobody in my own time has ever fully understood me.'

'Nobody in my time understands you, either,' I said. It was cruel, but I said it unthinkingly.

He looked up and frowned. His pure profile was silhouetted on the night sky like a cameo. He reached up a hand and pretended to pluck a star. 'I tried not to mind when my father beat me, or when my mother caressed me. I didn't care if my father called me a coward, or a ninny, or made fun of me. I wanted to read, not fight. I wanted to study the philosophies and become a healer. I loved medicine; does history tell you that? Do the historians say, "Iskander loved to read and wanted to become a philosopher"? Do they tell how I cried when my mother told me my baby brother died? She thought I would be grateful. Do they say how much I love beauty?' His voice paled and faded. 'Will you sing me one of your songs? Sing me one for your gods, if you have any left.'

I thought a minute, then sang an old song that was already a few centuries old when I'd learned it: *Let It Be*. I sang the Beatles to Alexander the Great.

Alexander had not moved, but his mouth curved in a smile. 'That's a very wise song,' he said. 'Mary. The goddess Mary. Mother Mary. Let it be.'

Night had claimed the sky. There were patches of stars and some low clouds. A small squall blew across the meadow, dropping a light rain upon us. Then the sky cleared again and the stars blazed.

'Zeus rained,' he said dreamily. 'A good omen. I think I'll found a city nearby, over there, where the rocks are gleaming in the moonlight. I'll call her Alexandria Margiane. Mary Alexandria. And then we'll go over the mountains.' His voice was soft and low, the breeze was cool, and the rain had made the earth and plants release their scent.

We wrapped up in his cloak, two naked humans under Uranus, the vast sky. Two specks of dust upon the face of Gaea, the mother earth. The night birds called to each other, the crickets chirped. Alexander put his face in the crook of my neck and cried. His body shook and I held him still. He was crying for his gods, for his mortality, and for the unfairness of it all. And for the wonder of it all.

'I always dreamed that I would rule the world,' he said, after his sorrow lifted. 'But it was the dream of a child. Now I am a man. I don't want to rule the world; I will let others rule it for me, my governors or my satraps. I want to *know* the world. I want to possess it. I want to see everything everywhere, to learn all the languages, speak to all the philosophers, and learn all the secrets the world has kept since the beginning of time.' His voice swelled and the earth beneath him vibrated with it. He seemed to grow beside me, to change. He was no longer a man, he was something else. He was pure energy, humanity distilled and refined into a single, concentrated essence.

I held him and felt his muscles tighten, as if he wanted to leap to his feet. He was shaking. Then he relaxed, and his arms went around me once more.

'I want to build a kingdom, I want to destroy nothing. Do your historians say that, when they speak of me?'

I took his face in my hands and I said, 'All your cities

will be like glittering diamonds set in the face of the earth. Everything you touch will be graced with beauty, and your name shall voyage three thousand years into the future. When people say your name, they will say it with respect and awe for what you've done. Even if they never know why.'

'Even though, for me, it is the why that matters the most?' he said.

'I'm sorry.'

He looked at me, and his parti-coloured eyes flashed, one light, one dark. 'Let it be,' he said, not without humour. 'Whisper words of wisdom. Let it be.' Then we kissed.

I could have kissed him all night. But a faint smell of smoke was in the air now and we had to go back to the camp, where sixty thousand men revolved like asteroids and planets around the sun that was Alexander.

End of Book One

Read on for an excerpt from Book Two
Heroes in the Dust

"As Children learn good manners
As Youth learn to control passions
In Middle Age be just
In Old Age be wise
Then Death shall bring no regrets."

Delphic Maxim engraved on monuments in the cities founded by Alexander the Great

"One day there shall come into the rich lands of Asia
An unbelieving man
Wearing upon his shoulders a purple cloak.
Savage, fiery, a stranger to justice. A thunderbolt
Raised him up, though he is but a man.
All Asia shall suffer; the earth shall drink blood
Hades shall attend him, although he knows it not.
And in the end those whom he wished to destroy
By them will he and all his race be destroyed."

Ancient Persian Oracle

Chapter One

Mist obscured the mountaintops. The path I was following rose steadily and was worn smooth by the passage of hundreds of feet and hooves. Taking advantage of a pause, I bent and scraped some snow off a boulder. Next to me, Plexis stopped walking, stretched, then caught sight of my hands. 'What's that?'

'A snowball.'

'What does one do with it?'

I smiled sweetly. 'One throws it! Catch!' WHACK! I threw the snowball as hard as I could, catching Plexis on the chin. His expression of shocked outrage turned to one of an avenging angel. He scooped up a handful of slushy snow and patted it into a snowball.

'Like this?' he asked, cocking his head to one side. His clear brown eyes were guileless, his dark brown hair curled in ringlets around his high-cheekboned face. He looked like a Raphaelite angel. Appearances can be misleading.

I giggled and dodged around the side of my pony. 'Sort of.' I peeked over the withers and received a faceful of snow. 'No fair!' I bent down and tried to make another snowball, but the fine, fluffy stuff was melting as fast as it fell and was starting to turn to rain. I looked up at the sky, soft and grey as the belly of a turtledove just over my head. 'Well, that was snow,' I said, licking the last of it off my lips. 'Haven't you ever seen it before?'

'No, I lived in Athens. It never snowed there. Iskander saw snow when he was a child in Macedonia. He was always lording it over me. He made it sound so wonderful.' His voice was wistful. 'I never thought it would look like ashes.'

I was startled. 'Ashes?' I looked at the snow differently now. The snowflakes, fat and gentle as feathers, did look like wood ash. I smiled. 'The first time I saw snow I thought it was bits of paper. I was sitting downstairs, and I fancied the maid was throwing torn newspaper out the upstairs window. I rushed to see, but nobody was there. It gave me a shock. I must have been only four years old, but I remember it clearly.'

'There you go again with your strange stories,' Plexis teased. 'I suppose I'll ask you what a newspaper is and you'll say, "I can't tell you," and I'll spend another day longing for death.'

I gave a shocked laugh. 'You don't really believe in the prophecy, do you? The oracle said I'd answer your questions on your deathbed, but did you ever stop to think that perhaps you'll be disappointed?'

'No, and I have a list somewhere – a list of things I'm going to ask you, so you'd better be prepared.'

'Well, a newspaper is a sort of papyrus with all the daily events written on it, like a journal.'

'Like the one Onesicrite's writing?' He wiped the last bit of snow off his face and pulled his cloak tighter around his shoulders.

'I don't know, is he writing one?'

'He's sending all the latest news to Athens.'

'I didn't realize that.' I frowned. Onesicrite had arrived a few weeks ago, as puffed up with self-importance as a ruffled chicken. He and Nearchus were always coming into our tent in the evenings. I had wondered why Onesicrite asked so many questions of my husband and wrote everything down on a parchment. I was used to the scribes and historians. I hadn't thought for one minute there would also be a journalist. 'I assumed he was just one of Nearchus's pals,' I said. Nearchus was the admiral of my husband's navy.

'Nearchus is flattered by him. The city of Athens has hired Onesicrite to write about Iskander's conquests.' Plexis narrowed his eyes as he stared at the sky. 'Snow is such flimsy, wet stuff,' he said, sniffing. 'I can't believe Iskander made it sound so marvellous when we were young.'

He called my husband Iskander, as did many people. In time, he would be known as Alexander the Great, but right now he was simply Iskander, king of Macedonia, Greece, Egypt and most of Persia. We were following him over the Hindu-Kush Mountains. The mountains were the Himalayas and we were still on the lowest slopes. It was autumn, and winter was nipping at our heels hurrying us along. We had hired guides to take us through the mountain passes, although we'd been warned it would be difficult.

Alexander marched at the head of his army. With sixty thousand soldiers, it was a formidable fighting machine. It was also a city unto itself, full of men from different countries with different languages and customs, all following Alexander like the tail trailing behind a comet.

The army carried along priests and whores, soldiers' wives and children, cooks, engineers, doctors, scribes, historians, diplomats, lawyers, botanists, astrologers, grooms, messengers, slaves, and – last of all – me.

I was born three thousand years in the future. I used to take a monorail to the city, and here I was on foot leading a pony, with the closest city some three hundred parasanges away. A *parasange* is a Persian measurement equalling twenty *stades*, or five thousand fifty metres if you prefer. The city we were heading towards might have a gym, a courthouse, a bakery, a temple, a fountain, and then again, it might not. It might be just a huddle of mud huts near a sullen stream. One thing it would not have would be a Tele-time station to send me home. Home was here and now, early December 330 BC.

Over my knee-length linen tunic and cotton shift, I wore a thick woollen cloak. Sturdy boots replaced my leather sandals for the march over the mountains. I had a knit cap with a jaunty red pompom, and I'd made myself mittens.

While I slogged through wet snow and mud, I daydreamed about the ten-bedroom house I was born in with its five maids and butler, and the cook, Daphne, who made such wonderful scalloped potato pie. Potatoes would make it to Europe in roughly one thousand five hundred years. I did not daydream about my mother, who had made my life hell, nor about my father, who was dead. I hadn't known him well enough to grieve. I'd seen him at most twice a year until he died of old age when I was ten years old.

My mother had been in her fifties when I was born. I

was an accident, and my arrival embarrassed both parents deeply. I spent my life in boarding schools until my mother managed to marry me off to a much older, brutal man. The memory of my parents and my marriage made me glum, and the grey sky was depressing enough, so I tried to think about something cheerful. Like my Brookner Prize. I'd won the coveted journalistic prize when I was still in Tempus University. Unheard of! Then I was chosen to participate in the time-journalism programme, to which most people don't get invited until they have been journalists for decades. And to top that off, I'd beaten thousands of candidates and was selected to go back into the past.

The smiles I received from my colleagues could have cut glass. Everyone was sure I'd bought my way into the programme, because my mother's fortune was colossal, I had a title, and my photo was often in the society pages. I didn't care. I was about to embark on a voyage to the distant past to interview the famous personage of my choice. I had chosen Alexander the Great, a childhood hero, and I would meet him in person.

Time travelling uses an extravagant amount of energy and can only be done once a year. The lights on the entire planet dim for the thirty minutes the magnetic beam is in use, and twenty-two hours later, when the person is picked up again, the lights dim once more all over the planet. Such is the power of the beam and the renown of the programme. No one can ignore it. The trip is a stomach-wrenching, head-splitting journey. You freeze solid, your bones and blood turn to ice, and you pass out while your atoms are disconnected and spiralled through the magnetic beam into the past. Sometimes they recover cadavers from the beam.

I'd survived. I was unconscious when I arrived in a secluded spot in the past, and I threw up right after I regained consciousness. It was an awful trip. No one had bothered to tell me. I bet they were all grinning, thinking about me writhing and shivering on the ground while my body thawed out and the frost left my veins.

I'd made my way to Alexander's encampment. I'd met him and made quite a fool of myself pretending to be a temple virgin, asking silly questions like, 'What do you want to do with your life?' I had a lot to learn about the people of that time. For one thing, they were incredibly sensitive to sound. They were careful about what they said, because the spoken word was the only way most of them could communicate. I was an enigma. Alexander loved mysteries. He proceeded to kidnap me.

He followed me when I had to leave and saw me being pulled into the frozen magnetic beam. It makes an eerie blue light and the cold is intense. He actually pulled me out of it, and somehow we'd both survived. But I was trapped in the past, and I couldn't let anyone know who I was. If I changed history in the slightest the time-senders would use the beam to erase me. It was incredibly precise. And so, with that Damocles sword hanging over my head, I lived with Alexander. He married me, which was sweet of him. He also thought I was Demeter's daughter being taken back to the underworld by the god of the dead, Hades. Everyone believed that. My stupid grass sandals that the Institute of Time Travel made for me, the ones that cut my feet and made me limp, were sitting in a temple in Arbeles being prayed over. I was known as 'Ashley of the Sacred Sandals'.

Only Alexander knew I was from the future. I had to tell him, we were making each other too unhappy with our secrets. He took charge of telling the scribes and historians not to write anything about me. That way I wouldn't show up on any ancient scraps of papyrus.

It's easy to get people to do as I like here. I threaten to turn them into frogs or owls. They are absolutely terrified of being turned into frogs, and owls run a close second in the nightmare race. With my reputation as a divinity, I am usually left alone. This suits me fine; I grew up alone. It's people that worry me.

I usually trailed after the second section of the army. The army was on foot. Even the cavalry walked because the horses were used to pull the multitude of wagons full of tents, weapons, food, and all the paraphernalia soldiers couldn't do without. I followed the wagons, at a distance, on foot or riding my little grey mare when I was tired of walking. I had a donkey, too, whose name was *Sibyl*. She was expecting a foal and I left her with the herd of livestock that preceded the army by about a day's march.

The army was divided into three sections. The first section marched a half a day ahead of the next and so on. Alexander marched at the head of the second section, which was the main fighting force. The first section was livestock and food wagons protected by the archers. Then came the foot soldiers, the weapons, the tents, and the last section was the rest of the army including the war machines, the engineers, the diplomats, and the phalanx.

There were even families voyaging in the general

direction we were heading, who joined us for company and protection. They formed the tail-end of the army, a noisy, squabbling gaggle of tinkers' wagons and gypsy caravans. They were usually two days behind us. We could hear and smell them before we saw them – dogs barking, men cursing, children shrieking and women scolding. It was a cacophony of bright sound closing the march.

When we camped, the last section arrived two days later and would leave two days after we left. It was like a huge inchworm that hitched itself forward and then pulled its rear end in before inching forward again.

I'd mimed that for Alexander one night in our tent. He'd nearly died laughing. If he had died I would have been erased, and time set back on track again. It would have taken an inordinate amount of energy and was used only in dire need by the time-sender historians. As long as I was careful not to affect history, I was all right. I couldn't change time an iota.

At night in the tent we played charades, checkers, dice, chess, backgammon, knucklebones, and guessing games. Our games were often contests with prizes. Most nights there were stories and songs.

In Alexander's tent were Alexander and myself – in the big bed, near the rear of the tent, Brazza and Axiom, Alexander's servants – not slaves, he had freed them, Usse, Alexander's army doctor and friend, and Plexis, better known in the history books as Hephaestion, Alexander's childhood friend.

However, anyone could come into his tent. Callisthenes, Aristotle's nephew and my tutor, was there nearly every evening. Lysimachus, the captain of the guards, would sometimes sleep inside the tent. And if one of Alexander's soldiers were dying, and we weren't in the middle of a battle, he nearly always ended up in the tent at the foot of Usse's pallet, with Usse and Alexander caring for him.

I don't know how he did it, but Alexander could give comfort to dying men. He'd hold their hands, and they looked into his eyes and found the solace they needed. Usse said it was a gift from the gods. I don't know how Alexander felt about this. He was drained and exhausted afterwards, refusing to talk or eat.

This snowy, grey morning was one of those days. A man had died the night before of a simple cut gone septic, and Alexander had been there to comfort him. Now he walked at the head of his army and his mood was despondent. He was wrapped in a grey woollen cloak, and his parti-coloured eyes were full of grief. Plexis and I knew enough to stay out of his way.

Plexis walked with me. He was one of the few people who had no fear of me. We had been lovers and we still loved each other, though now it was a deep friendship.

The sky was still dark and I thought it might be cold enough to snow. However, all we got for the rest of the day was slushy rain. It was a relief to reach the campgrounds where our tents were being set up, and where the cooks had prepared a warm meal for us. Plexis and I joined the long line of soldiers waiting for their bowls of hot lentil soup. It was invariably lentil soup with onions and garlic, and the smell of garlic would always remind me of the army. There was warm bread, which I chewed carefully, because the flour was stone-ground and sometimes had little pebbles in it. We drank water, hot water tonight as it was so chilly.

Each soldier had his own bowl, cup, spoon, and knife. They carried these in a large pouch they wore hooked over their belts. In addition, the pouch held a comb, a bag of medicinal herbs that they collected while marching, some linen bandages, and whatever amulets they thought necessary to protect themselves. The soldiers were unused to wearing any clothes, although they had new woollen capes for the mountains. Usually they went barefoot or wore sandals – now they had new boots.

I took my steaming bowl of lentils to our tent. Then I removed my boots, and shook the rain off my cloak outside. In the back of the tent there was a clothesline strung up next to a small brazier, and I hung my cloak over it. I stuffed some rags inside my boots to dry them, and then I sat down with a contented sigh on the rug. The tent was large, warm and cozy, being heated by two braziers and lit with an exquisite glass lamp made of delicately moulded glass. It was blue-green, and made everything look as if it were underwater. Whenever we moved, it was carefully lifted down, the oil was poured out, and it was packed in wood chips in a wooden box.

I sat cross-legged on a richly coloured Persian rug and set my bowl on Alexander's low table. The table was made of carved wood and inlaid with ivory and jet. If he saw my bowl on it he would frown, so I was careful not to spill anything. There was a jade bowl on the table, filled with fresh or dried fruit, depending on the season. Tonight it held walnuts.

Alexander had few belongings, although those he had were very fine: a priceless rug, a precious lamp, a beautiful table, and a bowl carved from apple-green jade. He also had a little earthenware bowl, the same as his soldiers had, to eat from. However, he drank from a solid gold cup that stood on lion's paws. There was a lion's head carved on one side, and two wings clasped the cup from either side forming the handle. The Persian king Darius had given it to him.

I was alone in the tent. Plexis had gone to see to his horses, and he'd kindly taken my pony for me. Axiom and Brazza were probably with their friends, gossiping in the mess tent. Usse was in the infirmary, most likely treating blisters from the new boots. Alexander was everywhere at once, seeing his men, talking to the families tagging along, reading the scribes' daily reports, or conversing with his many generals. He had to see to everything from the Royal Macedonian guard captained by his childhood friend Cleitus, to the cavalry, the navy, the engineers, the infantry, and the different tribes who were represented by different captains including the barbarians led by Pharnabazus, Alexander's brother in law.

I was Alexander's third wife. First he'd married Barsine, who was pregnant and expecting his child. Alexander already had a child. I'd borne him a son, Paul. Now we were trekking over the mountains in pursuit of a man named Bessus who'd kidnapped our baby.

Bessus was a satrap from Bactria. He'd betrayed Darius, the Persian king, and then killed him. Now he had our son and was fleeing.

Darius had kidnapped our son first; he'd meant to

bargain for his daughter's life with him. When he knew he'd lost the battle of Persepolis against Alexander, he'd sent our baby to Bactria, at the far reaches of his empire.

Not knowing Darius had kidnapped Paul, Alexander had married Darius's daughter Stateira; it was his second marriage. Stateira was also pregnant, and Alexander was confident this baby would be a son, because the oracle had spoken to him in Babylon.

He was a great believer in omens and portents, oracles and signs. He was forever glancing at the sky, searching for seagulls, swallows, eagles, or crows, which would mean various things depending on if they were flying, eating, or shitting on you.

I believed in none of this, which drove him crazy.

He would have preferred to be like me, but he couldn't. Everything he'd ever learned was based on fate, that men had no control over their destiny, and that the gods decided everything. Only by reading omens could men decipher the hints that gods were willing to drop.

I had never believed in fate. I'd always believed that I, and I alone, decided what my life would be. The idea of pre-destiny was ludicrous to me, which was ironic, as I was trapped with a man whose destiny was known to me. A destiny I could not change, no matter how much I wanted. So in a way, our beliefs were the same now, which drove *me* crazy.

About the author

Jennifer Macaire lives in France with her husband, three children, and two dogs. She grew up in upstate New York, Samoa, and the Virgin Islands. She graduated and moved to NYC where she modelled for five years for *Elite*. She went to France and met her husband at the polo club. All that is true. But she mostly likes to make up stories.

She has published short stories in such magazines as Polo Magazine, PKA's Advocate, The Bear Deluxe, Nuketown, The Eclipse, Anotherealm, Linnaean Street, Inkspin, Literary Potpourri, Mind Caviar, 3 am Magazine, and the Vestal Review. One of her short stories *Honey on Your Skin*, was nominated for the Pushcart Prize. In June 2002 she won the 3am/Harper Collins flash fiction contest for her story *There are Geckos* Her story *Islands* appears in the anthology 'A Dictionary of Failed Relationships' published by Three Rivers Press, an imprint of Penguin Putnam.

For more information about **Jennifer Macaire**

and other **Accent Press** titles

please visit

www.accentpress.co.uk

17700144R00242

Printed in Poland
by Amazon Fulfillment
Poland Sp. z o.o., Wrocław